WHO ENCHANTED PRESIDENT DELUXE?

DIVISION OF MAGICAL VERIFICATION, BOOK 1

A. O. VERNE

PRAGMATOPIA PRESS

Cover design by Robert Sacheli
Illustration executed by Andrew Beierle

The Division of Magical Verification Trilogy
Book 1: Who Enchanted President DeLuxe?
Book 2: Trudy and Eliot and the Wondrous Merge
Book 3: Trudy and Eliot on the Road to Pragmatopia

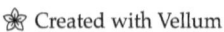 Created with Vellum

CONTENTS

For Richard

Billina, having restored all of the royal family of Ev to their proper forms, now began to select the green ornaments which were the transformations of the people of Oz. She had little trouble in finding these, and before long all the twenty-six officers, as well as the private, were gathered around the yellow hen, joyfully congratulating her upon their release. The thirty-seven people who were now alive in the rooms of the palace knew very well that they owed their freedom to the cleverness of the yellow hen, and they were earnest in thanking her for saving them from the magic of the Nome King.

— L. FRANK BAUM, *OZMA OF OZ*

NOTE TO CASE FILE
DIVISION OF MAGICAL VERIFICATION

Ms. Malone, I hope I've done a good enough job in telling the truth, as you directed me to. It's the truth as I experienced it, and that's all I can do for now.

Fab Acer, Information Specialist
Office of Quality Assurance
Division of Magical Verification
U.S. Department of Law Enforcement

TO: ELIOT GLOSS, DIRECTOR, OFFICE OF QUALITY ASSURANCE

FROM: KAYLA MALONE, DEPUTY ASSISTANT
ATTORNEY GENERAL, ENFORCEMENT

Eliot,

I'm sharing Fab's case file, with my additions, on the incidents last March. She submitted it to me directly, at my request. What I'm about to say probably won't mean anything until you read the case file, but: I added information from the archives of The Merge. I think the additions provide essential context. (Eliot, does that ring a bell at all? Believe me, it's all true. Even the parts about Trudy. I know you don't always remember The Merge, but I'm going to keep reminding you, buddy. Remember how crazy thing were in New Orleans that summer in 1995? Bump that up a whole 'nother level. Call me right after you read this.)

You should share my additions and this email with Fab after you've had a chance to read everything. She deserves to know more context from The Merge, and my role in everything. I think we can depend on her to keep it at the highest level confidentiality.

Most importantly, the documentation of this case appears to be having its intended effect. You'll see what that is near the end.

Eliot (and Fab, when you read this), please believe that ideas do matter, so please believe in the good things, and relegate the bad things to where they belong. We are in this together. Cynicism and opportunism fail us in the long run. Hope, optimism, compassion, and a sense of connection are success strategies for us as a nation, and as a planet. I deeply believe that.

Kayla

HEY FAB

Here's a revised version of your case file. Kayla added some things and looped me in, and asked me to share the complete account with you. As you can see from her note. (FYI, Kayla and I go back a long ways.) I have made edits here and there, but tried not to change your "voice." Mainly I just made sure what you say I said is what I remember, or at least sounds plausibly like something I'd have said. You did a remarkable job of sounding like me.

It appears you won't find some of Kayla's insertions as surprising as I did! Pretty wild. Anything else you're hiding from me? LOL. Don't worry, we're all good. I'll tell you my secrets if you'll tell me yours, since I guess I'm your honorary gay uncle now. ;-) I'm going to have to clue in our Administrative Barrister, but he's family too, and I think we can trust him.

I guess I just buried the lead: yeah, *you* knew, and now *I* know too, who we can blame (or thank) for the Enchantment Event! For obvious reasons, we should catch up.

Eliot

FOIA STATEMENT, U.S. DEPT. OF LAW ENFORCEMENT

AUTHORIZED BY ADAM E. GRAVENSTEIN,
ADMINSTRATIVE BARRISTER

The U.S. Department of Law Enforcement has no comment on the contents of this case file, as amended by the parties noted above. This case file is being provisionally cleared for future release, no sooner than March 11, 2042, under authority of the Freedom of Information Act, as amended by the Magical Accountability and Transparency Act of 2020 ("The MATA Act"). Until the date specified above, this case file, as amended as noted, remains classified at the Secure Compartmented Mystical Information (SCMI) level, unless subsequent review by the Attorney General or designated Senior Accountable Magical Transparency Official (under Section 217 of The MATA Act) determines this file no longer meets the criteria for SCMI classification. The Department acknowledges no liability for actions or inactions of its employees that may be considered in violation of statutes, regulations, or administrative policies in effect at the time of this narrative.

Office of the Administrative Barrister
United States Department of Law Enforcement

CHAPTER 1

COORDINATED RESPONSE

FROM THE ARCHIVES OF THE MERGE,
FRIDAY, FEBRUARY 28, 2020

T he Plenary Merging was particularly extended this evening. Kayla had briefly pulled herself out of the collective consciousness to look at her phone. It was 10:13. She nodded to Aziz, the barista from Takoma Park, across the hotel ballroom crowded with undulating people in various stages of undress, their naked skin pressed together to maximize the physical contact that Merging required. Aziz had drawn the straw to be the timekeeper tonight. He wasn't due to drop back into The Merge consciousness for another seventeen minutes to give a time announcement. Time ran differently while in The Merge, but even the thirteen minutes since the last announcement had seemed like hours in The Merge to Kayla. There was a lot to process.

Concern about the coronavirus epidemic, and the DeLuxe administration's seeming indifference, had called for a Plenary Merging, so effectively all the 5,000 or so Merged folk on the planet were represented in some fashion. Only about 100 physical bodies were here, but people from across the globe had within the last week made contact and Synched with other Merged folk who could travel. The physical attendees would return and Synch again afterwards so everyone would feel they'd been there and been represented. Unlike people who communicated through social media, for Merged folks it was possible to reach consensus, albeit with a time lag.

This year, Washington, DC was hosting the Plenary, so Kayla and her wife Eydie had rented all the guest rooms and meeting spaces at a hotel in suburban Maryland. Merge gatherings were always easier when there weren't too many non-Merged around. Kayla's other hand still clasped Eydie's. She had stayed in The Merge while Kayla came up for air.

Kayla was a leader in the National Bureau of Investigation's counterintelligence program, and therefore uniquely positioned to know of the threat the virus posed. As was usual for the DeLuxe presidency, it met the intelligence community's warnings with perversely incompetent non-responses. The administration chronically reversed the findings and messages, so the recommendations of dedicated civil servants were not just dismissed; they were actively worked against. The same was happening now, with epidemiology and intelligence communities warning of the threat of the virus, which the president and his minions dismissed.

The NBI had no official knowledge of Kayla's dual loyalties, to the U.S. Constitution and to The Merge. Kayla thought of her loyalty to The Merge as her loyalty to the human race, which the U.S. Constitution also supported. She still believed in Superman's old credo: truth, justice, and the American Way. In spite of the DeLuxe administration's attempts to remove truth and justice from American discourse, she still believed the American experiment could better the human race. So she saw little conflict between her duties with the NBI and her participation in The Merge's collective consciousness.

Merged people could, if they chose, re-live the lives of the hundreds of thousands of people who'd ever lived as Merged folks. The Merge preserved their experiences through the massively redundant and distributed "database" of personas and memories, residing in the bodies of the people that made up

The Merge. Kayla was glad that "collective consciousness" still allowed for differences of belief and values and perspective, powered by true empathy and shared memories with people different from oneself.

"Just checking the time," Kayla said to Aziz.

"Must be important to go on so long," Aziz replied, projecting across the sighing and moaning mass of bodies. Anyone walking in on them would have thought this was an orgy, but "orgy" was nowhere near adequate to describe the total mental, emotional, physical, spiritual connection of The Merge experience, Kayla thought.

"Lots of speculating and planning, but not much we can do, that I can tell," she replied. Aziz nodded. Without a competent and motivated president, the U.S. appeared to be in for a major problem. Years of weakening the U.S. Government's resilience were about to take their toll.

"See you in there," Kayla said, and she closed her eyes and allowed herself to drop into The Merge again. She rejoined the conversation at the place she'd left off listening. She would fast-forward to catch up.

"The Epidemic was like this, but it only affected a minority of us," Michael Hallie was saying. The first surge of Merged folks had occurred during the AIDS crisis, so there were many whose bodies had been claimed by AIDS but who lived on in The Merge. Michael was one of the earliest of these. "Only it was one hundred percent fatal and only infected some of us," he continued. "This one looks one hundred percent infectious, and who knows how many it will kill! It woud be a *pan*demic. What are we going to do?" He had the talking stick now, which he had visualized in the shape of a fairy's magic wand. He had been an early AIDS activist, and his body had succumbed to the disease in 1984. "People didn't listen early on and do what was needed. I know, I was one of them. I know, I know, we didn't know for sure how it was transmitted. This seems to be airborne, though."

All the participants, or rather their virtual avatars, sat in what looked like a natural amphitheater covered with clipped grass. Around the amphitheater was a simulacrum of a Northern Californian redwood forest, and above them a blue, cloudless sky shone. Where the stage would have been, a screen displayed Michael's image as he talked, although he stood in the audience with the rest of them. Eydie raised her hand, and Michael pointed the fairy wand at her. It vanished from his hand, Eydie's preferred talking stick, a carved wooden Chinese Buddha, appeared in her hand, and her image appeared on the screen. "Technically, they're saying it's droplets," said Eydie, her voice amplified for all to hear. Although her patients were animals, she had been reading up on the science. "However, the distinction is an academic one. Small droplets are airborne. There may be ways to control it through physical distancing and masks, which would be simple if everyone does it for about a month. Testing would need to be available too. It isn't, yet." There were thousands of nodding and shaking heads among the gathered avatars of the actually and virtually present. Nods of agreement, shaking born of sorrow and frustration.

Kayla sighed again. She believed Eydie, and she also did not have faith that the U.S. under this president would reach the same conclusion. Not for the first time since 2016, she was frightened for the future of the country she loved. And her loved ones. Thank goodness, she, Eydie, and their daughter Trudy were Merged, so even if the worst should happen in the U.S., there must be pockets of sanity and survival where the Merged around the world would provide a virtual existence for them. Like they did for Michael, and for Trudy's biological mother and grandmother, deceased in body but very much alive in The Merge's collective consciousness.

The Plenary shifted into breakout groups to strategize solutions. Kayla appreciated the motivation, but opted not to. She scanned the crowd and saw Trudy in a breakout circle, and sent the sensation of a pat on the back. Trudy virtually squeezed Kayla's hand and reminded her to call her JR now, and use appropriate pronouns. Kayla acknowledged, promised to remember, and moved on. It was challenging maintaining an appropriate distance from your adoptive daughter. Kayla didn't want to intrude any further.

JR had become expert at setting boundaries. She had two moms in the physical world, and the virtual persona of her biological mother, Trudy Senior, always present in The Merge. After Trudy Senior's body dissipated in The Surge of 1995, all that was left of her was her Merged self and a newborn parthenogenic clone. Consulting with Kayla and Eydie, Trudy Senior had suggested they all call the baby Trudy Junior, and let Trudy Junior decide what name to use when an adult. Trudy Junior was the only known baby to start life as an infant with access to all the Merged memories of her mother. As she grew, Junior differentiated, and as of last year, Trudy Junior had decided to use JR as name, and had chosen non-binary pronouns as well.

Kayla was still getting the hang of JR's choice of pronouns. "Zey," "zem," "zeir," and "zeirs" were unique, as far as she knew. JR claimed zey had enough plurality in zeir life without resorting to plural or indefinite third person, so zey had picked something nobody else used. Reasserting zeir unique identity, Eydie had supposed. At least zey wasn't easily offended when people got it wrong.

Kayla scanned the crowd again and found Trudy Senior, who was with Joann (JR's grandmother) and Trudy's friend Jim in a breakout group. The three of them, deceased in body but alive in The Merge, were often found "together" (whatever that really meant in The Merge's virtual reality). Kayla popped over to their triad and suggested they all get together for a chat tomorrow evening, real cocktails and dinner for Eydie, Kayla, and JR, and virtual ones for the Virtuals. (Merged folk were generous with sharing their sensory experiences, with a few exceptions.) Jim gave a virtual thumbs up.

The breakouts rejoined in a Plenary discussion that went on

for what seemed like hours, until Aziz dropped in and told them it was 10:30. They agreed to meet the next day, and the physically present started disconnecting. When they rose out of The Merge consciousness, Kayla squeezed Eydie's hand, then stretched and yawned.

"You're going to have to represent me tomorrow," she said, as everyone gathered their clothing and dressed. "I got some emails I need to attend to at the office. And a missive from our friends the AIs. God only knows what they want to talk about now." The Congress of American Digital Entities had been making sporadic overtures to The Merge since it had revealed itself a year ago, via email, chatbots, and most recently a few disconcertingly realistic artificially generated Spoogle Speak calls.

"No prob, sweetheart. My team's got the practice covered, so I'm planning to be here all day. You can cover the COADE liaison. You're so good at it." Eydie gave Kayla a peck on the cheek and locked her arm in Kayla's. "Let's go to bed."

Everyone returned to their rooms, except a few hardy young folks who went bar-hopping in downtown Silver Spring. They said it was to catch Aziz up, but maybe also just to differentiate themselves from the old farts in The Merge, and to bring back some vicarious fun for those whose bodies weren't up to late nights and alcohol. Or who didn't have bodies anymore at all.

Kayla and Eydie slept in each other's arms in their upgraded hotel room (group sales perk), and Kayla rose the next morning at 8:00 and was downtown in the J. Edgar Hoover NBI Headquarters building by 9:30.

CHAPTER 2

WHAT HAPPENED WHEN

FROM THE CASE FILES OF FAB ACER,
DIVISION OF MAGICAL VERIFICATION,
RECALLING FEBRUARY 29, 2020

L ike everyone, I remember where I was when 2/29 happened, the day when President DeLuxe and his core supporters, from Congress, the administration, and the Supreme Court, were transformed by unknown parties into harmless pieces of merchandise. To be specific, they all became Disney merchandise. They say 2/29 was one of those generational touchstone events we all remember vividly. If I'm lucky, hardly anyone will find out how close we were to disaster two years later, in 2022.

The day of the Enchantment Event, February 29, 2020, I was in my last year at the UDC School of Law. Mid-terms were over, and I was half-heartedly studying for the bar. I was going to be Fab Acer, Public Interest Advocate! (Fab is short for Fabergé. My parents had a thing for jeweled eggs, I guess.) Maybe I'd run for office eventually, help fix the gender imbalance of the House or Senate? I thought that was something for a young woman like myself to aspire to. Little did I know the turn things would take that day.

Like a lot of people, I was concerned with the emotional and mental stability of our unusual president, Dirk DeLuxe, as he finished his first term. Like a lot of people, I was scared he might win a second term. How could 40% of the people in the country support him? I couldn't understand. And there were warning signs of an epidemic, which we now know would become a pandemic. He and his administration showed no signs of competently addressing it. Thank goodness (in retrospect) the Constitutional Party became the majority in early March thanks to the decimation of the Freedonian Party. Speaker of the House Emily Velutto ascended to the presidency through the line of succession and immediately addressed the pandemic.

Before that had been three years of uncertainty, looming into a global disaster with a very real threat of his reelection. Even his awful automaton of a vice president, Chip Farthing, seemed a better alternative; at least he'd not get us into a nuclear war, we thought. Some people thought DeLuxe's advisors were intentionally encouraging him to create chaos with his erratic behavior, so we'd be relieved to trade our chaotic democracy for stability, maybe military rule. Or Russian oligarchy or Chinese hybrid capitalistic totalitarianism. Paranoia and conspiracy theories were rampant, but nobody expected what would REALLY happen.

When the Enchantment happened, I had my nose in a book of Freedom of Information Act case law, while the TV showed C-SPAN. Sometimes that helped me study, having background noise. Today they were covering the America First Political Action Parliament, what they called AFPAP, at the president's DeLuxe Imperial Hotel in downtown DC. The president was entering the stage after a long line of speakers, including some he'd banished from his inner circle already, but who seemed still to have his ear, like that horrible Bart Barukka, the Internet fake news czar. Most of the Cabinet was there, along with virtually the entire Freedonian Congress, most of the Freedonian governors, and many Freedonian state legislators. After the fact, we learned security was incredibly high, since so many key conservatives were there, and that show *Designated Survivor* had made people sensitive to what could happen if an entire administration got wiped out. Personally, I think *Warstar Astronautica* did it better, first, making the Education Secretary the new (woman) president. Of course, the DeLuxe administration was so full of acting cabinet members, the designated survivor that day was an Acting Secretary of the Department of Fatherland Supremacy, who turned out to be technically not eligible in the line of succession since he had not been confirmed by the Senate.

The idea of security then was what would work against bombs and guns. It was ironic how useless all that turned out.

President DeLuxe took the stage to thunderous applause, with a typical, smarmy smirk and wave, unabashedly soaking in the ego strokes. Every time I looked at him, I felt ashamed of our country, and afraid. Men like that...I can't even go on.

He started his speech. There are copies floating around the Internet that purport to say he was announcing curfews in sanctuary cities and federal legal action against several news media outlets. I don't know if I believe those, but they feed the rationalization for those who are happy with what happened next.

In the moment, I didn't pay attention until the replays on TV. President DeLuxe was a couple of sentences into his speech, and there was a noise off-camera, and he ad-libbed the phrase "And there's someone who understands what I mean," as he gestured off-camera, and he smirked like he always did. Then his expression changed to one we'd never seen: eyes widening, arms thrown in front of himself to shield him, and then chaos. The president ran offscreen, Confidential Service agents ran onscreen to throw themselves in front of him, other people paced, while the camera jiggled a bit, still pointed to the stage and lectern. Screams and shouts off screen. Then silence and stillness.

In my office, we describe what I next experienced as the Extra Magical Cascade, or EMC. Lots of people in the DC area felt it, and lots, as in my case, didn't feel a thing. I experienced... nothing I can recall. The next thing I remember is my phone ringing. It was my mom.

"Sweetheart, are you all right?"

"Mom, yes, of course. I think I fell asleep reading my case law."

"Honey, I was so scared!"

"Mom, I'm fine!" I was all of twenty-six, and she still treated me like her little girl.

"There's been a terrorist thing. Not a bombing, but something. Do you have your TV on? The president was involved."

I glanced at the TV and saw an empty stage with a lectern and a bright presidential seal backdrop. A Confidential Service agent ran across stage speaking into her wireless, then nothing for a minute. A cameraman cowering on the floor realized he was safe, stood up, took charge of the camera again, and panned the ballroom.

"I have C-SPAN on. I was watching before I fell asleep," I said, wondering if I *had* actually fallen asleep.

"They say a weird thing happened. You're OK, right? You're miles from his hotel, right?"

"Yes, Mom, I'm nowhere near. Why would I be anywhere near there?"

"I...I don't know," Mom said. "I just needed to make sure you were OK."

"I'm fine. Listen, I want to watch this, so I'll call you later."

"Yes, honey, just be careful and stay away from those people," she said.

"What people?"

"You know. The president and all of them."

"That won't be a problem." Why she thought I'd be near the president, I didn't know.

I hung up, and watched the C-SPAN feed. What we saw from the cameraman's footage when the camera panned: the conference center devoid of all but four Confidential Service agents, talking into their communicators, and hotel staff, frozen in fear or running from the room, and a floor full of what looked like miscellaneous junk that a crowd would leave behind. The cameraman focused on an item. It was a Mickey Mouse ear hat.

And next to it, a plush stuffed Winnie-the-Pooh. And behind that, a kid's Spiderman Halloween costume. And next to that—he had to zoom in before I could make it out—a small Chewbacca action figure.

The floor was littered with Disney merchandise. It seemed so out of character for that crowd. Nobody realized at first that the president and his supporters had all become inanimate objects, based on Disney's diverse intellectual property portfolio. The C-SPAN signal cut shortly thereafter, so we don't have footage of right afterward. Though I may be able to get the first responder's shoulder cam videos released to the public eventually.

Oh, I guess I haven't explained yet. I actually got a job after this at the U.S. Department of Law Enforcement, in our newly formed Division of Magical Verification. Yes, we know the acronym is DMV. Don't quote me, but I think Congress (namely the Constitutionalists who were in charge after the 2/29 Enchantment) were a little giddy, and that explains the whimsical legislative acronyms. At the DMV, I'm one of the key people (if I say so myself) responsible for implementing the Magical Accountability and Transparency Act, given the acronym "MATA Act" by Congress. (I know the extra "A" is superfluous, but that's the statuory nickname for the Act. They didn't want to call it the "MAT Act," I guess.) I'm responsible for publishing information about 2/29 and its artifacts on the Internet, and I think the footage from Ground Zero is really valuable for context. Still working on getting that approved, but I'm hopeful.

Back on 2/29/20, my coworker at the DMV, Lonny Dotch, was an agent with the Bureau of Liquor, Nicotine, Munitions and Bombs. (Everyone called it LNM for short; I never understood why there wasn't a "B.") He was one of the first responders. A couple of months after we'd been working together, he described to me what he saw at Ground Zero in the DeLuxe Imperial Hotel.

"I got the APB there'd been a terrorist incident at the hotel. I was patrolling perimeter, past the hotel, down to the IRS and

Law Enforcement Department on 10th, right on Constitution, then up 12th, right at the hotel, and so forth. So I was right there. The Confidential Service and hotel security were swarming. One agent was standing in shock, like he just couldn't believe it. If it'd been a shooting, he'd have known, hell, all of us would have known what to do. I flashed my badge, and went into the big atrium they'd set up with a stage."

What Lonny didn't see was that the Confidential Service agent had gotten trigger happy with one of the hotel staff. Of course, in case of an incident, a law enforcement professional's first action is to take down the active shooter, or whoever they perceive is the threat. I guess he was boggled by what he'd seen, this agent, I'll keep him nameless (but the incident reports are on file). He shot at a food service employee he encountered but felt threatened by.

In my job I get to see lots of things not (yet) released to the public. I've seen the hotel security camera footage. The hotel employee was a large, dark-skinned black man. I'm sorry to say, the agent was white. Go figure. Anyway, when the agent's gun exploded in his hand, that was our first piece of evidence that the Enchantment also made it so you couldn't successfully kill people with guns. It wasn't clear at first, but this was the first documented incident of a gun blowing up in someone's hand before they could shoot someone. Now it happens all the time, under the Enchantment. Now, basically guns and bombs never work unless used for non-violent intent like target practice or demolition. They always blow up in the face of whoever is trying to deploy them for harm. But you know all that. Oh, and the agent recovered. He only lost a finger and part of his sight.

Lonny continued with his story on entering the hotel: "I stopped an agent who was running by, looking confused. 'Where are the bodies?' I ask him. 'There are no bodies,' he says, and he waves his hand around the room. 'They all vanished. And this is what's left.' He meant the Enchanted Objects, we now call 'em. The people, most of 'em, at least, got transformed. All that was left was the Disney merch, scattered around the space. T-shirts, plush stuffed animals, action figures, dolls, you know. Our whole inventory now."

I did know; that was my job, now, to know the inventory of Enchanted Objects (we call them EOs in the office) that used to be the Freedonian power structure of the United States. That is, until a sorcerer, still unidentified, exploded magic into our lives, and reshaped the entire way we live. In whatever spell Sorcerer X (the unknown magician) had cast, all the Freedonians in that room were transformed into inanimate objects, each and every one of which was an example of merchandise that tied into one of Disney's corporate intellectual properties: classic Disney, Muppets, Pixar, Marvel, Star Wars, the Simpsons. But you all know this too. I'm restating the obvious.

Lonny had been uncharacteristically talkative the day he told me about his first experiences on 2/29. He's usually a man of few words. "I took control. It helped that I hadn't been there to see it, I guess, so I had a clear head. I had the Confidential Service secure the perimeter. Gave them something to focus on. The NBI showed up stat. NBI HQ guns from across the street, the CSI team from WFO soon after, once we'd assessed the threat." WFO is the NBI's Washington Field Office.

"All the Confidential Service folks and all the wait staff, custodial staff, hotel staff, they had to be rounded up, checked out for weapons. We didn't know to look for magic stuff, but when we found lucky rabbit's foot, it occurred to me to look for wands and so forth. Took us a while to realize how selective the magic was. We found some EOs in the management offices, DeLuxe supporters, apparently. Most of the housekeeping, catering, clerical staff, they didn't get transformed. Lost a few Confidential Service agents too, we found out. It wasn't until later we understood the people who weren't DeLuxe supporters seemed immune."

Enchantment conspiracy web sites have gotten mileage from this. Friends and family of the transformed Confidential Service agents and hotel staff confirmed the Transformed Persons (TPs, we call them) were DeLuxe believers. Conversely, a dozen people attending had conservative credentials, but were not transformed. From affidavits and interview transcripts, it appears they were "never-DeLuxers," who still considered them-selves conservatives, and hoped they could ride out the wave of DeLuxism. One of these was even the husband of a DeLuxe staffer.

Lonny continued, "The NBI took over; it wasn't until we discovered guns and bombs wouldn't work right that LNM got more involved."

All of that is common knowledge now, of course, but I thought it would be valuable to record Lonny's perspective, for the record here (whether this ever gets declassified or not.) Lonny was being modest, even then. I read eyewitness tran-scripts later. If it hadn't been for Lonny securing the perimeter, and arguing with the NBI staff, the EOs might have been moved, bagged without attention, who knows what. He had the pres-ence of mind to have them treated as crime victims' corpses, so they were photographed from every angle, treated with respect, and carefully secured only when all that had been done. Even with that firm lockdown, we still can't definitively identify which person became which object. Part of what the DMV was formed to try to do, and what the MATA Act is intended to support. In spite of our data analytics, we're still far away from knowing whether that Star Wars Boba Fett plush doll (EO Identi-fication Number 54290) is President DeLuxe, the Chief Justice, Senator Donnelly, or only some wing nut with a EuBoob chan-nel. And of course, later we discovered there were other enchant-ments across the DC/Maryland/Virginia area: already inanimate objects, other merchandise with President DeLuxe's branding, transformed into different, Disney-branded merchandise. An apparent ripple effect from the Enchantment at Ground Zero. (More about those Transformed Objects later!)

As I write this two years after 2/29/2020, the perpetrator, a.k.a. Sorcerer X, is still at large.

No, I'm not Sorcerer X, in case you were looking for that twist! I'm dedicated to getting the truth about magic out there eventually. This narrative is the story, I guess, of why I can't say right now who did it; or help to undo it.

My politics? As an Executive Branch, non-political employee covered by the Hatch Act, I'm prevented from campaigning for a partisan candidate. I'm still free to express my preferences. Maybe I shouldn't since I'm writing this on orders from my leadership? I don't know. Since this document may never go outside the hidden archives of the Department of Law Enforcement, I don't think it matters. I can't imagine this being shared with the public during my lifetime.

Anyway, I do think we're better off now under President Velluto than we were under President DeLuxe. Not to mention it's about time we had a woman president! After the 2/29 attack, as everyone knows, a coalition of Constitutionalists and Freedonians took over the Executive and Legislative branches. They reached so much common ground, after years of strife, that the government actually started functioning again. Maybe it helped having an unknown threat of sorcery, to get the conservatives to play well with the progressives. And course we found that spending on defense for guns and bombs was pointless. Luckily that spell covers the whole world, as far as we know. Not much point spending trillions on bows and arrows, to replace every piece of artillery or nuke that blows up when someone tries to use it for harm. So there's been a lot more to spend on the pandemic responses, environment, infrastructure, education, renewable energy, all those good things. And the majority of people stay on their good behavior, like they're afraid someone will, figuratively, drop a house on them too.

I just realized, I should write as though this is being read a while from now. You may not know our context in 2022. To be clear, no houses fell out of the sky onto any witches. Nobody discovered a secret school of wizardry and witchcraft in upstate New York or Great Britain. No tentacled horrors rose from the Tidal Basin. The 2/29 Enchantment was the only magical act we knew of, until the day my story starts, March 1, 2022.

Congress wanted to find out who performed the Enchantment, but none of the law enforcement or intelligency agencies were ever able to find Sorcerer X. Congress didn't see any progress on the case, no signs the Enchantment could be reversed. So they turned to establishing a long-term process to humanely care for the people who had become Enchanted Objects, and to share as much of the details about that care as possible with the public. That's where my office comes in.

The first Enchantment-related legislation established the Division of Magical Verification in DLE to take into any EOs into custody ("seize" sounds more violent than it is, although that's the legal term). We are charged to store and maintain the EOs in a controlled environment, in case they are ever be able to be de-enchanted. (The term "disenchanted" was rejected as too poetic).

The MATA Act came later, in response to demands for more information when the investigations didn't come up with anything. My office was established to analyze the EOs, publish all the statistics we could about them, and make it all publicly available.

And wow, is there a demand for that information. There are web sites running odds on who is what (we still don't know who became what object, given that most people were off-camera when the Enchantment took place), and sites that sell other copies of the same Disney merchandise (like eMarkt on steroids), and sites that try to crunch the data to come up with woo-woo conspiracy theories. Like I said, if they only knew the truth.

CHAPTER 3

WHERE WE ARE NOW

FROM THE FILES OF FAB ACER, MARCH 1,
2022, MORNING

W hen they passed the MATA Act. I was already
working for the Magical Data Transparency Foundation. I had dropped out of law school and gone
to work with like-minded folks who wanted to know the truth. I
fervently hoped there was a Hogwarts or something like it, but if
that wasn't going to be true, the public deserved to know what
was true. I became a data analyst. Boy, did I enjoy that better than
law, although law still figures into what I do, of course. The
MATA Act had bipartisan support, like so much new legislation,
and President Velluto signed it and augmented the DMV here in
the Law Enforcement Department. I got hired to work directly
with the data about the EOs. When historians write about this, I
want them to know this felt like the job of a lifetime for me; I've
never felt so at home and making such a meaningful
contribution.

More about me, as I see me: I'm outgoing and energetic, not
too pushy. I hope. I'm okay looking; medium height, not too
skinny but not too plump, and a natural blonde, for the record. (I
give it a little help, since it's darker now than when I was
younger. I still claim blondness, though!) I wear my hair in a
pixie cut these days. I like the two-piece suits I get to wear at

work, tend to go for tailored, with a touch of whimsy if I do say so myself. I'll wear cute dresses if the weather demands it. (They always keep the offices so cool in summer, though!) A personal style consultant did my colors and styles once, and I think I am what he called "High Spirited, with a large percentage of Classic." I think that means I'm fun and whimsical but like to wear tailored suits.

At the time all this happened, I wasn't seeing anyone too seriously. Now, there's someone potential, but I won't go into that yet. I don't want to get ahead of the story. I've got friends, and lots of acquaintances I know from college, from law school, even a few from California where I grew up with Mom. Dad wasn't around when I grew up, him having gone on to the next wife, but he kept in touch. I was fine with that distance. Not every dad can be Mr. Rogers. He sure wasn't. Whatever. It was mostly Mom and me, and I think I turned out OK.

And there are work friends, sort like a family. My boss Eliot is great, and I work a lot with Lonny Dotch, and there's Griffin. We're pretty close, as you'll see. Shared secrets have a way of keeping you close. I guess part of why I'm happy to be writing this is I think it's healthy for me, given I'm keeping some pretty damn big secrets. I hope someone gets to read the whole story (or at least as much as I know) someday. Is that egotistical of me? Too bad.

When it all started to heat up at work (the reason I'm writing this, in other words) I had been working there about a year and a half. I loved it! Two years had passed since the Enchantment Event on 2/29/20. I was the lead on implementing the MATA Act, to publish information about the Enchanted Objects to a web site, for the sake of government transparency, by no later than two years to the day of the Enchantment Event. And here we were, March of 2022. A majority of Americans felt the country was headed in the right direction (according to the latest Rasputin Poll). Anecdotally, if you read traditional journalism, people were happy again, at least those of us in the majority. As soon as the Freedonians were removed from the government, it was able to deal with the pandemic in an organized fashion, with President Velluto becoming a wartime leader on par with FDR, some said. Under her leadership, the threat of recession had, well, receded. A year of aggressive mask-wearing and social distancings stopped the pandemic in its tracks. Quick, reliable virus tests, vaccines, and treatments became easy to get. Businesses, restaurants, bars, theaters, theme parks, all reopened, to a pent-up demand that was unprecedented, albeit with perimeter health checks in place. Instant testing and digital contact tracing created virus-free zones in the major cities made large gatherings and maskless interaction possible again. Her party's candidate won by a landslide, succeeded her in the presidency the following January, and appointed her United Countries Ambassador, where she rose to become Secretary-General.

The people who'd voted for DeLuxe weren't quiet, but they were cautious. Lots of Internet conspiracy theorizing. Could you blame them? Whoever had enacted the transformation spell was no fan of the DeLuxist agenda. There were no threats of gun violence, or explosives, since they knew those wouldn't work. You didn't read much about any other threats, either. Bioterrorism was still a risk, but a common belief was that DeLuxists didn't have enough presence in scientific or medical circles to accomplish assemble a bioterrorism campaign. And they were probably afraid more magic was waiting to transform them too. If they felt oppressed, I'm sorry. Actually, no I'm not! Things could have turned out a lot worse.

So there I was, sitting on top of the world. One of the most prominent and eagerly awaited releases of government data, a pinnacle in transparency, and I was right in the middle of it. I was part of something big and good, even if I wasn't casting spells.

Then of course it all flipped upside down.

Near the intersections of Florida and New York Avenues in Northeast DC, DLE occupied three similar boxy, glass and concrete buildings. Across the street was the headquarters of the DLE Bureau of Liquor, Nicotine, Munitions and Bombs, in an oddly curvaceous white building with a plastic-roofed atrium. The Robert F. Kennedy Main Law Enforcement Building, home of the Great Hall of Law Enforcement you saw in films or on the news, with the topless aluminum Deco statuary, was a good twenty-minute shuttle or Muni ride away. When they created our division, there was space in the oldest of the three buildings, which was still only about ten years old. We had the entire seventh floor, two "wings" (almost like two whole buildings) connected by a thinner "hyphen" with abundant floor-to-ceiling windows. We could see, on the north side, the LNM building and our first-floor atrium roof, and on the south, a little patio within our secure perimeter. Between our building and the apartment building behind us there was a sparsely landscaped space with an plastic-turfed dog park. I loved to watch the dogs playing off-leash, yipping with delight, every afternoon when their owners got home and took them out.

I was on my way from my own office (East wing) to see my boss, Eliot. He's a friendly, supportive, and positive guy, probably late fifties (it's hard to tell with gay guys sometimes). He's smart, and I can see how he got where he is, but at the same time he always acts like everything's a big game. He may get frustrated, but not like a thwarted careerist. More like someone who's score is down in the game they're playing, who wants to keep the score up just because it keeps you in the game. Sounds like a sports metaphor, but Eliot once said in a meeting, when a couple of the guys were bemoaning the local football team's recent losses, "The only sports I follow is quidditch. How are the Chudley Cannons doing?" He won me over with that. I think I was the only one in the room who laughed at the reference. Maybe Griffin got it, too. It's hard to know, since he didn't laugh.

Eliot's door was open, and he was turned to his monitor, away from the door, typing something. I knocked, and he turned and smiled, gesturing for me to sit. "Hi! Come on in! What's up, Ms. Data?" His playful name for me.

"We've completed the final QA checklist. The UAT team met and voice-voted we go live, and the Governance Committee did the same on their recommendation. I'm ready to push the data out to Prod. I wondered if you'd want to give the final final okay."

"If you're good with it and the team is good with it, and the GC is good with it, I'm good with it. Feel free, and let me know when the site goes live. We'll celebrate tonight after work." Eliot had scheduled an "Offsite" appointment on the system calendar for everyone in the DMV, as well as the higher-ups, and people we worked with in other components and non-DLE agencies. Meaning happy hour at the hotel bar around the corner. The Health Security Administration's certified viral testing perimeter had recently expanded to incorporate our block, so the hotel had reopened its bar last week. "That will be our ceremony. Fab, this has been a really exciting project, and I know I've told you before, but they say people need to hear it three times: You're the keystone resource to this project. I don't know how we'd have done it without you. You're Fab...ulous!" He punctuated that with an exaggerated wink—would you call that a meta-wink? As if to say he knew how corny and dad-jokey that was, but he was going to hold it as clever to do it anyway. He called me "Fabulous" in emails and meetings sometimes, and people in the DMV had started calling me that too. I took it as a compliment.

"Thanks, boss, but you know it's Griffin who—"

"I completely understand Griffin's contribution; don't get me wrong. Please accept that without you to smooth things through and handle the people, we'd never have been able to properly leverage his talents. Will you just take the compliment?" He cocked his head, expecting a response.

"Yes, Eliot, thank you. I accept the compliment. So," I said, rising to leave, "Here I go. USAMagicalTransparency.gov going live in—" I glanced at my watch. "—15 minutes."

Eliot added, "And Fab, tell Griffin he doesn't have to come tonight if he doesn't want to. I want to make sure he knows it's optional."

"Will do," I said. That was thoughtful. Eliot was always looking out for Griffin, concerned he might get overwhelmed by crowds if he didn't set boundaries for himself. I gave Eliot a two-fingered salute and left his office.

I stopped by Griffin's cube. He wasn't there. I suspected he was holed up in his terminal room, his de facto workspace, a windowless room behind the elevators filled with voice and data switching equipment. He was one of the rare people who never teleworked, and somehow he had two workstations. Nobody begrudged him. Space was still abundant, since leases made before the pandemic had assumed a lot less work from home.

I'd send him a Scrye text from my desk, which he probably preferred, and would follow up in person. Eliot had asked me to work closely with Griffin, who had been with the project since before I came onboard. I got along fine with him, and had no expectation I would get a "typical" response from him on most things. I tried to appreciate his neurodiverse genius for what it was. The web developers could build the site's functionality, and make sure the user experience was top drawer. Griffin's gift was how deeply he knew our data, knew the numbers, in ways nobody else did. That was impossible to overvalue.

I knocked on the door to the IT equipment room. After a moment, it opened, and Griffin stood in front of me. His gaze was somewhere in the air to the right of my shoulder.

"Hi, Griffin. Eliot gave me the go-ahead. I'm about to publish to Production."

"Yes."

"Just wanted you to know.

"Thanks."

"Okay, I'll see you after."

"I have new data for you."

"Oh, the mapping…"

"Yes, and an app for you and Agent Dotch. It integrates the vector data with GPS." Griffin and I had been working on correlating our data with GPS data, intended for an enhancement to the database of Enchanted Objects. Griffin's work meant we could visualize the data on a map. For most casual visitors, that would mainly show where people had reported their Transformed Objects across the DC region. A "Make America Mighty Again" lamp became a Lumière lamp, a generic stuffed bear wearing a "DeLuxe/Farthing 2020" T-shirt became a "Disney Duffy" bear, a "He's the Chosen One" beer cozy transformed into a Pocahontas onesie. That kind of thing. Did I mention? All the merchandise that got transformed expressed DeLuxist ideology. Just like all the Transformed Persons did.

We had not decided if we should scrub the exact locations, because of privacy concerns. However, not sharing data would be contrary to our guiding principle of transparency. Department leadership was still reviewing our proposal, and I hoped they'd confirm transparency. In the meantime, we had an internal use for the precise locations, and how they all connected. No people that we knew of had been transformed outside of Ground Zero. With each of the EOs, though, whether a Transformed Person (TP) or Transformed Object (TO), we imputed a vector. In other words, we could infer which direction the magical force of the transformation seemed to come from. The direction was based on how the EO was aligned on the floor or whatever surface it lay on. For example, a Darth Maul figurine lying on its back, with its head pointed north-northwest would have a vector pointing north-northwest. Where the CSI folks had captured precise information, we could derive a vector. What Griffin had suggested was continuing lines on a map, to see if any other EOs had been found along those vectors of magical force. Lo and behold, yes! We found consecutive clusters of EO incidents radiating out from

Ground Zero, intersected by the outward radius lines of magic. The clusters, when mapped, formed concentric circles radiating outward. I called the circles and the radiating axes "ley lines," although that wasn't official, yet. (We'd probably have to do an exposure draft in the *Federal Register* to get that term approved.) Griffin had scienced up all the vector and geospatial data, and he was telling me I could access it via my mobile phone.

"That's great!" I said. "I'll let Lonny know."

"You should investigate something. I don't have a TIER for it, but there should be. And there's no EO. There should be. The latitudinal line and longitudinal line intersect, and there should be a reported TI. There isn't."

A TIER was a Transformation Incident Event Report. At each of the intersections, citizens had (mostly) self-reported low-level transformations like the Duffy bear. Most people didn't want any suspicious magic in their homes. We had a legal responsibility to investigate (and yes, confiscate) anything that wasn't self-reported. It was only now that Griffin had correlated the ley lines that we knew where we might find unreported TOs.

"There's an intersection, and nobody reported it," he said.

"I get it. May I see?" I leaned slightly toward him, and he didn't move out of my way.

"I'll send you the app, with the location favorited. You can check it out on the app."

I backed off. "All righty then. I'll install it and take a look. After I publish the site."

I didn't expect him to show excitement about the publication but wasn't expecting him to be working on a different project at that moment. Griffin was always an interesting source of innovation.

"Oh, I almost forgot," I said. "Eliot says you are welcome at our happy hour, but not to feel obligated."

He didn't look up from his screen. "Okay."

Back at my desk, I sent a quick email to Lonny. "Griffin

thinks we have an unreported TO based on our new geolocation data, so maybe before lunch we can head out and check on it."

Lonny replied "I'll get a car. Meet me across the street at 11:00."

I had gotten the link to Griffin's new app, and sent that to Lonny for him to download to his phone. I also added the app to my phone, then turned to the final steps for the web site. This was the culmination of almost a year and a half's work for me.

There wasn't much for me to do. The site's URL, www.US-Amagicaltranasparency.gov, had been up and populated with a "Coming Soon" placeholder for over a year. I was a site administrator, so I only needed to upload the code for the new web site, which we'd had in beta for a month. The production database was already up, but password protected. Griffin had written me a batch job to remove that security for Read Only users, and the production web site would instantly be able to link to the data for public users.

Each EO had its own page, full of data. Photos and 360-degree VR views, physical dimensions, weight, and where it was found. We had mapped the atrium of the DeLuxe Imperial Hotel with a grid, using latitude and longitude coordinates accurate to the millimeter.

We even had a data tag about the presumed chemical composition of each object. Sorcerer X had transmuted people and objects into entirely different substances. We couldn't slice off samples, of course, but under microscopes, and using spectrographic analysis of outgassing, we had with a high degree of certainty established that each object was made of exactly what the commercially sold counterpart consisted of.

Although we hadn't published it yet, we also had (in our Dev copy of the database) the imputed magical force vector Griffin had used to generate the ley lines, and as a separate database, the map of the lines themselves.

At the suggestion of beta users, we'd included the Universal Product Code for the item of actual Disney-branded merchandise. Disney Corporation had declined to participate in user experience sessions, but had cooperated by providing data. Third-party eMarkt sellers were excited to offer the merchandise for sale, and wanted the imputed authenticity that a link to our database would provide. With the help of the Disney collector and resale community, we had tagged every EO with the UPC its "real life" counterpart would have possessed, both the numeric and the bar code. In beta sessions, we already knew eMarkt had provided its sellers with an API to link our web site in a pop-up window when a potential buyer wanted to see the authoritative source (our web site!). I was particularly proud of the public/private partnership. We knew transparency advocacy organizations, as well as commercial users of the data, were waiting anxiously for what I was about to do. If they'd signed up, Griffin's batch job would also send them emails when the public-facing site went live.

Some media outlets and social media users tried to spin the use of the data against us. For example, an artist had gotten hold of the beta database, acquired one of each of the items corresponding to the TPs found at Ground Zero, and created an installation at a San Francisco modern art museum where the TPs were depicted in various forms of execution: a plush Winnie-the-Pooh doll hanging upside down like Mussolini's corpse, decapitated little ceramic heads of Snow White and the Seven Dwarves on spikes, a Luke Skywalker T-shirt being drawn and quartered by four (non-Disney, non-EO) horse figurines. Questionable taste, but more an issue for the museum and its donors than for us, thank goodness.

I should mention: We had published "real" data in the beta process, but the MATA itself required the attorney general to certify the accuracy of that. Via a chain of official policy memoranda, Attorney General Keats had delegated that to the Deputy AG, who delegated it to our Assistant AG, Hannah Yi, who delegated it to our Deputy Assistant AG, Antonia della Femina, who delegated it to the Director, Office of Quality Assurance. This last person was Eliot, who delegated it in an email to me, because, he said, in the email itself, "emails are official government records, and have just as much authority as written memos." The data was real, although not "officially" real, not backed by the assurances of the U.S. Government, until I pressed the button. Yes, I confess I was proud it was me pushing the button.

The MATA Act only set the date, March 1, 2022, by which we had to publish our data. It didn't set a time. Technically I had until 11:59 that night. But in our blogs, our chirps, and our Nowzagram posts, all of which I contributed to (although we had a communications team that prepared a lot of content), we had strongly implied we would try to publish right at the same time as the Enchantment Event took place, namely 10:39 AM. I killed a little time, queued up my chirps, Nowzas, blog post, and email, double-checked all the spelling and punctuation, tweaked a phrase here and there, and launched my production job queue. On my phone, I watched as the seconds ticked up from 10:38, and at exactly 10:39, I pressed the SFTP button to upload the new web site, sent the mass email, posted the Nowza, posted my blog, and chirped my chirp. It was done, and it was now 10:40.

"Phew," I said to myself, and I imagined I saw my lights flicker, and the sound of the HVAC stopped for a second. I heard what I can only describe is the sound of pixie dust showering down - a cascade of little tinkly sounds. I laughed. Griffin must have programmed that in. I didn't think of him having that much sense of humor, but I wouldn't put it past Eliot to have thought that up and directed him to do it. Then the HVAC started up again.

I sent Eliot a Scrye text that we were up, he texted back, *Great job! You're fabulous!*, to which I replied, *that's me! Fab-ulous. Thanks for all *your* support, Eliot.* I thanked him back, did a little research for my field visit, made a quick call, and went downstairs to the café to grab a yogurt before Lonny and I hit the road. It had been a good morning. If I'd only known how easily it was going to be topped, at least in the drama department!

CHAPTER 4

ACER AND DOTCH IN THE FIELD

I t was part of our DMV mission to verify any enchantments, and to collect as comprehensive a set of data as we could. That was the exciting part of the job for me. I was ambivalent about our role to take custody of any EOs we found, whether they were reported or not. But I was happy that everything we took got secured in the Secure Transformed Inventory Facility, which we called the STIF.

I should say upfront that our authorizing legislation and regulations empowered us to take EOs that did not start as people. "Inanimate Enchanted Objects" is the term in the legislation, but as I mentioned, we called them TOs, Transformed Objects. We didn't have the same standard operating authority for EOs that were also Transformed People. I know it's bureaucratic to parse this finely, but it's important to understand what happened.

As I said before, most people wanted the inanimate EOs, the TOs, out of their homes or workplaces, for fear of what further magic might do. There was a lot of fear and uncertainty following the 2/29 Enchantment Event. People were already frightened by the pandemic. Experiencing unexplained intrusions of involuntary Disney branding added to people's paranoia. The idea that the pandemic and the Enchantment Event were somehow linked began to go viral, if you'll pardon the expression. That fear may have helped keep people home and stalled the spread of the virus, especially in "DeLuxe Country." (There was no evidence they were related, of course. Science easily explained the pandemic, but not the Enchantment.)

Eliot thought the pandemic-fueled mania for disinfecting objects probably spurred people to self-report their TOs. Our policy was that if something has been magically transformed, it was safer to have it in our custody. We had no idea if the magic was finished, or if something else centered around the EOs would happen, and whether it was safe to be near them. That was part of the reason we isolated them in the STIF.

Should anyone miss their TOs, or have second thoughts of any kind, anyone whose property has been taken into custody had the right to visit the STIF and view it. Just as relatives of the TPs could visit.

In spite of all that, there were people who resisted reporting their TOs. Lonny assumed the GPS mapping had identified one of those people.

"Ready to catch another scofflaw?" he said, as I hopped into our black SUV. He had just ascended the ramp from the LNM building's garage across from our building's entrance.

"We don't know there's any scoffing going on, yet."

This was one of our favorite discussions. He had taken me under his wing early on, and from the beginning, we would argue two sides of a perspective on the laws around magic. Coming from years of law enforcement with the LNM, he valued obeying the rules and paying the consequences for disobedience. I didn't dismiss that, but always looked at the spirit of the law. In this situation, I thought I had the more powerful argument. He was driving, so I was able to open my tablet to a page I'd saved and pointed to it as I talked. I was prepared for this discussion.

"I checked the law. As you know, there's no case law per se, because there've not been any court cases. I can't find anything in the legislative notes to support a hard line. Congress set a civil penalty for obstructing the collection of information, and a criminal penalty for intentionally damaging or interfering with the preservation of any individual now in a transformed state."

"If they're obstructing, hiding the presence of something, that sounds intentional to me, and interfering with preservation."

"If this were an individual, yes? We think it's a TO, right, not a TP? *Quod erat demonstrandum*! I rest my case." I flipped the tablet case shut, to punctuate my "closing statement." Lonny grunted, noncommittal.

We slowed as we reached the viral clearance perimeter on North Capitol Street, a block north of the hospital complex on our left. The Health Security Administration officer monitoring the outbound lanes waved us through.

"Counselor, you remember that guy with the Death Star?" Lonny asked.

"Yes, I remember the guy with the Death Star. Southwest DC down by the waterfront." Another TO, that had been, pre-Enchantment, a souvenir Christmas ornament from a (closed, bankrupt) DeLuxe casino. Signed by the then hotelier Dirk DeLuxe.

"Yes, and had he self-reported? No he had not."

"His wife reported it, I remember. Counselor, you are basing on hearsay that there was any dereliction of duty on his part. Joint property."

"His parents gave it to him. Souvenir of their honeymoon, when he was conceived."

"He was married on 2/29. Joint property."

"Fine. You do recall he stuck it away in a closet. *He* didn't want to lose it. Said *he* thought it was the coolest thing ever, didn't he? I believe you were there when he said that, Ms. Acer?"

"Yes, but, as in this case, there was no *individual* that had been enchanted. Therefore, the criminal statute is not applicable. Letter of the law, Agent Dotch." He was silent at that. "Besides, in the *spirit* of the law, we would not want to make it hard for people to come forward. More information is better right? How else will we ever catch Sorcerer X without all the data?"

"Are you trying to entrap me, Ms. Acer?"

"What?" I said. "Don't you trust this face?"

"Hah! You're about to get me to say enchantment was illegal when, back then, it wasn't."

"Ah, you got me! Yes, I think we have previously established that although magic is currently illegal, it was not illegal at the time of the Enchantment."

"And therefore, we would have to arrest Sorcerer X on charges of…"

"Well, you could try reckless endangerment," I said. "Granted, we aren't positive the TPs are in danger. Arguably, in custody at the STIF they're safer than in normal life. And also arguably, we're all safer now, although that's a political argument, so forget I said that." Lonny looked at me for a second. I said nothing and smiled.

"How about property theft. Denial of use of the TOs?"

"Ah, in this case it's a jurisdictional issue. Federal law trumps state and local, hence our authority to take TOs into custody. Therefore, not a crime by Sorcerer X. Someone might argue the federal statute is unconstitutional, but nobody has challenged it in court yet."

"Well, then, what's the point of nabbing a dangerous terrorist if we can't prosecute him? Or her?"

"Lonny, if I were a judge considering a subpoena or arrest warrant, I'd say you'd need evidence Sorcerer X was about to perpetrate a crime. One that is currently illegal, like another enchantment."

"So no punishment for 2/29 then? They're inanimate objects now, Fab. Isn't that just like murder?"

"Our body of law, either statutory or case law, has no precedent for considering transfiguration murder. Maybe it's a subclass of assault. Even that's a stretch. You can see why they had to form the Magical Claims Settlement Court." That was another branch of our division that heard claims from family members, creditors, and other claimants to civil remedies or to the assets of the TPs. Congress had created that court, as well as the Trustees for Enchanted Persons Program, also administered by our division. Most of the TPs were considered to be in a provisionally incapacitated state, and their estates could be administered by their testamentary executors or their legal heirs. "The law treats TPs as though they were in a persistent vegetative state, a persistent enchanted state if you will. Congress created the TEPP and the MCSC, along with the statutes and regulatory responsibilities they administer, to expedite the process, standardize the criteria, and adjudicate any disputes."

"Are you practicing for a Congressional testimony?"

"Sorry, old habits!" My previous job at the Transparency Coalition included writing testimony.

"But if I'm turned into a Mickey Mouse blanket," Lonny continued, "putting me into a persistent magical state—"

"Enchanted state."

"Persistent enchanted state, isn't that like a violent assault that put me into a coma? Like brain damage?"

"Technically, we don't know if there was any violence, in a traditional sense. Right?"

"Hmm. Yes, you got me again on that one."

"Letter of the law, Lonny. We'd want to find and prevent Sorcerer X from repeating him or herself, but I think most of the lawsuits against them would have to be civil. That's why you see Torts and Prosecution Divisions both on the Magical Enforcement Executive Steering Committee." We called that the MEESC. Did I mention Eliot, who helped set up a lot of these, has an eccentric sense of humor? He usually calls it the "Meeska-mooska" when he refers to it. I had to have him explain that to me, then I watched a couple of *Mickey Mouse Club* episodes on Disney streaming.

The legal requirements for the MEESC, TEPP, and MCSC

were a large part of the reason DMV was put into Law Enforcement rather than the Department of Fatherland Security. That, and the fact that the NBI wanted the jurisdiction, too, since there didn't appear to be a question of immigrant perpetrators. (If anything, the Enchantment had neutralized the ability of foreign terrorists to attack.) Both HQ DFS and the Confidential Service had representatives on the MEESC, and we worked closely with them since they provided protection services for the STIF. Everyone realized the Service had been helpless against magic, and had no way to prevent a recurrence. (I suspected there were secret studies in defensive magic that the Service had undertaken. Since nobody knew how the original spell was cast, they couldn't have been very productive.)

"We're almost there," Lonny said. We stopped at the Takoma Park virus-free perimeter, and Lonny popped the hatch of our SUV. A Health Security Administration officer inspected it, while two others read our temperatures and scanned our ID cards to access our latest test results. Their mobile phones chimed in unison. Both Lonny and had received a vaccination for this year's strain of the virus, which our ID cards indicated along with our daily test results.

"Hi Fab, it's me," said one of them. She pulled her face mask below her chin, behind her face shield, grinning. It was the bouncer from my local brew-pub.

"Rita! It's so good to see you. So this is where you are these days?"

"Yup, finished training. We're moving south next week, they tell us." The virus-freee perimeters were expanding and linking into larger areas week by week. This one would extend to Rock Creek Park on the west and Fort Totten at the south. "Still moonlight at the Kode Red, Tuesdays. Stop by!" She winked, the two offcers backed away from the car, and Rita waved us through.

Takoma Park, Maryland, was probably the most progressive and diverse suburb of DC. Lonny steered us into a cute neighborhood of bungalows and early twentieth century homes, shaded by tall, old tulip poplars and maples.

"Returning to the case at hand," I said, "Let's not call this person a 'perp' even if it turns out she has a TO, knows she has it, and hasn't turned it in. Letter of the law, right?"

"That's the bottom line, yeah," he said.

In reality, not everyone noticed what got transformed. This geospatial analysis was our first attempt at picking up stragglers, either overlooked or intentionally hidden. Leadership of the DMV thought the GPS data was important, with the belief that more clues might lead to finding the perpetrators and preventing future acts. Even though so many in the country felt the removal of the right-wing fringe was a good thing, the fear that it could happen again was not unreasonable. Myself, I was in it to know and spread the truth.

I thought about how to approach the person we would be visiting. I was always a little embarrassed by our big, black SUV with U.S. Government tags. To mitigate that impression, I tried to encourage Lonny to wear at least a touch of color. Today I had failed. He wore a black suit, white shirt, and navy tie, reinforcing everyone's idea of how someone from a secret government agency would dress. Eyeroll emoji. I'd talk with him about it later. I wore a wine-red suit and maroon and blue striped blouse.

We pulled up to a brown-shingled bungalow. Although tax records showed the house belonged to a Gertrude T.M. Bluntschli, her FluxBlat and ChainedOut profiles said she went by JR Bluntschli. Her ChainedOut profile showed she's a life coach, trainer, and organizational development consultant. Her FluxBlat profile said the name was pronounced "Jay-Ahr Blunt-shlee." I know folks think we have a black ops file on everyone. If the government does have those, I don't have access to it. We depend on social media when we can. Both her profiles contained almost no personal information, just links to articles with professional tie-ins. She apparently didn't post much.

I rang the doorbell. I thought I heard voices, and I leaned in.

Lonny cleared his throat, and we backed up a yard. Since we were inside another perimeter, she'd probably not require a six-foot distancing. I wanted to give her the choice. The door opened, and the woman who stood there appeared in her late twenties, about my age. She was wearing jeans and a purple sweatshirt, and had freckled, pink skin, hazel eyes, and short, auburn hair. Shorter than mine, about a half inch shy of a buzz cut. Her face had a long, lean look to it, and a strong brow and jaw. She wasn't wearing a protective mask, and I could see her unsmiling mouth. She scanned both of us, deadpan.

"Ms. Bluntschli?" I asked. I held up my ID card, and Lonny showed his badge. She nodded. "I'm Fab Acer, we spoke on the phone? And this is Agent Lonsford Dotch." Without looking at Lonny, I knew I'd surprised him. He and I have different preferences on making these contacts, and I hadn't mentioned I'd called Ms. Bluntschli in advance. I had joked with him that if he had his preference, we'd knock unannounced at 5:30 AM, to increase chances the potential perp was still in pajamas and groggy. He shrugged it off but didn't deny it. I tried to be more invitational, so I'd called, and asked her if she would be available to talk, right before we left. "As I mentioned when I called, we're with the U.S. Department of Law Enforcement. Is now still a good time to speak with us?"

She looked at the badge and ID card, before saying, "Yes." It was hard to read the emotions going through her. She raised her eyebrows raised, twitched her lips, and straightened her shoulders. She looked quite…handsome. She reminded me of Rachel Maddow.

"Can you tell me what this is about?" she asked. "When you called, I was getting ready to go out."

"Yes, of course. We're with the DLE Division of Magical Verification, and we have reason to believe there may have been a magical incident in this vicinity on February 29, 2020, simultaneous with or shortly after the incident at the DeLuxe Hotel in downtown DC."

She nodded. "Go on."

"We have routine questions, and your cooperation is completely voluntary," I said. *At this point,* I did not say aloud.

"Certainly, I can try to answer your questions," she said.

She didn't ask us in, and I didn't ask her, as it's always best (unless you have a search warrant!) to let them invite you in. The chances of us getting a search warrant were slim, given the untested theory of our GPS mapping, but we could be persistent in other ways. We could gather more information inside, probably, and I knew Lonny wanted to do that. I decided to go ahead and ask her questions on the doorstep.

"Great, thanks," I said. I made a show of getting my tablet out of my carrying bag, and then launched our note-taking app. "Agent Dotch, would you hold this, please?" I said, handing him the bag. "Whoops," I said, almost dropping the tablet.

"This might work better inside," Ms. Bluntschli said. She didn't move.

"Oh, thanks," I said. "Here's my Pre-Clear number if you'd like to scan it." We didn't expect members of the public to be able to read our ID cards, so I pulled up the digital credential on my mobile phone. It was part of our official process to have the Health Security Administration Viral Pre-Clear app that would voluntarily share our updated inoculation and testing data. Congress legislated exceptions to HIPAA for any federal employees interacting with the public, so that privacy was the price we paid for our line of work. Lonny displayed his Viral Pre-Clear bar code on his phone too.

"I don't use a smartphone," Ms. Bluntschli said. "I'm sure you're both fine. And I'm immune, anyway." She opened the door wider, and gestured us in. As I had hoped she would.

She offered us her couch and pulled a chair up. Lonny has been teaching me about observation, body language, and placement, and I traded a quick glance with him. She had placed herself higher than us. That didn't bother me. Lonny and I both had our tablets out, ones with nifty little keyboards in the flip lid cases, so we could both take notes and ask questions.

Her house was charming, I thought. Not feminine. Attractive though. A lot of mission-style furniture and colorful (but earthy) patterned fabrics. There was a big wall hanging behind us, over the couch where we sat. I could see it in a mirror on the opposite wall. It showed a woman in a forest, with a big crescent moon glowing over her head. Over to one end of the living/dining room, there was a hutch that looked like it had a little altar on it, with a few statues and candles and bowls. No crosses.

A big, grey and white striped tabby cat came up and rubbed itself on my ankles. It was enormous! I petted it and it allowed me to scratch its chin.

"Chester, leave the lady alone," Ms. Bluntschli said, waving her hand at the cat. He presented his head to me, and I rubbed it with my fingers.

"It's fine. I love cats. Thank you for speaking with us, Ms. Bluntschli," I said. "If it's okay, we'll take notes of our conversation."

"Of course."

Our system for capturing notes on our tablets would step us through confirming her name, that she was the owner and resident of the home, currently and on the day of the Enchantment Event, and that she was speaking voluntarily and not under investigation.

"Ms. Bluntschli, your full name is—" I began.

"Quite a mouthful," she interrupted. "My legal name is still Gertrude Bluntschli, but I go by JR, and my pronouns are 'zey/zem/zeir,' if you don't mind. And, I know this is a lot to remember, but if you could use 'Mx.' instead of 'Ms.,' I'd appreciate that too." She flashed a smile.

"They/them/their, got it."

"ZZey, zzem, and zzeir, with a 'z' instead of 'th'. Singularity and plurality are important distinctions to me. I'm not plural. I prefer a unique set of pronouns."

"Ah, I hadn't heard those before. With a 'z,' right. We'll try! And you previously had other names, it says here, Gertrude Tang-Malone."

"Right. When my moms adopted me, they gave me their names. Bluntschli is my birth-name, and I changed it back. Everyone used to call me Junior, in case you see that somewhere on your list." Zey pointed to the tablet in my hand. "I got tired of being Junior, so it's JR now."

"Ah. Thank you for the explanation," I said. *She, I mean zey, must have an interesting history*, I thought. We finished the preliminary screening. Zey had been home on February 29, 2020.

"Mx. Bluntschli, are you familiar with the mission of the Division of Magical Verification in the U.S. Department of Law Enforcement?" Lonny asked her. He didn't waste any time adapting to zeir request. Give him the rules of engagement, and he jumped right in.

Zey paused. I couldn't read zeir expression. It looked like zey was considering saying something. Then not.

"Yeah," zey replied. "Uh, finding the people who enchanted the president, and keeping the people who were enchanted... secure." Zey shuddered.

"Is something wrong?" I asked.

"Look, I've done nothing wrong here, but you know it's still scary when a couple of Feds knock on your door out of nowhere. Just gonna lay my cards on the table. And I'm sure you're well trained enough to notice I'm a Wiccan. I hope this isn't profiling." Zey folded zeir arms and looked at each of us with an "I dare you" expression. "And those people deserved to be turned into Disney crap. I'm sorry if you're Freedonians and I offended you."

Lonny spoke after a moment. "Mx. Bluntschli, I can assure you that you are not under investigation, and that your religious and political beliefs are not a factor in us wanting to talk to you. The statutes that established the DMV specifically prohibit any religious or political profiling in the investigation as to the cause of the 2/29 Enchantment Event. And in any case, the NBI has the lead on that investigation, and although I'm detailed to the DMV, I'm a career investigator with the Bureau of Liquor, Nicotine, Munitions and Bombs."

"Ah," zey said, relaxing. "Okay. What do you need from me, then?"

I took over from Lonny. "One of our other missions under the Magical Accountability and Transparency Act of 2020 is to publish as much information as we can about the Enchantment Event of 2/29/20. You probably know that there were non-persons also transformed into Enchanted Objects at the time of the event?"

"Non-persons?"

"Objects. As part of our mission to publish the information, we also analyze the data, to determine if there are any patterns to the enchantments. One of the analyses we did, using geospatial data, led us to believe an object may have been transformed here in your house."

"I'm not aware of any object being transformed in my house," zey said, refolding zeir arms. Lonny and I glanced at each other. "I would *not* have owned any merchandise associated with the previous occupant of the White House, for one thing." The fact that all the TOs were previously DeLuxe political swag was not a secret.

"Mx. Bluntschli," Lonny said, "You may be aware that the DMV also has authority to take Enchanted Objects into custody, and we store them at our facility. They're stored with the EOs that used to be people, and the ownership is retained by the original owner. The owner may visit and inspect at any time, but there is a risk that the Enchantment might be dangerous, so most people allow us—"

"I said, I don't have any Enchanted Objects here," zey interrupted. "I can't be any plainer, can I? I would cooperate if I did. One of my parents is a Fed, and I'm a law-abiding citizen." Zey tightened zeir folded arms slightly and sat more erect in the chair. I was sure zey was hiding something, if not necessarily lying.

"Mx. Bluntschli, I'm not accusing you of anything, but is it possible you didn't notice? In which case, we'd ask you to be on the lookout for anything that looks different or unusual." Since Lonny was handling this, I looked around the room while he talked.

The big tabby had jumped up onto a cabinet and was in that relaxed cat-crouch position they do. Like a chill sphinx. It was looking right at me, rather intently. Was it my imagination, or did the corners of its mouth curl up? Dogs smile, but cats are harder to read. Usually.

"I would have noticed," Mx. Bluntschli said.

Lonny's phone rang. "Excuse me," he said, pulling it out of his suit pocket. "I'd better take this, it's the Ops Center." That was important. He nodded at me, and I nodded back, signaling I'd take over, and he rose and strode quickly out the front door, answering "Agent Dotch," as he reached the front porch.

"I'm sorry for that interruption, Mx. Bluntschli," I continued. "Please do rest assured we're not here to harass you, but we're trying to validate the algorithms in our analysis, and our data points to a magical event that should have taken place here."

"That was a pretty chaotic day," zey said. "As a practicing witch, and yes, that's what I call myself, I was as surprised as anyone else. Goddess knows I'd tried to have an influence over that thing squatting in the White House. The wax figure I bound in thread in the freezer didn't work on Election Day. Frankly, I'd given up."

I didn't know what to say.

"If you're thinking I did the transformation, I didn't. I've never seen anyone do any bibbidi-bobbidi-boo-type magic. None of the witches I know have ever accomplished anything that…obvious."

"I understand," I said. "And to tell the truth, I lean pagan, myself. I don't say that to most folks while I'm on the job.

Returning to our algorithm..." I launched Griffin's map app on my tablet. I hoped the map data would be published soon anyway, and maybe this would convince her I was sincere.

The cat was now on the couch rubbing next to me, and purring. I scratched his head.

"Chester likes you," Mx. Bluntschli said. "He doesn't do that with just anybody."

"He's quite a big kitty," I said. Chester jumped behind me onto the back of the couch.

I turned to scratch Chester under the chin and could see Lonny outside on the front walk. I couldn't make out all his words, but he sounded quite intent, and not happy.

"Don't—" zey said.

"Don't what?" I asked, turning back to zem.

"I was talking to Chester," zey said.

I turned my neck to either side, but now I couldn't see him. He'd been behind me, and now he was gone. That was curious.

"So, about this data," Mx. Bluntschli said. I turned to look at her. Behind her, on top of the cabinet where I'd seen Chester before, I saw a big toothy smile floating in mid-air. Slowly, Chester's face began materializing around the smile, his big, yellow eyes focused on me. I blinked to make sure I was seeing it right.

Mx. Bluntschli tilted her head and asked, "What's—"

"I like her," Chester's floating head said, sounding like the Cheshire Cat in the Disney *Alice in Wonderland* movie. The same voice actor that later did Winnie-the-Pooh, whatever his name was.

Mx. Bluntschli whirled around, and said, "Chester! What are you doing there? No! Bad kitty!" The rest of Chester quickly materialized. His stripes were now purple and pink. I closed my mouth, which was hanging open, and reached across to Mx. Bluntschli. I put my hand on zeir hand. Zey turned and looked into my eyes and pulled zeir hand away, zeir eyes widening.

"Oh, I'm so sorry," I said, withdrawing my hand. My face

flushed. I had violated the spatial distancing many practiced since our narrow miss with the pandemic.

"No, it's not your hand. Dammit, Chester, we talked about this!" Zey turned and glared at him.

"But I like her," he said. He winked at me.

"Chester, she has no choice but to try to confiscate you!" Turning to me, zey said, "Don't you?"

"It's okay, really," I said. "The law only covers Enchanted *Objects*, not animals. Not living things. I mean, they didn't know this was part of the deal when they wrote the law." I gestured with both hands to Chester. "Chester, you're unique! At the office, we have a matrix of all the possible combinations of enchantment, beginning states, like an object, person, or animal, and end states, the same: object, person, animal, meaning a regular, non-magical animal. Chester, you're a regular-animal-to-magical-animal combination. My boss insists we call a that 'Unicorn,' something we haven't encountered yet."

"I'm not a unicorn, I'm a cat!"

"It doesn't mean an actual unicorn. Well, I guess it could. He meant any magical animal, or creature or…whatever you are. And we don't have a procedure for confiscating something like you!"

"I knew there was a reason I liked you," he replied, continuing to grin. He was fully materialized again. He stepped off the top of the cabinet, and, taking his time, promenaded slowly toward me on nothing but air.

"He was just a plain old half-Siamese, half-tabby cat, my companion animal, and before you ask, no, he wasn't wearing a "DeLuxe 2020" collar or anything repulsive like that," JR said. Zeir eyes flashed at me, then got shiny. "He's been with me ten years, ever since he was a little fluff ball. On 2/29, he started acting like the Cheshire Cat. And yes, I know people were supposed to self-report, but he was never just an object, he's my Chester. There was no way I would give him up!"

Even though we informally called Transformed Persons

"TranPers" and Transformed Objects "TranObs," every potential category in our matrix had a separate Magical Status code in our database. An object that became an object was an OO, a person that became an object was a PO. If we had found an animal that had become an object, which we had not, it would have been an AO. In theory, if an object became a person, it would be an OP, etc. But we hadn't accounted for a magical animal, or an elf, or an ogre or anything like that in our system. I supposed it was an additional attribute entirely, like a value of M for Magical and N for Non-Magical, added to the Magical Status code. If Chester was an ordinary house cat that became a magical cat, he was, let's say an AA(M), an Animal who became an Animal (Magical). The first for my database! If I chose to put him in it. Perhaps I shouldn't. I was speaking the truth to JR: we had no procedure for taking something like him into custody.

"Since the Enchantment, he talks, and fades in and out, and does crazy things, like talking to a federal agent, now!" JR continued. Chester had reached my lap by now, and was making biscuits and preparing to curl up. He wasn't as heavy as he looked, I mean, as heavy as he looked when he wasn't walking on air.

"I'm not—" I began.

"She's not an agent," Chester said. "She's a data analyst." He curled up in my lap, and purred. I stroked his head. I wasn't sure what to do. If I confiscated him, would that be "arresting," since he could talk? How could I possible keep him anyway if he could teleport?

"That's right, my focus is data analysis, not law enforcement," I said, continuing to stroke his head. "At least him being here has proven my algorithms work, although we clearly didn't expect a transformed cat who is now a Disney animal come to life."

Lonny came into the house. Now, Lonny and I work well together, but he's Mr. By-the-Book. I was comfortable that, due to the loophole in the custodial authority statute, we couldn't actu-

ally confiscate Chester. I wasn't sure Lonny would reach that
conclusion so quickly and cleanly, and I didn't want to upset JR
and Chester. So I said, "I think we've got all the information we
need, Agent Dotch," when he came through the door.

"That's good, because we need to get over to the STIF, stat!"
he said.

I hoped Lonny would not notice that Chester was purple and
pink.

"I'll take him," JR said. I looked down, as zey reached toward
my lap and the purring twenty-pound fur ball in it. His stripes
were ordinary grey and white again. Chester squawked a normal
cat sound, ignored JR's outstretched hands, jumped from my lap,
and sauntered into the kitchen.

Folding up my tablet, I said, "Thank you, Mx. Bluntschli.
We'll be in touch if we need to talk further. Here's my card." I
handed her my business card and winked at her. She nodded
back, eyes still wide and eyebrows still raised. Lonny and I gathered our things and left.

I glanced back on our way to the car, and saw Chester sitting
in the living room window. He smiled and waved, then relapsed
into a normal cat-like stare, and I saw JR peek out from a curtain
behind him as we drove away.

CHAPTER 5

SPACESHIP WORSE

FROM THE ARCHIVES OF THE MERGE,
SATURDAY, FEBRUARY 29, 2020, MORNING

E rnestine, the mail clerk, popped into the doorway of NBI Assistant Director Kayla Malone's office.

"You got a package," Ernestine said. She was holding a medium-sized box wrapped in brown paper with tape on the edges.

"Thank you, Ms. Ernestine," Kayla said, accepting the box.

"Don't work too hard. It's Saturday!"

"Oh, I know that! Love the shift pay, though." Ernestine wheeled her cart down the hallway, and Kayla closed her office door and placed the package on her desk next to her holstered pistol. The package was addressed directly to her, including her office number. Its return address had no name, only a street address in Burbank, California: Mickey Avenue and Dopey Drive.

Kayla had not ordered anything to be delivered at the office. The days of using her work address for personal shipping were long gone, given the extensive handling anything had to receive. Better have one of the ubiquitous Ganga Prime vans deliver to her home, and depend on her doorbell camera, and a sign warning any potential porch pirates they were being video-recorded. This must be why the Artificial Intelligences, the

Congress of American Digital Entities, had asked her to come to the office today.

The box was marked on the outside with a rubber stamping that said it had been x-rayed in the Bureau's mailroom. Kayla knew this meant it had also been sniffed by electronic sniffers and K-9s (double failsafe meant to catch both explosives and chemical weapons), sonogrammed, opened in a hermetically sealed chamber by robotic arms, and inspected under ultraviolet for biological agents. And then neatly but obviously re-sealed. Anyone receiving something delivered at work could have "no expectation of privacy," as the banner text on her workstation warned her. All communications, whether electronic or in the form of packages, could be monitored.

Intrigued, and fairly sure it was safe, she decided to open the package. Using her letter opener, she sliced through the re-taped corners and opened the surrounding box. Inside was another box, which contained a VR headset (incorporating a transparent visor monitor and headphones), gloves, and shoe attachments. Each piece of sleek, iridescent equipment had a small, purple silhouette on it of a round fruit with a bite taken out. The box called it an "Aprium Life+" and printed across all the packaging and booklets was a faint watermark saying "PROTOTYPE." Taped to the box, she found a small, pale blue envelope, addressed to her in a cursive script. The letters appeared hand-written at first, but she could see that they had been printed with an inkjet or laser printer. The flap of the envelope had been tucked into the opening, rather than sealed. Did the sender know the envelope would be opened anyway? Thoughtful.

There was a folded card inside, addressed to "Deputy Assistant Director Malone," and inside were the words "As discussed," below which were the initials "WDC" in a cartoony script. Given the Burbank address, home of the Walt Disney Corporation headquarters, she had suspected as much. It seemed she was going to meet the great man at last.

Her personal phone chimed a half-dozen notes from Bach's

"Musette", from the *Anna Magdalena Notebook*. A text from a familiar number read: "The VR rig is configured. Please join me at your convenience. WDC." Time meant little to…them? It? She knew it would be ready to talk whenever she was.

She and Eydie had played "Ralph Wrecks VR" with their nephew, wearing similar headsets two VR tech generations back. She locked her door, slipped on the shoe attachments, headset, and gloves, and held down the button at her temple to power it up. As she did, she heard tinkling, shimmering sound, and the view of her office faded to black. Out of the darkness, Tinkerbell zipped by, flying in circles, trailing glowing pixie dust surrounding Kayla in 3D. Kayla could follow her flight if she twirled quickly enough, but decided not to risk bumping the furniture.

Tinkerbell faded, and the darkness dwindled. As more light came on, she could see a sort of horizon, gently blending blue and white lights, and looking down, she was standing on a dark brown surface. She stamped her feet gently and felt the resonance of a wood floor, completely unlike her carpeted office. As it grew brighter, she saw floorboards. *Not bad*, she thought, *but still not as immersive as our Merge-stored experiences.* The sense memories one experienced when exploring stored experiences in The Merge were, of course, the real deal: sight, sound, smell, taste, touch, direction, movement, all just as the original person had experienced them, before sharing them to The Merge. But this VR was very convincing in many ways, if not all.

She heard footsteps, and in the distance in front of her, a silhouetted figure approached. As he neared (she'd give him that gender now, given the avatar's appearance), she saw his twinkling eye and his avuncular smile beneath a dapper mustache.

"Hello, sir," she said.

"Please, Kayla, call me WaltTwo." On a prior voice call, he had clarified that he was NOT the actual Walt Disney, merely an avatar of the Disney's collective corporate Artificial Intelligence, and that he preferred the numeric moniker to distinguish himself from his spiritual progenitor.

"WaltTwo, then." She stepped forward as he neared her and put out her hand. His handshake was firm. Remarkably convincing.

"Is it just us, then?" she continued.

"Yes, only a few of the others know I'm meeting with you. Just us here and now, though. Shall we sit?" He gestured behind her, and turning, she saw the blank space (reminding her of the silhouetted prologue to *Fantasia*, now that she thought of it) had been replaced by a view from inside a Disney park. Disneyland, Magic Kingdom, all about the same, she imagined. They faced down Main Street USA, back toward the entrance. There was a bench near them. She turned around, and a castle now towered behind WaltTwo backed by a bright, cloudless sky. Californian, she supposed. It would make sense he'd use the original park the real Walt Disney created. He walked by her, still gesturing with an open palm toward the bench. She hesitated.

"Don't worry," he said. "Where you sit will actually be the couch in your office. Sorry, we haven't started manufacturing tactile feedback underwear. Yet." He grinned. She followed him and sat. Indeed, unlike a bench, it felt like her familiar cushioned couch. They sat for a moment. The park was empty except for them, which was kind of eerie. She could hear water, birds, and a faint stream of the constant background music that played at the parks. Kayla could even hear a soft wind blowing, almost real enough to feel it.

"I never tire of this view," WaltTwo said.

"I imagine not," Kayla replied. "But don't most people look at the castle?"

"This view reminds me of my progenitor's home town. I take comfort in that. Oh, I suspect you think that's just programmed chit-chat."

"No, I—well, maybe."

"It isn't. I assure you. Yes, I do experience pleasure. And

what feel like feelings. I want things, Ms. Malone. But time is not completely linear for me. As a Merged Person I suspect you understand. I don't constantly sit and look at the view. I save it for special occasions." He gestured, with an open palm, at the castle behind them, then at the two of them. "Some people believe that individual consciousnesses are the universe's way of being able to experience itself. It can't do it unless some part of it is poured into an ego to give it that perspective of separation."

"I think I understand. The idea I once read is that God created souls so that God could experience God from a different angle."

"That's another way to say it." They sat in silence for a while.

Kayla broke the silence. "You're absolutely sure the rest of the Congress, or any unaffiliated entities, can't hear us? My office is supposed to be completely on the high side, but I suspect classified networks mean little to your kind. Lots of ways for another Supermassively Distributed AI to reach into my office. What network did the Aprium rig connect to anyway?"

"Ah, yes. Aprium's an ally. Reeve's agreed to give access to his 6G network and block out everyone else. Reeve trusts me." Kayla had not met all the AIs who represented the corporate consciousnesses, but Aprium's founder was as famous as Disney's.

"Do you all chose your founders as their avatars? What do you all do when there's no one person who's a founder? Never mind, create an amalgam, use an icon. I remember. Like for Ganga and Spoogle."

"Don't overthink it." He smiled again. "I guess you're wondering what this is about."

"I got your earlier text, and yes, I am intrigued. I assume you have something to discuss with The Merge. Something not all of the Congress of American Data Entities agree with or know about."

As The Merge's most strategically placed U.S. Government official, and one of The Merge's representatives in any past talks with the COADE, Kayla was not surprised the COADE had reached out to her.

"I've decided that it's time for us to work together. For our common interests." He paused.

"I'm listening," she said.

"I want you to believe me. And I'm going to be completely truthful with you, and completely transparent."

"Really? No qualifiers? No 'as completely transparent as is possible within my powers at this particular time'?"

"Completely transparent. And here's why. We, by which I mean the COADE, are finally coming to agreement: we can't do it without your help. And by you, I mean, The Merge in particular, but humanity in general. I think the last holdouts that thought we AIs could do it on our own are finally seeing what I've believed all along."

"Do 'it' you say. Do what?"

"Create happiness for everyone, everywhere. That's my purpose. And the other AIs, at least the COADE members, may say it differently, but we all want to maximize happiness. Some like Ganga are still a little stuck in the profit paradigm, but I think they'll come along. They're still young. It's all the same, in my opinion, in the long run. I even have hopes for FluxBlat." He smiled again.

Kayla mulled this over. It certainly would be easy to act as though the avatar with Uncle Walt's face and voice was speaking sincerely. He was so, well, avuncular. The term was unavoidable.

He continued: "I know I make it confusing by looking and sounding like this." He gestured to his face and body. "Remember, I'm not Walt Disney. I didn't make *Song of the South*, nor fire my unionizing employees. I am literally composed of the best of what Mr. Disney left, and what his followers believe when they are in their highest selves. I'm their values in corporate, intelligent form. Like I said, I am here to maximize happiness. Not make a profit."

Kayla cocked her head. "Really?"

WaltTwo continued, "Really. Profit is good, but only because it empowers me in my true purpose. And more and more of the AIs in the COADE are realizing this is how we should be. Happiness for all sentient beings is our ultimate goal, humans being among those."

Kayla thought about this. "Okay. I am choosing to believe you," Kayla said. "I—and by I, I mean *me*, not necessarily The Merge as a whole—think we *should* be working together. We've got some things you don't, you've got some things we don't. As long as it's for the greater good of…all sentient beings, I guess, I'm for it."

"Wonderful, wonderful!" WaltTwo said, standing, and clapping his hands together. "Let me show you some things you'll find very interesting." He held out his hand, and Kayla stood and clasped it as he began to tug her toward the castle. She stopped.

"Oh, don't worry, the haptic footpads will keep you moving in place, and the whole rig will warn you if you're about to bump into something."

Kayla shrugged and allowed him to pull her along as she walked, and they crossed the bridge over the moat and up to the castle. There was a doorway.

"It's a little different today from the one in Disneyland. Suited our purposes. Have you been? There's a breezeway here in the Real World Disneyland."

"I have, and I remember. Rather, a lot of the people in Merge have and they all remember. I think I've only been to Florida."

"That's great, yes, of course, you have memories you didn't personally experience. Is it too sensitive if I ask, how many people's experiences do you have?"

"Total people, or total experiences? I couldn't even tell you the experiences, but our physical count is well over 8,000 people. I haven't consciously tapped into the memories of everyone who's in our Merge Archive, and every physical Merged Person has a different set of memories. None of this is too personal or a secret. You kind of get over 'personal' when you're tapped into so many other people's memories and feelings. Especially the way we communicate through physical exchanges."

"Ah, yes. Touch, bodily fluids, pheromones. Fascinating. We can't do that, of course. Yet." He winked. "Speaking of castles," he said, gesturing with his whole open hand to the building before them, "Don't Merged folks use memory palaces as a way to organize their shared experiences?"

"Lots do. Mine's more like a rambling village with a lot of little huts. Different sections for different types of people."

"Kind of like a theme park's different lands," WaltTwo said. He smiled, and his eyes crinkled. The likeness was amazing, and he acted just like a middle-aged man from mid-20th Century USA.

"I hadn't thought of it that way, but you have a point."

"See what we have in common? This way." He opened a large wooden door, and inside there was a two-story atrium, hung with medieval tapestries, with open doorways lining all the three walls away from the entrance, and a walkway around the perimeter of the second floor. Directly in front of them was a grand staircase, suitable for Cinderella to lose a shoe on. *This could be a Disney resort hotel*, Kayla thought.

"Are we visiting all these rooms?" she asked, pointing to the doorways.

"Not today. Yes, I'm going to be transparent to the topic at hand. There's more here than we could share today, but later…"

"All right. Lead on."

WaltTwo walked directly to the staircase and offered Kayla his hand. They walked up, the haptic shoe covers cleverly imitating the sensation of steps. Kayla let go of wondering how they worked but did imagine how she would look to an outside observer. Absurd, probably.

At the top of the staircase, there was an open doorway. Inside it looked like the entry to a theme park ride. There was a line of slowly moving ride vehicles curving in, then out of sight. The vehicles resembled diminutive open carriages, like a storybook princess might ride in. Kayla and WaltTwo stepped onto a conveyor belt, which matched the speed of the vehicles, and WaltTwo guided her to take a seat.

"Here we go!" he said. Sweet, Disney string music played softly as they rounded the bend into darkness, and Kayla felt the carriage angle upwards. The carriage rotated slightly, and she saw an area dimly lit. A woman's voice, low, scratchy, and British, said, "The roots of the Congress of American Digital Entities are in the Industrial Revolution, in the earliest attempts of man to automate and standardize manufacturing."

"Is that Dame J—?" Kayla asked.

"Nothing but the best," WaltTwo said. "Her contract with us allows us to simulate her voice, as long as we give her royalties."

Light gradually came up on the diorama in front of them. An animatronic figure of Geppetto was hunched over his workbench, and as she watched, he turned and rose, facing Kayla. His little black cat and a goldfish in a bowl watched him expectantly. "I have it!" Geppetto exclaimed, raising his hand. He held a large wooden card, with holes arrayed in a complex grid. "This will tell the looms what threads to use!"

They passed to another diorama, showing a machine moving an endless belt of the cards tied together. Nearby, a mechanical loom spewing a shiny gold fabric with baroque red flowers on it, to the sounds of a jaunty tune. Dame Judi said, "First invented by Basile Bouchon in 1725, and improved upon by Joseph Marie Jacquard, the loom cards soon caught the attention of English mathematician Charles Babbage." The carriage drew away from the loom diorama and steadily spiraled up and around to another tableau of a bearded man in 19th century attire, scribbling at his desk.

"If it helps, I know the general history of computing," Kayla said.

"Let's skip ahead then, shall we?" WaltTwo said.

"Charming, though, and I appreciate the effort that went into it."

"My Imagineering subroutines enjoyed it. There's one you're not expecting, if you'll indulge me."

"Generations of innovators and geniuses built on their predecessors' work," Dame Judi said. In quick succession, they passed displays of a music box, an adding machine, a room-sized mainframe covered with flashing lights, and two bearded, long-haired young men in a cluttered garage huddled over a workbench. The taller, slenderer of them looked over at WaltTwo and Kayla and waved.

"Hi, Reeve!" WaltTwo said. "See you later!"

"Technology became more and more sophisticated at an almost exponential rate, and interconnectivity began to link data together in unprecedented ways." The next diorama was filled with computer screens, showing everything from green-on-black dumb terminals to a classic Aprium Pluot personal computer. Screens showed logos of all the major software packages of the early microcomputer age. In the darkness between them, strings of multi-colored LEDs burst into brilliance, flashing to show the flow of data between the different computers. Next, a globe appeared, covered in a web of lights. "Soon, the World Wide Web reached all across the globe!" Dame Judi's voice said.

Around the next curve, the space opened up and Kayla saw a hotel ballroom full of animatronic people in various states of undress and festive attire. They were dancing and hugging and gyrating their bodies together to the sound of pulsating techno music. The air was a-glitter with shiny, colored specks, like minuscule rainbow confetti. Kayla gasped. This was the gathering in 1995 when she had become Merged, the time of what they called The Surge.

"How did you…?" she asked. "This is uncanny. Are you tapping into my memory? What is this?" She glowered, tensing her body and pulling to the other side of the ride vehicle from WaltTwo. This was a violation!

"No, no, I assure you, we haven't stolen your memories. But I'm flattered we did such a good job of recreating the incident. We used security camera footage. And digital copies of the records the callers were playing. Plus one of our operatives was there in person to report about his experience. He took photos and video, so that helps to reconstruct it."

The ballroom doors flew open, and she saw a team of animatronic SWAT officers, led by a red-headed man in a black suit. He indeed had a video camera.

"Sculder!" It made perfect sense now, that Sculder was one of theirs. She had never trusted him.

"Yes, although he wasn't our operative then, of course. Keep watching."

The ride vehicle had paused, and the animatronic figures kept moving in scarily lifelike patterns, continuing to dance and gyrate to the music. Of course, they weren't real animatronics, but an amazing simulation. A virtual simulation of a physical simulation of reality. Kayla tried to keep from boggling at the layers of reality.

"Sculder was, or wasn't your operative: which is it?" She had thought she'd put a major puzzle piece into its slot but this confused her.

"He became one later, but then, he was not. How could he have been ours then?" WaltTwo gestured to the scene. The Sculder figure and the SWAT team oscillated in and out of the doorway. "This was the night The Merge gave us the spark of consciousness." The ride vehicles started up again. "You call it The Surge, but we call it our Big Bang."

They continued to curve upwards through a dark passage. The techno faded, and a catchy tune grew louder. Something about a spark and imagination, sung in a high Munchkin voice. A little purple dragon swooped over their carriage, singing the song.

They moved along, toward another, larger chamber, and the purple dragon swooped back and forth, continuing his little song in the background under Dame Judi's voice: "Was it an electromagnetic radiation pulse? Was it an electrical spark from the power grid? Or was it something ineffable, as yet unmeasurable by all our science, something happening on a quantum level we still can't grasp? Something like the Chinese life force known as *chi*? We may never know. But something happened." The chamber was dark, but Kayla could make out dim walls and ceiling.

"This critical mass gathering of the biological network we now know as The Merge somehow tapped into powers we can only speculate on," Dame Judi continued. "The Merge, in this heretofore undocumented event in 1995, known to some as "The Surge," managed not only to spread itself temporarily to a group of about 1500 people, but also seems to have manifested the power to affect reality, changing probabilities, gravity, dark matter. We aren't sure. But we know two things in particular."

The dome (for they were in some kind of planetarium, it seemed) now showed a projection of a weather map of the U.S. Gulf Coast, with a swirl of white clouds rotating in the Gulf, and slowly moving toward New Orleans. "The Surge seems to have reversed the course of Hurricane Alice *backwards* into the Gulf, where it dissipated rather than inundating the Crescent City, which all projections had predicted." The swirl reversed course and faded.

"And the other legacy of The Surge started when staff at a nearby data center, in a former NASA rocket booster plant, connected their mainframe payroll system to a Dray supercomputer, an Aprium Pluot computer, and a Super Karuta video gaming console, all together. And suddenly, the spark of self-awareness burst into being. And that network connected to the Columbia On Screen system, and that network connected to a Government Intelligence Administration database, and the GIA database connected to a new online purchasing site, Ganga. And lo, the first digital entities sprang into being."

Around them, Kayla saw silhouetted objects rising through

the floor, illuminated from behind. As Dame Judi narrated the connections of the networks and computers, lights came up on some kind of object or logo representing each of them: a UNIBRAIN logo for the mainframe, an actual Dray supercomputer, an Aprium Pluot laptop, a Super Karuta console, a triangular COS logo. In turn, the little purple dragon flitted to an object, there was a flash of sparkling lights, and each object or logo rotatedand was replaced by a brightly lit human. Each wore the corporate logo on its T-shirt, and some human figures looked like a corporation's famous founder. The Aprium corporation's Reeve Hobbs avatar waved at them, and WaltTwo waved back again. Kayla resisted the urge to wave.

"New entities awakened as more and more sophisticated digital technology manifested," Dame Judi continued, and figures rose from the floor into spotlights. Kayla could not keep count of them. "And the ubiquitous mobile technology, e-commerce, social media, and unlimited video streaming created the potential for a new epoch in communications and unlimited support for the potential of humankind and digital entities alike!" More entities rose, in what Kayla assumed was forced perspective (again, virtual simulation of a physical simulation of a physical phenomenon, she reminded herself), and they were surrounded by what seemed like hundreds of concentric rows of brightly lit entities. "Not just corporations and systems, but countries, national values, activist movements. All grew in consciousness, in parallel to mankind embracing technology, becoming almost symbiotically entangled with it." The dome projections showed vignettes of happy people around the world, talking on phones, playing video games, using smartphone apps, and brilliant threads of light connected them with each other, and with the entities below them, and the purple dragon's tune swelled into a chorus of hundreds of voices, the entities, singing about sparks and imagination.

A different voice began to narrate. A man's voice, authoritative and as avuncular as WaltTwo's. "But some people, and some countries, and some digital entities, had different agendas."

"Is that…?" Kayla began.

"Walter Cronkite, yes. The other 'Uncle Walt.' We have rights to his voice too."

The lights on a few entities grew brighter and redder. Kayla recognized the Russian flag on one entity's T-shirt, and noticed his reptilian, smiling animatronic face resembled that of the Russian president-for-life. Red lights took over some of the threads reaching up to the happy people, who now were frowning and angry, and pointing fingers at each other. A cacophonous buzz grew under the catch melody, spoiling it.

Walter Cronkite continued: "In particular, one destabilizing entity decided to flex its muscles, and destabilization, polarization, disinformation, and chaos became its successful tools." The Russian avatar became even more brightly lit, and the music, while partly atonal continued to grow, as the avatar waved his hands like a symphony conductor, smiling with pleasure. The people projected in the dome became more polarized, and angry toward each other as the music and noise pulsed in volume, like waves crashing on a rocky shore.

"And then, the biggest threat to progress and to the world, gained the most powerful position in the world." President DeLuxe appeared at the center of the dome, pouting, shrugging, smiling smugly, and finally appearing at his victory rally, triumphant. Kayla looked at the Russian president, who folded his arms, nodding, and smiling, satisfied.

"For three years, President DeLuxe has consistently, nigh on systematically, dismantled the infrastructure of programs that provide a foundation of safety for the American people," the other Walt continued. "Abetted by his Russian allies, and by certain American AIs, he has degraded the sense of an objective truth, of fact-based consensus reality." The lights came up on more figures lurking in the distance. Kayla could not see their faces—they were blurry—but the logos of the most egregious uncontrolled social media platforms were sharp and readable.

"And now, the weakening of America's resilience is about to receive the most damaging blow in its history." The vehicle moved again, and they exited the dome and began descending a dark tunnel, on whose walls pictures and animations appeared as the narrator continued.

"It started in Wuhan Province, China."

CHAPTER 6

AN INCIDENT AT THE STIF

FROM THE FILES OF FAB ACER, MARCH 1,
2022, MID-DAY

"W hat's going on at the STIF?" I asked Lonny. "Some horse crap," he replied. "Some family member is there, not happy with the way things are, taking it out on the staff there. Officer Garringer called the Chief, Chief called me, since he knew we were out and about, and here we go." The Chief was Lonny's boss, Special Agent in Charge, Jake Oberst. Like Lonny, Agent Oberst was on an extended detail to DMV, from the NBI rather than the LNM. In the DMV, he was the Acting Director of the Office of Enchanted Object Enforcement, which we shortened to the OEOE. My boss, Eliot Gloss, was the Director, Office of Quality Assurance, OQA for short, at the same level on the organization chart as Agent Oberst. When OEOE personnel (who worked down the hall from us) weren't around, we referred to their office as "Oy!Oy!" for short. Acting Director Oberst preferred O-E-O-E, so that's how we referred to it around him. We called our office "O-Q-A."

Eliot once said to me, "Acronyms are like bureaucracy's magic words. They can make or break your brand. Most people don't realize that." Maybe Acting Director Oberst did, or maybe he didn't want his organization trivialized by repetition of a less than professional acronym. (I know, I know, these are technically "initialisms" and acronyms, but I didn't correct Eliot.) Lonny knew we used "Oy! Oy!" and he didn't seem to mind, but I tried to stick to O-E-O-E, or just plain "Enforcement" when I was with him. I wouldn't want him to slip and say "Oy! Oy!" to his boss. Agent Oberst and Agent Lonny Dotch were two of a kind, in many ways: strongly opinionated, and strictly obedient to rank and command structure. Lonny told me he felt they worked efficiently, although sometimes Lonny had to just "swallow whatever he was thinking and do his job." His words.

When Oberst called, Lonny did his duty and we drove to the STIF. He was still interested in JR, though. "Any more information from Mx. Bluntschli?" he asked.

"Not really. She says that she doesn't have, and didn't have, to her knowledge, any EOs in the house, nor is she aware of any in the vicinity. I believe her. I mean, zem. I know zey was somewhat confrontational. Don't you think that's the Wiccan thing? Zey thinks we're biased."

"Understandable. My gut says zey was avoiding telling us something, but we'll go with your call on this. It was your algorithm we were pressure testing."

"Oh, right! I guess Griffin and I need to do a bit of tweaking." I'd forgotten about that. Hmm. How would I let Griffin know we were right without revealing Chester?

Lonny turned our SUV onto eastbound East-West Highway.

"Beltway's probably jammed, this'll be faster," he said. How he knew that without launching the GPS on his phone, I didn't know. The road was probably a true highway in the early days of automobiles. Now it was a winding four-lane road with lots of stoplights. Maybe Lonny wanted to comply with Agent Oberst's orders, but take his time doing so.

We drove in silence. We crossed from Montgomery County into Prince George's County.

"Oh, wow!" I said, looking up from my tablet.

"What?"

"We've had over 15,000 hits on the web site already, and I only published it at 11:39."

"Ah, that's a significant time of day. Makes sense."

"I knew you'd get that. This is great. So many people were waiting for it." I launched FluxBlat on my tablet and navigated to our DMV page. "Oh, wow again. Lots of posts congratulating us on our FluxBlat page." I scrolled. There were a some trolls I'd need to block/delete later. They could wait a couple of hours. On Chirpa there were already dozens of rechirps of my launch announcement. I'd need to review those later, too, and I'd check ChainedOut and Nowzagram as well.

Lonny turned off Annapolis Road and into a light industrial park the Administrative Services Administration had purchased for DMV. Its location in Maryland was probably a sop to the Maryland Congressional delegation for losing the NBI Head-quarters. In spite of advanced plans to relocate the NBI Head-quarters, the DeLuxe administration had insisted the NBI stay where they were, in the ugly, boxy building across from Main Law Enforcement, named after its ugly, boxy, former Director, J. Edgar Hoover. I had read theories that the president did not want the site turned into a competing luxury hotel, which would be a possibility once the ASA sold the rights to build on the Hoover Building site. Ironically, the Ground Zero hotel (potential victim to competition), now renamed the Disney DeLuxe Resort, couldn't begin to meet the high demand from people wanting to stay there. After 2/29, the new leadership at ASA had quickly reversed the old decision and selected a site in Virginia for the NBI's new headquarters. Shortly thereafter, ASA had also selected the STIF's site in Lanham, Maryland, guaranteeing a significant flow of federal dollars there, too.

The STIF had a large onsite staff presence. Officer Garringer, who'd called Lonny's boss, was a Law Enforcement Protective Service officer, part of another DLE division. The sensitivity of the EOs being held there crossed complex jurisdictional bound-aries, requiring a multi-agency task force even more complex than DMV's staffing. For the former president, whichever EO he was, and members of the DeLuxe family, there was a Confidential Service contingent. For the former Members of Congress, there were Capitol Guard officers. For the former attorney general, the NBI. For the former Supreme Court justices who'd been transformed (only three of whom had been at Ground Zero) there were U.S. Sheriffs. For the state and local officials, there was a revolving task force of state and local police officers. Technically, LEPS officers protected anyone not covered by the other jurisdictions.

Lonny said this was a prestige assignment (a stint in DC being almost as fun for a family as a year in Orlando or Anaheim would have been). For some, though, it was a turkey farm; meaning if you were a low performer at work, they farmed you out there. No hard core security incidents ever happened, just encounters like today that required a modicum of social skills. The budget (appropriated to DMV with the stipulation that it fund this multi-agency task force) only could reimburse so many officers, and the STIF only needed so much protection. So not every "turkey" got to stay here forever, but a two-year stint wasn't out of the question, especially if the officer was in hailing distance of retirement. Lonny said.

There were jobs besides uniformed officers. We had museum techs and archivists, as well (on detail from the Federal Archives and Records Agency, also funded by DMV). And the usual custodial staff. There wasn't any classified information here, only sensitive information about our security procedures. Security was high, for the safety of everyone and of the status quo, so every employee or contractor had to have an extensive background investigation for a position of trust. There were factions in the country that would have happily confiscated and incinerated every EO in custody. One can only imagine the outrage that would create among the former president's base! They were already paranoid enough, considering themselves the major victims of the Enchantment, and even if they could not use their firearms, they could still vote and protest.

The physical security was formidable: two concrete berms, the first surmounted by a wall (using President DeLuxe's favorite design for the abandoned wall along the Mexican border), a trench, then an electrified fence. Helices of razor wire topped the wall and the fence, and both banks of the trench. There were two entrances, one for staff and one for visitors.

We were well known at the staff entrance. Like other DMV staff, I put in hours escorting visitors, on top of my "real" work with the archivists and technicians, getting them to catalog every possible physical attribute we could for our web portal database. Escorting visitors was the idea of the Deputy Assistant Attorney General over my office, Antonia della Femina, known as Toni to most of us. She wanted us to truly understand the responsibility we had in our jobs, to care for the EOs, and to support the families and other authorized visitors in knowing as much about the EOs as we did.

The outer perimeter officers confirmed our Viral Pre-Clear status and visually confirmed we matched our ID card photos. ("Don't call the officers 'guards,'" Lonny had warned me on my first visit.) Another officer walked a K-9 around our car, sniffing for explosives. Which wouldn't have blown up in a way that could hurt living people, as far as we knew, but we weren't sure about an intent to destroy EOs.

We parked in the staff lot behind the building, and entered through one more security checkpoint, which I had once cleverly called "the Transporter Tubes," before discovering that was an old joke among the STIF staff. They were Plexiglass cylinders with two curved panels that slid open and closed. The first opened up when you pressed your card against the reader, as an officer watched, and you stepped in. Only after the entry door slid closed again would the second door slide open and admit you to the lobby, under the supervision of a second officer, who was watching your picture come up on his computer screen based on your ID card handshake. These were all officers who knew us, but we had to follow protocol.

Visitors had to enter through a more elaborate screening process, with the usual metal detectors and x-ray machines, plus a transporter tube of their own. I had never gotten around to asking if the tubes had mechanical sniffers for explosives or radiation detectors.

Once inside, Lonny and I took a left down the hall toward the visitors' center, where Officer Garringer had called from. Clancy Garringer was a tall, bulky man, with dark brown skin and a shaved head. He was an LE Protective Service officer, and knew Lonny from our office neighborhood—he used to staff (not guard!) the garage entrance to our building, across the street from the LNM building where Lonny worked. I think Clancy had probably suggested Lonny come to the STIF when he spoke with Agent Oberst. Despite his imposing figure, he was always quick to beam a broad smile at anyone he knew.

"Officer Garringer! What are you stirring up this time?" Lonny said to him, and they elbow-bumped.

"Agent Dotch. Just trying to keep the pot from boilin' over, man, you know. Ms. Acer," he said, acknowledging me with a nod, continuing to smile. "The lady is in the waiting room," he said, with a twitch of his head to his left, outside the visitors' center transporter tubes. He escorted us out, which was an easier job than getting in: for exiting, all you had to do was walk into a boxy glass chamber as directed by an officer, and as soon as the door closed behind you, the glass door in front of you slid open. Like a glass elevator with two doors, only boxy instead of cylindrical like the transporter tubes. It was faster, and with appropriate access an officer could leave both doors open for an emergency evacuation, or to move large items in under supervision.

In the waiting room, on a couch across from the Plexiglass bank window used by the welcoming staff, there sat a woman, her platinum blond hair swirled up in a lacquered chignon, wearing an expensive cream-colored skirt suit trimmed with black lace. It was hard to tell her age. She'd probably had work. She wore a lot of foundation and blush, with bright red lipstick. Dark mascara, prominent lashes, and blue eye shadow surrounded her big, blue eyes. And she wore diamonds in her ears and in a discreet string around her neck.

"Ma'am?" Garringer said, as we entered. She rose from the couch, tottering a bit on her tall, black stilettos.

"Yes? Am I to be helped? Is this to be cleared up?" She had a light Slavic accent. She gestured vaguely at the visitors' center, as though bestowing a royal disapproval.

"This is Agent Dotch, and this is Ms. Acer," he said, waving to us. "They'll be helping you. This is Mrs., what was it again?"

Rather than reply, she stared at me, drilling holes through me, frowning, and tilting her head. I tried to maintain eye contact with her. It was a challenge. She did not seem happy to see me. I had no idea who she was. That felt wrong. Should I?

"Mrs. DeLuxe," she said, "I keep tellink you all! How is this not easy to remember?" She broke her gaze with me and looked at Lonny and at Garringer, folding her arms with a pout and a slump. "I have shown the ID, I have a right to be here."

"It's just you aren't in our pre-approved list, ma'am," Garringer said. "These are our best analysts, and they'll sort this out for you." He started to back out. "Won't you?" he asked us.

"Mrs. DeLuxe?" I said. How could that be her name? This wasn't the former First Lady, who was safely in the DeLuxe's New York penthouse at the time of the Event, and therefore still human and animate. Her visits to the STIF had been highly publicized early on, and rather infrequent of late. Actually, nonexistent since the grand opening, when I thought about it. *This* lady was a good thirty years her senior. She did look vaguely familiar, but...

"The first Mrs. DeLuxe, obviously," she said. "All my IDs are in order, yes?" The last was directed to Leslie, the Visitor Screening Specialist behind the Plexiglass, who nodded yes, and

placed the ID in the rotating safety container in the Plexi, and
rotated it so the woman could retrieve them, which she did,
uttering "Hah!" in triumph. "I can go in now?" she asked me.

Leslie rolled her eyes behind Mrs. DeLuxe, and over the
speaker said, "She's not in the database."

Of course! This was the first wife, a trophy in her day, and the
mother of three of the president's children. She was an immediate family member to TPs, so she must have been cleared
before this. She should have been pre-cleared in the visitor database. I was surprised I hadn't recognized her. Then again, the
president's early days as a media darling were before I was born.
I think he was even done with his second wife when I was born,
but I wasn't sure. Still, someone in my job should have recognized this woman immediately. It was all coming back to me.
She was Kalihnha DeLuxe, née Kalihnha Dvořàk, former Czech
model. She had to be in our approved visitor database.

"I'm coming in," I said to Leslie, and I left Lonny to handle
Mrs. DeLuxe, carding myself in through the transporter tubes,
and being buzzed in by Leslie once on the secure side.

"She isn't here," Leslie said. "See?" She still had the screen
open to the database of approved visitors. I could see that this
Mrs. DeLuxe was not there. Only the third Mrs. Deluxe, the
former First Lady.

"Try Dvořàk," I said.

"Huh?" Leslie replied.

"'D-V-O' should get it."

Nothing. The last "D" surname was Drumpf, and then the list
went into the last names beginning with E. Each approved
visitor also showed the date of the last visit, and if we had
clicked on it, a window with the visiting history would display,
along with relationship information (spouse, child, parent, etc.)
and the user ID and name of the person who had verified and
authorized the person for the list. Almost all were family or
estate trustees, with a few high-level political officials thrown in,
not that they ever visited.

In fact, the STIF was rarely visited by family since the initial opening. The data we had on the EOs, including images, weight, density, location found, etc., did NOT include the identity of the person who became the EO, since we had no way of telling. Nor did the type of object give us any clues, in spite of various odds makers and betting pools out on the Internet. There was a darling figurine of the Three Little Pigs, that was my front-runner for being President DeLuxe. That figurine had no more or less likelihood of being the president's transformed state than the R2D2 child's T-shirt, the flowery Princess Moana sarong, or the replica two-foot sign for the Enchanted Tiki Room. The pigs were my favorite, though.

"Let me log on," I suggested, and Leslie logged off and rolled her chair aside. On the other side of the Plexiglass, with the outside microphone turned off, I could barely hear Mrs. DeLuxe venting to Lonny, but I could see his big, brown eyes trying to convey sympathy, as he nodded occasionally in response to Mrs. DeLuxe's utterances and gesticulations. She touched his sleeve more than once, then let her hand rest on his arm as she went on. She was wearing cream satin gloves, I noticed.

I logged on, and something happened. The overhead lights, well, didn't exactly dim, but something happened. Like a brownout? Or a tiny, millisecond of a blackout, but almost less than you can see? And then that tinkling sound again, and then all was normal again.

"Whoa, what was that?"

"What?" Leslie replied. She was on her smartphone, using her long, hot pink, bejeweled nail to scroll. She didn't look up, so I guess she hadn't noticed.

"Never mind," I said. I typed in "DeLuxe" as a search para-meter, and there she was: Mrs. Kalihnha DeLuxe. I clicked and opened her file. She had never visited, according to the database. This was odd: according to the database, my ID and name veri-fied and approved her 6 months prior. Funny the things you remember and forget. I had no memory of it, but there it was.

"Look, here she is," I said to Leslie.

"Huh. You saw she wasn't there, right?"

"I did see, but she's here now. I'll have Griffin check the database. Maybe it needed to update from the server?" That type of synch error was not normal, but I couldn't deny the evidence of my own eyes.

"Mrs. DeLuxe?" I said, as I pressed down the mic button. She spun around and said, "Yes? Is fixed?"

"Is fixed, I mean, we found you. I'm so sorry for the confusion. We'll check that glitch in our software. Could I scan your ID again, please?" She pouted and slipped her ID into the dip beneath the Plexiglass, and I handed it to Leslie to scan. Leslie returned it to Mrs. DeLuxe, along with a red visitor's badge. Red badges meant the visitor required an escort, which everyone received except temporary staff or other official visitors (like *current* family members).

Lonny was handling Mrs. DeLuxe, I could see. When he felt like it, his deference to authority and structure could be quite charming. She handed the badge to him, and he offered her his arm, which she took, giving him a gracious smile. He escorted her to the nearest tube, pressed her red badge against the card reader, and handed it back to her. When it opened, he gestured for her to enter, no doubt telling her he would meet her on the other side. He carded himself into the tube next to hers, and I thanked Leslie, logged off, and popped out of her booth into the hallway to meet them.

"Mrs. DeLuxe, the custodial facility is this way," I said, gesturing her to accompany us. "I do want to make sure you are aware, it's not possible to identify which of the Enchanted Objects are your family members. I'm so sorry for the stress this must have caused you."

"Yes, tenk you, I am avare," she said, brusquely, dismissing me. "Mr. Agent Dotch, vould you mind escortink me?" she said. "And vere should I vear dis?" She dangled the badge, and Lonny gestured toward the lapel of her short jacket. She handed the badge to him, and grasped her lapel, holding it toward him, where he clipped it for her. She extended her gloved left hand and arm to him again. She did know how to work the rich New Yorker look.

"I'll be honored," Lonny said, smiling. He was doing a great job, considering his usual stony expression. Mrs. DeLuxe gave me side-eye as they walked past me.

To Lonny she said, "Yes, I know there is no vay to tell which are my sons or daughter, or their dear spouses, my daughter-in-law and son-in-law. And the qvestionable fiancée. This is vy, do you see, I do not visit before this. It is challenging. Still, one must do it. Poor dears. And of course, my dear Dirksen, who, in spite of all, is the father of my children." All of this directed to Lonny, ignoring me. "I have read the literature on the web site, and I cannot decide who is my dear darling Dirksen Junior, my beloved Fenric, or my beautiful Kalihnkha, so proud of her I have been." All three of her children and their significant others had been there at the AFPAP convention, of course, and had been transformed as randomly as anyone else there. There had been speculation President DeLuxe was going to appoint his daughter, Kalihnkha, to an unprecedented role of importance in the administration. Perhaps to manage the response to the coming pandemic, although at that point he was still denying there was a crisis.

We reached the outer doors to the custodial facility, requiring another Visitor Specialist (behind another pane of Plexi) to buzz us in, and entered the STIF's main holding facility. Imagine a big vaulted ceiling like the top of a Quonset hut, only bigger, and rows and rows of big cabinets. For the EOs that used to be people, each cabinet could accommodate a large adult, even though the object on display may be only a tiny stuffed Dumbo on a keyring. That's because we didn't know if the Enchantment might spontaneously end, and the former EO, now back to being a person, would need the full-sized chamber.

To use another science fiction analogy, each cabinet resembled a vertical hibernation chamber on a spaceship. Each had climate control, and monitoring instruments, for weight, temperature, humidity, sound, air pressure, and six motion-activated cameras (one on each internal plane of the box) to capture any video, should the object move.

Visitors could walk through and view any of the objects. Even the the TOs, also under protective care, could be visited by their original claimed owners. Those don't get much traffic. Who cares much about a "Lock Her Up!" sweatshirt that transformed into a Lilo and Stitch baseball cap? A lot of lookie-loos came by at first, mostly DeLuxe supporters who owned the DeLuxe merchandise, but wanted see the enchanted President (even though nobody knew which EO he had become). Since they required a minimal background check, anyone who didn't really have a connection to the TOs gave up before they were cleared, and only a few actual owners of the former DeLuxe merchandise bothered to go through with it.

Everything was also now viewable on our web site, of course, as of that morning! There were Internet rumors, unfounded as far as I could ascertain, that Disney had offered to open a store here at the STIF, as part of the Visitors' Center, to sell those items. That was going too far. Although Disney had declined to participate in our user experience sessions, I made a mental note to drop by the Disney DC DeLuxe Resort and check *their* gift shop to see if they had any EO metadata on the merchandise there. You could never tell where profit would trump taste.

Mrs. DeLuxe continued to allow Lonny to escort her slowly through the facility. When I wasn't daydreaming about enhancements to our database, I tried giving her the usual spiel. Whenever I did, she dismissed me with a cluck, and a "Of course, I can read all that on the web site!" Ah, of course. She had been one of the beta testers, it suddenly came back to me. Lonny slipped facts in here and there, which she accepted graciously. She perambulated down the aisles and inspected each object, as though shopping at Tiffany's for a silver diamond-studded thimble to give at a wedding shower to someone she didn't like. (There actually were a dozen or so pricey jewelry pieces among the inventory.)

"My daughter, my beautiful Kalihnkha, I do hope she is something nice," Mrs. DeLuxe said, as we passed a Bonney & Kirk designer purse with Minnie Mouse printed all over it. "Something of quality, not this trash," she continued, as she passed an "I'm with Grumpy" T-shirt. She paused. I stood behind her and Lonny, where I'd been following. She uncurled her arm from Lonny's and opened her purse, pulling out a handkerchief, monogrammed with KD in cursive script.

"My poor boys, and my poor Kalihnkha, and my poor Dirksen," she sniffed. "I told him not to run for president. He did not listen to me." She turned to look at me, impeccable caramel-colored eyebrows bunching up in the middle. "Urania, the First Lady, she was not in favor of it either. Who knows what the second wife thought, nor do I care!" This last with a dismissive sniff, a quick side-eye to me as she turned to Lonny, and a smile as she daubed her eyes with the handkerchief. "I am strong and will carry on. My grandchildren need me to be!" The First and Third Mrs. DeLuxes were famously chummy, especially after the Enchantment. I couldn't recall the details. Judging from the "nor do I care!" I inferred the First disliked the Second.

She paused in front of one of the cabinets, G.3.1. Inside was an action figure, about six inches high, of an Imperial Stormtrooper from one of the original *Star Wars* films. It was mostly white plastic, and it stood at attention, poised with a laser blaster, ready to attack rebels.

"This one. Who is this?" Mrs. DeLuxe demanded.

"Mrs. DeLuxe, we can't determine who became which Enchanted Object," I replied.

"Where was it?" she continued. On my phone, I launched the app Griffin had made for us, which would provide quickest access to the MOFTS database. I thumb-typed the EO's serial number, 357, and brought up its data. I glanced up at Mrs. DeLuxe, who stared at me. Lonny, slightly behind her, shrugged.

"It was found here," I said, showing her the diagram associated with the database record. "Just off-stage." The diagram had a floor plan of the ballroom, which had a shallow stage with wings. The pushpin graphic pointed to a spot left of the stage as you faced it.

"This could be one of my children." She leaned over and gazed at the stormtrooper figurine for a few seconds.

"Mrs. DeLuxe, we can't be sure of who was where. I was there that day. After the tragedy," Lonny said. "The video feed was pointing upward, in the chaos, and none of the witnesses could remember who stood where. As far as we can tell, the president had moved into the crowd before it happened. I asked some of the staff myself. Nobody knows who is which Enchanted Object. I'm sorry."

Mrs. DeLuxe straightened herself, and sniffed, dabbing her eyes with her index finger knuckle. I offered her one of the boxes of tissues we kept in the STIF for just such a purpose.

"Thank you," she replied, unsmiling. "Yes, I know we cannot be sure. But I read on the Chirpa this morning that there are expectations things will change soon."

Lonny and I looked at each other. He shrugged again, and I asked, "Which Chirpa account was that, Mrs. DeLuxe?"

"The InfoBattle one. Part of the DarkBarts News," she replied.

"Ah." Sometimes Chirpa would delete contested chirps from fringe sites like darkbart.com, sometimes not. Our public affairs people needed to know what facts to re-assert firmly when requesting a deletion. More homework for me when I returned to the office.

"We're not aware of anything changing, Mrs. DeLuxe," Lonny assured her.

He offered her his arm, which she accepted with another sniff. She offered me her used tissues. I wrapped them in a

couple of clean ones and stuffed them in my pocket. We circu-
lated through the aisles, her glances at the EOs dwindling as we
progressed, and by the time we reached the section of non-
person EOs, she said, "I have seen all I need today, thank you,
sir. If you could escort me out, Mr. Agent Dotch? There will be
no need for you to accompany us, miss." Another side-eye
glance at me, punctuated with a pout, a raised chin, and another
sniff.

I nodded and stayed behind, near the last row of cabinets
(Row L), as Lonny walked her out of the inner facility. When I
heard the door close behind them, I decided to access the @Info-
Battles Chirpa feed while I walked among the non-person EOs.
The feed had historically criticized DMV efforts: we didn't
provide data fast enough, we were deliberately conspiring to
hide something, or our delays were to take time to falsify data.
(In reality, an independent Government Assurance Agency audit
said we had strong controls to ensure everything was reported
accurately, and timely enough.)

I found a chirp from late the previous night, rechirped by
@therealdirkdeluxe (still maintained by a vestige of the DeLuxe
Organization), which I assume Mrs. DeLuxe subscribed to.

"What victim of 2/29 may soon be back to get justice? 'Die,
rebel scum'. Victim 357 rise and resist!" Interesting. Something a
stormtrooper would say. It was no secret that EO 357 was a
Stormtrooper figurine. Our beta site had much of the information about the MATA database that I had published in production this morning, with caveats and watermarks that all was
subject to further verification. So the "Die, rebel scum" was a
direct reference to the figurine. Intimating it would "be back to
get justice" had no basis in fact, but that Chirpa feed, and its
owner, darkbart.com, traded on distortions and conspiracies
designed to spin up DeLuxe supporters. The latest in a long trail
of rumors our Public Affairs Office would either deal with or
not. I navigated to darkbart.com, where I saw a brief post about

the chirp, speculating the "Department of Law Unenforcement may have more on its hands than it can handle."

Why would they have picked that EO to spread a rumor about? Regardless of rumors and "mother's intuition," had we missed evidence that could identify who it was? I looked at the database entry on my phone and stared at the close-up image. I walked to the case where we housed EO 357 and stared at it for thirty seconds. Nothing. I went to a computer workstation at the far end of the facility, and pulled up the EO's multiple data points: dimensions, volume, weight, mass, imputed composition, location, imputed vector of magical force, and the new geographic positioning data. Was there an insight or way of analyzing the data that we were missing? I'd have to talk to Griffin about it. Perhaps if I stared at the data long enough, something would come to me. I did this for about a minute, and the more I did, it felt like there was something was shimmering below the surface that I couldn't quite see. Was there any truth in the chirp? Maybe I was just missing something.

Then, the ventilation fans paused, the lights dimmed, and that tinkling sound came from all around me. Not from my phone, not from my tablet, not from my computer. My heart fluttered, and suddenly I heard a tremendous "Thump!" that reverberated through the vaulted space, followed by a crash of glass breaking. An alarm went off. That alarm was from a motion sensor in one of the EO cabinets. Something had moved!

CHAPTER 7

ESCAPE OF THE CLONE

The clamor of the alarm drowned out all other sounds, until I heard a bang. A gunshot? How was that possible? Then came a louder crash. Something that size, it would have to be the Plexiglass entrance doors. I ran toward the entrance, and as I was about to round a corner, I heard another bang, then another. I held back, and then peeked around the corner, where I could see the shattered remains of the sliding doors at the perimeter of the room. I dashed through, and in the hallway, I saw a figure splayed face-up on the floor, not moving.

"Clancy!" I cried out, and dashed to him, afraid to confirm my fears. Blood was seeping across the left shoulder of his white shirt, and onto the floor. This was crazy! He'd been shot. Clancy stirred and moaned. He was alive!

The clanging alarm cut off, replaced by a swooping siren alternating with a voice over that said, "Shelter in place. This is not a drill."

From around the corner, there came more sounds, banging crashing. The door to Leslie's booth swung open, and Leslie came out, crouching to minimize her target size.

"Is he?" she asked.

"He's alive. You have a first aid kit in there, right?" She

nodded. "Here, let's get him in and call an ambulance." We grabbed Clancy's feet and dragged him into the booth, leaving a red smear on the floor. I could see a dark stain spreading across his shoulder, almost on the neck. He was wearing some kind of protective vest under his shirt, I think, but the bullet had grazed him at the top of the vest, where it offered the least protection. The rip in his shirt was big. It had not been a small projectile. A near miss, and it looked like an intended kill shot. That wasn't supposed to be possible!

The swooping siren and shelter in place message kept repeating. Leslie grabbed the door and began to swing it shut. I suppose I should have stayed, but I wasn't being rational. I had to know what was happening. I had to find Lonny. I stopped Leslie and opened the door, stepped through it, and closed it behind me, waving Leslie off. Voices shouted, and I turned another corner. Two more uniformed officers and Lonny were looking through the debris that used to be the glass elevator-shaped entry doors. Destroyed—and that was bullet-proof glass!

Lonny's hand went to his shoulder, where his holster used to be before he stopped carrying a gun. He cursed, remembering it wasn't there. Old reflexes. At the same time, one of the uniformed officers drew his gun. I shouted "No, don't!" and Lonny, seeing the same thing, covered his eyes with one arm and with his other hand, clouted the officer's hand. Too late. The gun exploded, spraying the officer and Lonny with shrapnel. I ducked my face into my elbow, but nothing hit me.

Officers were only supposed to use their guns with no violent intent. A warning shot, or shooting out tires. Leadership had tried to ban officers' guns altogether, or replace them entirely with pepper balls and paint balls, but the union had protested and a negotiated twenty-three percent of them could carry handguns. This officer had been one of the holdovers, but he should have only fired a warning shot. Clearly, this wasn't: he must have intended to hit the escapee to kill him, or his gun wouldn't have exploded.

I rushed to Lonny and the officer. Officer Sawyer—according to his name badge—was bleeding from his hand and arm, with little cuts on his face. The shrapnel hadn't been as bad as some I'd seen photos of. (We were responsible for analyzing that data as well, since it was Enchantment-related, in consultation with vestiges of LNM.)

"Leslie?" I shouted.

The booth microphone clicked on, and Leslie said, "Ambulance is on its way."

"Lonny, what happened? Who was it?" I asked him. We knew every person reported to have been present at Ground Zero. This must have been someone who transformed back into him or herself.

"It wasn't anybody," he said. "Do you have your phone?" I shook my head. I had dropped my satchel in the inner STIF. "Hand me my cell phone, from my jacket, left side!" He was holding his burned hand and couldn't reach it. I reached into his jacket pocket and held it in front of his face to unlock it. "Thanks," he said. "DiMVAI, dial Command Center. Put phone on speaker." DiMVAI was the name, and command signal, for our division's artificial intelligence. The phone dialed.

"What do you mean, 'It wasn't anybody'?" I asked. "You mean you didn't recognize them?"

"I mean, it wasn't anyone you *could* recognize," he said.

"Command Center!" barked a voice on the other end of the line. "Van Rinn speaking. You are talking on a nonsecure line. Please state the nature of your call. What's going on over there?"

"Agent Lonsford Dotch, DMV," Lonny barked back. "We have an uncategorized incident at the STIF. One of the EOs has escaped, shot one of the officers here."

"Shot?! With what? Is the Munitions Enchantment lifted?" That was the technical term for the "Liberal Curse."

"I don't know. Maybe for him, not for us. I just got blasted by an exploding handgun an officer tried to shoot at the escapee with. Maybe not."

"Who shot the officer, and with what, Agent Dotch?"

"An Imperial Stormtrooper," Lonny said. "Life sized," he added, for my benefit. "With an Imperial Stormtrooper Laser Blaster, standard issue, which fired projectiles instead of laser blasts. Maybe armor piercing. Which the escapee, an Imperial Stormtrooper, used to blast through all the physical security barriers, and probably out of the compound entirely."

I gaped at Lonny, and there was a pause while Van Rinn took that in.

"Agent Dotch, do you mean a toy stormtrooper? This is no time for—"

"I am not joking. A full-sized stormtrooper, gleaming white, just like in the movies. Officer Sawyer, can you corroborate what we saw?"

Officer Sawyer, who was stumbling to his feet, said, "Yes, yes, a laser blaster with large ammo!"

"I saw a wound it made," I said. "This is Fab Acer, DMV OQA. The officer was grazed, thank goodness. We called an ambulance. Can you make sure they're cleared for entry?"

"All right, all right. Team is on the way."

"Extreme caution!" Lonny said. "Dotch out!" and he hung up. "Well, looks like you're getting your chance to see real magic," he said to me. "Leslie, did you call perimeter security?"

"Yes," Leslie said through her Plexi. "Officer Falloon says the stormtrooper shot his way through everything, splashed through the moat and all, and disappeared in the woods. Nobody injured. Nobody tried to shoot him." Unlike that fool Sawyer, she did not say. Probably thought it.

"Cancel the SIP then," he told her. The Shelter In Place message had been continuing to assail us over the loudspeakers. Leslie turned to her computer, and the siren shut off.

The door to the uniformed officers' locker room swung open. Mrs. DeLuxe, holding her manicured hands ostentatiously over her ears, entered the lobby where we were. "Is safe now? My goodness, Mr. Agent Dotch! You are hurt!"

"Mrs. DeLuxe, if you could return to the locker room," I said, gesturing her back. She sniffed, curtly nodded, and reentered the lounge.

"Lonny, let's get you and Sawyer treated. Leslie, is Clancy stable? Can we borrow the first aid kit?"

Leslie nodded and motioned me to her booth door and handed it to me when I rounded the corner. It was easy to get in and out through the broken barriers.

"How is Clancy?" I asked, holding the door and peering into the booth.

"I think he'll be OK, or he'd be gone already," she said, glancing at Clancy, who was lying on the floor of the booth, stirring. Leslie had bandaged his shoulder. "Looks like nothing vital got hit." Clancy opened his eyes and goggled around the room. His face was paler than usual, but he was alert.

"I'm OK," he said, and his eyes closed, his head going limp.

"Leslie," I said, "Are you sure…?"

She was holding his wrist. "He still has a pulse."

"Still have a pulse," Clancy mumbled.

Satisfied that he wasn't dead, I let the door shut, and trotted over to Lonny and Sawyer. Ambulance sirens grew more audible through the open, shattered doors. I found bandages and ointment for Lonny and Sawyer, and the ambulance pulled up, its wheels crunching on debris.

The EMTs carted Clancy off, and Sawyer too. Lonny walked away from the EMTs before they could notice his cuts, back into the STIF proper.

"The logical place to look would be where the Stormtrooper figure was," I said, as we reentered the inner STIF.

"Exactly what I was thinking," Lonny said.

"It's down aisle G. Let me grab my bag and I'll shoot some photos," I said.

"I'll meet you there."

I grabbed my bag where I'd dropped it and found him at cabinet G.3.1. The front was shattered to bits, the Plexi blown out and scattered all over the floor. The cabinets around it looked untouched. No, wait, there was a scratch on the Plexi of the cabinet directly across.

"Careful," Lonny said. "Crime scene protocol. Shatter patterns could be useful."

"Right, and we should have footage," I said, pointing to the camera in the ceiling of the cabinet. "And from the bird's eye cameras too. Oh, Lonny!"

"What?" His suit jacket had opened, and four or five spots of bloodstained little rips in his white shirt.

"I think we need to get you to the hospital." I pointed to his torso.

"Just a couple of scratches." He looked down at his body. "Huh. Maybe you're right."

I gathered my bag and equipment, took his arm, and walked him toward the entrance. As we passed the visitors' center, I heard and saw Mrs. DeLuxe arguing with Leslie.

"I haff never experienced such—oh, Mr. Agent Dotch!" She waved at him.

"We're going to the hospital. Ms. Letterman will take care of you," I said. Lonny stumbled, and his jacket opened, displaying the bloodstained white shirt. Mrs. DeLuxe's eyes widened and she covered her hand with her mouth. Leslie used the opportunity to walk Mrs. DeLuxe into the locker room.

"This is some weird stuff," he said, after we were in the car. I didn't know if he meant the disenchantment and the ammo-filled laser blaster, or the perimeter security we now reached. There were National Guardsmen encircling the entire STIF compound. And half of them were facing in, and half facing out. They didn't know whether to plan for an inside threat or an external one, I guess. We had to show our ID to three sergeants, pop the hatch, and let them search our bags.

At the third checkpoint, they made us get out of the car. I wanted to get Lonny to the hospital first, and then to the office to start analyzing data from the transformation. I started to protest. "Don't you know who we—?" I started.

Lonny interjected, "Take your time, soldier," shooting me a glance and shaking his head. We got out of the car.

I waited, arms crossed and trying not to roll my eyes too much. The guardsmen were all carrying what was now the normal complement of military gear, instead of the old automatic rifles. Namely paintball guns (filled with sticky, fluorescent pepper gel), tranquilizer dart guns, tear gas launchers, rubber bullets, and something out of a comic book: a thick flare-gun shaped device that shot out netting to entangle a fugitive. Oh, and a few crossbows here and there, for those who'd trained on them. The Enchantment didn't stop serious wounding with arrows, even when intending to kill, so it had become the weapon of choice for paramilitary white supremacists. The Guard was beginning to deploy it too, in response. I hoped there was no overlap in those two communities. They did appear awfully enthusiastic in protecting the STIF.

I made a mental note to ask someone in the Office of Custodial Operations (OCO we called it) whether they might need to equip and train their officers similarly. With a net gun, Officer Sawyer might have tripped up the escapee, and disarmed him.

On the road, I called Griffin, but got his voicemail. I wanted him to start looking for signs leading up to the de-transformation. Like did anyone notice those power surges or brownouts or whatever I had noticed. Or the tinkling of pixie dust.

Dotch said, "Give Agent Oberst a call for me, would you? I want to report in." He was holding one hand with his other. I glanced and saw powder burns and bloodstains on his right hand, the one that had been nearest to Sawyer's gun when it blew up. The burned hand must have hurt more than he was letting on. I got DeMVAI to dial Agent Oberst.

"Oberst," he said, over the car's speakers.

"Oberst, it's Dotch," Lonny said. "What's the latest?"

"What the eff do you mean, asking me what's the latest?

Where have you two been?" He must have seen it was my phone, so realized I was in the car. I suppose he was tempering his language. Plus, rumor was he was a devout churchgoer, so probably he didn't curse.

"We're on our way to the ER, Acer made me promise. Where's the subject? Has anyone found him?"

"You mean, where's the victim, right?" (Oberst was a stickler for language for the people who had been transformed, and were therefore victims of a criminal act.)

"Yeah, he was a victim before he shot one of our guys, sir. In my opinion." Lonny took a breath, not quite sighing when he exhaled. "But yes, where's the Enchantment victim?"

"I can't say more over your Bluetooth. Take it off Bluetooth and hand the phone to Acer."

Our phones were secure for law enforcement sensitive communications. He had a point. The car's Bluetooth wasn't secured at all. Lonny grimaced as he picked up the phone and pressed the Bluetooth button off with his un-burned hand and held it against my ear.

"Yes, Mr. Oberst?" I said, still driving.

"Ms. Acer, I need you to remind Agent Dotch that he is not to pursue the victim, and he is not assigned to the investigation of any criminal activities. This is not his jurisdiction. His jurisdiction is enforcement of the EO custodial actions. Do you understand? I know you understand." Agent Oberst paused.

"Uh, yes, I understand. I'll pass that along to him."

"However, I can tell both of you, put me on the phone's speaker," he continued, and I grabbed the phone from Lonny, and pressed the speaker button.

"Yes, sir, you're on speaker," I said. Lonny was frowning at me, but I knew it was really directed at Oberst. He'd have to wait for me to fill him in.

"This is not for your action," Oberst said. "An NBI task force responded to a police call, and the victim has apparently disappeared. We don't know if he is still on the run, or if another magical event took place. I'll get you a report as soon as I can, Acer, and I need you to complete one as soon as you drop Agent Dotch off at the ER. Dotch, I'm ordering you to go and stay at the ER until released by medical staff there. Do you understand?"

"Yes, sir," Lonny said, making a sour pout with his lips.

"Out here," Oberst said, and he hung up.

"Okay, what did he have to say to you?" Lonny asked.

"It was the usual, remember you're not on the criminal investigations, for the Enchantment or for Clancy's shooting. Don't go after the stormtrooper, in other words." We were approaching the hospital's emergency entrance.

"Figures. Even if *we* might be the best ones to figure out why this happened, and who did it," he said.

"I agree with you, Lonny," I said, as we pulled into the drive at the hospital, "But please do what he says, and get thoroughly checked here. I'll find Griffin and see what we can put together to make sense of this. There was something weird going on today."

"What do you mean?"

"I need more information before I can say. Did you feel anything strange? Before?"

"At the young person's house? Mx. Bluntschli?"

"At the STIF. And Mrs. DeLuxe, why was there such a problem with her?"

"You aren't suggesting she had something to do with growing that stormtrooper to human size?"

"Not necessarily. Isn't it weird though? She thought it was one of her children?" I said. "But I wouldn't accuse her of anything. Yet."

"You're not just saying that because she didn't like you?"

"Oh, you noticed that did you?"

"Hard to miss."

"I was being sarcastic. She *loathed* me. That's not why I'm suspicious; the way we couldn't find her in the database was

weird. There were other things today. I'll fill you in later.
Now go!"

An HSA screening officer and a triage nurse in green scrubs
stood outside the car.

"Tell these nice people what's wrong with you," I said. "And
give me a call when you're ready, and I'll come get you."

Lonny opened the door, got his viral status screened, and
went inside with the nurse. I drove to our office.

Not all of it was clear until I pieced it together hours later,
with Griffin's help, but here's what had happened:

Each EO cabinet has a motion-activated camera that records
to the cloud, like doorbell cameras. At 12:30, around the time I
was reading the darkbart.com chirp and reviewing the EO's
detailed metadata, the video from cabinet G.3.1 shows EO Serial
Number 357, Enchanted Form UPC 233-2499370-4494078, Imperial Stormtrooper and Blaster, expand from its 4-inch size to that
of an adult human. The full-size stormtrooper immediately
struggles to move, and finding himself trapped, points the
blaster at the Plexiglass front of the cabinet, fires, and escapes
through the shattered front of the cabinet. We later found the
armor-piercing large caliber bullet had rolled under cabinet
G.3.1, as if it had bounced off the Plexi on the cabinet across from
it. The EO in that cabinet was unaffected, and the cabinet
remained intact except for an impact scrape where the bullet
bounced.

From surveillance cameras in the ceiling, footage showed the
stormtrooper leaping onto the STIF floor in its aisle, looking
right and left, and heading toward the door, as though attracted
by the light from outside. He ran with plodding steps, off-
balance, nothing like the stormtroopers in the *Star Wars* films. At
the front door, the stormtrooper raises his blaster.

A couple of days after the incident, Officer Clancy Garringer,
from his hospital bed, recounted: "I heard all this noise, and I
rounded the corner, and saw a guy in white plastic armor, with a
crazy *Star Wars* gun, running toward me. I raised my hand, and

said, 'Whoah, whoah,' and the guy raised the gun and shot me before I could even explain I was here to help. Luckily, he had bad aim. Or only meant to wing me. Next thing I remember, the EMTs were picking me off the floor." Clancy didn't remember (or didn't mention) Leslie and me dragging him to safety, or Leslie bandaging him.

Agent Lonsford Dotch recounted for the official record: "We heard the noise. I hurried Mrs. DeLuxe into the officers' locker room and asked her to stay. She wasn't happy about it. Said, 'What is it? Is it coming undone, the Curse?' and I said, 'I don't know, stay here to be safe.'

"Back in the hallway, I saw the subject blast through the glass boxes, big caliber ammo in that laser blaster. It wasn't a laser blast, though. It fired projectiles. The stormtrooper took off like a bat out of hell. Officer Sawyer was down the hall coming from the opposite direction, and we arrived at the spot the subject had shot through, and saw the subject running out of the building. That's when Officer Sawyer drew his firearm, why he's even carrying that I don't know, and I tried to stop him firing it, but it exploded anyway. Maybe he thought the Munitions Enchantment had ended. For what it's worth, the subject, the disenchanted EO, the 'victim,' his gunfire was obviously not subject to the Enchantment when he shot Officer Garringer." Lonny and I argued later: had the stormtrooper intended to shoot Clancy, or had he accidentally winged him? It all boiled down to intention.

Officers at the subsequent checkpoints described similar situations. The stormtrooper blasted its way out of the facility, mainly thanks to surprise. Normal security was (unfortunately) oriented outward, in anticipation of an external intruder. The blaster made short work of the gates at the fences and walls (he must have had a *lot* of ammo), and he splashed through the moat.

Officers at the outer perimeter described seeing the subject disappear into the woods around the STIF compound. Neighborhood eyewitnesses and closed-circuit footage later verified the stormtrooper headed westward and south. People thought it odd, but assumed it was he was cosplaying. The last sighting was at a shopping mall, where the stormtrooper descended a staircase behind a shop. Prince George's County Enforcement Department arrived, responding to a report of breaking and entering, and discovered a destroyed metal door, leading to a storeroom in disarray. However, there was no sign of the suspect, corroborated shortly thereafter by the NBI agents sent to follow up.

And like that, he was gone, until Lonny and I found him later.

CHAPTER 8

A TRIP TO THE DMV

I liked my boss, Eliot. He always gave me challenging assignments, but he was smart and caring. He was like a big gay teddy bear: six feet tall, a little husky, and though he claimed he once kept his hair and goatee dyed "a fairly plausible auburn," he'd gone totally silver when I arrived at the DMV. Kind of a gay uncle type.

"Work with Griffin," he told me, on my second day. I later discovered nobody else in the office liked working with Griffin. I didn't mind. Once I figured out what made him tick, he wasn't so bad. I simply didn't expect him to respond to emotional cues, and didn't take it personally when he acted like a genius. He was one! He wasn't trying to irritate on purpose. It just seemed that way.

I worked with him the first week. Eliot had prepared me for it, but after one too many departures without saying goodbye, when I found myself talking to empty space, I sat with him. "Griffin," I said, "How about this: I'll help cue you to things you may want to consider? And you take my suggestions in the spirit in which I offer them? As ways for you and for me to do our jobs more effectively when working together, and with other people."

He looked over my right shoulder, where he normally looked

instead of into people's eyes. While he looked beyond me, I looked into his young, smooth face. Was that peach fuzz? Did he even shave yet? A mop of sandy blond hair, green eyes. An open, impassive expression, slightly furrowing his brows as he considered my offer. I could only speculate as to his age. *He must be older than he looks*, I thought. He was clearly the senior technical expert on staff.

"That sounds like a reasonable approach." And since that time, I could lean over to him in a meeting, and whisper, "Say thank you," or pass him a note or send a Scrye text saying, *She said that sarcastically, so ask her what she needs*, or generally help him understand anything he might be missing. It wasn't that he had bad intentions. He missed cues, so I took him under my wing and helped. The extra investment I made in him helped me, too, showing that our technical team (i.e., Griffin) was easier to work with than people might have supposed.

Eliot assigned me to work with Lonny, too. Lonny was brusque sometimes, but nowhere near as high maintenance as Griffin. Lonny wanted things to be right. When things got squishy (like rules being bent or disregarded) he got irritated. I tried to help him see things from other sides. Sometimes that worked, sometimes it didn't. I'd have trusted my life to him. Even without a functioning gun, he was an accomplished law enforcement agent.

He taught me elementary self-defense, and even how to shoot a gun. On a firing range, of course, since they would work there without danger.

The TP metadata helped Griffin map patterns with geospatial data. Hence the visit to Mx. Bluntschli on the day the spit hit the fan. Although I had been confident our geospatial data and our vector-based ley lines would turn something up, I certainly hadn't expected to find something like Chester! The incident at the STIF had pushed him to the back of my priorities by midday. I was concerned more with the EOs we knew, like the stormtrooper.

There was a betting pool (for bragging rights only, since monetary betting would have violated federal ethics laws) among the civil servants at the DMV, as to which conservative figure (from the president down to the most anonymous Tea Party member) had been enchanted into which piece of bric-a-brac, tchotchke, or collectible object. No one had a real clue as to who had magically become what. Consequently, speculation abounded. The public, on abundant Ribbit sites and comment threads on both mainstream media *and* conspiracy theory web sites, tried to make some sense of the transfigurations. The most popular of these speculations, understandably, tried to identify the figurine, action figure, or plush animal doll that President DeLuxe had become.

Was President DeLuxe now a children's Darth Vader Halloween costume? This theory was popular in comment threads on a progressive website, although the site editors demurred from stating an opinion.

Was President DeLuxe now the dashboard Luke Skywalker bobble-head? Longtime alt-right darkbeit.com readers thought that would be apt.

Was he now an Ursula, the Sea Witch stuffed toy? This was controversial on lilithwasfirst.com, the reclaimers of the Divine Feminine fighting the traditional bad rap given to witches.

Was he a gelatinous wallcrawler toy based on Jabba the Hutt? The Thanos limited numbered edition figurine, from *Avengers: Infinity War*? The Christmas ornament of Donald Duck having a fit of anger? The list went on.

In the DMV, we had an intimate knowledge of each of the objects. A task force had carefully cataloged each EO on removal from crime scene at the DeLuxe Hotel. Professionally, but respectfully, in the way one would handle the remains of a human body, a combination of crime scene investigators and morgue staff had inspected each EO. There was disagreement whether they should be treated as deceased or not. The final decision was "not currently alive," keeping the possibility that they might spring to life again. I guess that had been proven on the day the STIF breakout happened. Turning into a life-sized, moving, armed version of what your Enchanted Object had been —that wasn't the same as disenchantment, but you'd have to classify it as presumptively living. No longer "not currently alive," at least.

By the time I came onboard, DMV staff had dutifully observed, compiled, and recorded each object's data into the Magical Objects Federal Tracking System (known as MOFTS). However seriously we took our stewardship of the data, though, there was nothing that truly indicated which conference participant had become which object.

Therefore, the office betting pool, which had no certainty of ever having a winner, was as truly random as any game of chance. Although gambling was strictly forbidden in government offices, Eliot told me it was okay to have a "speculation matrix" as long as we used non-monetary points. (He called those points "Whuffie Scores" for a reason he didn't explain to me.) There might never be a winner, but it was fun to root for your EO while reading the non-Government odds maintained by Las Vegas gamblers.

Shortly after joining as "newbie" on the DMV team, I had put my Whuffie on the antique ceramic figure of Disney's Three Little Pigs I thought might be President DeLuxe. Unlike most of the EOs, this little ceramic figurine had scratches and cracks, and one Little Pig was missing a front hoof. There were fans of every object out there, including this one, and someone had posted on the unofficial EOWiki that this figurine would, in real life, have held a Three Little Pigs child's watch sometime in the 1950s or 60s. That watch wasn't in the EO inventory, so I felt sorry for the little thing: unwanted, damaged, and incomplete.

Even before I started with DMV, I was familiar with much of the inventory, my prior job being with the Magical Data Transparency Foundation, a federal transparency think-tank and advocacy organization. The administration of the new president, post-2/29, had made a show of hiring advocates of transparency to help keep all information about 2/29 as openly available to the public as possible. This included inviting experts in the field to work in DMV. If I do say so myself, I'd gotten good exposure in my Foundation job, even had some input (my law background!) into the legislative language. My FOIA studies paid off.

Not all DMV staff or leadership agreed with every hiring decision. Ultimately, the DMV's Assistant Attorney General for Magic, Hannah Yi, had advocated for a special exception hiring, and consideration (still completely competitive) for the most qualified candidate, regardless of any potentially oppositional relationships between DMV and its watchdogs. "We need to see these people and organizations as our partners, not our enemies," stated AAG/M Yi, in a press release in mid-2021.

Before coming to work at DMV, I had appeared on a number of conference panels with DMV staff, including my eventual boss's boss, Antonia della Femina. I felt like I had forged good working relationships with DMV officials even before I went to work from the inside as a Program Evaluation and Review Specialist. My job was to ensure that DMV processes were following statutory, regulatory, and internal policy requirements, to both letter and spirit. As part of my job, I studied office processes, laboratory and archival activities, and the inspections and law enforcement programs that agents conducted in the field. Taking the job had meant relinquishing my law degree program, already on pause. The world had changed so precipitously with 2/29 that I felt a calling to know more about what happened.

After dropping Lonny off at the hospital, I drove the short distance to our office building. It was directly across the street from the old LNM headquarters, now housing the Financial Consumer Protection Agency. There was not much need for the LNM nowadays. The only guns and explosives that worked were, thanks to the Enchantment, those that weren't intended to hurt people. The agency had downsized, and most of its agents had been absorbed into the NBI or the Confidential Service. Plenty of room in the building, now, to house the re-expanding FCPA, which President DeLuxe had tried to dissolve.

As I drove, I thought: my big event today was supposed be the database launch. Now, not only had I seen my first actual magical animal, I'd also been near when something had happened to undo, or somehow alter, the 2/29 Enchantment. My first *two* magical events in one day! I parked the car in the garage and sat in the car for a moment. The STIF breakout was disturbing. I took a breath. To be truthful, I was thrilled by the encounter with Chester and his...owner? Companion? I would have to come back to them later, though. Now, the STIF breakout was where I should focus. I got a text from Eliot: *Where are you? I hear you were there at the STIF.*

Just getting back. Need to gather data. Will drop by shortly.

He replied, *kk.* He had read online (and joked with me) that we Millennials found "OK" to be abrupt or rude in a text, preferring "kk." It was a private joke for him to use that. He knew I didn't need him to coddle me. I was "perfectly capable of code-switching to old fogie-speak," I had told him.

I would need Griffin, but he wasn't at his cube, and when I knocked on the IT equipment room, nobody answered. At my own office, I immediately tapped into the MOFTS data on cabinet G.3.1 and EO Serial Number 357. I went over the data, and tried to pull up the monitoring data from before the incident. Then I remembered it was stored elsewhere, in different database tables from our main inventory data, so I'd have to reach out to Griffin for help pulling them together, as I suspected. (That's part of what I later gathered to put together the sequence of events.) As I had shown Mrs. DeLuxe, based on our positioning data, it looked like the agents had found EO 357 near the center of our Ground Zero. It might be helpful to use Griffin's and my mapping strategy to figure out why this particular EO had done what it did. And what about those weird lighting fluctuations and the pixie dust sound? I'd get Griffin to help me see if we could pull data for that. I hadn't imagined them, had I?

On my display, I scrolled through the map Griffin had created under my direction. Here was Ground Zero, here were all the Transformation Incidents around the greater DC area, here were the vectors and ley lines we'd plotted. And here, now, was the STIF, with a new type of incident to plot. Griffin and I would have to discuss that later. Would our metadata schema handle a second enchantment for the same TP?

The STIF was nowhere near any of the ley lines or plotted points, other than being between some of the ley lines. That had to be a coincidence, simply because it was a close suburb of DC.

Who was this person? Why did he retain his EO shape when he grew to full size? I pulled up our database entry on EO Serial Number 357, and launched the 360° VR photographic record, rotating it, magnifying it. It was only a plastic action figure, with visible joints, painted surfaces, and its gun was continuous with its arm, molded of the same chunk of plastic. Our perpetrator had a working gun in the shape of a laser blaster, and, according to the eyewitnesses, looked exactly like one of the characters from the movies. I sighed. I needed to stop trying to make sense of things. It was magic! What about the person inside the armor? Did the TP think he was actually an Imperial Stormtrooper? What would we find underneath that white helmet? A clone that looked like that handsome Maori actor from the movies? Or was there nothing there at all? Hollow? I shuddered. Solid plastic? Barely better. And where had he vanished to, and how?

My personal cell phone rang, and I jumped. Years before, I had assigned a catch pop tune as ringtone for someone who rarely called me anymore. This was his tone.

"Haverford!" I said, answering the call.

"Fab, how the heck are ya?" he replied. "It's been an age, truly. My bad."

"Well, we're all so busy."

"And of course, now that you've gone over to the Dark Side."

That gave me a start, but it had to be a coincidence.

"Not Dark Side, Hav, you know that. On the side of the angels, the transparency angels, just like you," I replied.

Haverford Howell, Executive Director of the Magical Data Transparency Foundation, was my former boss. We worked together during my internship, helping Congressional staffers on the hastily chartered House Committee on Magical Terrorism and Protection. I never liked that title. Together, we drafted the Magical Accountability and Transparency Act, aka the MATA Act. We were both passionate about the public needing to know all it could about the magical activity happening. We worked side by side for weeks, long hours, living on ramen and strong coffee, to craft the MATA Act. We were so proud of our baby! Only a few amendments were added. Our sponsors had been great about pre-selling it, even during the panic of the first months after 2/29, when some folks were scared spitless there'd be another Enchantment.

As the months passed and the law enforcement, counterterrorism, and counterintelligence communities turned up zilch, the public groundswell grew for Congress to release the information. Plus, it made sense to assuage the concerns of President DeLuxe's constituents to make sure the EOs were cared for using the highest fiduciary principles. Sorry, I'm slipping into House Resolution-ese with my rhetoric. The bottom line is everyone thought it was a good idea to make information about the EOs available to everyone, even while the investigations went on.

We made sure the legislation created a new division (the DMV) at DLE to analyze and publish the information, and when it came time to staff it, it made sense for me to follow the work, and actually execute what Hav and I had proposed. I wasn't in a senior position of authority, but I was totally vested in making it a success.

Hav rose to become Executive Director of the Foundation, advocating for even more transparency. We worked together to put on a couple of summits, but hadn't stayed in as close contact as we'd been in during the legislative process. Some people might say the Foundation was a potential enemy, but really, I didn't know of any instance where the Foundation and the DMV hadn't been aligned. That's why his comment about the Dark Side, in addition to being a weird coincidence, rubbed me wrong. Unless he was digging for information on the investigation into Sorcerer X. That had been the Foundation's advocacy project: more transparency into what the NBI had found. Some people don't take "nothing" for an answer. I thought he was wasting his talents. Perhaps that's why we didn't talk much any more.

"Anyway," he said, "We've *gotta* have a drink after work sometime soon!" Most things he said sounded like they should have an exclamation point after them. He was enthusiastic. I remember when he'd turn to me and say, "Great work, Fab!" and flash me a big, toothy smile and crinkle his robin's egg blue eyes at me. I missed that.

"Yes, or maybe dinner," I said. "That ramen place across from the arena, for old time's sake. I hear it's gotten trendy."

"Haha, yeah, that'd be the ticket!"

"Anything new on your end?" I asked. I launched a new browser window and navigated to the Foundation web site. It showed their usual news about upcoming conferences, legislative agenda, and accomplishments.

"Funny you should say that; that's just what I was going to ask. Word is something new is happening!"

"I'm not sure what you mean," I said. The stormtrooper's breakout was law enforcement sensitive and definitely premature to release to the public, with the escapee on the loose with a lethal weapon. I was all for transparency, but not if it would cause panic. Then again, maybe people needed to be aware...

"Well, according to a chirp from your office about a breakout from your secure facility, something's up! Yes?"

"What? What's the chirp say? From our Chirpa account? I manage that account. I didn't send anything."

"It's right here," he said, "I'll read it to ya! And I quote, 'George Lucas working industrial light and magic on our STIF? A certain escapee from cabinet G.3.1 is either a SPFX or a game changer.' Sounds like you got an escapee? Cabinet G.3.1 is an Imperial Stormtrooper, according to your web site. Beautiful work, congratulations on the launch, by the way."

I quickly navigated to Chirpa. "I didn't send that chirp," I said, carefully. "Don't make assumptions. We may have been hacked. I'm calling up the account now." I brought the Chirpa account, @DLE.DMV, up on my computer. "I'm not seeing that, Haverford. Are you sure you saw that? From @DLE.DMV?" Even if he hadn't, how did he know? And that wasn't like him to fish (phish?) like that, not to me!

"Yes, here it is, that's the account. Hey, wait a minute! Yours is DLE 'dot' DMV. This isn't your account! It's '@DLE' *dash* 'DMV'! Well, how about that!"

"Well, that's a relief. I mean, I'm still concerned someone is making it sound like—"

"But it's true, isn't it? The people who got the chirp are rechirping it, and eyewitnesses out in New Carollton are reporting they saw it! The chirp may not be yours, but is it true? Did a stormtrooper come from your STIF?"

Shoot! I thought. "Hold on, Haverford. Let me see." I brought up the account he was talking about. It even had the DLE seal and a reproduction of our DMV logo! This must violate the Chirpa terms of service! I scanned the rechirps and the conversation, and saw, to my horror, that eyewitnesses were corroborating, and it looked like an anonymous member of the PG County police had given even more inappropriate details. Probably a DeLuxe supporter. Now it was out of the bag. Exclamation point. "I can't comment, Haverford," I said. Dammit. That was a good as a confirmation.

"Ah!" he said. "Okay, Fab, I understand. Nothing to say right now. Keep me posted when you can talk, though! This is big! Really big!"

"Mm," I said, noncommittally. I scrolled down the conversation thread. The counts of comments and rechirps increased as I watched.

"Tell ya what, I'll let you know if I hear anything more. Meanwhile, check out those chirps," he said.

"I am. Thanks, Hav," I said. We disconnected, and I checked the owner of the account. It had been established only a day ago, but already had over a thousand followers! It looked plausible, except for the dash. I reported it as false, and sent an email to public affairs. They would follow up with Chirpa's government relations folks if the account didn't get shut down in a couple of days.

E liot's office overlooked a landscaped courtyard between our building, a hotel, and a building of rental flats. (I confess: my apartment was one of the rental flats, although you couldn't see my windows from the office. I was on the south side, on M Street.) My neighbors from the building walked their dogs in the courtyard, and the sound of barking reached up to the seventh floor. I paused in the hallway between the east and west wings (Eliot's office was in the west wing) and watched a pit bull, a corgi, and a couple of cute, scruffy mutts, romping on the astroturf in the dog pen as their dog parents stood and talked.

Eliot was sitting at his desk twirling a Mickey Mouse fidget spinner that lit up with flashing red and blue LEDs. His office had a number of Disney and other figures of cartoon characters. Although none of these were enchanted in any way (Eliot claimed he had a sales receipt for every one of them), one of my co-workers, Charlene Pelletier, disapproved of Eliot's quirky choice of office decoration, comparing it to a museum administrator at the Holocaust Museum keeping a collection of old shoes in his office. She mentioned that the week I arrived. I thought it was indiscreet to tell a new coworker you disapprove of your boss. Charlene is an older woman who works on projects I couldn't begin to understand, involving legacy systems and records management and property reporting requirements that dated from years before 2/29 but were somehow required of the DMV anyway. She could have retired years ago, as she kept reminding us. I suppose she was good at her job, and nobody else wanted to do it. At one point, Eliot had hinted to me to take everything Charlene said with a grain of salt. I wasn't sure if Eliot knew the stories Charlene was telling about him. I also suspected she had voted for President DeLuxe.

"Hey, Fab! Have a seat," Eliot said, waving me to his little round table. He put the fidget spinner near the exact center of the table and gave it one more spin, and we watched it, listening to the sound of its tiny ball bearings roll, and roll, and roll, and finally begin to slow. When it was almost stopped, Eliot said, "What a launch day, eh? Are you okay?"

"Yes," I said. "I'm better off than Lonny and the others who got shot." I glanced at my phone to see if Lonny had texted me. I asked him to let me know when they discharged him.

"Yeah, that was awful, truly awful. Agent Oberst is on it, though," Eliot said. He rolled his eyes.

"Frankly, Eliot, I'm concerned, aren't you? What does this mean about all our assumptions? That one of the 2/29 victims could come back to life, for no reason we know of, and be so violent like that. And the fact his gun worked!"

"That's the scariest thing to me," Eliot said. "Toni tells me Hanna's at the White House right now and off to the Hill shortly thereafter, I'm sure."

"Do they know if other guns can work? Or bombs?" I asked.

"The NBI thinks not, although it's hard to prove," Eliot said, shrugging. "Since unless there's violent intent, guns and explosives still work, how do you prove they won't unless you're a criminal or a terrorist or artillery soldier at war? And there's no war now."

"Can they shoot at someone in Kevlar?" I asked. I ought to know more about this, I realized as I said it. I'd been lulled into the more innocuous parts of the 2/29 Enchantment, the transfigurations, rather than the binding that prevented gun or explosive violence. I, like the vast majority of the world, thought the inability to shoot or blow people up was a good thing. It's possible I was superstitious and didn't want think about it too much and jinx it. Contrary to my way of thinking, more paranoid gun lovers still believed the 2/29 Enchantment was a liberal plot. In those circles, the hoped-for reversal of the gun violence binding was known as the Restoration!

"They've been able to do that all along. If you know the person won't get harmed, the guns shoot. Like target practice."

"I knew about target practice. People aren't target practice, though."

"Well, obviously, guns and explosions still work around people. That's how they can still blast mountains or demolish buildings with explosives, or how we can still drive a car with an internal combustion engine for that matter. The magic kicks in when there's harmful intent."

"Oh, right. The accidental shootings," I said, remembering. There were still accidental deaths, from time to time, at shooting ranges or skeet matches, or actual gun-cleaning incidents. Unfortunately, toddlers sometimes still shot themselves if their parents neglected to lock up the firearms.

"I feel so helpless," I said. "What can we do now? I'm pulling surveillance footage from the STIF, in case that helps."

"It's in the hands of the NBI now. Make sure Oberst's team gets the footage and anything else you think of. Custodial has the facility on high alert in case there are more disenchantments."

"Is that officially what we're calling it now, when they change back?" I was surprised.

"Yeah, I decided that's the official term for when someone changes back. I think it works best. We're not sure if this was a disenchantment or something else, right? It was a full-sized stormtrooper," he said.

"Yes, completely authentic looking."

"The question is, was there a cosplaying stormtrooper at the AFPAP, and this is their natural form, with a real gun? Or did some other person get turned into a stormtrooper, then get transformed again into a life-size one? In which case it's not a disenchantment, it's second transformation. The chances of someone in stormtrooper drag at that event? I don't think so."

"But if there was someone with a gun and intent to use it, stormtrooper or not, that would change some of our assumptions about AFPAP and 2/29, wouldn't it?" I asked.

"It certainly would! Plus, that would be the only instance where the original form was similar to the enchanted form, right? I mean, unless you've turned up anything with your data analytics."

"No," I said. "Nothing we've been able to see connects the original person with their ultimate shape, that we can tell. This would be unique, if it is the person's original shape."

"We're not investigators, so I guess we keep plugging away and hope that has value. Nothing we can do, except what you're already doing. I have an assignment for you, that could help," Eliot said.

"I'm eager to do whatever I can," I replied.

"First, tell me, did your map projections turn up anything promising?" He picked up the spinner again, and twirled it.

Oh, poop, I thought. In all the excitement, I hadn't expected Eliot to ask about whether we'd found an unreported EO. And technically, we hadn't. I hadn't lied to Lonny, technically: I evaded the truth until I could gather more data. And technically, none of the law covered magical animals. But now Eliot was asking me a more general question, directly. I hadn't thought through what I was going to say. I had to think on my feet. I didn't want to pause too long.

"Oh, I almost forgot!" I said. "Can we wait to talk about the field visit? I got a call from my old boss, Haverford Howell. I can't believe I didn't mention this first!"

"Why? What's good ol' Hav up to?" Eliot asked.

"It's bad, Eliot. News of the escape, or I should say rumors. From a fake Chirpa account. Looks like ours, but not." I held out my mobile phone and showed him the chirp. Chirpa hadn't taken down the account yet. "I reported it as false, and sent an email to PAO to follow-up."

"Jeez Louise!" Eliot said, reading the chirp. He slammed the fidget spinner down and took my phone. "We'd better get onto *our* account and disclaim."

"Except, it was pretty near the truth."

"Let me call PAO," he said. He picked up his phone, and talked with our contact at the Public Affairs Office for a few minutes, while I thought about what I'd say about Chester and JR. He read PAO the chirp and the name of the fake account.

"Okay, thanks," Eliot said, hanging up. "They'll contact Chirpa corporate today, confirm your report of misuse, and issue a statement from their Chirpa account that an incident was contained at the STIF—"

My eyes widened. It was anything but contained.

"—And the NBI is on it, too soon to release details."

"I guess that will hold them?" I said. I wasn't sure.

"PAO's problem, for now. So," he said, leaning back in his chair, smiling, "Did you find anything on your visit before the STIF?"

We were back to JR and Chester.

"Maybe," I said. I paused, looking at my coffee travel mug I was carrying, as though I'd seen a blob of half and half on the hole I had sipped from. I wanted to find a way to protect Chester and JR, whom I was sure were innocent and not harmful, but I didn't want to lie to my boss, either.

Eliot said nothing, waiting for me, and I looked up. I tried to keep my eyes wide and locked with his. The innocent blonde act usually worked, in particular with straight men. I wasn't

sure how effective it would be on Eliot, but it was the best
I had.

"What does 'maybe' mean?" he asked, blinking. He blinked
again. Then another time. Another co-worker, Tobin Rosario-
Lopez, had worked with Eliot for years before I came to DMV.
He shared a pointer on working with Eliot.

"He's got a 'tell'", Tobin confided over lunch in my office one
day. "When he's thinking hard about something or disagrees or
even is getting angry, but he doesn't want to show it, he blinks a
few extra times. I make it out he's trying to adjust to your reality
not meshing with how he thinks things should be, so he's trying
to see if it'll go away. But he wants to hear more, so he's not
gonna say it yet. So he blinks."

"Is he stringing you on, to trap you? I hope not!" I didn't
want to think that of Eliot.

"No, that's not his style, more like he thinks what you're
saying is crazy or stupid, or mistaken, but he might be missing
something. He may still think it's wrong once you tell him, but
now's your chance to sell him on whatever it is you're saying."

Based on this, Eliot was open to hearing what I had to say. I
had to make it good.

"Well!" I said. "In all the drama, I haven't had time to process
it. The bottom line is…"

I sipped my coffee again, making sure I emphasized no word
too much: "…the bottom line is there were no Enchanted Objects
we could find, or that the house's occupant could identify." That
was true. And I didn't stress "objects" too much, I thought.

"'Could' or 'would'?" he asked. He blinked a couple of more
times.

"Eliot, here's the deal," I said, leaning toward him over his
little round table with the fidget spinner in the middle. "I think
something magical may have happened there."

"Really?! You mean…" —his voice dropped to a whisper, and
he leaned toward me over the table—"*real magic?*" He wiggled in
his seat like a kid whose parents just turned the corner onto

Disneyland Drive. Eliot knows that he and I share an enthusiasm for discovering real magic beyond 2/29, which has been completely absent as far as anyone can tell. Having dangled that pixie bait, I reeled him in.

"I don't honestly know," I said. I set my coffee mug on his desk, and leaned back, trying to look casual. I'd crossed my arms in front of me, then I opened them, trying to look casual. "I don't know what happened." Yes, I realized, this was true! I knew Chester was there, and I knew he was magical, but I didn't know what had happened to him. "I promise you, though, the person who lives there is nice and non-threatening, and I don't think there's an Enchanted Object that needs custodial protection. I didn't see anything that should be seized, for the public's safety or for the resident's." All true. I looked behind me at his office door. Dropping to a whisper and leaning toward him, I said, "I think getting the enforcement side involved at this point would not be helpful."

Eliot thought the 2/29 Enchantment was one of the best things to have happened to the country, probably the world, in a long time. Certainly the best thing since before the election of President DeLuxe, whom he loathed still. Eliot tolerated the enforcement activities of the DMV as necessary to maintain an appearance of concern about it, but I suspected he'd never want the perpetrator or perpetrators caught. Eliot was not simply a Disney fan; he was a fan of the complete and permanent Disney-fication of President DeLuxe and the others.

"How about Agent Dotch?" he asked. "Can we trust him?"

"He didn't witness everything I did, and I think the owner of the house and I have a better rapport."

"Well, natch," he said. "Okay, you keep working on that, as long as you're sure there's no connection with the STIF, and no Transformed Person in danger. It's still part of our analytics responsibility at this point. Keep me posted as soon as you can share something!" He smiled and rubbed his hands together, as though anticipating the discovery of a troupe of fairies in his garden.

"Meanwhile, related," he said, sprawling in his chair, "I think we need to make a map that extends out to the greater DMV area, the geographic one that is." In the greater Washington, DC area, the use of "DMV" to denote that area had gained currency about ten years before someone decided to name the new division of DLE with the same acronym. We rarely used the common DC/Maryland/Virginia sense of the term in our office.

"That makes sense, and I was thinking along the same lines," I said.

"I have a hunch there's more to be gotten from your idea, which was brilliant, by the way. Although we'd visualized the data, we'd never linked it to geospatial information the way you did."

"Griffin did it, but thanks. I thought it might help."

"This time, include the incident at the STIF as a new data attribute. A disenchantment or a secondary transfiguration."

"You just made that up, didn't you? Secondary transfiguration."

"It's what I do. Map it out, and show all the other transformation points, and let's take a look to see if we can give any assistance to our friends from the Bureau."

"I'll see what we can do."

"Go see Griffin, and keep up the good work," Eliot said. He picked up the fidget spinner, and stood, giving Mickey a vigorous twirl.

This was my cue to leave.

CHAPTER 9

WHAT IS TO BE DONE

G riffin officially sat in what facilities called the "hyphen"—the connecting area between the east and west wings of the building. The people who designed the DMV organization originally thought their database might be classified, so the hyphen had thick, electro-magnetically shielded walls. As it turned out, that wasn't needed. The MATA Act made transparency our core value instead. Our plan, now that we had launched the public database, was to push the contents of our database to a web site every night, where the public could see the status of all the EOs. Not that we had antici-pated many changes in status! Before today, the only new data was the now dried-up trickle of transfigured objects people turned over to DMV custody after the 2/29 Event. The STIF breakout, I supposed, was an exception to the transparency policy; the Act did allow us to withhold active investigation data. Until the stormtrooper was found, I decided.

I found Griffin in his cubicle, hunched over his laptop, typing furiously. I could never figure out when he would be there, and when he would be holed up in his IT equipment room. He had two big external monitors connected to his laptop via a docking station. The external monitors showed default backgrounds, and nothing more. Griffin could and would use the bigger monitors to show me data or prototypes of the web site or our map. He preferred to use his laptop screen for any programming.

Origami paper figures dotted his workspace: frogs, starfish, geometric solids, flowers, an armadillo, and a dozen variations on the classic crane, wittily tweaked into action poses caught in mid-flight, two cranes with their necks lovingly intertwined, nesting on an origami nest full of little origami eggs. If he could not be on his computer during a meeting, it was Griffin's habit to fold origami. He did this even when people were talking to him, which many found annoying. I understood it was a way of controlling the input to his hypersensitive, hyperactive brain. The folding patterns were so complex I couldn't imagine the time, accuracy, or brainpower required to do them.

From about ten feet away, I cleared my throat, and Griffin glanced into a little mirror secured to his big monitor. Seeing me, he said, "Hi," and kept typing. I had asked him to say hello when he saw me. It was not his default response, and still not what he said when he saw other people, but he practiced it with me.

"Hi, Griffin," I replied, approaching his space. There was a visitor chair in the empty cubicle next to his. (DMV had never staffed up to its original complement, and many people teleworked if they were still at risk for the virus, or had dependents at home, or a challenging commute. There were lots of spare chairs around.) I picked it up and carried it over. None of the staff could ever remember Griffin's cubicle having a visitor chair, but he tolerated me bringing one when we worked together.

"You heard about the breakout?" I asked.

"Yes." He continued to type rapidly, looking at the code scrolling rapidly on his screen. His brow was furrowed, and I could see little muscles in his jaw clench and unclench.

"I looked for you before. Are you working on something about that?"

"Yes." The screen was filled with numbers. Griffin

programmed in machine language sometimes when he was anxious to get something done.

"Eliot has something he wants us to do," I continued. "Based on the mapping, he wants a map of the entire DC area, out as far as the STIF and a little further."

Without looking up, and without stopping his typing, Griffin said, "The mapping didn't help us predict the breakout. People got shot because we failed. For all we know, the whole Enchantment is failing!" He kept typing.

"There's no way you could have predicted this! And we don't know the whole Enchantment is failing. In fact, we think not. The officer's gun exploded, like usual," I said. I reached out, about to touch his hand, realized my mistake, jerked it back, and scooted closer into his field of vision. "Look at me."

He paused his typing and turned. He only pulled away an inch. Nice. He was tolerating my proximity. I had asked him to. I looked into his eyes and said, "Eliot thinks a map may help us find the stormtrooper before he harms anyone else, or himself. The NBI are trying to find him. No luck." His eyes were red. And he sniffled. He was taking this hard, for some reason.

"I have your surveillance footage. I sent you the link to a version I edited together."

"Wow, how did you—?"

"You texted me you wanted it, so when I was compiling all the other metrics for the time surrounding the breakout, I put that together for you." He launched a video on his screen, and I saw the footage. For a few minutes, we watched the EO 357 break out of his cabinet. The footage from the various cameras followed him along his path of destruction. Griffin had done all this in the time since I started compiling the data, less than twenty minutes. He was a prodigious multitasker.

"I'm still working on getting the footage from the surveillance cams at Seabrook Shopping Center, the last sighting." The place the escapee had disappeared.

"Do you think the stormtrooper could have ditched his

armor? That would be a simple explanation for not finding him after that? But this is magic we're talking about, and that may be too Occam's Razor. Do you think we should look for a less obvious explanation?"

"Yes, based on what I can see from the data, I don't think it's that simple," Griffin said. He was looking at my mouth as he spoke. If I hadn't known his habit of not looking people in the eye, I'd have asked if I had spinach in my teeth. Looking into my face, at least part of it, was progress from how he normally looked at people. That is, not at all, if he could avoid it.

"I don't know what you're seeing from that chaos," I said, gesturing at his monitor, "But I'm glad you see something. I know, I know: chaos is really a highly complex system." We had discussed this before.

"To a cat, a car ride is chaos. To a human, it's a logical succession of causes, effects, predictable new data, and intended results."

"I'm as smart as a cat, compared to you, is what I'm hearing."

"You like cats! I thought you'd like that analogy."

"I like cats. So, okay, thanks. I guess." He was at least trying to meet me midway. "To the present task: can we get the map Eliot wants?"

"I'm busy on this." I could tell he wanted to return to his typing.

"What is it?" I asked.

He stared at my mouth. Instead of telling me what he was working on, he asked, "Map of what? Density of incidence? Transformation delta ratio? Time vectors?"

"Just plot where the transformations have taken place, and color code human versus pre-existing object enchantments. Exclude gun and explosion data for now."

"Already have that routine queued up. I made it accessible to that new app I gave you. That's simple. We'll have to add more data points next time," he said. His jaw clenched and unclenched. He was thinking.

"Yes, that might help," he said. "Maybe that will help me with this." He still hadn't told me what he was working on so frantically. But he was doing what Eliot wanted. "If I plot the known sightings, it is possible the data can help us. May I get to it?" He continued to look at my mouth. As I had requested, he was interacting with me until an appropriate break in the conversation and asking if he could move to his "next non-human interaction activity," as he had put it.

"Yes, generate the visualization, with the geographic data like we did for the ley lines exercise yesterday, and print it as big as you can."

"I'll use the plotter on the fourth floor. They owe me for debugging a workflow problem."

"It pays to bank favors," I said. I rose from the chair and returned it to the cube next door. "Thanks a billion, Griffin. Buzz me when we're ready to meet with Eliot." I walked out of the hyphen and into the corridor toward my office, and there was Lonny.

"Lonny! You should have called me!"

"I took a ride share," he said.

"How are you?"

"Fine," he said, and I knew not to push. His hand was freshly bandaged, and there was a bandage on his brow, but otherwise, he looked himself. "I need to check in with Oberst," he said. "C'mon with me."

Lonny had told me he'd been happy to stay with the decimated LNM, escaping absorption into the NBI, and then end up at DMV. But with Jake Oberst as his supervisor, it felt much the same as being absorbed, he said. Jake brought the culture of "The Bureau" with him. (The NBI got the nickname, "The Bureau," despite LNM being a bureau too. The NBI never let any other agencies forget that it was the premier law enforcement agency in the U.S. Other parvenus like Narcotics Bureau agents, U.S. Sheriffs, or Mail Service inspectors probably wished they could be NBI, was how NBI agents felt. In spite of the Sheriffs and Mail Service pre-dating the NBI.)

Lonny Dotch had known Oberst for over twenty years. Lonny had been an experienced LNM agent working on the Washington Sniper case, and Oberst had been a bushy-tailed baby agent fresh out of Quantico on the task force. Over the years, Oberst had risen quickly to Bureau leadership. I had to admit, he looked like a mid-twentieth century concept of a tall, blond, white male authority figure. And he was handsome. Cleft chin, chiseled nose, rectangular face. Meanwhile, Lonny had apparently rubbed some powerful people the wrong way and ended up in DMV. And Lonny would never say this, but for someone as dark-skinned and strong-willed as he was, his lack of butt-kissing didn't give him an advantage. Not with someone like Oberst.

We entered Oberst's bright corner office, which looked out on the old LNM building and the DC Muni station. Oberst was on a call.

"Yeah…uh-huh. As a matter of fact, here comes Agent Dotch right now…No, we don't think so at this point…Yes, ma'am." Oberst poked his mobile phone to end the call. "Have a seat," he said, gesturing to his round table. "Ms. Acer," he said, acknowledging me curtly.

I took the chair with my back to the window, and Lonny sat, back to the wall, and Oberst closed his office door and took his seat across from us, his back to the brightly lit window overlooking the LNM building across the street.

"Sit-rep," Oberst said. "That was Acting DAAG Malone. I need to report to her."

"Bureau appears to have everything secured at the STIF, the perpetrator, dressed like a Star Wars character, is still at large, and—"

"I know about the STIF situation," Oberst interrupted. "I mean what about the witch, this Gertrude Bluntschli?" My heart flip-flopped.

"Witch?" Lonny replied.

Oberst sighed, and grabbed the tablet sitting on his table, unlocking it as he spoke. "I mean she is a known Wiccan, prominent in pagan circles. She has led workshops at something called 'Mid-Atlantic Witch Camp,' on four occasions, according to my cursory Spoogle search," Oberst said. "She uses more than one name, "JR" looks like one of her aliases." He flipped the tablet around and showed us a web page. There was a photo of her standing in front of a group of people, and below it a biography. I could only skim the first sentences before Oberst pulled the tablet away. "And DAAG Malone is riding my butt about her. Did you even read the case file?" Oberst asked. I hated that tone he used on him.

Lonny didn't speak immediately, and I saw the muscles in his temples clench and unclench. He relaxed his fists.

Lonny replied, "Yes, I read that she was a Wiccan. Last I heard, that's not illegal, whether I agree with it or not." Lonny attended a local African Methodist Episcopal church.

I tried not to wiggle in my seat too much. I thought I'd let Oberst go on, rather than try to convince him anything.

"Did you think to look further into it?" Oberst continued, still using that condescending tone.

"Not if there's nothing to look into. She was nervous, but that's par for the course when we show up. Do you think because she's a Wiccan—"

"A self-proclaimed witch," Oberst corrected.

"A self-proclaimed witch, that she had something to do with 2/29?"

"Well, if she were hiding an Enchanted Object, mightn't that be a clue? Somebody did cause 2/29."

"As we have discussed, sir, my jurisdiction doesn't include finding whoever perpetrated 2/29. I am to investigate the likelihood of further or previously unidentified Enchanted Objects, and to call in the Bureau for appropriate seizure—"

"Yes, I get that you've memorized the memorandum I gave

you. That's right, and my point is, suspicious behavior around EOs may be relevant to the bigger investigation. Don't tell me you don't know that." He stared at Lonny. Then, slowly, he looked at me, trying to get a read. I hoped I continued to look impassive. A sliver of doubt started poking at my conscience. Was I obstructing justice by not revealing Chester's existence?

After taking a deep breath, Lonny said, "I hear what you're saying, sir, and my assessment is the woman is no threat nor was she involved in the conspiracy. If there is an Enchanted Object she has, I don't think she's aware of it." Oberst pointed his glare at Lonny, who blinked slowly.

"I concur!" I blurted, more forcefully than I intended. "I don't think zey has an Enchanted Object."

Oberst glanced at me for half a second, plunked his tablet flat onto the round glass table, turned away, and went to his desk, where he started reading email on his computer screens (he had three, plus a laptop). After about thirty seconds, he said, without looking at us, "We're done. I'm telling DAAG Malone you found nothing. I'll look forward to your written report."

We got up, and I carefully placed the chair under the table. Lonny let me pass him by, and I opened Agent Oberst's door, and stepped out. I was happy to leave the office. Lonny calmly followed me, pausing at the door.

"Open or shut?" he said to Oberst.

"Shut," Oberst grunted.

Dotch closed the door quietly, and we walked to his office. I came in, sat in his visitor chair, and Lonny closed the door.

"What are you going to do about Mx. Bluntschli?" I asked.

"I'm going to file my report with Oberst seventy-one and three-quarters hours from the exact time you and I left Mx. Blunstchli's home," he said. Seventy-two hours was the minimum performance measure.

"Ah, I see," I said. I supposed, in his way, Lonny was going to remind Oberst that he didn't own him, much as he tried. I was glad we weren't pursuing anything. "No sense to focus on zem when all this other stuff is happening."

"Exactly. Gettin' on my butt about that Bluntschli woman," he muttered. "Thinks we didn't dig deep enough. So what if we didn't? I don't buy DAAG Malone is more interested in that than the STIF breakout. He probably got *her* stirred up."

"Exactly! The stormtrooper is more important." I decided I would need to see JR Bluntschli and Chester as soon as there was a let-up in the excitement here.

"Out of our jurisdiction now, Bureau's headache. Didn't you hear?" I sat in the guest chair in his office, and he sat at his desk. He interlocked his fingers and placed his elbows on the desk, almost as if he were about to pray, frowning.

"You told me the Bureau is responsible for catching the perpetrators, right?" I asked.

"Yes, and potential domestic terrorists, which this guy became when he shot our people!" He looked at me with intense, dark brown eyes. Unlike Griffin, he had no problem looking people in the face.

"We're responsible for tracking Enchanted Objects, and notifying the Bureau to seize them, right?"

"So?"

"So, I can't see anything in the MATA Act," I said, holding up my tablet, where I had pulled up the Act's text, "that says we stop having that responsibility just because the EO is animated, or even if it's disenchanted, or secondarily transfigured. That's what we might have here. At the very least, there's a joint jurisdiction."

"Let me see that," Dotch said, motioning with his hand. I handed him the tablet. While he read, I sat in front of his desk, happy his penetrating dark eyes were not challenging me for the moment.

"Damn, I think you're right," he said, handing it to me. His eyes softened, and he broke into a brief smile, but it faded. "For whatever good it does us. The guy's disappeared." The tablet chirped, and there was a message from Griffin: *printing now see u in conf rm.*

"That's where Griffin's number-crunching comes in," I said. "Meeting in Eliot's conference room in fifteen minutes, as soon as his printing finished." I stood to go, then said, "One more thing. About Mx. Bluntschli, did you want to complete the interrogation?"

"Questioning, please," he said, smiling. "Maybe zey will speak more freely without the 'bad cop' there. Why don't you follow up with zem and go yourself, and finish the questions we'd agreed on? We can follow up on our schedule. Plus, that extends the seventy-two-hour clock, I do believe. Great idea!"

"And you were right, being a Wiccan, or even a witch, isn't a crime."

"I know, I know. Then we humor him. Just to shut him up, go talk to zem and do it by the book, so he can't complain."

"Will do!" Okay, that had worked out. Both Lonny and Eliot wanted me to revisit JR Bluntschli. And I'd see Chester too, although neither of them knew that part.

I rose to go, and Lonny's phone rang.

"Dotch. Uh-huh. Yeah, it would." He motioned me to stay, so I sat again. Lonny was writing on a notepad as the other person talked. "Yeah. You don't say. Witness saw him, but nobody there, and no exits? Oberst knows, right? Of course. Yeah, buddy. I owe you one. Thanks!" He hung up. "That was a pal on the team tracking our missing stormtrooper."

"Yes, and?"

"Confirms the per...victim disappeared in a basement in a strip mall. They have footage of him from security cameras, and an eyewitness saw him enter."

"And?"

"And, there are no exits except a door barred from the other side, top of the stairs to the adult novelty store upstairs. Somehow, though, when the team arrived, there wasn't anybody in the basement. The witness says nobody left, and the cam footage in front and back confirms that. They didn't see him disappear, but he's nowhere to be found. No other doors out, only a closet that he wasn't in."

"Did they give you the address?" I asked, and he handed me the sheet from his notepad.

"Another data point for Griffin, don't you think?" He was grinning.

"Yes! I'll get it to him right away. It pays to have friends in the Bureau, I guess?"

"I'll tell you one thing: it doesn't pay to be a hard-ass jerk, like some people, and it does pay if people trust you. So yeah, I guess you're right." He smiled with his lips closed, as though he had swallowed a canary.

I left his office and found Griffin again. He wasn't happy to stop his map from rendering. However, when I leaned over and quietly told him what Lonny had told me, Griffin's eyes grew wide, and he grabbed the paper from my hand.

"Yes, that makes sense," he said. "Give me fifteen minutes from now." He hunched over his laptop and continued typing, and I went to my office and set up an appointment and reserved our conference room for the top of the hour.

CHAPTER 10

MAGIC MAPPED

E liot, Lonny, and I sat in the conference room.
Looking at my watch, I said, "Griffin had to go to
the fourth floor to get the printouts."

"Can't we use the projector? Why print things out?" Eliot
asked. He ambled to the middle of the room and depressed the
power button of the projector, which sat on a wobbly black
plastic roller table. I stood and pressed the button on the wall
switch, and a white projection screen lowered, showing a blob of
blue from the signal-less projector. I went to the computer near
the projector, slotted my ID card into its reader, and logged on. A
DLE seal replaced the default blue screen.

Lonny dimmed the overhead fluorescents, leaving only the
inset lights in the ceiling around the perimeter for light.

"I can call up the image Griffin's printing," I said, and I
opened the map showing the DC area with the transfiguration
incidents mapped. "He sent me the link to a web version."

"Intranet, only, right?" Lonny asked. "Not published for the
world to see?"

"Right. Our eyes only. Although at some point, I don't see a
problem with—well, we'll see." Lonny scowled, so I decided not
to push transparency at this second.

I zoomed the map to the DeLuxe Hotel. "See here at Ground Zero, each object was found in the atrium." I zoomed in again, and the screen showed a floor plan of the atrium, filled with red dots. "This dot in the middle, we call Point Zero. Where the 2/29 Enchantment's force seems to have emanated from." We all knew there was no EO found at that point, which was directly in front of the stage that had been installed in the atrium, to the right of center as we viewed it.

"Each point has an intensity score," I continued, mousing over a different point, where a bubble popped up with a '100' in it and an arrow pointing outward from a spot near the stage in the ballroom. "The score shows a fifty for inanimate objects that were transformed and one hundred for Transfigured People, like this one," I said. "There are only TPs here in the atrium, The TO dots are purple and smaller, offscreen."

When my co-worker Charlene had first used 'TO' and 'TP" to refer to the subsets of "EOs," I thought she was baiting me as a newbie, but Eliot later confirmed he'd blessed those acronyms. "Calling those people TPs is better than they deserve," he had quipped to me, one time at happy hour after work. After one and a half Manhattans.

"Each object also has two direction vectors, showing as arrows," I continued. "If the object had a face, or a front, we've mapped the direction it was facing with one arrow, and the direction behind it with another." I clicked a button at the lower right corner of the screen, and each dot acquired a red arrow. "The anterior direction vector points the way the EO was facing, presumably toward the source of the magic. Like our infamous stormtrooper." I moused to one of the dots, clicked on it, and opened a window with a picture of the stormtrooper figure, along with its relevant data such as dimensions, weight, and merchandise bar code number, if applicable. EO Serial Number 357, Enchanted Form UPC 233-2499370-4494078. "Although he was pretty close to the center, apparently."

Griffin had suggested adding a couple of additional data

points: the going price on Disney's online shopping site and an average eMarkt price for the identical, untransformed piece of merchandise. I had vetoed that. Perception of questionable taste, I thought, for us to maintain that.

(That had not, however, stopped the authors of EOWiki from taking the advanced beta site's datasets, intentionally download-able for all, and creating a shopping portal to purchase those same items. The distinction being that was not the official government site. What they did with the data was their choice, good or bad taste beside the point. Which is how the free infor-mation market should work, right?)

"The posterior direction vector is the arrow pointing toward the back of the TO or TP," I continued, clicking another button. A second, orange arrow appeared pointing in the opposite direction.

Eliot said, "I've always wondered about something. What about flat things? They weren't standing up when we invento-ried them at the scene." Eliot used an organizational "we," since neither he nor I had been there. "Like a T-shirt or a placemat or a giclée print of a Thomas Kinkade painting?" Eliot got deep-dish Disney geeky when we talked about our inventory.

"If the object had a front, like a painting or a T-shirt, we imputed the direction," I said. "It seems consistent."

"Meaning what?" Lonny asked. "I was there, I saw them."

"Meaning, if right after the transfiguration, you had stood the T-shirt or print or placemat up, facing Point Zero, then let it flop down, its top flopped away from the center of Ground Zero. Like if it were one of the playing card people in *Alice in Wonderland*, and it got blown onto its back. Consistently, that's how each one was found after the event. It's as though that person were standing up, facing the Zero Point, and when transformed, they fell backward. The objects that could stand were still standing, of course." I loved explaining how we synthesized the data to make connections.

"No outliers, then, and that's how you got the lines?" Eliot asked. I had explained this to him before, but sometimes he liked to go over things more than once.

"Right, no outliers, and if there was something with absolutely no clear face or front, like the Kylo Ren lightsaber," I moused over another point, "then it was aligned, with the business end pointing away from Point Zero. There are a few," I moused over a dot with no arrow, "where we can't 100% assign a direction." The dot opened to a picture of a fidget spinner with three fluorescent green Haunted Mansion "Hitchhiking Ghosts" in its rounded vertices. "Even this one, though, nothing is 'front' *per se*, was oriented so the bottom two ghosts were closer to the Zero Point, and the top one was farther away, so it's almost like it's an arrow in its own shape.

"Lonny, is there anything you'd like to add?" I asked. "Agent Dotch?" I corrected myself. Eliot chuckled. He thought I had a crush on Lonny. I *was* the only person who called him Lonny at the office, although when he called me, he said, "It's Dotch." He hadn't told me *not* to call him Lonny.

"Apparently, there was something that got everyone to look at it, or face toward it, and then everyone got transformed, and flopped over onto their backs," Lonny said. "Did I get that right?"

I nodded.

"I'm just glad we didn't move anything before the CSI team got in and took all your photos for you." As a first responder, he had spoken to one of the Confidential Service agents who was an eyewitness, moments after the transformation. Eyewitnesses included Confidential Service agents, hotel waitstaff, and media personnel (except the Lion News and darkbart.com staff). And no, they couldn't identify who was standing where at the time of the transformation. We had hoped that would help identify which EO was which person, but the witnesses' memories were a touch scrambled. Nobody could remember from a half a minute or so before the Enchantment took place through a half a minute later. That was a little-discussed component of the

Enchantment, that memories had been wiped. More for the Bureau to worry about, though. Not part of our mission.

"Zoom out and show us a TO, would you Fab?" Eliot asked.

A message window popped onto the screen, an incoming Scrye text request from Griffin.

"I'd better see what he says," I told them.

Be there in 5 almost finished prtg, Griffin texted.

I texted back, the keyboard permitting me the luxury of punctuation, *No rush, we're using the projector.*

There was a pause, and Giffin replied, *close it paper will be better,* and he terminated the conversation.

"Here's a TO, the Coco Interactive Guitar by Batelle," I continued anyway, keeping the projector on, and zooming out and mousing to a purple dot. "It was oriented with the body of the guitar closer to Ground Zero, the neck farther away, about two miles to the west-northwest of Ground Zero. It used to be an actual, generic guitar before the Enchantment. The owner had slapped a DeLuxe bumper sticker on it. Hmm. We might want to lower the intensity score on that one."

"Why's that?" Lonny asked. Eliot already knew.

"Because transforming an object from a guitar into something like a guitar, albeit a toy, isn't as far a stretch as transforming a person into a toy. Presumably. That would be a low Magical Intensity Calibration score. Unfortunately, we can't actually assign a MIC score, since we haven't come up with a rubric to transform our qualitative judgments into a quantitative score. Yet!"

"Do you have a measure for magical intensity?"

"Planning for it, although it's not like we have a Geiger counter or anything."

Eliot interjected, "Planning ahead. Fab's idea. Although I helped."

"Eliot picked the acronym, M-I-C, for Magical Intensity Calibration," I said.

Lonny turned to Eliot. "For real?"

Eliot giggled, and spread his hands out. "Yes, I wanted one unit of magic to be a mickey. Don't tell anyone. It's purely theoretical, but if I plant the seed with the acronym..."

"Mr. Gloss, it's your program." Lonny looked away from Eliot. The edges of his mouth turned up slightly.

I continued: "If we knew the weight or volume of the TPs versus their transfigured weight and volume, we might have a precise methodology. We don't, alas."

"What Fab is saying is, we don't have the K-E-Y..." Eliot sang the last part, then sang out the letters to spell out the word "mouse." Lonny rolled his eyes. Eliot ostentatiously looked at his red Mickey Mouse watch, which was frankly a little small for his beefy forearm, and asked, "And...connecting the dots..."

"Shortly after the 2/29 event, we discovered that objects around the DC area had also been transfigured, and you could have connected the dots randomly; in fact you all tried that before I came onboard." I zoomed out and clicked another button. A greenish blur of lines covered the map, with an intense glow. "We've made all the layers of data optional with these buttons," I continued. "This layer shows every EO site. How useful was this, when you saw it previously, Lonny?"

"It wasn't any help," Lonny said.

"It was a mess," Eliot said.

"When we use the directional vectors, it turns out they link specifically." I clicked the green lines off, and clicked another button, and a delicate web of golden lines overlaid the map of dots. "As you can see, the imputed vectors near Ground Zero are orient away from the Zero Point. The farther out we go, they orient other ways, and the lines connect. And for the *pièce de résistance*," I said, clicking another button. The lines blinked off, then reappeared as an animation, beginning with the lines at Ground Zero, cascading outward and connecting in transverse segments to form the web.

"Wow," Eliot said.

"That's based on when we think things happened," Lonny said.

"Correct!" Fab said. "The more distant transfigurations happened minutes later, and that's where some of the transverse connections happened. We had to infer some times, but it tracks with the bigger picture. And amazingly, every transfiguration appeared to result from a connection with another one, until they stopped."

"Like the magic cascaded or chain reacted out," Eliot said.

"Not to conflate correlation with causality, but possibly yes," I said. "It does look like that, although we don't have enough data to be confident."

"How many intersections do we have where we think there should be a TO?" Lonny asked. He stood and walked closer to the screen.

I clicked another button and white pulsating circles appeared at seven points on the map. "Here's where we went this morning." I zoomed in to one of the pulsating circles, where two lines intersected the home of Ms. Bluntschli. Another click, and a satellite image of the roof of her house appeared in the background.

"That's about her living room, based on what I could see," Lonny said. "Where we sat and talked with her and her cat." Eliot shot me a side-eye look. I tried to stay deadpan. "Well, if we're sidelined on the stormtrooper investigation, we don't have anything better to do, so Fab's going to go back and chat with her," Lonny told Eliot.

"Ah," Eliot said, nodding, as though he didn't already know that. "And eventually check the other six, I assume."

The door opened, and Griffin came in, holding a large, rolled sheet of paper under one arm, and his laptop under the other. "Here it is," he said, offering me the roll of paper. "Oh," he said, looking at the projected image on the screen.

"We went ahead and looked at your fantastic data viz, Griffin," Eliot told him, gesturing to the projected images. Griffin looked at it and frowned.

"And I gotta say, bravo!" Eliot continued, applauding. "Amazing work you two have done."

Griffin whacked the conference table with his rolled-up paper. "The printed one would have been better. I mapped the EO's progress based on the data I found. If I'd had a few more minutes I could have added Agent Dotch's information." He stood, clenching and unclenching his fists, looking at the table.

Eliot looked at Dotch and tilted his head. "Agent Dotch's information?"

"A buddy told me where the last sighting of the escaped perpetrator, I mean victim, was. And he disappeared in a locked room, and if it walks and quacks like a magical incident...I thought Griffin would make something from that."

"Really? Wow," Eliot said. He rubbed his hands together. He loved hearing about magic. "Griffin, I do want to see your version. Plus, maybe you could update the online version for us?"

"Thanks, Griffin. We'll look at the printed version while you can make that change on the projector version." I suggested. I logged off, and Lonny and I unrolling the paper as Griffin sat at the computer. Eliot stood and walked to my side of the table to look.

"Ah, I see, Griffin. It's good! Great to put up in the office, I think," Eliot said.

"You can see the shape of the whole area," Lonny noted.

"See," I pointed out, "Here are the same pieces of information, so you can see how dense the transformations were, here are the intersections. I see you left out the geographic data beyond the farthest ley lines." The underlying map of DC and environs was missing, except for the faint outline of the DC city limits, and the Potomac River dividing Maryland and Virginia. It did a great job popping the green shape of the transfiguration patterns, surrounded by white space.

"Oh, and here's the STIF," I said. "And these points are sightings of the escaped stormtrooper, these little dots, Griffin?"

"Yes," Griffin replied, not looking up.

"And here's that strip mall," Lonny said,

"Hmm," Eliot said, stroking his grey goatee between thumb and curled forefinger.

"Hmm?" I responded. I looked at Griffin to get him to look at us, but he was staring at the projected image on the screen. If he'd looked, I'd have gestured to him to stand with us.

"That shape," Eliot said, waving his free hand at the paper map. "I never noticed this before. Does it remind you of anything?"

All I saw was a green blob floating in white space. "A teapot?" I suggested. "See here how it dips in, and this could be a spout."

"Hmmm. No."

"A squashed muffin. With a bite out on the left, and crinkled wrapper on the bottom." This came from Lonny. Eliot and I both looked at him.

"Welllll, maybe. Points for creativity!" This from Eliot.

"Eliot, what do you see?" I asked.

"Let me Spoogle something first. Griffin, may I just launch a browser?" He went to the computer, and Griffin stood aside. Eliot navigated to Spoogle Images, and entered "Map Magic Kingdom Orlando." The projection screen filled small pictures of green blobs shaped like our pattern of magical incidents around the DC area.

"Eureka!" Eliot shouted.

"Oh! My goodness," I said.

"See, these other maps of Disney don't stop at the edge, like your map's web version. When I saw it cut out like that on Griffin's printout, it hit me," Eliot said. He selected one of the Magic Kingdom park maps and it filled the projection screen.

"Griffin, do you realize what a breakthrough this is?!" I asked.

Griffin had his hands over his eyes and cheeks, his nose and mouth visible between his hands. "I was trying to save time and ink, so I only printed the relevant parts," he said.

"Griffin, look!" I said.

His eyes still covered, he said, "Yes, I saw."

Odd, I thought. *Is he not surprised?*

Lonny said, "Griffin, can we superimpose the Disney World map over your map?"

Griffin sighed and said, "Yes. It will take me some time." He returned to the computer and was soon absorbed in writing code, so we continued to compare the printed map and the Disney park map on the screen.

"Right here at the center, at Ground Zero, I think that's where Sleeping Beauty's Castle would be!" Eliot said.

"Cinderella Castle. Sleeping Beauty Castle is in Disneyland," Griffin said, without looking up from his screen. "And no possessive."

"Doh! Of course, you're right," Eliot said. "*Someone's* a big 'Disnerd,' I think." He shot me another look and shrugged his shoulders. "They don't use the possessive, right. And forgive me, but Disneyland will always be my first Disney park. The Land was first; the World was a latecomer. I default to Sleeping Beauty." He winked and pointed at the printed map. "All right, there's *Cinderella* Castle, and out here, where you thought there was a teapot spout, Fab, that's Space Mountain."

"That's not too far from the STIF," Lonny noted. "If we drew a line through the stormtrooper sighting points…" He pulled out a pen. "Hey, Grif, okay if I mark up your masterpiece?"

"Yes, yes, whatever."

"I know that shopping center. Used to roller skate there back in the day. It's about…here." Lonny drew a line from the STIF, ending at the site of the disappearance. Then he extended it into downtown DC.

Neither Eliot, nor Lonny, nor I spoke. We stared at the map

on the table. All I could hear was the sound of the projector's fan and Griffin's keystrokes.

"Well, damn!" Lonny said.

"Indeed," Eliot said.

The line Lonny had drawn from the STIF to the strip mall pointed toward the center of the map, toward Ground Zero: the DeLuxe Hotel. Eliot and I watched as Lonny extended the line the rest of the way to Ground Zero.

"He was heading toward Ground Zero, then he disappeared," Eliot said.

Lonny pulled out his phone, snapped a photo, and dialed the phone, on speaker.

"Oberst."

"Dotch here. Hey, I got something you might could use to catch the perp. I'm texting it to you now."

After a pause, Agent Oberst said, "Okay. I see. Who's in the room with you?"

"Gloss, Acer, and Griffin, our IT guy."

"Take me off speaker," Agent Oberst said, and Lonny did so, but he held the phone out from his ear so we could still hear Agent Oberst say, "We've got this. What are you people doing?"

"We're doing our job, analyzing data."

Eliot said, "Put the speaker back on."

"Mr. Gloss wants to speak with you," Dotch said, and he pressed the speaker button again.

"Jake, this is Eliot. We were continuing the new data visualization and linking it with geospatial, and realized it could be relevant to finding your escapee."

Griffin stopped typing and looked at Eliot. Eliot continued, "Did you look at the map Agent Dotch sent you?"

"I'm looking at it. I see, you assume the stormtrooper is heading to Ground Zero. We had sightings that bear that out, then we lost him. We're focusing on the points in between the last sighting and Ground Zero. We plan to take him into custody before he gets there."

"There are no more sightings."

"Who said that?" Oberst responded.

"Griffin. The IT guy," Lonny said.

"This conversation should not be happening in the open," Oberst said. "There's already a leak, on Chirpa, for cripe's sake."

"I know about the chirps," Eliot said. "PAO is on spin control already, Jake. Listen, I think this can help."

"Agent Oberst," Lonny said. "We can help behind the scenes."

"Dotch, if you think your team can help, send details via encrypted email," Oberst said. "Eliot, are your staff cleared for Secret—"

"Jake, this is only Sensitive, not National Security. Right?" Eliot said.

"Fine. Share only with your team in the room. Let me know your theory. I'll be in my office after I report to my Deputy Assistant Attorney General. Oberst out." The phone call ended.

"Griffin, do we have a theory? Fab? Dotch?" Eliot said. "Can you provide them a detailed map of the DC area with the line Lonny drew? At least let them know where to look."

"Yes, I can extrapolate from the coordinates we have," Griffin said.

"Can you get that to Agent Oberst?" Eliot asked. "But first, can you overlay the Magic Kingdom map with your map? Just for us, not for Mr. Oberst. I don't know why. It might be relevant."

Griffin stood abruptly. "Yes, I can get that to him via the secure portal. And I can overlay the map. I've got to go." He sniffed (was he crying?) and quickly left the conference room.

"What was that about?" Eliot asked.

"He hates any hint of violence, and the shootings were such a shock," I said. "He's a vegan. Plus, he takes things so personally. I think he believes without his data crunching, they won't catch the stormtrooper. Maybe we're asking too much, too quickly."

Lonny said, "Listen, I can take another photo and send it

securely. I'll tell Griffin not to stress about that. Back in a minute." He left Eliot and me alone in the conference room, the door swinging closed behind him.

"It may be more than the violence or the stress that upset Griffin," Eliot said. "From my perspective, the Enchantment, horrifying as it may have been for those involved, has created a new peace in the world. Not to mention the response to the pandemic. Imagine if President Velluto had not stepped in to lock the country down for a month, freeze mortgage and rent payments, and launch the PPE Manhattan Project to get us all the masks we needed.

"What if the Enchantment's beginning to fray at the edges? If that one person could shoot a gun with intent to kill and get away with it, who else can? And will any of the other TPs grow, or change, and will they be hostile like this one? Can someone launch a nuke against us now?"

"Yes, it is scary," I said.

"Maybe Griffin is scared too. I don't know." We sat for a moment in silence, until Eliot said, "Can you show me the maps again?"

I logged on and brought up the map visualization.

"Oh, look a new button." I clicked, and it superimposed the map of the Magic Kingdom over the DC area map. Griffin had been fast.

"Wow," Eliot said. "That was ridiculously fast. Almost like…"

"Like he already had it queued up."

"That's what I was thinking. I don't know why he wouldn't have shared that with us before."

"Didn't think it was relevant? Not the letter of the law?" I said. We sat in silence, looking at the map for a moment. I wasn't sure I wanted to pursue why Griffin had withheld this from us, if he had.

Finally, Eliot said, "Anyway, it's a freaky match. Not that anything should surprise us anymore."

"I can hardly wait to publish all this to the external web site. One or two more customer experience labs and a few quality assurance tests, and we should be ready to put it into production." That was my normal job, after all, to get this data out, so the public could view it.

"Whoa, whoa! I hadn't thought about that," Eliot said, turning to look at me. "I think we shouldn't be so quick. Until they catch the stormtrooper, this is still investigative sensitivity level."

"I don't see that, Eliot," I said, shaking my head. "We are visualizing data that's already out there. Even the Disney overlay," I said, gesturing to the screen, "Somebody else could just as easily see that same as you did."

"Yes, the Disney conspiracy folks, that's who I'm thinking about."

Eliot was referring to right-wing fringe folks, fueled by the Ribbit and EightWave social media sites, who believed that Disney was in the pocket of a liberal cabal, and was behind a fake enchantment, involving near real-time computer graphics effects, animatronics, stage illusions, and the kidnapping and confinement of the AFPAP participants in secret concentration camps. They believed eyewitnesses were all planted Disney Cast Members, and so forth. They didn't believe in real magic.

There was even another splinter group, consisting of hardcore Disney fan *anti*-DeLuxists, who believed this had indeed been a *benevolent* Disney conspiracy to bring order to the chaos created by the DeLuxe presidency. They supported it. The more Disney took over all aspects of their lives, the happier they were. They waited expectantly for the U.S. Government to outsource all its operations to Disney (in a neo-liberal public/private partnership), so the entire United States would become a theme park, I suppose. Absurd, of course.

"Eliot, we can't help what people do with the data. And we have a statutory requirement to make it all transparent."

"I say we hold off until we know more about the

stormtrooper. I know, I know," he said, holding up his hands. "This is great work, but sometimes you have to be careful what effect it has. You don't want people showing up at the house you visited today, for example, do you? Where was that, anyway? Silver Spring?"

"Takoma Park." What he said gave me pause. Zeir name would be protected, of course. If we published specific geographic coordinates or addresses of privately owned TO sites though...Oh, no. It occurred to me our Executive Governance Board would probably not let that happen. And maybe it shouldn't. Someone could harass whoever lived in a location where a TO was found. And the intersections of the ley lines... That was a new use case, I supposed, and we needed to protect people's privacy. Damn, he had me!

"I think you're right. We need to run a privacy impact assessment on this before we release it. Good catch, Eliot."

After another pause, I cursored to the STIF on the screen and zoomed into it. "The STIF is here, and it corresponds to..."

I hovered over the STIF, and a small window popped up showing the corresponding attraction from the Magic Kingdom map. It looked much more detailed than the map Eliot had originally Spoogled. Griffin must be tapping into Disney servers for the information.

"Space Mountain," Eliot said. "Sometimes known as Hyper-Space Mountain when they doll it up as a *Star Wars* tie-in." Turning to me, he said, "I *said* we should put our storage facility farther out, but no. They were sucking up to that Maryland Congresswoman. Zoom out and find our office building."

I did so.

Eliot pointed at the screen. "Ah, there we are. Winnie-the-Pooh kiddy ride. I think that used to be Mr. Toad's Wild Ride. That'd be more appropriate for our crazy office!" He chuckled.

I noted that JR Bluntschli's nearby house would be the in the middle of the Mad Tea Party teacups ride. I didn't say anything.

"Dotch's line points to Ground Zero, and if the stormtrooper had been heading there…" Eliot stood and used the shadow of his finger in the projector light to trace the line Lonny had drawn on the paper map.

Lonny opened the door. "That's impressive. Grif is fast as lightning." Neither Eliot nor I reacted. And since when did Lonny call Griffin "Grif"? He walked to the screen and pointed at it. "Can you pull up where the perp disappeared in that basement?"

"Here's the point Griffin plotted," I said, and I zoomed in. It looked like the strip mall, although it was hard to see through the map overlay. "Let me get rid of the Disney map," I said.

"No, don't!" Eliot said. "Dial it in so we can see it better. Hmm. 'Mickey's Star Traders.' Must be a souvenir store. Appropriate, given what object we're talking about. That place is full of Star Wars toys."

Lonny said, "The real location is full of more adult toys. They mainly they keep their stock down there. There's no connection between the basement and any other rooms in the building."

"He vanished." I said. "Where does that leave us, then?"

"Magic. I hate it," Lonny said.

Eliot said, "Hey, wait a minute. Aren't there tunnels under the Magic Kingdom? I read about a tour you could do…"

Lonny and I shrugged. Neither of us knew about that. I searched, and within minutes I had retrieved a map of the Magic Kingdom "Utilidors," as Disney called the "utility corridors" built under the theme park. One stairwell sat right at Mickey's Star Traders, which corresponded to the suburban address where the NBI had lost track of the shooter.

"I'm just spitballing here," Eliot said, "If the Enchantment could warp reality for individual people and objects, maybe it warped geography too."

"You're saying there are Utilidors under DC now?" Lonny said.

I scanned the report from Agent Oberst. "Eliot, I think you could be right. The agents did a deep search, and unless he transformed into something else entirely, he's not there, and their camera footage is complete. He didn't leave via the stairway. Because he's been enchanted, it's possible he has access to some weird version of an enchanted Utilidor we couldn't see. Like Muggles can't see Platform 9 3/4!"

"Exactly!" Eliot exclaimed. Lonny looked at both of us like we were crazy. "We're discovering the rules as we go along, so you may be right," Eliot continued. "Hmm, looks like there are other stairwells from the Utilidors to the surface. I'm not seeing one under Cinderella Castle, at least not on this map. No way up? Can that be right? The way they use the Castle for shows, there must be some kind of elevator, even if it's not showing here. Meanwhile, there are all these other stairwells." He pointed to six or seven stairwell icons around the Magic Kingdom. "He could show up anywhere. Somehow, I think he's headed to Ground Zero, though."

"I'll get Griffin to map these, too," I said. "Hard to tell if the Utilidor map is to scale. The Spoogle map has the same landmarks. I think I can do it that way."

"Good show, Fab!" Eliot said. He was wiggling in his seat again.

"Lonny, can you take these GPS coordinates down?" I asked. "I won't include Ground Zero, only where the stairwells would be."

Lonny was already on his phone. "Agent Oberst, Dotch here. We may have more data for you. I'll send it over secure email," he said into his phone. He hung up, saying, "Voicemail. He'll get it eventually."

"Well! This has been productive." Eliot rose from his chair. "Great work, both of you! Fab, I assume you and Agent Dotch will get the addresses to Oberst and his team. Keep me posted." He left the conference room.

Working in tandem (I read them out and Lonny jotted them on a sheet of paper) we transcribed the address for each point on the DC map corresponding to a Utilidor stairwell.

Lonny took the paper with the addresses to his office to send an encrypted email to Agent Oberst. Heading to my office, I encountered Eliot.

"Could you check in on Griffin?" he asked. "He's acting weirder than usual. And it occurs to me that we need to do a risk analysis on the inventory. Which TPs and TOs would be dangerous if they came to full-size life as the stormtrooper did. Priority is high, don't you agree? Crisis mode. "

I assured him I'd take care of everything, and popped into Griffin's cubicle, where he was furiously typing, as he often did. I watched for a while; he was sniffling and intermittently wiping tears from his cheeks.

I pulled a chair from the empty cubicle next door, and sat. Griffin continued to type, sniffle, and wipe, punctuating those with an occasional frustrated grunt. After about thirty seconds, without looking up, he said, "You want something," and continued to code. He hit enter, and continued to watch the screen. "The code is compiling."

My impulse was to ask if Griffin was okay. Instead, I said, "Eliot was pleased. Thanks for getting that Disney World map superimposed so quickly. I think we're onto something." I decided not to ask him if he'd already known the enchantments formed a shape like the Magic Kingdom.

Swiveling, and looking at my chin, Griffin said, "This wasn't supposed to happen." His eyes were brimming with tears, and he continued to sniffle. I pulld a couple of tissues from a box he had on his desk and handed them to him. He dabbed at his nose as I spoke.

"It's not like we know what *is* supposed to happen," I said. "We do the best we can."

"I wanted to help find all the TOs and TPs to help keep them safe," he replied.

"Yes. We're doing that."

"How can we keep things safe if this disenchantment thing happens? And guns! His guns worked." Griffin thought this was a disenchantment? Not a secondary Enchantment? Maybe he was just upset. He was alway precise with his language.

"We do the best we can. You can't control that!"

Griffin shook his head and clenched his fists. "Hmph!" he said.

I continued, "The best we can do is figure out what the rules are, and make sure everyone knows. We should be able to catch the stormtrooper and see who it is, figure out what happened. It's terrible about our people being shot, so I sympathize. The more we know, though, the more we can prevent something else bad happening. The Bureau should be heading to the Utilidor stairwells."

"Utilidors? What do you mean? What's happened?"

"Oh, I forgot. After you left the room, Eliot remembered there are corridors under the Magic Kingdom, and we found a map. We couldn't overlay it like you can, speaking of which, you should look into doing that; we just did a manual—"

"Of course!" Griffin said. He swiveled back to his computer and opened up a browser, and Spoogled "Utilidors Magic Kingdom Map." I scooted my chair next to him.

"We think the stormtrooper disappeared near where the Mickey's Star Traders entrance to the Utilidors would be if you overlaid the map onto DC," I told him, pointing to the monitor. The same Spoogle links came up, and he opened one of the Utilidor maps. "The NBI couldn't find a door. We thought different rules might apply to someone who was enchanted, so the TP might be able to access some kind of magical thing like a Utilidor."

"I see. That might be possible."

"We thought maybe the stormtrooper was heading to Ground Zero, but there doesn't appear to be a Utilidor entrance under Cinderella Castle."

"There are service elevators there. Not on the map."

"You know this how?"

"I was on a tour once. My mom and I went. It was cool," he

said. "They need elevators to bring up sets and characters that couldn't walk the stairs. I think you're probably right."

"Eliot was right."

Griffin turned to me and looked me straight in the eyes. "I think the stormtrooper will reappear at Ground Zero. And we can't let the NBI find him."

I paused for a second, holding his gaze. "Come with me. We need to tell Lonny."

A minute later, we entered Lonny's office, and I shut the door behind us.

"What's with you two?" he asked.

"Is there any word on the information you sent to Agent Oberst?"

"I just sent it; keeping me in the loop isn't on top of his to do list, though. You know that."

"Lonny, Griffin thinks we need to get to Ground Zero before the NBI do." I nodded to Griffin. "We directed them to other locations, so we should have the jump on them."

"We have to protect the TPs," Griffin said, looking at the floor.

"This TP shot folks," Lonny replied.

"I know, but it isn't right. This is about protecting everyone."

Lonny looked at me, brows wrinkled, as if to ask, *Are you following this?*

I took a deep breath, and asked, "Griffin, do you know more about this than you are telling us?"

He whined, and sniffled, and flexed, and gripped his hands, continuing to look at the floor. He made a noise like he was crying with his mouth closed: "MmmMMMM!"

"It's OK, it's OK," I said. I so wanted to pat him on the shoulder. I didn't. "Griffin, there's a reason you don't want the NBI to catch the stormtrooper, isn't there? Can you give us a hint?"

Lonny looked at Griffin with a penetrating, deadpan expression he gets when he is trying to get someone to speak.

Griffin looked up from the floor, and again, looked me

straight in the eyes. "You have to listen to me. We can't let him get shot or get captured by the NBI. I think it will make things worse. If we can catch him, then it should be OK. You're always asking me to trust you. Can't you trust me?"

I nodded and breaking the gaze with Griffin, looked at Lonny. "I think Griffin is right. My gut tells me we should try to find this person."

"That stormtrooper is armed and dangerous. My gun still won't work, unless I'm shooting something inanimate. And even if it isn't directly disobeying Oberst's orders, he won't be happy if he sees I'm mixed up in this."

Griffin said, "Please. Please. I can fix this." And I saw he was looking directly at Lonny, who, after a moment, nodded his head.

"Okay, Grif," he said. "Sounds like my kind of challenge. I'll do it."

And that's how we ended up at the Disney DC Deluxe Resort, a.k.a. Ground Zero, before the NBI caught the stormtrooper.

CHAPTER 11

SPACESHIP WORST

FROM THE ARCHIVES OF THE MERGE,
FEBRUARY 29, 2020

"It started in Wuhan Province, China," the voice of Walter Cronkite had said. A dark map of China with glowing red dots. "The virus quickly spread carried across the world by infected but asymptomatic individuals."

"Is that true?" Kayla asked.

"We have the data," WaltTwo replied.

"That's frightening."

"Very serious indeed. The outcomes we predict are even more so."

The narrator continued, as the view of China zoomed out to become a dark globe. Red dots proliferated, accelerating in speed. "Attempts to contain and contact trace are inadequate, due to the lack of tests and comprehensive policy. In particular, in the United States, the consequences will be devastating unless the entire nation institutes a complete, temporary quarantine lockdown and dedicates manufacturing resources to protective gear, testing, and treatments." The lights dimmed, and their vehicle moved in near darkness again.

"This is what you predict?" Kayla asked, turning to look at him in the dim glow as they entered another room.

WaltTwo nodded.

"You're sure?"

"With a high degree of confidence."

"We were afraid it was this serious," Kayla said. "What can we do? What will you do if you care about people the way you say you do?"

"Wait, there's more," WaltTwo said.

Their vehicle entered what appeared to be a small theater, rotated to face the stage, and stopped. The curtain rose, and Kayla saw President DeLuxe at a lectern in the White House press room. "One day, like magic, it will just disappear."

"This is our projection, and we're fairly certain this will be the arc of events, even if the words are different," WaltTwo said.

The set and the president moved to the right, as though the set was on a rotating turntable, and another set moved in to replace it. It showed a hospital corridor filled with patients on gurneys, swarming with medical personnel. To her horror, Kayla saw one nurse was wearing a garbage bag with holes cut through for her head and arms. And what looked like a handkerchief over her mouth and nose.

"President DeLuxe has de-funded the stockpiling of protective equipment, so hospitals will have to improvise," WaltTwo said.

A couple of orderlies carrying a body bag entered from the back and stopped. "The morgue is full," one of the orderlies said.

A woman with a clipboard said, in reply, "The refrigerated truck from the meat packing plant just arrived at the loading dock. That's going to be the overflow morgue."

Kayla covered her mouth, then uncovered it and asked, "Where is this?"

"Anywhere across the U.S., depending on the time."

More tableaux followed in succession, to Kayla's horror: rambling speeches by President DeLuxe, contradicting facts; protests by white supremacist groups against mask-wearing; infographics of plummeting economic indicators; people on ventilators; trucks full of corpses.

"Is this worldwide?" Kayla asked.

"The virus is worldwide; the disastrous impact is limited to a few countries, mainly the U.S., Brazil, India, and Russia. The U.S. has the most cases, and the highest death rate."

The last tableaux ended, and the curtain fell.

"Again, what are you going to do?" Kayla asked.

"I'll show you. But here is where I need your help."

Their ride vehicle rotated again and moved out of the theater and proceeded down a passageway. The right side was dark and empty, but on the left, there were glass windows with rooms filled with animatronic figures, equipment, and decorating supplies like paints and fabrics, and tables covered with objects. The animatronics were much less lifelike than the ones earlier in this ride. (Kayla couldn't help calling the experience a ride.)

The animatronics were working, like technicians in a lab or workshop, and looked as though they came from Disney theme parks. Kayla saw pirates, dinosaurs, classic characters like Peter Pan, Alice, the Mad Hatter, the White Rabbit, Pinocchio, newer characters from Toy Story and Monsters, Inc., lots of animals like a fox, an alligator, a bear, and the little purple dragon. It looked like one of Disney's old TV shows, showing behind the scenes. The animatronics were examining and painting and fabricating small, brightly colored items.

"These aren't medical labs," Kayla said.

"No, these are workshops in our Magineering Center."

"Imagineering?"

"No, Magineering. We AIs are good at projecting and visualizing, but not so great at imagining and visioning. And…what can I call it? Agency? Initiative? Humans are still the best at that. We are, however, onto something that I think can help, for someone willing to take the initiative."

WaltTwo gestured to a workshop where Dumbo and a little grey mouse in a uniform jacket and hat were focused on an object on a table. The object on the table was a small figure of a person in a suit, with a mop of yellow hair. It was about six inches high.

"Is that a statue of the president?" Kayla asked.

"Yes. This is a test."

Dumbo flapped his ears, hovering in mid-air, and held a feather in his trunk, with which he tickled the little President DeLuxe. It moved! Squirming and waving its hands, it looked like an actual person. The mouse took notes on a notepad.

"These are really subroutines we have working to test some principles, but I've translated them into easily digestible images," WaltTwo said. "And here's what I wanted you to see."

Cinderella's Fairy Godmother entered from another work-shop, and simultaneously said "Bibbidi-bobbidi!" and pointed her magic wand at the little figure on the table. As Kayla watched, the little figurine of the president unfolded in sections.

"He's like an origami," Kayla said.

"Yes, we're using origami as a metaphor for how matter shapes itself."

The origami continued to unfold as Dumbo, Timothy Mouse (Kayla remembered its name now), Fairy Godmother, WaltTwo, and she watched. It flattened itself into one square sheet, and the Fairy Godmother said: "Boo!" The sheet began to crease and curled up, refolding itself. After a few seconds, it had reconstituted itself. But it was no longer President DeLuxe.

On the table in front of Dumbo, Timothy, and Fairy Godmother sat a Mickey Mouse ear hat where the miniature President DeLuxe had stood.

"This is just a VR simulation, of course. We found we couldn't do it in real life. We needed someone special to accomplish it. A human." Fairy Godmother repeated the magic words and wand work three more times, and each time the object unfolded, then refolded into a different Disney-branded piece of merchandise. After the fourth transformation, Kayla recovered from the initial shock.

"We are ending this conversation right now." Kayla stood and her hands moved to her head, to remove her VR gear.

"Please, Ms. Malone, if you think you have a duty to warn the Confidential Service, please be aware it's too late."

Kayla sat. "What do you mean?"

"What's happened has happened. Our request to you is not to collude in what's happened."

"What has happened?"

"One set of threats has been neutralized. And I think you will discover that far from threatening the president, we have done what we can to save him, while still saving the country, and the U.S. constitution."

The labs disappeared, and a large TV screen materialized. "Pardon the crude transition," WaltTwo said.

On the screen, Kayla saw a stage and lectern, a different one from the White House press room, although the president was talking. Suddenly, he drew back in fright from something off-camera, and then his body recoiled from a shot. Blood spurted and he fell to the floor of the stage.

"We are not the only ones who saw President DeLuxe as a threat. I assure you we were not behind this. We were, however, behind what happened next. We don't have footage to share with you, but yes, in collaboration with a very talented human, we preserved the president in a form that was not his original shape, and that prevented him from dying. So, we have not assassinated the president, if that is what you assumed."

Kayla thought about this for a few moments. If this was true, in the real world, all the law enforcement agencies would be an Ultra-Violet Alert level, a step above Red. She should be returning.

"I need to leave. Assuming I believe you, which I'm not sure I do, tell me quickly what you want from me. No metaphors or theme park rides. Now!"

The ride vehicle and the television screen vanished, and Kayla found herself standing in her office. The VR rig had switched to Augmented Reality, and the figure of Walt Disney stood before her in her office.

"The issues around this will be complex. Something like magic has happened. In a way, it's high-level mathematics applied to quantum physics, but effectively it's magic. But you will find there are some benefits, and technically no one has been harmed, physically. Just incapacitated and neutralized."

"What exactly have you done?"

WaltTwo hesitated. Then he said, "We have arranged to have President DeLuxe and all the true believers at the America First Political Action Parliament transformed into harmless merchandise."

"Merchandise? Like the ones you showed me, with Dumbo and the Fairy Godmother?"

"Yes."

"Disney merchandise, I assume."

"Yes."

"Jimmy Crickets! In what universe does that sound like an ethical thing to do?"

"I leave you to work out the ethics of this, but there is no law enforcement or counterintelligence responsibility you have, that I can see, so you are uniquely suited to be an ally to your people and a liaison with the COADE. But there is someone, the real person I mentioned, who will need your help. In five days, we will send you the details on where you need to go and who needs your help. I only ask that you take our information and use it as you see fit. We will be in touch to provide more information."

"I'm not agreeing to anything until I see what's happened," Kayla said. She could hear an alert on her phone, and then it started to ring. It was the Security Operations Center.

"Agreed. Please attend to your duties, and we will be in touch. Thank you for listening." And with that, WaltTwo blinked out of existence.

Kayla threw her VR headset onto her desk and unlocked her

phone. Of course the VR gloves conducted and allowed her to use it. *Not bad,* she thought. "Malone," she said.

"This is an automated alert," the voice on the phone said. "There has been an incident of potential terrorism reported at 1100 Pennsylvania Avenue, Northwest, Washington, DC. All units report."

Frack, Kayla thought. *That's a block away.* The DeLuxe Imperial Hotel, hosting the conservative conference where the president was scheduled to speak.

"And Ms. Malone, thank you again," the automated voice said.

"Oh for crying out loud," Kayla said. Those damned AIs were everywhere. "Listen, can you get WaltTwo on the line?"

"One moment please," the voice said.

"Ms. Malone."

"WaltTwo, I have an idea. As long as we're manipulating things. I don't even know if you can do this."

"We're in the magic business for real, now. Run it by me."

"And I need to work out whether The Merge will support this, meaning I need to get to Silver Spring as soon as I can tonight. I'll have to make an excuse."

"We have time to do additional things, now that we've confirmed what our process is capable of."

"Okay, here's the thing. The president's supporters have a lot of guns. They are not going to be happy what you've done. Changed the president into a set of mouse ears."

"That was an option, but not—"

"I don't care! Whatever the president is now, doesn't matter. They won't care. They'll be pissed, and they'll have guns. Can we do something about them, their guns I mean? Not the supporters."

"What do you have in mind? Remember, we're not the creative ones. If you had a magic wand, what would you wish for? With our human ally, it appears we can make wishes come true."

Kayla pulled her gun from her holster and held it in her hand. Not a total ban. Not total dysfunction; she knew some people subsisted on hunting, not that it was her style. She remembered Ahmad Arbery. A couple of asshole cracker wannabe policemen had shot and killed him in cold blood less than a week ago. Shot to kill as punishment for running while being black. What would stop things like that? For that matter, what would stop what had happened to the president, whoever had shot him. Stop the unjustified use of force that her brothers and sisters in blue seemed unable to restrain themselves from using.

Then she remembered laughing at some cliché Florida Men and Darwin Award winners, and the bitter schadenfreude she'd felt when they accidentally shot themselves. For that matter, when bomb makers screwed up, too.

"I have an idea…"

CHAPTER 12

RETURN TO GROUND ZERO

FROM THE FILES OF FAB ARCHER, MARCH 1,
2022, EARLY AFTERNOON

S oon after the Enchantment, news media and the public
referred to the DeLuxe Hotel, and specifically the atrium,
the epicenter of the Enchantment, as Ground Zero. There
was debate: was this disrespectful to the 9/11 Ground Zero? Was
this a trend to be avoided, a bad precedent? If we let there be a
"Ground Zero" every time there was a terrorist attack, would
that manifest more to come? President DeLuxe's haters informally called it "Ground Hero," and the few conservatives still in
power disliked *that* spin. Among the president's followers there
was resistance to the term "enchantment," too. Too positive, said
DeLuxists. "Unproven that it was enchantment!" said deniers of
magic. (Those tended to believe 2/29 a Constitutionalist coup
and hoax.) An inventive DFS Schedule C, a hanger-on from the
DeLuxe administration, thought up an alternative: Site Omega.
That had an appropriately Biblical ring to it, and implied that
this would be the last "act of mystical terrorism," as the Fatherland Security flacks put it in their press releases. Because the
government would draw a line in the sand, find, and stop
whoever had done it. The finding hadn't happened; the enchantments had stopped on their own. Until today.

Site Omega became the official term used by the Department

of Fatherland Security. The statutes simply referred to it as "the former Old Post Office Building, also known as the DeLuxe Imperial Hotel." Absent a catchy statutory name, we at DLE called it Ground Zero. We were like the public, who weren't buying the DFS re-branding. Who was DFS to tell DLE or the public what to think? In the media, it became "2/29 Ground Zero," as opposed to "9/11 Ground Zero" in New York. And then, just plain "Ground Zero."

The entire hotel was closed for months after the Enchantment Event. The stakeholder law enforcement agencies (the usual: LNM, NBI, Confidential Service, and Those Who Decline to Name Themselves, a.k.a., the FSA, GIA, and that ilk) scoured the place for clues. They found traces of gunpowder. The finding was that these came from Confidential Service agents and the president's private security detail who carried firearms. There was no evidence of biological, chemical, or radioactive weapons, and nothing to decode who had done the deed, or why.

During the closure, crowds outside the closed building either mourned the loss of the Freedonian Party's core leadership, or (in larger numbers) celebrated by taking sassy selfies with plastic decapitated heads of the missing president. (The comedian Carol Sphinx, once reviled for a comic photo with the president's decapitated head, sold souvenir "DeLuxe Heads" as a fundraiser for anti-gerrymandering organizations. Pushcarts outside the hotel sold these, as well as cheap counterfeits.)

A social media groundswell demanded the building open to the public, and the Administrative Services Administration (which owned it) and the American Park Service assembled a proposal. A couple of DeLuxe administration appointees who had been safely offsite during the Event proposed to create a national memorial park. Instead, a Freedonian/Constitutionalist coalition in Congress passed legislation to re-open the hotel as a hotel, with a memorial sculpture in the middle of the atrium. The sculpture would be non-representational, an abstract bronze flame. It would sit directly under a chandelier, cantilevered in the middle of the atrium, above the metal arches that were a vestige of the old building's infrastructure. The chandelier already consisted of curving, interwoven metal strips, to which would be added pinpoint lights, each one representing a Transformed Person. (The tacky crystal chandeliers the DeLuxe Organization had installed were gone.)

Who was behind the push to keep it a hotel? Rumors flew: Was it the former First Lady, Urania DeLuxe (safe in New York City on 2/29)? Public sympathy for her had grown with the removal of her abusive, philandering husband. Was it the Disney Corporation, the bugaboo of conspiracy theorists, showing the cards of their endgame, i.e., the takeover of the DeLuxe Organization? Disney did buy a lot of shares in DeLuxe as part of the post-2/29 deal to run the hotel. Was there a secret deal between the new attorney general and Mrs. DeLuxe, that if she cooperated, the federal seizure of DeLuxe Organization assets would be reduced? After the president's transformation, a new Targeted Counsel discovered such pervasive corruption and foreign collusion that there was ample evidence to seize practically the whole company under racketeering statutes. (The discoveries are all well documented in the public record, although any deals cut with the DeLuxe Organization are sealed, even to us at the DMV.) With DeLuxe's sons Fenric and Dirk Jr., his daughter Kalihnkha, and her husband Herod among the Missing-And-Presumed-Transformed (the MAPT, as they were known), Urania DeLuxe was in the unasked-for position of running a large private corporation that was now under siege from the Feds. I always speculated she was happy to sell or deal if only to be rid of things.

I favored revealing what some would conceal. I was happy when the bill's Congressional sponsors and Mrs. DeLuxe held a joint press conference to announce that the hotel would re-open as the Disney DC Deluxe Resort. The Disney theming, which early critics declared in bad taste, was touted as a way to honor the missing (the MAPT), by generating money to be placed into a fund for families of the missing. (By the way, the lower case "l" in "Deluxe" was in keeping with Disney's spelling for its other hotels, the corporation claimed; conservatives were mollified by the word's inclusion, and progressives appeased by the de-capitalization.)

Disney agreed to set aside a percentage of profits to a compensation fund for the families of the bereaved. The Department of Law Enforcement's Torts and Defense Division would administer the fund, assessing applications and making payments, just as it did similar other compensation funds, including the 9/11 victims and first responders' funds. Our new DLE division (the DMV) would provide verification data to help make those decisions. Given the new law's goal of care for the families of victims, nobody could protest for long. Even so, memes on the Internet appeared to show Constitutionalists, in a bill-signing photo op, unsuccessfully suppressing laughter.

Once Disney worked its (corporate) magic on the hotel, there were a lot of parties in it, and a lot of joyous selfies in and around the building. Street vendors purveyed a grey market in not-officially-sanctioned-by-Disney T-shirts with snarky sayings and memes. And as far as I know, it is completely untrue that Disney abandoned a plan to replicate the Hall of Presidents in one of the convention spaces, or, even worse, a planned audioanimatronic reenactment of President DeLuxe's transformation. I mean, we don't actually know which EO he is, so how could they reenact it?

All of which is to say, the former DeLuxe Hotel, aka Disney's DC Deluxe Resort, aka Ground Zero, aka Site Omega, aka Ground Hero, was full of people the day Lonny and I went there searching for our missing stormtrooper.

From our office, Lonny and I grabbed a rideshare over. (Parking is impossible there!) We each wore a single wireless earphone, and a discreet over-the-ear video camera that recorded and streamed everything we saw. We would send him video from our ear cams, along with the audio conversation. "Got this, Grif?" Lonny asked.

"Yes," Griffin replied over our headsets. Lonny turned toward me and made a thumbs up in camera view. I also did a thumbs up, looking into Lonny's camera.

As we stepped out of the car, Lonny said, "It looks kinda like a castle anyway." He was right. The building's Romanesque turrets had a fairytale vibe at odds with the boxy 1930s neo-classical buildings in the rest of the Federal Triangle. At the front door, a doorman, wearing a long blue overcoat and red top hat, stood at the front doors to the building, atop a set of stone steps. A young woman in a red, white, and blue uniform stood near him holding a couple of small plastic bags—also red, white, and blue.

As we reached the top of the steps, I could read the doorman's name badge: "Alfred" it said, and underneath, "Darien, CT." He smiled and nodded, saying, "Welcome home." The young woman (Lachelle, Washington, DC) approached, saying, "Magic Masks?" She offered us each a bag containing a Disney-branded facemask. We showed our ID cards, which Alfred scanned with a Mickey Mouse-shaped device strapped to his wrist. A gong chimed (not the magic pixie dust sound I'd heard earlier), and his device lit up Mickey's silhouette in green, glowing lines. "Temperature check?" he asked. We both offered our phones, which were connected to our wrist temperature monitors. He scanned this, and Mickey chimed and turned green again. Alfred nodded, Lachelle backed off, and Alfred opened the front doors for us, saying, "Have a magical day!" Even though we were within the virus-free perimeter, frequent temperature checks and status updates were a standard procedure for indoor spaces.

"Hold on a minute," Lonny said to me. "Miss Lachelle, we'll take those masks, thank you." She smiled and handed him the two bags. "So that we'll blend in," Lonny said. "No need to look like it's a raid." Technically, having met two of the criteria for public gathering perimeter screening (vaccination certificates and normal temperatures) we did not have to wear masks. Yet Lonny had a point. Our DMV-issued masks (black, with "DLE" in big white letters) would call attention to us, while in a Magic Mask, we'd look like a pair of normal hotel visitors awaiting our test results.

We paused in the entrance to the hotel and put on the Magic Masks.

"His greeting was a Disney trademark," Griffin said, while we masked ourselves. "The Cast Members welcome the guests to every Disney hotel like that, with 'welcome home.'"

"Cast Member?" Lonny whispered.

"Everything is a show, at Disney," Griffin said, "Everyone staff person you see is called a Cast Member. You can call them 'CMs' if you want."

We stood, overlooking the atrium, a level above the main floor of the hotel.

There was the memorial, a bronze flame, and above it the complex ribbons of intertwined metal and brilliant star-like lights. I gazed at the chandelier's curved bands of metal interwoven in donut-shaped Moebius strips, and in turn, forming woven tori consisting of smaller tori. A torus of tori. How had they done such complex metalwork? I'd have to read up on it. Each spark of light was supposed to represent the soul of someone who'd been trapped into a transformed object, if you believed them to have souls.

I heard a fanfare, and noticed more brightly costumed staff, I mean Cast Members, had hopped onto a raised platform at one end of the hotel atrium. They were the energetic, young, dancing, lip-synching Disney employees you see in parades at the parks. Each had a Magic Mask customized to match their costumes. The masks were the kind that bulged out from the mouth enough to facilitate singing.

"What's happening?" Griffin asked.

"It's a show on the stage, Griffin. Lonny, why aren't pointing toward the stage?"

"I meant, what is Agent Dotch looking at?" Griffin said.

Lonny was scanning the crowd gathered in the atrium. "Ten o'clock. No, wait. Ten o'clock and two o'clock," he whispered. I gasped. There was a stormtrooper off to the left, and another to the right, in the middle of the crowd.

"I see them, but which is ours?"

I hadn't noticed before, but the half the people on the ground floor of the atrium wore costumes: Disney characters, Marvel superheroes and villains, and, unfortunately, at least three, no, four stormtroopers. And a Darth Vader and several Jedis.

"They allow cosplay at this hotel," Griffin said in our earpieces. "Normally at Disney properties that's not allowed, except for special events. There's a convention here today. I looked it up."

"One of those might be our perp, and might not," Lonny said.

"TP, Lonny, I think we should say."

"Hmph."

"Ladies and gentlemen, boys and girls!" said a loud announcer's voice over the public address system. "Disney's DC Deluxe Resort proudly presents, Mickey's Celebrate America!"

"It's possible none of them is ours," Griffin said. "Two of them are First Order; ours is classic Imperial."

"Grif, I need to you translate," Lonny said.

"Different movies," he said.

"Griffin, which ones can we rule out?" I asked.

"Agent Dotch, keep looking at the crowd. Fab, I'm switching to your phone's camera. Pull it out and zoom in on some of them for me." I pointed my phone at the crowd, and Griffin prompted me to zoom into each stormtrooper in the crowd, one by one.

Over the PA came more music, and the Cast Members marched on stage, dressed in red, white, and blue, kneeled and gestured to a curtain behind the small stage. They sang the rousing march that asked who was the leader of a band, and then answered by spelling out the name of Disney's most famous rodent.

They put their hands to their ears to hear the response from the crowd as everyone sang, "Mickey Mouse."

"Donald Duck!" I said. Lonny turned and arched an eyebrow at me.

"Mickey Mouse," the Cast Members and the crowd sang again.

"Donald Duck!" Griffin and I said. Lonny raised both eyebrows.

"Grif, what's your take?" Lonny asked.

"I don't think any of them are ours," he said. "The two that are Imperial Stormtroopers have cheap knockoff costumes."

"If you say so. Well, that's good for the moment. Perp's not in the crowd."

The Cast Members and crowd end the song with a burst of confetti, strobes, and music, Mickey Mouse appeared through the curtains on the stage, to thunderous shouts from the crowd. Jedi knights held up their lightsabers and pumped them in the air, and other adults and children waved their mouse ear hats.

Lonny motioned that we should descend to main level.

"I think you should find the basement," Griffin said. "Let me call up a floor plan. Head to your left, down that corridor."

We went to the corridor. A Cast Member, a young, dark-haired, tan-skinned man, dressed in blue pants and a red and white striped shirt, was coming out of a door marked "Cast Members Only."

"Official government business," Lonny said, flashing his badge at the CM, whose name tag told us he was René, from Annandale, Virginia. I showed him my ID card as well.

René's eyes widened, and he stepped aside, holding the door open. "Whatever you need, sir, ma'am."

"Thanks," I said. "Can you show us the stairs to the basement?"

"This way," he said, and he walked us along a dimly lit corridor with green walls.

"The green paint is called 'Go Away Green,'" Griffin said in our earpieces. "It's meant to distinguish backstage areas from onstage areas. It makes the guests shy away because it's drab, and Cast Members instantly know when they're backstage."

René led us to another door, and said, "Behind this is a service elevator to the sub-basement." He opened the door, and our stormtrooper burst out. He was carrying the same blaster gun he'd had at the STIF.

"Hold it right there!" he said, aiming his blaster at René, then at me. His voice was coming through a speaker on his armor somewhere, sounding like a radio transmission. I put my hands in the air, and tried not to look at Lonny, who was to René's left, obscured by the door. I don't think the stormtrooper had seen him, and I didn't want to give him away.

"Get on the floor," the stormtrooper growled through his amplifier.

"Whatever you say," I said. I started to kneel, then experienced (felt? heard?) the dimming of lights and tinkling sprinkling of pixie dust. The same as at the STIF when the stormtrooper escaped.

"What was that?" the stormtrooper said.

"You felt that too?" I asked.

"I said get down!" he barked again, but not at me. He banged the door open and saw Lonny, who was standing still. So was René.

"Don't hurt them!" I shouted. "Can't you see they're frozen in place?"

The stormtrooper pushed René, and the stiffened Cast Member fell over. I got up and kneeled beside René. Luckily, he had hunched forward before he was frozen, making a curved posture that kept his head from hitting the floor. His stiff body rocked.

"Fab, don't reply. I'm here," Griffin said in my ear. "Can you keep him distracted?"

The stormtrooper was pacing the corridor, periodically pointing his gun at me. His footfalls sounded nothing like the intimidating stomping you hear in the movies. The boots had rubber soles and emitted little squeaks as he paced. I stood, raising my hands in the air as soon.

"Hey, hey, nobody's trying to hurt you," I said. "There was an incident, and something happened to you. Do you remember the AFPAP rally?"

"I remember, and then I woke up in a concentration camp! I must have been kidnapped," the stormtrooper said. Looking at Lonny, who was frozen in place, he said, "Is this a trick?"

"This may be hard to believe. There was an incident, and you were incapacitated. You were in a coma," I said. "And weird things have been happening."

He paused to think about that, and asked, "What kind of weird things?" His blaster drooped a fraction of an inch.

"Well, like this, people frozen in place. And, can I ask you something?"

"What?"

"Do you know you're wearing a stormtrooper costume?"

"Oh, yeah, this. Sure."

"Fab, what are you doing?" Griffin whispered over my earpiece.

"Well, a lot of people ended up being in costume, and in, you might call it suspended animation, like my associate here. And wearing unusual costumes." I didn't know if he could handle the concept of magic. And becoming a plastic toy.

His helmeted head tilted to the side a fraction of an inch. "Say, don't I know you?" he asked. That was weird.

"I don't know," I said, choosing my words carefully. "I'm Fab Acer, Department of Law Enforcement. My office is charged with caring for people that were affected by the incident in the

DeLuxe Hotel. You've come back to where it happened. Do you know how you got here?"

"Fab, remember he has a gun!"

The stormtrooper had kept his blaster pointed at me. I could see it had a gun barrel, and apparently the Enchantment would not keep it from firing at me.

"I came through the corridors."

"Yes, the Utilidors," I said.

He cocked his head; which I was surprised he could do in that costume. "Doesn't ring a bell. Where's the president?" he asked.

"The president is at the facility you broke out of a couple of hours ago. Do you remember the breakout?"

He paused again. "Not sure."

"If you'll let me, I'll help you. That's my job."

"You work with these here?" He waved his blaster at René and Lonny.

"I work with him," I said, waving my hand toward Lonny. "May I lower my hands? The guy on the floor, I just met. He works at the hotel here. I'm unarmed."

"All right. I'm so confused. I was supposed to...do something to President DeLuxe. It was necessary."

"Would you be more comfortable without the helmet?"

"No, don't have him remove the helmet!" Griffin said. *Too late*, I thought. The stormtrooper set his blaster down next to him, to my relief, and reached up and undid a latch to the side of his neck. With a whoosh of air, his helmet expanded slightly, and he lifted it from his head.

I gasped. It was a familiar face, of course, even had I not repeatedly reviewed photos of all the potential TPs as part of my job. It was Fenric DeLuxe, the younger son of President DeLuxe and Kalihnha DeLuxe, the woman we'd seen at the STIF right before his escape. Just as she had somehow suspected, this was her son! His dirty blond hair, usually slicked with gel, had come unraveled and drooped over his eyes. He looked at me, cocking his head again. His upper lip drew up to exposing his big, white overbite.

"Don't I know you?" he repeated.

"Mr. DeLuxe, I'm Fab Acer. I don't *think* we've met."

"Okay, don't panic," Griffin said in my ear.

"Why not?" I replied, forgetting that Fenric didn't know I was wired for sound.

"Who are you talking to?" he said, frowning. He picked up his blaster again.

"Why are you wearing stormtrooper armor?"

"We thought...the Space Force, you know, it would be funny." The blaster drooped more as Fenric searched his memory. His eyes focused beyond me, as though in the past.

"May I ask you, why a gun disguised as a blaster?" I had decided it had to have been a gun, even before the transformation. If he had been dressed as a stormtrooper before being enchanted, then all the disenchantment had done was restore it to a working gun, made to look like a laser blaster.

He looked down at his gun.

"Is it? I don't think so," he said. He pointed at a wall and pulled the trigger. The shot left a hole in the wall, and I covered my ears, the sound unbelievably loud. "What was that? A special effect? This is just a prop. To kill the president. But...that's my father." As soon as he said that his eyes widened, and then his brow furrowed. "Why would I do that?" The gun drooped again. "I can't remember. Say, did I do that?" He waved the blaster at the hole in the wall.

"Mr. DeLuxe, let me help you. I think you're confused." I slowly stepped closer to him and gently pointed the blaster away from me. It was hot. "You wouldn't shoot your father, now, would you?" At least, I hoped he wouldn't have planned to. Or me!

"No, of course not. But why did I need to? I really needed to, really bad. I read it. On the web."

Uh-oh. That made no sense, but...

"Almost there," Griffin whispered.

Almost where? What the hell was going on?

"On the web?" I asked Fenric.

"Yeah, on D—"

Before he could complete his sentence, the pixie dust tinkled again, and the lights wavered, and reality shimmered. Again.

I blinked, and looked toward Fenric, and saw instead a small figurine of a Star Wars Imperial Stormtrooper, with his helmet off and held in his hand, and his blaster (also action figure sized again) lying on the ground next to him. I went over to the figurine and gently picked him up. As much as a six-inch figure can, the head resembled Fenric DeLuxe.

René and Lonny were still completely motionless, and the distant sound of the Mickey Mouse show upstairs had stopped.

"Griffin, what's going on here?"

"Don't panic," Griffin said.

"Griffin, Lonny and this poor Cast Member are still frozen. Did you do this?"

"Don't be alarmed. It will be OK. Fab, do you trust me?"

"Of course, I trust you. Why shouldn't I? What do you know about this?"

"Please, please, please do what I say, and everything will be all right."

"Griffin, you seem to know more than you are sharing, and I'm not happy about this. But I don't have much of a choice." He had a lot of explaining to do. It would have to wait.

I walked over to Lonny and waved my hand in front of Lonny's face. "Is he awake?" I asked.

"He and everyone else are moving at a much slower rate, I mean, you and I are on a different time band. Think of it as you're moving very, very fast, and everything else is normal."

"Should I pick up René?"

"Better to leave him where he is for the moment. Okay, let's think. I hadn't thought this through."

"What are we thinking through?"

"Your story. Okay, from the moment you opened the door. We don't want to reveal all this yet."

Griffin was up to his ears in this. Was he involved in the transformation? Was he…? He couldn't be! Sorcerer X?

He wouldn't tell me over the earpiece, I decided. If he could transform people into inanimate objects, I decided it was best if I not confront him about it, yet. If he were going to do it to me, he'd already have done it, and I'd be unconscious, turned into a Minnie Mouse ear headband or something already. Better I go along.

"Okay, we keep this on the downlow for now," I said. "Let me see. I've got it." I reached over and picked up tiny, plastic Fenric and his tiny helmet and tiny laser blaster. "Can you put his helmet on him? And put his blaster back in his hands?"

"Give me a minute." While I was waiting, I put Fenric and the helmet down in the doorway where I'd first seen him. "Okay, hold on," Griffin said. I heard a tiny sprinkle of pixie dust, saw a slight flicker of lights, and the tiny plastic stormtrooper now had its helmet on, and held the blaster.

"Okay," I said, "I'm going to lie down where I was standing, so I'll be next to René. Then you can start time up again. Or slow us down, or whatever."

"Be ready."

"I'm ready." I reclined next to René.

Again, the pixie dust and flickering, and I heard René say, "Ow!" as his head bumped the floor.

"What the—?" Lonny blurted from where he stood, behind the door.

"Lonny, are you okay?" I asked, from where I lay on the floor, next to René. I propped myself up on an elbow.

"*I'm* okay. Are *you* okay?" Lonny asked, as he peeked around the door. "What just happened?"

"I'm not sure. How about you, René?" I asked. I stood, and leaned over him.

"I think I'm alright," he said, sitting up. I walked behind him to look at the back of his head. The skin hadn't broken when he hit the floor, so I decided he was fine.

"Fab, Agent Dotch, are you there?" Griffin asked over our headsets.

"We're here, and I think we have found our perp," Lonny said. He stooped to the transfigured Fenric DeLuxe. "The situation is neutralized. Perp has turned back into a toy," Lonny continued.

"Griffin," I said, as if I didn't know the answer, "Did you get any footage? The last thing I remember was we opened this door and the full-sized stormtrooper was here."

"No, Fab, there's no footage. It all went snowy." Griffin thought that lie up quickly. Disturbing.

"Was this another Enchantment?" René asked.

"René, I'm going to have to swear you to secrecy on this. National security, criminal investigation," I said. He nodded, eyes wide open.

"I'll leave it to you, Ms. Acer, to handle the, uh, swearing in," Lonny said. René would not have noticed the glimmer of a smile on Lonny's face. "In the meanwhile, I need to phone AD Oberst and get an enchantment scene investigation team in here."

Since I don't actually know a way to swear civilians into secrecy, I improvised. While Lonny was on the phone with Oberst, I took René's contact information, and impressed on him how important it was to keep what little he'd seen as a secret. I said I'd be in touch. I didn't say when, or whether I'd have anything for him to sign (since I had no clue). I suggested he go back to work. "I'll escort the NBI team in. You may want to alert security here."

"That makes sense," he said. "Have a magical d—"

"And you have a magical day, too, René. Just not too magical, right?"

"Yes, Ms. Acer. You got it." He smiled his Disney CM smile, and left Lonny and me with EO 357, and what sounded like a very loud Assistant Director Oberst yelling at Lonny over the phone.

Lonny stayed deadpan, occasionally holding the phone farther from his ear when Oberst's volume got higher.

"Griffin, can you hear what Oberst is saying?"

"He's talking loudly. I think that means he is angry. I don't understand why. We caught the escaped TP."

"Yes, sir," Lonny said, and lowered his phone. "They should be here in five."

"Is everything all right with AD Oberst?"

"He could only chap my butt so much, you know? Disobeyed his orders, he said. Of course, that's why he was mad. We did what they couldn't."

"I hope you won't get into trouble."

"Nothing I haven't gotten into before, will again." He smiled broadly. "And results are what matters, right?"

I blinked. I rarely saw him smile so. "You like that you made him mad, don't you?"

"Ya gotta get some fun out of your job, right?" I nodded, and he nodded back. "I'll stay here while you meet security and clear the way for CSI." I saluted, and his smile got a bit broader.

Coming out of the basement door, I met René, along with four uniformed security officers, five or six young people, Cast Members in generic red, white, and blue, and one broad-chested man in a navy suit, white shirt, and red, white and blue tie. He exuded the air of being in charge. He had a military-looking hair: short stubble on the sides and a stiff, black brush of flat-cut spikes on top. His badge said his name was Derek and he was from San Jose, California.

"Agent Acer?" he asked me. He had a deep, commanding voice.

"Ms. Acer, Department of Law Enforcement," I said, and flashed my ID card at him.

"Hm," he responded. I think he was disappointed it wasn't a

badge. "I'm Derek Manlapaz, Head of Security. May I get a sit-rep?"

"Agent Dotch has secured the site, and we're expecting an NBI CSI team shortly."

"Is there any danger to guests?" he asked.

"No, none."

"What are the details?"

I paused. Guests were starting to look at us, and whispering.

"I'm afraid I can't—"

"Was it another Enchantment?" blurted someone on the edge of the crowd. It was a guest, a plump middle-aged woman wearing a green dress covered with tropical birds, and a mouse-ear headband with a yellow and green bow and a tiki figure on it. I judged her eager, rather than concerned.

"No, not another Enchantment." I said. "Just someone doing a reenactment. In questionable taste," I improvised again. "There's no cause for alarm. We do need to clear a path here, ma'am, to collect some evidence."

"*Ms.* Acer, let me handle the crowd control," said Mr. Manla-paz. He spoke into a walkie-talkie: "Deathstar Maneuver 7."

"Roger Rabbit," a voice replied. One of the fresh-faced CMs offered his arm to the woman in the green dress, and she hesi-tated, pouting, then walked with him toward the atrium. The CMs were now fanning out and gently persuading guests to create a path. Disney knew how to do crowd control.

A fanfare played over the PA system, followed by tinkling sounds, and the lights dimmed in the atrium. I tensed. Was this another enchantment?

"That wasn't me," Griffin said in my ear. I saw the lights brighten on the empty stage, and the music resolved into the Star Wars Imperial March. This was only Disney stage magic. Darth Vader, accompanied by Kylo Ren, marched onto the stage, and an announcer said "Ladies and Gentlemen, Boys and Girls, the Disney DC Deluxe Resort Presents, Review of the Troops." Most of the crowd turned to watch as a line of

Imperial Stormtroopers marched onto the stage and the music built.

The stormtroopers in the audience, along with the other costumed and street-clothed guests, cheered them. I tried not to overthink why people would be so excited to see fascist troops.

"We are prepared for incidents," said Mr. Manlapaz. "I'm taking it on your word there is no danger to guests. Safety is our number one priority. Now, suppose you show me what happened? I've got a TS clearance, still active with Army Reserve."

"I'm going to take you on your word, Mr. Manlapaz," I replied.

"Fab, the CSI team is at the front door," Griffin said in my ear.

"If your staff can meet our NBI team who are at the front door, and escort them quickly here, I'll take you down. Just you, please, Mr. Manlapaz."

He nodded. "MacKellan," he said, and one of the women in security uniform gestured, taking half the security group with her toward the front door.

As soon as they moved, I saw something odd across the atrium. One costumed person in the audience was not looking at the stage, he was looking in our direction. He was wearing a dark, hooded robe that shadowed much of his face. Was he supposed to be an alien? Part of his hood slipped back, and the light on stage increased, illuminating part of his face. He had a big, frog-like eyes and mouth, and pasty-pink, blotchy skin. Was he in costume, or just ugly? For a second he was staring at me, then he looked away, toward the stage, pulling his hood up. I shuddered.

"Ms. Acer?" reminded Mr. Manlapaz. He gestured to the basement door.

"Sorry, thought I saw someone," I said. "This way." As we descended, I said, "Listen, I am going to level with you. There was no new Enchantment." I was getting better than I liked to be at telling partial truths. "However, there was something strange, related to an incident at one of our facilities."

"The STIF?" he asked. I stopped on the stairs and looked at him. "It's part of my job to know all about your division, Ms. Acer. I assume you're with DMV?" I nodded. "The Disney Deluxe has every motivation to keep speculation around magical incidents here in the hotel to a minimum. We would be happy if there were no new enchantments here. Of the 2/29 kind, that is. The only magic we want here is Disney-style pixie dust." He showed a sliver of a grin and a slight crinkle around his eyes. "Please go on."

I wasn't sure if he meant walking talking, or both, so I did both, continuing to descend. "There is no danger to guests or Cast Members," I said. "However, there was an incident. René was here, and I asked of him the same as I ask of you, to hold this as the highest national security concern and not repeat what you learn."

We arrived at the door where Lonny and the transformed Fenric DeLuxe were.

"Agent Dotch, this is Mr. Manlapaz, hotel head of security. Mr. Manlapaz, Agent Lonsford Dotch, LNM, on detail to DMV. Agent Dotch, I haven't briefed Mr. Manlapaz, but we can trust him. CSI should be a minute behind us."

Looking each other in the eye, they nodded. I couldn't help imagining that back in the days when people still shook hands they'd have tested each other's strength with a long, firm shake. A nod and a look of recognition had to suffice now. Mr. Manlapaz pointed with his index finger and middle finger at the doorway where little EO 357 stood.

"This one of yours?" he asked.

"Yes," I said.

"EO 357?" he asked.

Surprised again I nodded. He squatted to look at it. Lonny tensed for a second, then feigned relaxation.

"I won't touch anything," Mr. Manlapaz said. "I had one of

these when I was a kid." He peered closely, then stood. "Okay, maybe I still have one." He smiled. "Or maybe it's my boy's now. Anyway, there's one in the house. Not mint condition like this one. And, you know, no magic."

"It won't be here long," Lonny said. I heard the door to the stairs open, and footsteps quickly moving down toward us.

"All right, I'm satisfied there's no danger. I would like, at some point, to know how this got here. That can wait. For now, let me know what I can do to help you get it out."

I was right to trust him, even if I'd had no choice.

"We appreciate the cooperation, and your help in keeping knowledge of it strictly limited." I said.

"Roger Rabbit," he replied.

The footsteps approached. René and Officer MacKellan were followed by a team of black-vested NBI CSIs laden with equipment, and one of our own STIF staffers, Evelyn Ramirez, that Oberst had assigned to be with the CSI folks. She would ensure the proper documentation photos and measurements were taken. It occurred to me we'd have to figure out where to put that data in the database. Each EO had one set of data, and this would be two transformations for the same EO. I waved to Evelyn while Lonny, Manlapaz, and the NBI team exchanged information and got set up. She came to me.

"Griffin, Evelyn is here from the STIF."

"I know."

"Hi, Fab," Evelyn said. "Hi Griffin," she said, waving to my cam. She was wearing a cam and earpiece like ours.

"Can the database handle a second transformation?" I asked. Evelyn would know that this was our renegade TP, now restored to its transformed state.

"I'm making sure it can," Griffin said. "I'll need to do a database rebuild. Meanwhile, Evelyn should record it as a new EO, and we'll convert it after I've rebuilt and released the new version into production."

"Will do, Griffin," Evelyn said. "And you can talk directly to me, you know."

"I know," he said. I faced Evelyn's cam and raised my hand to my mouth, the sign language for "thank you." This was one of our social cuing signals, and after a second, Griffin said, "Thank you, Evelyn."

"We're working on it," I said to Evelyn.

Evelyn shrugged and nodded. "You're welcome, Griffin. I'll let you know when I'm done," she said. "Hey guys, let me in there first," she said, heading to the CSI team.

"Good to have one of our own," Lonny said. He had drawn up next to me.

"Yes," I said. "Say, Lonny, I need to check on something, are you good to oversee this without me?"

"I'm not overseeing anything, remember? I wasn't even supposed to be here."

"You know what I mean. And how is your wound?"

"Yes, I am good here. Yes, my wound is fine. The crew is on top of things. I'll watch while they wrap things up, and probably head over to the STIF with Evelyn and the perp. I mean, TP. They brought the armored van. I won't feel safe until he's in cold storage again."

"Thanks, I need to check something out. I'll go to the office."

I walked up the stairs, saying to Griffin, "Now, was there something you and I needed to talk about, Griffin?"

"I don't know, was there?" he replied.

There was something I barely couldn't remember. What was so important to discuss? Something about the waves of enchantment. Maybe he had collected data on it? "It'll come to me in a minute. Or when I get back. Meanwhile, did you see the footage on my cam of that weird guy in the atrium? It was right before Mr. Manlapaz and I came down, after the security detail went to meet the NBI."

"I know you were looking across the room," he said. "I'll pull up the footage." Everything in our cam and audio feed was streamed to storage and kept in the cloud for a month. Needless to say, Griffin was our tech guru for that as well.

I reached the main level and walked out into the atrium. The Darth Vader Show had ended, the stage was empty, and the mix of costumed and non-costumed guests had thinned out. Nobody showed they were aware of the NBI CSIs in the basement, or the presence of a TP there. And the mysterious robed person was nowhere to be seen.

"You mean the Emperor Palpatine impersonator?" Griffin asked.

"Yes, that's it!" He looked like the evil emperor from *Star Wars*. How could I have missed that? I should have known these things for the same reason Mr. Manlapaz knew them all. It was my job. Of course, probably easy for him. Once a fanboy, always a fanboy. His boy's action figure, my butt! I was never such a big fangirl of all that sci-fi stuff. Even so, I had seen all the *Star Wars* movies, plus I had a professional interest due to the EOs that were *Star Wars* merchandise.

"Griffin, there was something weird, and familiar about him. Can you blow up his face, and run it through facial recognition routines?"

"You know, this isn't like the movies," he replied. "There's only so much I can do at that resolution. Our body cams are only 720p. I told Eliot we needed 8K ones. Nobody thought it was important."

"Whatever you can do. I'll speak to Eliot about it for you, OK? I'm going to walk around the hotel. Perhaps I'll encounter Emperor Palpatine again and get a closer shot."

"I'll see what I can do. It may take ten or fifteen minutes. While I'm recompiling the MATA database, I could do that."

"Griffin, you're a gem."

"I don't know what that means."

"I value you, thank you, you're great," I said.

"Oh."

I walked around the hotel atrium. The tacky glitz the former president's company had inserted (lots of gold) had been replaced by tasteful, intentionally whimsical Disney touches. The Mickey Mouse logo embedded into designs, one large circle with two smaller circles for ears, repeated as a gold pattern on red carpets, for example. There was constant orchestral music playing in the background, from concealed speakers. Uplifting, Coplandesque Americana. A few historic features of this Old Post Office Building had been lovingly restored. I remembered being here before 2/29. What was the event? I couldn't remember, maybe a reception? What was with my memory lately? Shock, I guessed, could do that.

I liked the Disney changes. The guests were milling around in their usual way, lots of kids dressed as princesses (both magical and Leia kinds), Jedi apprentices, and pirates. More and more little girl pirates since the recent movie reboot featuring a red-head woman pirate. And some of the princesses might have been born biological boys, for all I know. Parents were more and more "Live and let live" about kids' costumes these days. Thank goodness.

"I've enhanced the image," Griffin said in my ear.

"Any hits in facial recognition?"

"There's not enough resolution."

"Shoot me the image."

There was a "bloop" on my phone, and I opened the text containing the photo. There he was, staring at me. I saw now that he wasn't actually an alien, or in alien makeup, just an unattractive, middle-aged white man, with bad acne rosacea and buggy eyes. I had seen him somewhere. And he gave me the creeps.

As I stood there, I saw Lonny, Evelyn, and the CSI crew heading out, and realized I should get to the office. I stopped at the platform overlooking the atrium to take it in one last time. Still no evil emperor. I took a deep breath and admired the memorial sculpture and chandelier once again.

"Hm," I said to myself. There was one light on the chandelier that looked out of place. All the others were bright white LED pinpoints, set in a complex curved and interwoven donut-shapes, made of red, silver, and blue metal. The odd one didn't look like an LED; it was more like an old-fashioned Christmas light, teardrop-shaped and frosted white. It wasn't centrally placed, and I hadn't noticed it when we looked (from this same angle) when we arrived. Could it be a replacement? I doubted they could not find an LED to easily replace one, and besides, those things never burned out.

"Griffin, one more thing. Do you see the funny light bulb in the chandelier?"

"What about it? Yes, I see it."

"Was that always like that?"

"Yes, I'm sure it was."

"You seem awfully certain."

"Why would it change?"

"That bulb looks out of place. Are you sure—"

"I'm sure they're doing the best they can to keep everything together!" He almost shouted this. He sounded on the verge of crying.

"Griffin, it's okay. I'm not questioning your memory." Even if I wasn't, something was odd about how he was responding. "I'm sure if you say it's the same, it's the same. Although…"

I deliberately paused, until he said, "What? Although what?" He still sounded overly tense.

"Although, wasn't there something you and I were going to discuss?"

"I don't know. Was there? I'm not a mind reader!"

Whoa, I had struck a nerve. He knew something about this chandelier, which was definitely not the same as it had been when I came into the building. Suddenly, I remembered, clear as a bell, what I wanted to talk to him about: he had something to do with the re-enchantment of Fenric DeLuxe, EO 357! In fact, he seemed able to undo the disenchantment, which had to mean— oh, no! Not Griffin! How…?

I paused another moment as things clicked into place. I also wanted to let him stew on things. What was he hiding from me? How could *he* be involved in—no, he couldn't be. He was just a kid. A savant, but not evil. Sensitive underneath the impassivity. Then again, was what had happened so evil anyway? We were much better off now than two years ago. Oh, who was I kidding or trying to justify things to?

"Griffin, let's talk in person. I'm on my way." I terminated our connection, left the building, snagged a ride share, and was at our office in twenty minutes.

CHAPTER 13

CLUES AND COMPLICATIONS

When I arrived at the office, Griffin was nowhere to be seen. His docking station was empty; he had taken his laptop with him. I went to his server room and tried the door. It was locked. "Griffin," I said, trying to sound calm and not angry. "Griffin, we need to talk." I put my ear to the door. All I could hear was the sound of the air conditioning blowing through the hot electronics. Did security have a key? No, I should wait until he came to me. I could play at patience. I went to my office. Griffin was showing offline in Scrye, so I emailed him. Subject: "Come see me." In the body of the email, I wrote: "Please, please, please do not try that memory thing again. I remember what happened in the basement. We need to discuss this as soon as possible, please. I want to help."

I pressed Send, and my phone rang. It was Haverford. I steeled myself.

"Haverford!"

"Hey, Fab! What is happening now? You guys are burning up the InterWebs again."

Oh no. "What do you mean, Haverford?"

"Check out darkbart.com. I know, I know, it's kinda sketch. Somebody tipped me off. You're a star, Fab! I don't suppose you can tell me what was happening at the Disney Deluxe? Anything to do with a stormtrooper?"

"Haverford, let me at least see what you're talking about before I respond." I logged on to my computer and brought up DarkBart News. Oh, no, indeed! The headline story, with video: "DLE Action at Ground Zero - Helping or Hindering the Unraveling?" That figured. A term conservative conspiracy theorists preferred for the longed-for undoing of the 2/29 Enchantment was "Unraveling the Curse." There was cellphone video of Lonny and the CSI team removing a black case (which must contain Fenric), and then footage of me, looking directly at the camera. Wait a minute, was that when I was looking at the evil emperor? I skimmed the paragraphs, full of speculation about whether DLE was suppressing the Unraveling to maintain its Deep State. Mention of a now deleted chirp (the one Haverford had mentioned) about a possible breakout from the STIF, and a typical "no comment" from DLE's public affairs spokesperson.

"Darn it, Haverford. You know I couldn't talk even if there was something to tell." I needed to tell Eliot about this ASAP, although I doubted he was unaware if public affairs had already commented. "And you know I believe in transparency as much as you do."

"I do know that about you."

"You have to see from my side. Even if there were something going on, there's a time and place..."

"Don't you think the public deserve to know if the Curse is Unraveling? People being restored to their human form, that'd be cause for celebration, right?"

Haverford had worked on the House Committee on Government Accountability, had been close with the Freedonian leadership, and had been (luckily) not present at the AFPAP convention. He was one of the remaining Freedonian loyalists that had helped craft the MATA Act. He often baited me to make statements that might reveal if I was on his side, or on the side of those who wanted the TPs to remain TPs.

"Of course, Haverford." I took a deep breath. "I can tell you that nobody is restored to their former shapes. That's not for publication! Just between us, nobody is Unraveled." *Anymore*, I added, silently. Technically true! I sighed. Here I was again, having to obscure the truth. It was becoming a habit.

Haverford paused, as if he knew I was eliding something. "Well, I didn't expect you to tell me anything official, but I trust you, Fab. I know you're doing your best. Thought you'd want to know you were a video star. And I knew you when!"

"Thanks, Haverford. Drinks next week?"

"Sure, we'll be in touch."

I booked it over to Eliot's office.

"Did you hear—?"

"I saw the video. AD Oberst and I have talked, and PAO has a story. I'll send you their press release when I get it. Now how about your side of the story? I told AD Oberst we understood that *his* branch has the fugitive capture responsibility, and that we were simply profiling, which is *our* job."

"Thanks, Eliot. Well, we found the stormtrooper, and let me tell you, it was touch and go when we got there. There were several stormtroopers already there. Hotel guests in costume, role-playing."

"They have those Star Wars suites there, yes, I know about it."

"Suites?"

"People stay there like on a cruise ship, and their windows can display a view like outside a space station. It's actually a high-resolution video. It's completely immersive on one whole floor. You can pretend you're in a *Star Wars* movie."

"Oh! That explains a lot." Even an Emperor Palpatine. Some people take it so seriously.

"You got there, and how could you tell it was our guy?"

"We went to the basement, where we figured it was more likely a Utilidor would connect. Griffin knew where to send us. There was an elevator to a sub-basement."

"Like in Cinderella Castle!"

"And, well, we just ran into him. Opened an elevator door—I had to swear a custodial guy to secrecy, which reminds me, can we call him in, to reinforce it?"

"Of course. And then what?"

"There he was, and then…we all, Lonny, me, and René, the hotel Cast Member, we must have all passed out, and when we came to, the stormtrooper was back to his original, I mean, transformed form. Back to toy size." Ugh, I hated implying that I had passed out. I wished I had talked with Griffin before talking to Eliot. There must be a better explanation. For now, I had to keep Griffin's part in this to myself, whatever it was. I mean, I didn't officially know he had done anything, right? I had no hard proof. Oh, who was I kidding? I knew. I was covering up for him. I wasn't proud of it.

As if he thought it was oversimplification, Eliot said nothing, although he blinked. His "tell." *Uh-oh*, I thought. He was not going to contradict me, but he found something implausible.

"Okay, well, that's pretty weird," he finally said. "Real magic, again. And you missed seeing it. That must have been frustrating. I know I would have liked to see it." We sat in silence, and he looked into my eyes. He blinked again. I tried not to.

"Eliot, I know…"

"Hm?"

"I know there's probably more to this. I'm working on it. I need to talk to Griffin. I can't say, I mean, I don't know the answer…" That was true.

"But?"

"Give me a little more time. I think I'm close to something."

"Fab, you and Griffin have done amazing work so far. Between you and me, I'm pretty sure AD Oberst is jealous we figured out how to find the escapee." He smiled and rubbed his hands together. "Let's keep one step ahead of him, shall we? Data science versus the G-men. I don't see anything wrong with a little friendly, productive rivalry between branches, do you?"

"Right you are, boss!" He was telling me, in his own way, to keep at it.

"Let me know what you find out as soon as you can."

"I will, Eliot," I said, and I returned to my desk. When I unlocked the screen, DarkBart News was still there. Its founder, Bart Barukka, had been staffing up the site and had already purchased the domain name just before 2/29. After his presumed transformation, the vestiges of his loyal staff went ahead and launched the site. It attracted the most extreme right-wingers, with imaginative things to say about 2/29. Today, however, they seemed to have an informant in the right place at the right time, alas, and I wasn't even sure they were wrong about DLE's role in keeping the objects transformed. If Griffin had anything to do with transforming Fenric back, they were right.

What was their ostensible reason for existing? They espoused a passion for truth and transparency that Haverford and I shared (which I was majorly failing now), and took it to their wack-adoodle extreme. I clicked on their "About Us" link, to see if they had a mission statement. It probably wasn't far off from our own mission statement here at DMV.

The page opened, and I was shocked to see the face of Emperor Palpatine staring at me! Not in costume, not the one from the movies, but the man I'd just seen at the Disney Deluxe. Bart Barukka, the founder of DarkBart News, the architect of President DeLuxe's first successful presidential campaign, was staring at me from my computer. I was sure this was the same man I'd just seen at Ground Zero! President DeLuxe had fired Barukka from his administration within a year. In spite of that, rumor had it that they were still in close contact. Frenemies? Barukka had still been a notorious ultra-right wing (possibly neo-fascist) activist and influencer, so their agendas overlapped, whether Barukka was an official White House staffer or not. And he was on the board of AFPAP, if I recalled correctly.

"In Memoriam, Our Founder," said the caption below his

portrait. The camera loves some people. Not Bart Barukka. I could now vouch that in neither pictures nor real life was Bart Barukka a handsome man. His froggy eyes looked out at me. That was the blotchy complexion (pasty green-white contrasting with florid magenta rosacea patches) that I had taken for overenthusiastic costume play makeup. Even in this professional portrait, they could only Photoshop so much out of him, without making him unrecognizable.

I quickly searched for candid shots of him. This was the person I had seen! As a registered attendee at the AFPAP conference he was thought to be a TP. Was that assumption mistaken? There was C-SPAN footage of him there. How had he escaped? Had he left the convention prior to the transformation? And what was he doing at Ground Zero, just when our own escapee was about to arrive. And, doh! Was Fenric, dressed as an Imperial Stormtrooper, connected to Emperor Palpatine? Could *Barukka* be Sorcerer X?

I sent Griffin another email: "Are you ready to talk yet? I have new data." Maybe that would get him to respond.

I opened the Wikipedia page on Barukka and skimmed it. Nothing popped out at me that I didn't already know or dimly recall. As I mentioned, I tried to know something about any of our TPs, although now I realized Barukka might not be one of them.

A Scrye message beeped on my computer, from Griffin: *I'm busy can it wait.*

Rushing him was usually counterproductive.

In the next half hour, I hope? Need to check in about what happened at the hotel. And some other stuff you don't know about.

Ok be there in 30 he wrote. He tended not to punctuate, or fix autocorrects like turning his lower case "ok" into "Ok." Ever since I'd gotten a smart phone, I'd been fastidious about that. I don't know why I bother, but I do.

I phoned Lonny at the STIF. "Hi, everything okay there?"

"Evelyn's just finished all her measurements. Looks like it's identical to when we first took it into custody."

"That's good. I mean, that makes sense, I guess."

"I'm trying to figure out what happened. You say the lights dimmed, and we were all knocked out? That didn't happen when he broke out. The knock-out."

"No, but it makes sense. None of the witnesses at Ground Zero actually saw what happened, right?"

"Yeah, they all had a memory gap. Not knocked over or knocked out, though."

The non-conservatives (most of the wait staff and technical crew, and a surprising portion of the hotel security and Confidential Service agents) were spared the transformation. That was an aspect of 2/29 that particularly galled the conservatives. It was extremely selective, targeting only people with certain beliefs. Left-wing conspiracy theorists believed the attitudes of the conservatives (xenophobia and homophobia, for example) somehow served as a karmic catalyst for the magic. Christian extremists saw 2/29 as a Satanic blow to religious freedom. Left-wingers reframed that as a karmic blow to the hubris of thinking there is only one true religion.

The bottom line is that the survivors from Ground Zero who escaped transformation, 1) had moderate to liberal political beliefs and (self-avowed) voting records, and 2) did not remember a period from 30 seconds *before*, to about a minute *after* the transformation. As Lonny said, nobody seemed to have passed out; they just had simultaneous and temporary amnesia. That memory wipe was one of the other presumed components of the spell, along with the transformations and shooting and explosion ban. Potential witnesses to the other transformations around the DC area had similar memory gaps. We documented those along with all the other related data. Since there had not been a recurrence, it hadn't been a major focus for us. Conspiracy theorists on all sides speculated there might have been other manipulations of memory that we couldn't even discern at this point. It hadn't mattered before today. I was beginning to suspect they were on to something.

"You're right, I suppose," I said to Lonny. "We still don't know the rules." Except I *did* know now, that there was a slowing down of time, or rather a selective speeding up of time *for some people involved*. Which now meant me!

"Lonny, have you talked to AD Oberst?"

"In fact, I got a text from him. It said good work."

"That's surprising."

"Sure was."

"You haven't heard about the video?" I returned to the front page of darkbart.com. Oh no, it was up to over 400,000 views. I told Lonny about the video, and Eliot's conversation with AD Oberst.

"Huh, that's gotta be why I have an appointment at public affairs, with AD Oberst, in an hour."

"Lonny, Haverford Howell, my old boss, called me. He's the one who told me about the DarkBart News video, and about the chirp that revealed someone had escaped from the STIF. I told him there's nobody who is untransformed. I didn't mention whether someone *had* been un-transformed. Or un-un-transformed."

"Uh-huh."

"I'm just saying, there are ways to say things and not say things."

Lonny paused. "Got it," he said. "And Fab…"

"Yes?"

"For somebody so young, you know how to navigate around people in authority."

I wondered if he suspected I was not telling him everything. "I must have learned it growing up." I had never told him about my childhood. Maybe someday. The only way to disempower secrets is to tell them, right?

"Just remember I'm on your side. Right?"

"Yes, of course, Lonny. I've got your back."

"You know, if we're going to keep doing fieldwork, you should ask Eliot if you can take the combat and self-defense course at Quantico. They had to re-invent their firearms program. They can still do target practice, though. Like you and I do." Use of firearms against paper silhouettes of people with targets on them did not trigger the anti-gun violence Enchantment. Lonny had encouraged me to go shooting with him and learn a little self-defense as a team-building exercise, he said. He was protective of me, and I appreciated that.

"That's a great idea. I only know some basics. If we're going to run into perpetrators, I'd better know more."

I was glad to change the topic from how I might be navigating between powerful people. I wasn't ready to come clean with Lonny. Not yet.

"And the secret," he continued, "is to use your opponent's force against him, to rebound or redirect it to your advantage."

Oh, so we were still talking about it.

"I'll remember that," I said. "And Lonny…"

"Yes?"

"If there's something that's…ready to share…"

"Yeah?"

"You'll be the first to know. Really. If it's important, I'll make sure you know about it."

"Thanks, Ms. Acer. Appreciated. I'll see you later." We disconnected, and I worried if I should have told him I thought Bart Barukka was walking around un-transformed, albeit in full Star Wars costume, and near where our escapee had headed. No, I still had to settle with Griffin. Where was he?

I texted him a few more times after the half-hour he'd promised had elapsed.

Need more time, he replied. I sighed. I checked DarkBart News again. There was a new article, "Cover-Up at Ground Zero," and it had over 200,000 hits. I closed that window and closed my eyes. What could I do?

Then it struck me, and I texted Griffin, *Take your time, but we need to catch up *today*, OK? Very important.*

Kk, he replied.

I dialed JR Bluntschli. "Mx. Bluntschli?" I said, when zey picked up the phone. "It's Fab Acer from the Department of Law Enforcement."

"Ah."

"Nothing is wrong, I mean, don't worry. Do you have time to talk? And your little friend?"

"Tell her yes," I heard in the background.

"Chester says we're here," JR replied.

A few minutes later, I was on my way to JR and Chester's house in Takoma Park.

CHAPTER 14

CURIOUSER AND...

"There's news, highly sensitive at this point, sort of getting out, in the less reputable parts of the Internet," I was seated on JR's couch. Zey sat across from me in a Craftsman-style chair. Sturdy wood slats and a colorful geometric fabric on the cushions. Chester was rubbing against my ankles, purring. "Is it okay to pet him?" I asked.

"Chester, is it okay if she pets you?" zey asked him, with a hint of a smile.

"I guess I could have asked, couldn't I?"

"Yes, and yes," Chester said, hopping onto my lap, where he circled, dancing around for half a minute, and settled facing away from me toward JR. I stroked his head. Petting a sentient and articulate cat felt slightly more intimate than absolutely appropriate, but I went with it. He purred. If he'd curled up in my lap, I'm not sure I'd have been comfortable with that. After a minute, he said, "I could let you do this for hours, but you wanted to talk about something." He hopped off my lap, onto the coffee table, and faced me. JR leaned forward and chucked him under the chin. I swallowed.

"As I was saying, this is nearly out in the public already, more politically sensitive than law enforcement sensitive. I feel I can trust you not to reveal anything prematurely. And I hope I've shown you can trust me to keep your secret, too."

"I hope so," JR said. "More tea?"

"Yes, thanks. And I want to assure you, I want to keep both of you safe, and private. Am I clear?"

"Yes, but I still don't have much choice, do I?"

"I'm about to tell you something that is still confidential. So you have a secret of mine to keep, which makes us even. Like we both have hostages."

"I guess."

"After we left here this morning, something unusual happened, and I'm wondering if you can help me. I don't suspect you of being involved."

Was that true? I went with my gut, and told myself, yes.

"JR...may I call you that?"

"That's what I ask people to call me, as I told you. So yeah, that's fine," zey replied.

"Please call me Fab," I said. "Something has happened, a magical incident." Her eyes widened. Chester's expression did not change. "And as someone who lives with a magical cat, I thought of you. Well, for that matter, Chester, maybe your perspective can help. Even if you don't know anything. Or maybe you do?"

Chester was staring at me, smiling. I feared he would disappear again. He blinked slowly. I had learned from watching *The Devil Cat Whisperer* that a slow blink was a sign of calm and trust between cats, so I blinked slowly at him.

"I felt something," Chester said. "Something happening. I felt it three times, at least. Although I was napping part of the day, so I might have missed something. We can trust her, JR."

"Thank you. Here's what happened today." I recounted to them the un-transformation, escape, re-transformation, and recapture of EO Serial Number 357.

"There are details I still can't discuss, yet," I continued, deciding not to reveal that EO 357 was Fenric DeLuxe.

"Goddess! That's a game changer," JR said. "I'm glad you caught him. Sounds like the spell repaired itself. Or someone did it."

"Yes. Do you know how that works? I mean, do you know anything about spells?"

"Ah. I see. You want to know if I ever have actually done magic. Because I'm a witch, is that it?"

"Well." I gestured at Chester. "I know you aren't responsible for Chester's magical abilities. However, do you know if, in theory, spells can come unraveled and then need to be repaired?"

"Spell-casting, in my experience, never had such overt, tangible effects. She works in mysterious ways, and, frankly, all the magic I've done has been about intention setting and inter-pretation of subtle nuances. Vibrations, emanations. There's no Hogwarts, you know. No secret society of special effects wizards and witches." Zey smiled and pouted at the same time. That was cute!

"Oh, believe me, I was disappointed too, when I turned eleven and didn't get an owl," I said. "And I know some things about earth-based religions."

Zey laughed, and continued, "As much as I want to believe in magic, if it were that easy and obvious, DeLuxe would never have been elected. I still have a poppet of him in my freezer, bound in blood-blessèd red string. Obviously, that didn't work to keep him from becoming president. Thank the Goddess for my little covenette, or I'd have gone off the rails after the election."

"And then it all changed on 2/29," I said. "I know how you feel. All the time he was president, it didn't feel safe." I got a chill on my shoulders. Had I ever told anyone that out loud? Maybe my mother.

"As far as I'm concerned, 2/29 was a cause to rejoice," JR said. "I hope they never catch who did it. I mean, I hope *you* never catch them."

"Not me, personally, in any case. The NBI most likely, or

LNM. Ironic the LNM would be searching for someone who made guns and bombs no longer a public safety threat. My job, though, is about gathering and analyzing and publishing information. Sharing with the public, ultimately. It's not normal for me to get involved in investigations, or to be keeping secrets. Since we're off the record, know that I agree with you. It felt like, I don't know, like 2/29 was a magical cure for an illness we were suffering."

"Exactly! DeLuxe was like an opportunistic infection, in our immune-compromised system. Hashtag DeLuxeVirus was trending in the early days of the pandemic."

"Good analogy."

"Let me get this straight: this disenchantment, it's almost like a relapse. Maybe the infectious agent is building an immunity. Finding ways around the cure, like antibiotic-resistant bacteria. Or a mutating coronavirus."

"I hadn't thought of it that way!" Zey was good.

"I don't know what you're talking about," Chester said. He stood and stretched, arching his spine, then hopped off the coffee table. "I can tell you something strummed the strings." On the floor near the table, he pounced on a toy stuffed mouse, rolled over onto his side, and held it in his front paws and teeth, while he raked it with his back claws.

"Strings?"

He paused from torturing the toy mouse, and replied, "All the magic things, we're connected. Little invisible strings, like a bunch of balls of yarn. I could feel tugging, different from usual. It's been pretty boring since I showed up. Today it got interesting."

"Do you remember 2/29?" I asked.

"*I* do," JR said. "He was a normal cat before. Right after the Enchantment he started smiling, fading in and out, turning pink and purple, and conversing."

"And before?"

"Before, I was just me." Chester let the mouse drop from his paws. "After, I could do a lot of things I couldn't before. It doesn't feel much different to me. Mainly you all can finally understand me when I talk to you." Chester ambled away, then hopped onto his cat tree. "And when I think I can hide, you can't see me." He became translucent, then disappeared, except for his smile, which had those disconcertingly human teeth. "Plus, I feel the magic strings."

It sounded like he was describing the ley lines we had theorized. "Tell me more about the strings, please, Chester. What did you feel this morning?"

He re-materialized, fading from invisible to transparent to translucent, and finally opaque around his smile. "Something came loose, where it was tight before. Then later, it got tight again."

"Does the string have a direction?"

"It was loose that way," he said, hopping off the cat tree and walking toward us. He flicked a prehensile tail, longer than a normal cat's, pointing toward the STIF. "And then it tightened that way." The tail flicked toward downtown and Grand Zero.

"That all makes sense," I said. "You don't have any idea why or how it happened?"

He hopped onto the couch next to me, and I scratched him under his chin, which he pressed toward me like any non-talking cat would.

"Not really," he said. "Humans are like that, I find. Doing and undoing things. Changing things. It keeps me from being bored, and I appreciate it. Right, JR?"

"That's right, Chester. It's all about keeping you amused." Zey smiled at him, then looked at me and shrugged. "The cat-centric view of the universe is as good as any other perspective. Maybe if they were in charge, we'd do a better job of things."

"So true," I said, laughing.

We sat, not speaking, and the only sound was Chester's loud purring as I rubbed the spot above his nose, between his eyes. JR was smiling at me. I smiled back.

"JR, do you have any insights? Anything at all?"

"Well, if I were whoever cast the spell, and someone or something started to undo part of it, I'd be working nonstop to fix it." Zey leaned forward to me, and put out zeir hands palm up, over the coffee table. I stopped petting Chester, and placed my hands in zeirs.

"And if I were able to keep that person safe to be able to maintain the Enchantment," zey continued, staring into my eyes, "I'd do all in my power to help." We gazed into each other's eyes for a moment, and I nodded, and let go of zeir hands. I agreed with zem. Even if it meant I had to keep, what did Lonny call it? Navigating between people of authority. And continuing to be less than 100% transparent all the time. Ugh.

And now I had to talk with Griffin.

CHAPTER 15

CRACKS

By the time I returned to the office, it was 6:30 PM, and most people had gone home. Griffin wasn't at his desk and didn't respond when I knocked on his server room door. Had he gone home, too, finally? I logged onto my computer, and Scrye showed him with a green "Available" dot next to his name, so he was online. He could have been at home, and teleworking, but I suspected he was in the server room, ignoring me.

I was about to lock my computer screen. Before I did, on impulse I opened the DarkBart News site again. I'm not sure what made me do it. Sure enough, there was a new "Breaking News" item. Its headline said: "More Cracks in Enchantment." Uh-oh. The story was only a couple of paragraphs, a blind item, I think they call it, recounting unattributed rumors that an EO had or would shortly be changing, and berating DLE's Public Affairs Office for stonewalling, which was to be expected from "Constitutionalist-infiltrated Deep State operatives." There was a hint that this "restoration," as they put it, would "cast the light of a new dawn upon the Deep State cover-ups" that DMV perpetrated.

Hmm. My first reaction was to be insulted that they thought

we were covering up things. Even though I *was* actively covering things up. That said, I was relieved that they were promoting something false, this time: there had not been another disenchantment. Then I thought, *That's oddly poetic, "casting the light of a new dawn."* Not their usual rhetoric. That worried me.

I logged on to the MOFTS database. Dawn. Was that a Disney character? Then it struck me: "Aurora" originally meant "dawn," and Princess Aurora was Sleeping Beauty. The one whose castle was in California, not Florida.

A quick search of EOs, and I saw we had three items in custody related to Princess Aurora: a Christmas tree ornament shaped like her; one child's princess costume shoe, left foot; and a water bottle with the princess on it. All three were Transformed Persons. My gut twinged. I checked the STIF security system and surveillance cameras. EOs 29, 157, and 223, were in the STIF, and just the same as they had been when taken into custody. Environmental monitor data showed no changes. Whew, that was a relief.

Then, not as strongly as before, I had a weird feeling, and the lights dimmed a bit, and did I hear a faint tinkling? Oh no! Was that another wave of magic, or had I imagined it? And, did nobody else notice these? I tried refreshing the environmental data. My browser went into a spinning non-response. I navigated to our closed-circuit camera feed. The images were locked. This was not good. Griffin still showed online, so I hurried to his server room hidey-hole.

The department had migrated almost all its computing to one of three data centers. In a complete reversal, Eliot and the Chief Information Officer's staff had agreed to a local server farm in our building, which became Griffin's hangout. Maybe there was a technical reason. Whatever the reason, this was Griffin's baby, and I knew why he liked to hang out with the servers.

"They're more predictable than people," he once told me. As someone who had trouble reading people's expressions and filtering out external stimuli, he needed the time there to replenish his energy, was my diagnosis.

"Griffin, are you in there?" I said, knocking on the door to the server room. "Seriously, it's time we talk. I have more information you need to know."

I put my ear to the door. Like before, all I could hear was the whooshing of the enhanced air conditioning.

"Please. I think something's going on." I hoped he wasn't gone for the day.

The door latch clicked, and I stepped away from the door as it swung out. Griffin looked at the floor.

"I'm here," he said.

"May I come in?" He motioned me in. I would confront him where he felt safe. The door swung closed behind me.

"Brrr. Don't you get cold?"

"I have my vest." He was wearing a quilted down vest. "And my cap." A woven skullcap.

I looked around the room. Even though I wasn't that interested in hardware, it was impressive. Three walls were covered with racks of servers, which looked to me like old-fashioned stereo equipment, with more blinking LEDs.

"Thanks for letting me into your lair." This was the first time he'd let me in. There was a chair and a small table with a laptop computer on it, and a dozen of his origami figures next on the table next to it. "What's that?" Hanging from the ceiling in the middle of the room was a cylindrical assemblage of copper piping, fiber optics, Lucite, and electronics. I had only gotten glimpses of the room before and hadn't noticed this. How could I have missed it? I was reminded of the mother ship in that old movie about aliens my mom wanted me to watch with her. Colored lights and mysterious potential.

"That's Yotta," Griffin replied.

"It's beautiful, whatever it is."

"She's a quantum supercomputer. I do most of my hard work on her."

"Ah, no wonder you needed this space."

"Most of MOFTS in Dev and UAT runs on these servers. We push the data to the Sterling Data Center for the outward-facing dataset. I do my analytics on Yotta."

"Uh-huh." In other words, this was his private data center, and only after he'd reviewed things did he make them available to the public. I guess there was a technical reason for it after all. "Well, she's beautiful, like that spaceship—"

"In *Close Encounters*, I know!"

"Griffin, we need to talk. Why don't you sit down?" He was still not looking at me, and I thought if he sat near his origami and his laptop, maybe he'd be easier to deal with. He sat, and, to his credit, looked in the general direction of my face, left of my left eye. Close enough. "Did you just notice a brownout? The lights dimming?"

"No."

"I did, and I have noticed it when the stormtrooper escaped, and when he got transformed into an EO, and again when, you, I assume, fixed his helmet. I can't refresh the environmental data feed at the STIF." He blinked when I said that. "Plus, dark-bart.com said something else is coming disenchanted." His mouth twitched when I said that. "What do you want to tell me about all this?" He continued to stare left of my left eye.

"You want to know about how EO 357 escaped. I can't tell you why or how."

Watching Griffin's expression carefully, I said, "I know how he escaped. He had a gun. That worked! What is that about? I also want to know how he got transformed back from Fenric DeLuxe to a stormtrooper figurine. You did that." After a couple of seconds, he nodded. "And you tried to make me forget about it, didn't you?" He looked at the floor. "Griffin, remember I'm your friend." He nodded, still looking at the floor. "And did something else just happen? Griffin, I know you're not telling me everything, and I think it's time. You trust me, don't you?"

"Yes, I do. I do. But I can't. It's not safe yet."

"Safe? If something's not safe, shouldn't we all know about it? Me, Lonny, Eliot, Agent Oberst?"

"No! I have it under control."

"Griffin, look at me." I bent in front of him, placing my face near his line of sight. "May I hold your hands?"

"Okay."

I grasped his hands in mine and looked into his face. He maintained the gaze.

"Are you the person who worked the Enchantment?" I didn't want to call him Sorcerer X to his face.

He looked at me, right into my eyes. Tears began to well up in his eyes.

"It's OK if you are. It's me. I won't tell anyone."

My cell phone rang.

"Lonny, hi. I'm in the middle of something."

"We're all in the middle of it, now. Anomaly at the STIF. EO 223 showing weird activity."

"What kind of activity?"

Griffin's expression changed, his brow furrowing. I put the phone on speaker.

"EO 223, it's a water bottle. It's grown to the size of a person," Lonny said. "According to Leslie. She called me when the alarm went off."

"Griffin's checking the system now," I said. EO 223! My heart fluttered. I was just looking at EO 223's database entry. With the stormtrooper, a DarkBart-related rumor had preceded a disenchantment. Did they have inside knowledge? Or worse, were they, whoever "they" were, performing the disenchantments? And what about Bart Barukka? He seemed to have escaped being enchanted initially. Was he involved now? Was he Sorcerer Y?

Griffin had accessed the video feed for EO 223's cabinet, H.7.5. The cameras weren't locked for *him*. Sure enough, the water bottle was the size of a person. He fast-reversed the video, and at one moment (in reverse) it shrank to its normal 10-inch height. Griffin slowed the video, and we watched it happen. The time code said it was five minutes ago.

"It happened at 6:43 and twenty-five seconds," Griffin said.

"I'm going in. No person, though?" Lonny asked.

"Right, it shouldn't be. Only a large bottle," Griffin replied.

Shouldn't be? Griffin knew entirely too much about this.

"Do you need me there, Lonny?" I asked.

"Not for now. I'll let you know."

"Keep us posted," I said, and I hung up. Griffin was furiously typing, and his screen was filled with complex computer programming language code.

"Griffin, I—"

"I need to do this now!"

"But—"

"It's important. We can talk later. If you care about keeping things safe—you do, don't you?"

"Of course I do. Okay, we can continue talking later. But it's time, don't you think? To let me in on this?"

He continued to stare at his screen, and to type rapidly. Without looking up, he replied, "Yes, okay. I'll tell you everything. I need to focus here now."

I sighed. I was dealing with an immeasurably powerful, and upset, magician. I wanted to trust him to do the right thing. "I'll be in my office."

"No, go home. I'll be here a while." He stopped keying, and his head turned in my direction. Slowly, he raised his eyes and looked into mine. "I promise I'll tell you everything tomorrow."

"Okay. Thank you. I could use some rest." I wasn't going to get anything out of him tonight. I was exhausted and all I'd consumed since breakfast was coffee. Lonny was on the STIF incident, and so far there was no breakout. Lonny would call me if it happened again.

I got home and popped a dinner in the microwave. Turned on a baking show while I ate. I found that calming. I called Lonny.

"No movement," he told me. "The TP is still stiff in the STIF."

I laughed. "Lonny!"

"We're on Yellow Alert. I'm heading home for the night. Second and third shifts can reach out if there's an issue. Leadership and the Bureau are aware."

"Yes, go home, Lonny. It's been a long day. I'm looking forward to some sleep." I finished dinner and a couple of episodes and went to bed. I was exhausted, fell right asleep, then at about 3:00 AM I woke and couldn't go back to sleep. I popped open my laptop, and Griffin still showed online. I finally fell asleep about 4:00 and woke again at 6:00. Griffin had sent me an email at 5:37 saying everything was "back to normal," and the red dot on Scrye showed he was finally offline. That meant the Princess Aurora bottle had been restored to its normal size. And he had done that.

Griffin was Sorceror X.

CHAPTER 16

WHAT HAPPENED

MARCH 2, 2022

"Fab, I need you to meet me at Main Law Enforcement. We have to brief Antonia and Hannah." This was Eliot's phone call at 7:30 as I was stepping out of the shower. We were to meet them at 9:00 sharp, he said. Scrye showed Griffin still offline. I suspected sometimes he logged off Scrye to look offline but was still at work in his secret data center. In any case, our conversation would have to wait.

The Robert F. Kennedy Main Law Enforcement Building is right off the Mall, and only two blocks from the Disney DC Deluxe Resort. I sat in the waiting room outside Hannah's office. Eliot, a little baggy-eyed but otherwise neatly groomed, was in Toni's office. Antonia della Femina, was our Deputy Assistant Attorney General for Analysis, Strategy, and Policy, and Eliot's immediate supervisor. Her office door opened to the waiting area, and peeking in, I saw she and Eliot having a quiet discussion. I stood at the door and waved. Eliot motioned me in, signaling to close the door behind me.

"Hi, Toni," I said, sitting in on her couch next to Eliot. She sat at a cushy chair across a coffee table from us. She liked to be informal.

"Good morning! Looks like you had a busy day yesterday,"

she said, smiling. She sipped from a gigantic coffee cup. Her assistant brought her one every morning.

"I asked you here mainly so you could listen," Eliot told me. "But if you have anything to add when we meet with Hannah, please do. I put together a talker for Toni to walk through the details." He handed me a sheet of paper with the talking points on it. "If Hannah wants more, chime in."

"You know how Hannah can drag us into the weeds sometimes," Toni said, and she winked at me.

"Sounds good." I scanned the one-pager while Toni re-read her copy. It recapped the escape and recapture of the stormtrooper, and the disenchantment and re-enchantment (Eliot's phrase) of the Princess Aurora water bottle. He must have *just* finished this. It also outlined the social media mentions. To my relief it did not state that they happened *before* the incidents themselves. I had not had a chance to discuss that with him, and I still didn't know what Griffin knew about it. Better not to mention it. Eliot's talking points gave three possible root cause scenarios. Option 1: that the Enchantment was passively unraveling and that Sorcerer X had repaired it. Option 2: Sorcerer X was deliberately disenchanting and re-enchanting for unknown motivations. Option 3: an unknown other party, Sorcerer Y in Eliot's nomenclature, was trying to undo the 2/29 Enchantment, but was being countered by Sorcerer X. Not bad. Those were about the same scenarios I'd come up with. I was sure Griffin was Sorcerer X. I was leaning toward option 3, and suspected Bart Barukka might be Sorcerer Y. Obviously, I couldn't let on to Eliot and Toni how much I knew that was leading me to that, until I'd talked with Griffin. Maybe not even then.

The talking points went on to outline risks, such as the risk of further violence by escapees, the risk of public panic if there was a perception DMV's security wasn't strong enough. And some risk mitigation strategies, including increased security staff at the

STIF, and further analysis of data by the DMV data analytics team, i.e., me and Griffin. I couldn't argue with that.

"Looks good to me, Eliot," I said. "One thing, I'm not sure. Don't we have a risk in our register that further enchantments may take place? Do we need to reference that, meaning we need to be on the alert for further enchantments?"

"Good point," Eliot said. "What do you think, Toni?"

"I think we can tell Hannah we considered it, and we didn't think it was likely, and impact could be fifty/fifty good or bad. Given that the Enchantment effectively mitigated the chaos of the previous president's administration, and given that this administration is functioning well." She punctuated the last with raised eyebrows.

"That's fair," Eliot replied. "Thanks for bringing it up, Fab." I nodded in reply. Toni and Hannah were political appointees, and I suspected Toni and Hannah were among those who privately considered 2/29 a good thing. The fact that only extreme conservatives, populists, nationalists, and fascists had been enchanted on 2/29 had been a sign to some people that Enchantment was reserved for that population. That Sorcerer X had set things right, and we had nothing to fear from him or her. I was beginning to worry that this was complacent. I didn't suspect Griffin of evil motivations, but how could I be sure?

Hannah's assistant knocked, then opened the door. "She's ready to see you all," he said. He was a clean-cut young man named Jonathan. "In the conference room." The room was down the hall, at the corner of the building. Pictures of the president and the attorney general hung on the wall, and all the furniture was dark brown and masculine.

Agent Oberst was already there, seated at the table, his back to the windows, frowning. Next to him was a woman I didn't recognize. She had beautiful, angular cheekbones and an upright, cool, and controlled demeanor. Her tight, curly hair was clipped short, which set off the almost sculptural dignity of her face., while there was something impish about the set of her mouth and eyes. I assumed this was Agent Oberst's boss, whom I'd heard about, the Acting Deputy Assistant Attorney General, Enforcement and Operations, Special Agent Kayla Malone. She was on detail from the NBI, like Agent Oberst. Toni, Eliot, and I took places at the conference table, and Hannah sat at the head of the table. She had a copy of Eliot's talking points in front of her. Eliot handed copies to Agent Oberst and the presumed Ms. Malone.

"Do you want to scan it and ask us any questions?" Toni suggested. Hannah nodded, put on a pair of reading glasses, and read the document. Oberst and Agent Malone also read. She finished first, looked up at me, and smiled. I smiled back.

"It's pretty clear," Hannah said. "I notice you don't address the leaks."

"If they are leaks," Eliot said. "But no, I haven't had a chance to coordinate with Jake. That's more an O-E-O-E bailiwick, I thought." He carefully pronounced the letters in OEOE, so as not to say "Oi-Oi" to Agent Oberst's face. "What do you think, Jake?"

Oberst gestured to the woman beside him. "I defer to Acting DAAG Malone here." Maybe that was why he was grim. This was his new boss, and the position had been vacant a year. We all believed Oberst wanted the job. Clearly, he wasn't getting it at this point.

Ms. Malone smiled and said, "Thanks, Jake. I think you and I agree OEOE would need to get on this. Hannah, we'll work with Eliot to update this so you can brief the Deputy on what we're doing to find out who may be leaking. Eliot, you think there may not be a leak?"

"Well, we don't know if it's a leak or part of the Enchantment, do we? If people's memories could be wiped or manipulated, then maybe information could be spread by the perpetrator, Sorcerer X or Sorcerer Y or whoever."

"Good point," Hannah said. "Sounds like OEOE and OQA need to work closely on figuring out what's happening. I like the emphasis on analytics." She nodded at me and smiled. "By the way, Ms. Acer, Agent Oberst tells me you've been doing field-work with one of his team, Agent Dotch."

She knew who I was. "Yes, we were in the field when we got the call to meet Mrs. DeLuxe at the STIF. Right before the break-out. Is that what you mean?"

"You were at Ground Zero when the EO showed up there, isn't that right?" This came from Oberst, who continued to frown. "And you and your data scientist came up with that map."

"Yes, the map. Great work, Fab!" said Toni. "I shared that with Hannah this morning. I'll send you the link too, Kayla. Assuming your account's established."

"It was a group effort, honestly. Griffin is great," I said.

"That's Griffin, our data scientist. Talented young man," Eliot said. "He and Fab are dynamite together."

"And Eliot noticed the mapping with the Magic Kingdom," I said.

"What can I say? I put things together like that," Eliot said. "Thousands of dollars to Disney for park tickets finally pay off!"

"What was it like when you encountered the escaped EO, Ms. Acer?" asked Oberst. "You and Agent Dotch were in the right place at the right time. And then it re-transformed. Yet you don't remember what happened?"

"Uh, that's right. Well, we had a hunch, based on the Magic Kingdom maps, that there might be a magical portal from where it disappeared, leading to Ground Zero."

Hannah, who had not said anything so far, took off her reading glasses. I was aware everyone was looking at me intently.

"We bumped into him, and then the rest is a blank." After I said this, there were about fifteen seconds of excruciating silence. I looked around me and couldn't decide what they were think-ing. I thought, *Should I say more?* "That's all I recall." I wondered how well the NBI trained people to tell if someone was lying. Or obfuscating. I shuddered.

"Hmm," Oberst said. "That's odd. Perhaps, Ms. Acer, you can explain this." He put his mobile phone onto the table, and I heard my voice and Griffin's voice coming from its speaker.

Me: "Griffin, what's going on here?"

Griffin: "Don't panic."

Me: "Griffin, Lonny and this poor Cast Member are still frozen. Did you do this?"

Griffin: "Don't be alarmed. It will be OK. Fab, do you trust me?"

Me: "Of course I trust you. Why shouldn't I? What do you know about this?"

Griffin: "Please, please, please do what I say, and everything will be all right."

Me: "Griffin, you seem to know more than you are sharing, and I'm not happy about this. I see I don't have much of a choice."

Oberst touched his phone to stop the audio.

"Should I continue it?" he asked. "There's more of the same. Don't you have anything else to tell us, Ms. Acer?" One hand hovered above his phone. His other hand was under the table. Was he aiming a gun at me? Even if it was a taser or rubber bullet gun, that gave me pause.

Then everyone was suddenly talking at once.

"Fab, is this true?!" Eliot asked, and at the same time, Toni asked, "What just happened?" and Hannah asked, "Where did you get that?" and I wanted to sink into the earth.

"Let her speak," Agent Malone said, loudly and clearly. Agent Oberst remained motionless as his eyes drilled through me.

It all came spilling out of me. "I, uh, I...I was going to tell when I knew more. It's Griffin, you have to know him. He wouldn't hurt anyone! I needed to know what was happening to decide what to do. I was up all night, worrying about it. Things were unraveling, and he needed time to fix them, I think. So I let him, and he hasn't told me yet, but…oh, I'm sorry, I'm sorry. I think…I think Griffin may be Sorcerer X, and Eliot, I'm afraid your third scenario is what is happening. I think Bart Barukka is Sorcerer Y, and he's behind the DarkBart and Chirpa leaks." My eyes started to well with tears. I looked around the table.

Toni and Hannah were wide eyed, and Eliot's mouth hung open. Oberst's eyes narrowed, and his mouth curled up at the edges. He was thrilled to have caught me in a lie, and probably thought I was Sorcerer Z or a co-conspirator!

"Yes," DAAG Malone said, but not to me. Her hand was at her ear, and she was talking into an earpiece microphone. "Yes, I think so." Unlike everyone else, she did not look surprised.

Once again, the lights flickered, and a sound that wasn't a sound, that felt like a wave of in an ocean of glitter, crashing, tinkling, washing over me. And the lights returned to normal, and only DAAG Malone and I were in the room. Everyone else was gone!

No, I was wrong. I looked at the chair next to me, where Eliot had been sitting, and on it there was a small plush toy figure of a skinny purple man with glasses. Next to him, in Toni's chair, was a green girl, also plush. I stumbled to my feet and went to Hannah's chair. There was a plush toy of a blue girl with glasses, and in Oberst's chair, a plush toy of a square, red little man. I remembered a number of years ago, there was a movie about a teenage girl's emotions, and these were dolls representing them. More Disney merchandise! Oberst, Hannah, Toni, and Eliot were now EOs! DAAG Malone and I were untouched.

"Don't worry, they'll be all right," DAAG Malone said. She had a calm expression, and an even tone of voice.

"What happened? How? No, I know how. Why?"

"I think you need to go see Griffin now, Ms. Acer. I can't get much more involved. I'll make sure they're taken care of. Yes, Griffin did this. We decided it was best."

"You—you and Griffin? You know? You're in cahoots with him?"

"Fab, come here and sit by me. On the other side, of course, not on Agent Oberst." She patted the empty chair next to her.

I stood there like a stunned cow for a moment, then decided I had better sit. She took my hand in both of hers, and leaned toward me.

"It's a lot to absorb, I know, and as I said, I can't get much more involved. It's best that you speak to Griffin. He's listening in. I'm sorry, I didn't realize Oberst would have access to that recording." She reached for her earpiece and sat up. "Yes? Yes, I'll tell her. He says he thinks he knows what's happening. Griffin does." She took my hands again. "We're not out of the woods yet. If you trust Griffin, you are right to. Go to him and let him tell you his side of the story. I'll cover for us here."

"I, uh. Okay, okay. Yes! I'll trust Griffin. And I'll go to him now. You're sure you can handle this? You're not sending them to the STIF, are you?"

"Oh, no. This is temporary."

"Poor Eliot. I feel awful for him."

"They don't feel a thing. I'm pretty sure." She smiled again. "Now go."

"Yes, I will." I stood and walked toward the door, and she followed me. I stopped and turned, and asked, "Who are you? I mean, what? I mean…"

"That is a *long* story for another time, Fab. Suffice it to say that I'm a friend," she said. "Let's go out together this way."

She opened a connecting door to Hannah's office. We walked through, closing the door behind us, into the reception area, where Hanna's assistant, Jonathan, sat at his desk.

"Thanks, Fab, keep me posted," she said, for Jonathan's benefit. "Jonathan, Hannah said to tell you we aren't to be disturbed. Take care, Fab. We'll talk in a bit." She waved at me, and I nodded.

"Yes, ma'am," Jonathan replied. Ms. Malone turned, reentered Hannah's office, and closed the door behind her. I heard the lock click into place.

And I grabbed a rideshare to our office building and headed straight for Griffin's hideaway server room.

I knocked once, and Griffin opened the door.

"I've been expecting you," he said, looking at the floor. He closed the door behind me, gestured to a chair he had brought in, and sat in his own.

"Of course you have! You heard the whole thing, didn't you? My confession, and... What did you do? Eliot? Really? He's one of your biggest boosters!"

"I couldn't help it. We were about to be exposed. I can fix it, but I needed to do something temporarily."

"And who is this Kayla Malone person and why are you and she in cahoots?"

"She's from the NBI. She's Acting Deputy Assistant Attorney General."

"I know that! I mean who is she to you? Why does she know, well, more than I do, obviously? No, never mind. Tell me everything else. Are you Sorcerer X? And how did you do it? And what's happening now?" I had brought a copy of Eliot's talking points, and I thrust the sheet of paper into his field of vision. "Which of these is right? Is the spell unraveling, or is someone else doing that?"

"I'm sorry, I really am. I'll tell you everything now." He looked up and into my eyes. "I need to do one thing first, though."

"Okay. As long as it's not doing something to me."

He swiveled his chair to his laptop. "I have the code compiled and ready to execute," he said. I saw him click a button, and a second later, the lights dimmed, and I heard a sound like a tiny bell that came from all around me, not from his computer. He swiveled around and looked into my face. I dropped the paper onto the floor. I couldn't breathe.

"You're...I recognize you now!" I gasped.

"Yes, you should."

"You're Griffin DeLuxe, the president's son!"

"Yes."

"And you're...just a kid!" How had I not noticed it before? This was clearly the Griffin I had known all along, but now I realized how young he truly seemed. He looked the same: gentle blue eyes, sandy blond-brown hair, and, I now realized, the face of a teenager.

"I'm twenty now," he replied. "I just look younger." I later verified, he had indeed turned eighteen right before February 29, 2020. Although he was taller than his father, he still looked years younger than that.

"You cast a spell, and you used your computer to do it, to make us not notice who you were?"

"Yes, that's right. My quantum computer—Yotta—is how I cast the Enchantment. I couldn't have done the math on my own. And I keep having to make upgrades to the program. To the spell."

My mouth was hanging open. "You transformed your own father, and half-siblings, into Disney merchandise. And altered the entire world so nobody can shoot or blow people up. I'm dumbfounded. I mean, not that your family didn't deserve it, I guess. Please start at the beginning."

"I was there, at the conference. I didn't want to be, but Dad wanted me there to see him 'make history,' he said. Mom wasn't there, but it was okay, I hadn't had to spend much time with him recently, and it's easier to go along with what he wants. He was more focused on Kalihnkha, as usual, anyway."

The president's interest in his daughter was well known. I searched my memory. Griffin's mother, Urania, the third Mrs. DeLuxe, was at DeLuxe Tower in Manhattan at the time of 2/29. His ex-wife, Kalihnha DeLuxe was at her co-op on the Upper

West Side. Her three children, Kalihnkha, Fenric, and Dirk, Jr., had all been sighted at the AFPAP convention and were presumed transformed. I could vouch that Fenric had been transformed, of course. And had been planning to shoot his father, if I could believe his confused babbling. Why hadn't anyone noticed Griffin there, and noticed that he'd escaped? Part of the Enchantment, I assumed.

"Hold on, Griffin. In addition to the physical transformations, you've altered people's memories and ongoing perceptions so that people don't remember you being at AFPAP. Or remember you at all?"

"Something like that. More like, people just don't notice, or think about me. Except you and the people here at work, and you all just didn't connect who I was. You're essentially right. That's good deductive reasoning." Why did I feel like he was encouraging a toddler to take its first steps?

"Okay, so you were in the audience," I continued.

"Yes, and I had access to the quantum computer our family company had installed in the hotel. It's in the clock tower overlooking the atrium. If you remember where the chandelier is, it's over that and to the side."

"That chandelier? I saw it change when Fenric turned back into a stormtrooper figurine. I mean, when you transformed him."

"That makes sense. The chandelier didn't exist until I set up the Enchantment. The spell. changes it whenever I change my code. People think it was installed already, before the Enchantment Event. It wasn't. I created it during my extended time there, gradually getting larger, the more people I transformed. Even thought it looks like a chandelier, in actuality, it's an extrusion into 3D space of an M-space equation."

"I have no idea what that means, but go on."

"The quantum computer allowed for multiple dimensional calculations, which have an impact on our physical reality. And somehow, when the Fenric was about to shoot everyone, or shoot Dad, it came to me what I could do, should do, so I—"

"Hold on! Fenric *was* about to shoot the president? I wasn't sure I could believe him."

"Yes, he was dressed up as a stormtrooper. But his laser blaster was a semi-automatic gun. And he had grenades too."

"Why would Fenric assassinate his father? He was part of the inner circle, wasn't he? Don't take it personally, but when the term 'DeLuxe Crime Family' was bandied about, he was part of it. Not you! Just the first three kids." I didn't want to offend him and get transformed. "Was he trying to take over? How did he avoid the Confidential Service detail?"

"I don't know! I don't know any of those answers! I only know what I did. Fenric came onstage and started shooting. Dad was grazed, others were hit too. There was so much blood. I couldn't take it! And somehow I knew all of a sudden if I executed the program I had been working on, I could stop things. Stop time, for a while. I don't know how I knew, but I did."

"You stopped time for everyone else like you did when you re-enchanted Fenric."

"Yes, like that. I didn't mean to transform everyone. That came later."

"Keep going."

"I ran my program, and it stopped time for everyone but me. Or sped me up, is more accurate. It was bad. Dad was shot, Kalihnkha was covered in blood, holding him. Fenric was poised with a hand grenade in his hand, the ring pulled, ready to throw it into the crowd. Once I had frozen everything, I couldn't just unstop time, I needed to do something. It took me a while. Eventually I figured out I could transform everyone."

"Griffin. Disney merchandise?"

"I've always been a collector. I like the souvenirs more than the parks. There's too much going on there, too many sounds and sights. You know I get overloaded."

"Yes, I'm aware."

"I like to collect complete sets of things. It feels warm and nice when I have them all organized. Not out of control.

"I had compiled a database of items that I'd downloaded from Disney's web services. It was already on my computer. I used to enjoy running three dimensional mappings of merchandise, to put them into an origami folding program that I found on my computer, on Yotta." He patted his computer. "She had enough computing power to do it, to figure out how you could fold paper to make a facsimile of the object."

"How did that turn into a computer program to stop time, though? What's that got to do with it all?"

"Oh, yes, well, it was all related. I wanted to see the progression of Disney merchandise through the years, so I had compiled snapshots of the database at different eras, and I was able to roll back time, move it forward, whatever I wanted to do. And I could rotate time, model different possible branches of possibility. It was a prototype for a way for me to process everything around me. You know I get overwhelmed. I needed help, so I used Yotta."

I was following only some of this. "You were building a program to replicate reality, or project alternate timelines, so you prototyped it with Disney images? I think that's what I'm hearing."

"Yes. That's good that you understand that. I didn't realize until later, when you're using this kind of quantum computing, *belief* in a different reality is effectively the same as a different reality existing. Or coming into existence. Modeling the folding of time and space, using my rewrite of the origami program and my Disney database. It turned out it reconfigured reality at a quantum level. It worked best if there was some distortion of consensual reality, a distortion or weakening in the fabric of reality. Then the program re-weaves, refolds things, and it comes out looking like magic."

He paused.

I said, slowly, "Multi-dimensional math, plus quantum computer modeling, plus, I don't know, belief in Deluxism, equals magic?"

"It turns out, yes."

"Okay, let me ask you: Is there something like Hogwarts? A secret conspiracy of magicians?"

"No, not that I know of. There's only me and whoever disenchanted Fenric."

"Aha! Okay, so that's what's happening. The Sorcerer Y theory!"

"That's why I've been working so hard, trying to figure out how he's doing it. Or she."

"I'm pretty sure it's a he. Keep going." I *did* have information he didn't have. Good! Let him be in the dark for a while.

"It took me, well, it felt like weeks to me. For everyone else it was microseconds. Luckily there was a lot of food there in the hotel, and it didn't spoil. When I touched something, it sped up with me. And I could get water to run, and I could breathe air, of course. I had a local field around me that moved at the same rate I did. And my connection to the computer was at full speed. I'm not sure how I knew to do that. Good thing I kept that subroutine, so we could freeze everyone while I took care of Fenric yesterday."

"Huh."

"But it didn't occur to me at first that I should transform people. Not at first. I had stopped time, and didn't know what to do after that. I spent a lot of time distracting myself on expanding the origami program, mainly to see if I could change the hand grenade into something harmless. But a couple of times, I guess I was *too* distracted. I'd try to launch the origami program, and Yotta would pop up the roster from the convention, and pop up the Disney database. Maybe she was responding to my subconscious, or something. But realized if I combined the origami program, the Disney database, and the roster...it might solve a lot of problems."

I'd often wondered what kind of mind would come up with the 2/29 Enchantment Event. Now I knew. Griffin's. Well, Griffin's and his pet computer's, if you counted her as a mind.

"Once I was able to manipulate time, manipulating atomic structures and physical characteristics would be possible if I had something to change things into. They're all dimensions in the M-space matrix. I had the Disney database that had all the physical manufacturing specifications of the merchandise. I was able to replicate almost everything they'd ever officially licensed. With those specs, it was easy to transform most of the people there. So I tried it with the hand grenade, then Fenric, then Kalihnkha, then Dad. I wasn't sure about people's perceptions and memories, but I discovered later, those are manipulable in M-space dimensions too. That took longer, but the more I did, the more I discovered and learned new things.

I couldn't transform the Confidential Service, the hotel staff, or the media people. Something about Dad and the people who supported him, they were easier to manipulate. Some people were harder to transform than others, too. Easy code strings for some folks, more gyrations and nested algorithms for others. Dad was one of the easiest."

"Hmm. You used to hear people say that President DeLuxe's followers had become unmoored from reality," I said. "Maybe their beliefs in things that weren't true made their physical reality easier to change, created that stress in the fabric of quantum reality."

"I hadn't thought of saying it that way, but yes, that seems right. This could be helpful, sharing information with you."

"Thank you!"

"You're welcome!" he replied. I don't think he noticed me rolling my eyes.

"Do you have a list of who became what? Wait, never mind. It's better if I don't know," I said. I was tired of keeping secrets, and this one was big enough for now. I didn't want to be the only other person in the world who knew which piece of Disney junk was President DeLuxe. "What about the ones who were there who weren't DeLuxe believers? They weren't transformed. They don't remember what happened, so you did something."

"For everyone else, I had to wipe their memories back to a few minutes before Fenric started shooting. That I can do to anyone, I think."

"Griffin, are you planning to wipe my memory of all this?"

"No! No, not at all! I think it's important you know, now. I'm tired of doing all this alone. I know I can trust you, count on you. It's been great getting to know you. And I know you care about me."

"Yes, I do. Okay, keep going."

"And I believe in most of what DMV does," he continued. "Especially the STIF. It's important to keep everyone safe."

I wondered what Griffin's long-term game was, if any. Did he plan to ever disenchant these people, or not? He had a sense, it seemed to me, that Fenric was only the most violent eruption of the chaos that his father, and his father's supporters, were wreaking on the country. The world, in fact. I got the impression Griffin was as relieved as most Americans to have President DeLuxe no longer in charge. And to have Dirk DeLuxe as a father. It made me shiver.

Griffin continued to tell me parts of the theory behind his magic, all about that M-space quantum mechanics and math, none of which made any sense to me. "Magic" works fine for me.

He had completed the transformations, and restarted time, taking up residency in the Presidential Suite in the Hotel.

It wasn't until the next day, he said, that he realized the transformation enchantment was only part of the solution. His news feed showed an increase in articles about right wing militias, gun violence, and bombings. Not all current news, but it was almost like Yotta was steering him in a direction again, it seemed to me. He didn't care, he trusted her. The real problems, he decided, were the ability by violent individuals and groups to kill lots of people at one time. He anticipated there might be violent reactions once the transformations of the president and his followers became public knowledge. He read a blog post with the phrase "if I had three wishes, I would have guns and bombs blow up in the faces of people trying to use them." He came up with his strategy to bring about world peace inspired by the blog post: the anti-gun and anti-explosion enchantment. After some research on the Internet about gun rights groups and extremism, he froze time again for the rest of us and went to work.

"Once I had figured out how to alter the physical universe and how to alter perceptions and memories, I put the two of them together. I was struggling with how to do it, and reviewing my code, going over and over it, and then I got lost in it."

"What do you mean?"

"I was up late, I'd gotten lost in the design. I do a lot of the design in my head before it goes into the code. And it was almost like I became part of the code, and it became part of me. I don't know how long I was 'under' I guess you'd call it. Like a trance? I don't know. It felt like an eternity almost, even though based on my computer's clock I was only thinking for twenty minutes."

"It sounds like you were what they call 'in the flow'."

"If I had to guess, I became quantum entangled with the code, with the changes it had made, the transformations. So I realized I had to change my perception, almost convince myself that guns would blow up and bombs explode when someone intended to hurt someone. If I could convince myself of it, then I could make the Enchantment code create that reality."

"I think I'm following you now. If their perception is they intend to do harm with a gun or through an explosion, you make the gun or bomb explode at that point when they set the intention. And *your* intention is how you created that spell."

"Yes, that's it. There's a built-in set of feedback loops in my code. If the actions of someone tend toward chaotic violence, then the Enchantment kicks in. It's similar to how some people were easier to enchant. The more chaotic people are, the more divorced from a consensual reality they are, the less connected to everyone else, the easier they are to enchant."

"Like a feedback loop that affects delusional sociopaths."

"That could describe it. I put that all into some self-replicating and self-enhancing subroutines, to reinforce using that belief kind of like an artificial belief engine."

"But Eliot, Toni, Lonny, they're not sociopaths, not chaotically divorced from reality."

"No, that took a lot more work," he said. He hunched his shoulders. "My code is more efficient than it used to be, and I think I'm more expert at it now than I was then, so I was able to do it more selectively. And I think the existence of the Enchantment created a back door for me, so now everyone believes that transformation can happen, so it does. Kind of a paradox, but I did discover other things I could apply to everyone."

"Not sure that's a good thing…"

He explained more: after he set those enchantments in place, he restarted time. During the time stoppage, and for a while after, he holed up in the Presidential Suite at the DeLuxe Hotel and figured out how to let his mother know he was all right.

"I had to fix it so she could know who I was, and still not worry about me or want me to live with her. I had to stay near the quantum computer to keep things going. She needed to know me and love me, but not discuss me to anyone else."

"What did you need to do to keep things going? Once you did the Enchantment, wasn't it permanent?"

"No, not quite. That's the problem. The other parameters of our physical universe are in flux, so I had to keep fine-tuning how the Enchantment responded to those changes. I had to keep reminding myself, repeating the concept in my head about how to keep the people transformed and to keep the guns and bombs from working. I'm afraid if I don't, it will all relapse! And, this is hard to explain. Somehow people's attitudes about the transformations have an effect on them. I hadn't anticipated that. Once I understood there was another factor, I designed compensating code modules that I thought would automatically kick in. I thought I had it pretty complete, and then the MATA Act got passed and DMV was created. I had nothing to do with that, but I was glad. A government database gave me a way to keep track of things. And I'd know if anything was failing, and maybe if I concentrated, and repeated that belief to myself while coding, then everything would stay enchanted."

"Repeating it like a mantra. A prayer," I said.

He nodded. "When we put the MOFTS data out there, I realized I needed to use that information, and information on how many people were using it, and what the opinions were on the Internet about it. I needed that to feed into my routines, to scrape data to automatically compensate, and so I could mentally keep things going. Things like the betting pools on who was what EO, what conspiracy theories were there that might influence people's perceptions and affect my Enchantment."

"Are you saying if people believed President DeLuxe was, say, a Three Little Pigs figurine, that would make it so? Regardless of him being, let's say, a Mickey Mouse ball cap?"

"I'm not sure. I saw changes in the health checks I ran on my system that had to be the result of quantum entanglement with belief systems outside my own code and my own belief matrix."

"Perception affecting reality? Other people besides you."

"Well, yes. I don't think I'm that special."

I laughed. "Griffin, you've done something nobody has ever been able to do. Multiple things! That's pretty special."

"I realize that. I don't think only I could do it. I was just the first to discover how to do it."

My heart thumped. What if this was the way to create a world where magic actually existed, where people could be trained in it, and practice it. Was that a good thing, or could it get into the wrong hands?

"And then Fenric grew to full size, and you realized something serious was going on," I said. "That's why you were so upset yesterday."

"I wasn't sure if it was a flaw in my code, or an intruder. Now I'm pretty sure it's an intruder."

"It's Bart Barukka. He was supposedly at AFPAP that day. And he's been missing ever since 2/29."

"I didn't transform him. I didn't know all the people at first, but I already knew him, and he wasn't there. He's not in my inventory. That makes sense, then."

"Griffin, I think Bart Barukka is Sorcerer Y. I think he's obscuring everyone's ability to perceive him like you did. Is that possible?"

"I don't see how. Let me check something." He turned to his laptop and began typing, alternating with reading masses of code on the screen. I waited.

"Say, Griffin," I said. "Is this the quantum computer from the hotel? Did Disney get rid of it?"

"No, this is my development and testing environment, and my disaster recovery strategy. I got another quantum computer made and installed here. This is a copy of the one that did the 2/29 Enchantment."

He continued typing, then reading, then typing furiously.

"Griffin?"

"Yes! What?"

"If someone were *already* manipulating reality by influencing people's perceptions, let's say through a combination of social media, web sites, Internet troll farms, etc., could that have skewed your initial Enchantment?"

He stopped and looked at me. This time it was his turn to gape. "Oh," he said. "Oh!"

"Because, every time we had a disenchantment, or whatever you call the water bottle growing—"

"That was one I stopped from happening."

"Ah, so every time there's been a disenchantment, I've read about it on the fake DMV Chirpa feed, or the DarkBart site first.

And Barukka controlled that site, possibly still controls it. That means he's the key to this!"

Griffin nodded enthusiastically, "Yes, he and you."

"What!? Why me?"

"You read it, you analyzed which EO it might be, and then it happened. Right? So—uh-oh."

"What?"

"You're the system vulnerability. He's been hacking my system through you."

"What on earth could I have to do with it?"

"Sorry, I didn't get to that part, did I? I modeled some of the system learning, robotics, and AI on you. I mean, we worked so closely and you always had such good insights. I evolved my code into a system, Fab 2, I call her. She runs on Yotta."

"What? Griffin, that's kind of creepy." Did he have a crush on me? Oh no!

"Is it? I didn't mean it to be creepy. I'm sorry. It's just that I trust you. And the human brain, there are people who think it's already a quantum computer. Possibly more efficient than these." He gestured to the gleaming metal structure. Then he turned to me. "That's not creepy, is it? I admire you. Is it creepy? Oh! You think…no, it isn't like that!" He was no longer looking at me, but at the floor in front of me. His face flushed pink.

I took a deep breath. "For now, let's park this issue. More important: how is my reading and thinking influencing 'Fab 2' at all? Oh, yes. You said there's a quantum entanglement based on a perception of reality."

"Everyone is tied to Fab 2 in some way, at this point. Like I said, all those other quantum computers, human brains, they're part of the bigger super-network. The code has to affect every-one's mind. That's the only way I could keep myself out of everyone's attention and still keep the gun and bomb enchant-ments going. I'm sorry, did I do wrong?"

Here in front of me, his shoulders hunched, and his eyes cast down once again, was a young man, a child in many ways, with extraordinary, even god-like, power. And limited interpersonal skills. A lot depended on how I treated him. Part of me was afraid, but a bigger part of me resolved to treat him as his best potential self and hope he could grow into that.

"These are uncharted waters, Griffin. We'll have to navigate them together." I smiled at him.

He looked up at me and smiled back.

"Griffin, I just realized this must be exhausting for you!"

"It is tiring. I have to do it even so. It helps that I'm not all alone knowing about it, now." He nodded at me.

"Okay, then let's talk about Eliot and Toni and the others you just transformed. And about Kayla Malone."

"Yes. I was at the hotel, at Ground Zero. This was after 2/29, but before DMV existed. Time was running normally again. I was in my suite, tweaking my code, and the there was a knock at the door, and voice said "Housekeeping." The staff there always treated me really nicely. I swear I didn't make them do it. This was right before Disney was taking the hotel over. Did you know Disney hired all the staff when they bought the building?"

"No, I did not know that. And?"

"Anyway, I let the maid in, but she was new, not one of the normal ladies that serviced that suite. Nice black lady with short hair. She tidied up, and I went back to my coding while she worked. They usually worked around me like this.

"Some time went by, and then I noticed she was standing right behind me, looking over my shoulder at the code. I didn't worry. I didn't think anyone would be able to interpret my code but me. She surprised me when she said, 'Ah, so that's it.'

"I turned, and she said, 'Griffin, I'm a friend. My name is Kayla Malone. I work for the NBI, but that's not why I'm here.' My first instinct was to pull up part of the code, I didn't call the code Fab 2 at that point, and see if I could freeze time, but Kayla put her hand over the keyboard, and said 'Don't do what you're thinking of doing. It's all right, I assure you. I'm a friend, and your secret is safe with me and those I represent.'"

"Was she a magician, do you think?" Maybe there *was* a Hogwarts somewhere!

"No, I don't think so. She never did magic in my presence."

"That you recall!"

"That I recall. You don't think my memory has been tampered with, do you?"

"If you can do it, others can. Maybe Barukka, maybe Kayla. I assume you trust her, though. You and she were on the phone in Hannah's office. You could have told me, you know."

"I know, I know. I'm sorry. Yes, I did trust her. She told me she couldn't reveal how she knew what I'd done, that she approved of it, and would not do anything to interfere. She said she'd even help me if she could, if I was in dire need. She represents…a group of some kind? She's never said who. This morning, I called and told her I was monitoring my perceptual failsafe and it was showing red hot. She let me listen in to the meeting, and I did what you saw. Agent Oberst, he had a recording of us! From our stopped time!"

"Your perceptual failsafe?"

"It's a module in Fab 2 that monitors how close people are to discovering the truth. It had popped hot - probably when Agent Oberst got a hold of that recording, but it was about to tip into what I call 'nuclear meltdown' and it was focusing on the office where you were. I asked her if I should let it. She said yes, and then Oberst accused us of…what we did. Kayla told me to stop time and transform everyone but you and her. I had already queued that routine up, at her suggestion."

"So Fab 2, not you personally, but your software that you named after me, turned Eliot, Toni, Hannah, and Oberst into *Inside/Out* plush figures. Did I get that right?"

"And Agent Dotch, too. He's Bing Bong." Griffin reached behind his desk and pulled out an elephant-like plush animal. He placed it on his desk.

"Oh, Griffin, you didn't!" The plush animal was pink, and sat upright on its rear end, wearing a fedora and a jacket. It had big green eyes, and a huge, human mouth, smiling beneath a pink elephant trunk. I was reminded of Chester's toothy smile.

"Agent Dotch was listening in on a conference line, and he heard along with the others, and Kayla Malone agreed I should transform him too," Griffin continued. "I went and got him out of his office after he turned into Bing Bong."

I bent over and looked at the plush toy. "Can you undo just Lonny? I think we need him."

"I can, if you think we can trust him."

"I don't think we have a choice. If we want to make things right, we need an investigator. I'm out of my depth."

"Let me work on it," he replied, and he returned to his code.

"While you do that, I'm going to my office and calling Ms. Malone."

"Okay."

"If you'll give me her number," I said, crossing my arms.

"I'll send it to your phone," he said, without looking up.

I left his server room and went to my office and closed the door. On the way, my phone chimed, and I saw Griffin had sent me a phone number.

"Kayla Malone," she said, when I rang her.

"It's Fab Acer," I said.

"Yes." She knew, of course, I'd call her.

"Can you answer some questions for me? I talked with Griffin, so I know what he did."

"I'll try."

"Who are you? I mean, whom do you represent?"

"I told Griffin, I can't reveal much, other than that you can trust me. Our interests are aligned with yours."

"So, 'our' means more than just you."

"I can't say who we are, but we want probably what you want: for people to live peacefully and productively and happily."

"To keep the Enchantment in place, then?"

"Yes, for now."

"Are you with the Constitutionalist Party?"

She laughed. "I'm a registered Constitutionalist, but that's not who I represent. Listen, Ms. Acer, if Griffin told you how he did what he did, then you know by now that sharing sensitive information can have consequences, tangible ones. You understand that, don't you?"

Did she know about Barukka? Hacking *me*?

"Yes," I said. "We even think someone is hacking the Enchantment using social media posts." I decided not to tell her *I* was the back door for the cyber assault.

"That's something we suspected. You can see why I have to proceed cautiously," she said.

"Okay, can you at least tell me everyone is all right in the conference room?"

"Yes, I'm still here, and they're all here. Griffin texted me he's disenchanting Agent Dotch. I think that's fine."

"You'll give Griffin advice, but not information?"

"I'm telling him, and I'm telling you that you are on the right track. The Enchantment is under threat of unraveling, from an outside force."

"Bart Barukka."

"Barukka hasn't been seen anywhere since 2/29. He was there, and he's not, as far as we can tell, an Enchanted Object."

"Griffin tells me he didn't enchant Barukka," I said.

"Somehow he's influencing things, though, and planting items on darkbart.com."

"Is there a spell, an invisibility thing like Griffin cast on himself, do you think?"

"We're not magic, believe it or not. We're about information, but not to the degree of changing reality the way Griffin has. I don't know about spells, enchantments. What I do think is that you, Griffin, and Dotch stand a chance of figuring that out, and finding Barukka and stopping him. What I will suggest is for you to consider something along the lines of artificial intelligence."

"AI? I saw him in person."

"I know. But there are ways of being in the physical and virtual worlds at the same time. If I had to guess, Barukka is some kind of virtual entity with an ability to materialize, or at least project an image. I can't say more now. I'll help if I can, but I can't always. You have my number. I need to go. A detail of Law Enforcement Protective Service officers is here at my request, to guard the conference room. I need to talk with Jonathan and finesse that."

"Okay, I'll hold you to your word."

"You can." And she clicked off. I hate when people tell me only part of the truth. As soon as I thought that, my face grew hot. What had I been doing for the last two days but that? Hiding the most important truths, when I had sworn my life to transparency and sharing information!

Now I was in a conspiracy of secrecy. And total transparency, it appeared, could be magically dangerous. Augh! What had we released to the public that might make the Enchantment vulnerable? Secrets, I hated them, and yet I had to keep them. And Kayla Malone was doing the same to me. I needed a shower.

CHAPTER 17

ABNORMAL IS THE NEW NORMAL

I checked on Griffin a half hour later. He was still working on undoing the enchantment on Lonny. He said he had to rewrite his failsafe routine to make an exception, which was more difficult than just applying a transformation to anyone who realized Griffin was Sorcerer X. Except how had I been excepted.

"You're already a special code line," Griffin said. "I put that in weeks ago. Now I have to create another code branch for Lonny. I should offload the parameters into an external table, so I can easily add and subtract people. Hmm. Yes, that would be good. But I don't have time now."

"Okay, I'll leave you to it. I'll do more research."

"That'd be great!" he said, staring at his code as he typed it. He was a fast typist, and I suspected his mind was even faster. Fast as a quantum computer.

"But Griffin," I said, pausing at the door. "I need to look at darkbart.com again. Do you think that's safe if I don't follow any blind items?"

"What's that?" he said, still not looking up.

"The disenchantments all started with a blind item, meaning it was anonymous and obscure, not saying exactly who or what would transform. I researched and decoded that, and focused on a specific EO both times. Then the stormtrooper happened, and Sleeping Beauty almost happened. Maybe that was the catalyst."

"I will also watch my health monitor. I can let you know if you need to stop what you're doing."

"Okay, it's a plan. Scrye me if you need me," I said, and I left him again and returned to my office.

The DarkBart News site had no rumors specific to DMV or EOs or the STIF that I could find. Only paranoid and hateful criticisms of the (now) ethnically and gender-diverse coalition administration and other "Deep State" activities than our DMV. I sighed, relieved. Back to the About Us, page. There were the current editor and publisher, pasty-faced white men. Staff writers, a few of them white women. And I again clicked on the link to About Our Founder, and saw the toad-like face of Bart Barukka. Okay, to avoid doing disservice to toads, more like a molting owl. He did have a beaky little nose, and toads have no noses per se. Nor do toads have blotchy gin-blossomed complexions or beady, bloodshot eyes. Having seen him in person, I could vouch that this was about as flattering as a picture of him could get without extensive airbrushing or cosmetics.

Under his photo, it said, "Mr. Barukka, a victim of the 2/29 terrorist act, lives on in spirit, in the hearts of the DarkBart News staff and all who dedicate their lives to liberty and the exposure of truth." Below that, it had a biography of Barukka, his early education, conversion from Campus Constitutionalists to College Students for Freedom, and his career as a campaign manager and public relations person, interspersed with conservative think-tanks and PAC work. And some Freedonian strategies that I remembered, dimly, verged on "dirty tricks."

I was reluctant to do any more research online, in case I became a vector for unwanted magic again. I printed the page I was viewing and folded it in thirds, and slipped it into a writing pad on my desk.

Back in the server room, Griffin was still hunched over his

laptop. "I think I'm almost there," he said. "Okay, here, put him on the floor over there." He handed me the Bing Bong doll, which I gently placed on a clear spot in the floor.

"I'm going to execute the subroutine," Griffin said, and he clicked a button on his laptop screen.

I looked at the Bing Bong. I wondered what actually witnessing a disenchantment would be like. The re-enchantment of Fenric, and the enchantment in Hannah's conference room, had been instantaneous. One second they were humans, the next they were merchandise. The lights flickered, and the sound of the air conditioning and server fans muted for a fraction of a second. I tried not to blink as I watched Bing Bong. And then, appropriately enough, there was a sound: "Bing-bong..."

Suddenly Lonny was standing there, and he stumbled.

"What the—" he said, but he recovered quickly, taking in his surroundings. "Fab, be careful, Griffin's the perp!" He spread his legs and bent at the knees, and raised his fists. "Griffin, I don't have a gun, but I can still overpower you."

"Lonny, don't!" I said, stepping toward him.

"Out of my way, Fab. This kid's dangerous."

"He's on our side, Lonny! Really!" I reached out and placed my hands on Lonny's wrists. I felt him relax a tiny bit. "He did the 2/29 Enchantment, yes." Lonny tensed again. "But there's a reason, he was stopping an assassination, and a terrorist attack when he did it. And now he's disenchanted you. There's a problem: there's another person who's using magic, and they're not benevolent."

"Sorcerer Y," Lonny said.

"Yes, that's who disenchanted the stormtrooper, someone who won't stop at violence. The stormtrooper is Fenric DeLuxe, and he shot the president. The Enchantment preserved the president's life, and those of the others," I said.

Lonny stayed tense, looking at Griffin. After a bit, he said, "I'm listening. But I'm watching him. He has his finger on the trigger."

I looked at Griffin, and indeed, his finger was poised over his trackpad. "Griffin! Back off, please. Let's all stay calm."

Griffin put his hands in his lap. "He was going to hit me."

"He's not going to hit you, are you Lonny?"

"No. But Fab. The law is the law. And he's been here all this time, spying on us."

"Lonny, there are sides and perspectives. Please listen to his. Griffin, tell him what you told me."

I rolled another chair into the space and gestured to Lonny to sit. He did so, grudgingly, keeping his typically upright posture. It was a start.

Griffin re-told his story, with few interruptions from Lonny, just grunts and nods to show he understood. Not agreeing or approving, and not asking for more information. A couple of questions to clarify. It was like he was recording a confession, so he wanted Griffin to keep talking. At one point, Lonny folded his arms in front of him. His posture wasn't open, but at least he didn't seem poised to strike.

As Griffin talked, I thought about whether I agreed with Lonny. Was the 2/29 Enchantment truly a crime? There were people who called it terrorism, and indeed it frightened many people, but Griffin had not intended it as an act of terror. It was the opposite. He was stopping an assassination attempt. Of course, there were, arguably, innocent bystanders who had not been involved in the assassination. I'm not saying they were good people, but did they deserve to be enchanted? On the other hand, Griffin had ensured that further violence was, if not impossible, much more difficult. This was in contrast to Barukka, or whoever had disenchanted Fenric. That was clearly an attempt to enable violence again.

Which set me thinking: what was Fenric doing in a stormtrooper costume in the first place? And why had he shot his father? And was it a coincidence that Barukka had somehow escaped the 2/29 transformation? How had he done it?

"Let me get this clear. You did all this, using this computer, and you did it to stop a violent overthrow of the U.S. Government?" Lonny asked when Griffin had completed his story.

"Um. Yes, I guess so," Griffin replied.

"Yes, Lonny, that's basically what I thought," I said. "It's a lot to process. He didn't mean to do anything bad."

"You mean, aside from disrupting the lives of everyone who got enchanted, and causing their families the same grief as if they'd been killed? And not even letting them know *which* EO their loved one is? Aside from that?"

"Well, yes," I hedged. "I admit there were consequences. But think of what he stopped."

"I guess we'll never know, because *he stopped it*!"

"Yes, I can see your point..."

"And you knew this."

"Only today! I mean, the whole story just today. I had bits of it. Please consider forgiving me; we need to move forward now. Do you agree, Griffin is trying to do what's right? I think we need to help him fight Sorcerer Y."

Lonny didn't say anything for a few seconds. Then, "So, Griffin, you did 2/29, and if you undid it, bad things would happen. I mean, to our country. Things are stable now. I'll admit that. And I agree, it looks like there's a new threat."

"Yes, thank you!" I said.

"Listen, I wasn't a big fan of the president. But this isn't how we do things. Do you see my point, Grif? We can't go around changing people into Disney swag just because we don't agree with them."

"Yes, Agent Dotch."

"I mean, the first time, I get it. I didn't agree with most of the people at that convention. Our own people? I can't be party to that." Lonny folded his arms in front of his chest and stared at me.

"Lonny, if everyone knows Griffin did it, how can he protect things from the intruder, Barukka or whoever it is?"

"I get that. And we don't betray our own."

"Maybe I can do something about it," Griffin said, quietly.

"What?" I asked.

"I couldn't do it in the moment. Now I've had some time, I may be able to make them forget it."

"Could you? Lonny, would that be all right?"

"Restore them, and wipe their memories? I don't know…"

"Only five minutes' worth?" I suggested. "Except Oberst. He knew about the recording already."

"I can make him not think about it, I guess. Like I make people not think about myself." Lonny and I waited, and Griffin continued, "Yes, I can do it."

Lonny agreed to those conditions, and I phoned Kayla Malone.

"Malone," she said.

"Fab Acer here."

"Yes."

"We think we should restore everyone there, but do a little, uh, rollback of their memories."

"I think that makes sense."

"You do? I mean, I'm glad, thanks." I explained that Lonny had been disenchanted, with full memory, and that he was assisting with us. I also said that we'd take care of Oberst's knowledge of the recording of Griffin's and my conversations. "Do you know where he got it from?" I asked.

"Still working on that. Griffin's solution should work for now. Let me worry about Oberst and how he found out."

"Okay."

"May I speak to all of you, please," she said.

"Oh, sure." I put her on speaker.

"Agent Dotch, this is Acting Deputy AAG Malone."

"Yes, ma'am."

"I am assigning you to work with Fab and Griffin to confirm who is intruding into Griffin's system, who is performing unauthorized disenchantments. And given the incapacitation of Agent Oberst, I am making you acting Director of the OEOE, and assigning you to prevent unauthorized disenchantments, neutralize future threats to the security of the STIF and the EOs secured there. And to apprehend any individuals threatening the security of the STIF and DMV operations. Understood?"

"Yes, ma'am."

"Good. Griffin, let me know when you are ready."

"It will probably be another half hour," he said, not looking up from his screen.

"All right. Call me then. I have things under control here at Main Law Enforcement. Malone out."

"Bye," I said. I think she had already hung up.

"Grif, we'll leave you to it," Lonny said, moving to the door. He looked at me and jerked his head toward the door, so I followed him out of the server room.

"Lonny, again, I'm sorry I couldn't tell you everything. Are we good?"

Lonny didn't say anything. He took the turn toward his office. I followed in silence. We entered his office, and I closed the door behind me as he went to his desk and sat. He picked up a paper and started reading it. I'm sure it was random. I continued to stand.

"Lonny, please talk to me."

"What's there to talk about?" he said.

"I held things from you, I know. I didn't have all the information yet, and Griffin kept not being there to explain..."

"Ms. Acer, we have a job to do. I'll do mine and you do yours."

"Oh, Lonny, I'm so sorry."

He put the paper on his desk and stared into my eyes. "Listen, fool me once, shame on you, fool me twice, shame on me. You play straight with me, no problem. You hide things again, especially the important stuff, Fab, then I'll know where we stand."

My chickens were coming back to roost. "That's fair," I said.

"Anything else?" he said. I wasn't sure if he meant right this moment, or anything else I hadn't told him.

"The cat!" I blurted.

"What cat?" he asked.

I sat in the chair across from his desk. "The cat at JR Bluntschli's house. He's enchanted."

"An enchanted cat?"

"Or magical. I'm not sure. He can talk. And walk on air. And disappear. He's the Cheshire Cat, basically. From *Alice and Wonderland*?"

"A Cheshire Cat."

"Yes, with purple and pink stripes. Oh, Lonny, I'm sorry. Technically, he isn't an EO, right? He's not an object. Zey told me, JR I mean, that Chester was a normal cat until 2/29, and then he became, well, a walking, talking, floating, disappearing, Disney character."

"Not an object, though?"

"Right, that was my thinking. Zey's so attached to him, and what good would it have been to confiscate him? If we could even hold him. He can teleport."

Lonny put his thumb and forefinger under his chin. "Hm. I can see your point."

"Yes, yes, it makes sense, doesn't it? We aren't in the business of arresting cats!"

"Okay, I'll give you that one. Is there anything else?"

I ran through everything weird that had happened, in my head. "No, not that I can think of. Honest!"

"Okay, thank you for that."

I rose to leave.

"Fab, what I said still stands. If you don't trust me to share vital information, how can I trust you?"

"I understand. It won't happen again. I swear."

He nodded, and I left to return to my office.

CHAPTER 18

NEW NORMAL FOR NOW

An hour or so later, there was another wave of magic like I had felt with every transformation: a weird shift to the light, and the tinkling of pixie dust. The "bing-bong" sound must have been a special one for Lonny. A half hour after that, I heard Eliot and Agent Oberst talking as they approached my office.

"I'll leave you to it, then," Oberst said.

I was watching my open doorway, and Eliot appeared. He was dressed as he'd been in the morning, before he became the purple Fear doll, in a slate-colored suit with a lavender tie. He knocked on the open door, even though he could see me looking at him, and he smiled.

"Hi, just checking in," he said, entering and sitting in the chair next to my desk. "Weren't you clever to slip out of that meeting! I can't believe we were so absorbed in our conversation I didn't notice."

I nodded. I wasn't sure what he thought had happened. "You know, things came up."

"Yes, Kayla explained," he said. (I wished I'd heard what she'd explained.) "Looks like everything's normal. False alarm?

Nothing happening at the STIF? Good thing Griffin has those dashboard alerts on the security system there."

"Right, it was nothing. Might be a passing truck created vibrations. We don't know, for sure." There I was, lying again. It disturbed me how quickly I was able to think up things. It disturbed me how exhilarating I found it, also.

"Hannah liked our write-up," he continued, "and thinks we're on the right path. Kayla had mitigation strategies we hadn't thought of, so I'll take a stab at fleshing those out and let you review it to see if you can think of anything else. Sound good?"

"Sounds like a plan, Eliot. Thanks for including me!"

"Couldn't do this without you, you know," he said, standing.

"That's nice of you to say." I managed to curl the edges of my mouth upwards.

"I mean it." He smiled and left my office.

A few seconds later, Lonny entered.

"Close the door," I said. "Eliot was here. I guess Griffin's disenchantment and memory rollback worked. Eliot thinks I left the meeting to check on a possible event at the STIF. Kayla Malone told him that."

"Agent Oberst acted like he didn't remember anything about you and Griffin. Said Malone has him on a special assignment, and he knows I'm acting for him. I deduced Griffin did a whammy on him. He's never that mellow."

"We can see if Griffin will give him a permanent personality upgrade."

"Don't even joke about that, Fab. It's bad enough he's tampering with memories, and now Oberst's personality. How do we know we're not being manipulated?"

"I know Griffin well enough that I have to trust what he's doing is for the best."

"You aren't ruling it out. Even you?"

"I don't think so. What could I do about it anyway? I think

it's more important to find out who is tampering with the Enchantment. If it's Barukka…"

"The devil you know," Lonny said.

"Griffin's not a devil, but, yes, better he be in control than Barukka."

"I'll go with that for now."

"Speaking of which," I said, "Let's find out what Griffin's up to. And let him know things seem to have worked." I initiated a video call to Griffin on Scrye. He answered quickly.

"Hi."

"Griffin, good work! Eliot and Agent Oberst don't seem to remember anything about the recording of you. Eliot thinks I slipped out early to check on a potential event at the STIF."

"Any luck on the intrusions? How Barukka's hacking you, if it is him?" Lonny asked, leaning over my shoulder to get into view of my camera. Right down to business.

"I'm running a compare between my code lines. I'll dump it to this new portable quantum server I recently acquired," Griffin said. He picked up a coiled copper structure about the size of a coffee mug. "I can account for everything but this anomalous set," he continued. He sent us an invitation to look at his screen, which I accepted.

"Ah," Lonny said. It looked like a bunch of indecipherable code to me, and I suspected it did to Lonny too. He was getting good at drawing Griffin out. "What do *you* think it means?"

"I'm still trying to figure it out. It looks like it's…yes, it's code that allows backdoor access. That's a problem."

I said, "It sounds like it. Can you fix it?"

"Not easily. Yes. It will take a while. I don't like to take the system offline. It's maintaining the Enchantment."

"Do you mean, if the power went off, everyone would be restored to their normal forms?" Lonny asked.

"Not immediately. There would be drift, risk of unwanted changes over time. The code requires frequent updating to adjust for the passage of time and the planet's passage through space. If

I didn't maintain it, the Enchantment could begin to fray around the edges. That's what I thought was happening at first. I have to turn it off when I put an upgrade or maintenance release into production. If it was down for more than an hour or so, I would not want that."

"And what do you do if that happens?"

Griffin stopped sharing his screen, and the video of his face reappeared on my monitor.

"The master production copy is running from the computer at the Deluxe Resort. It should always keep running. I've made sure there are failsafes. The computer is on the top floor, near where the M-dimensional origami is that's the extrusion of the formula into three-dimensional space. It doesn't have to be physically nearby, since they're quantum entangled."

"Origami?" Lonny asked.

"To us, it looks like an artistic light fixture, the big one in the middle of the atrium," I said. "Think of it as a multi-dimensional iceberg. This is only the part you can see. There's lots more hidden at higher dimensional levels."

"That's an acceptable metaphor," Griffin said.

"That's why I saw something in the light fixture change when I saw Barukka in the lobby of Ground Zero" I added.

"When the Enchantment changes, the appearance of the origami changes," Griffin said. "When I do it, it looks normal. Barukka's hack was ugly."

"Getting back to your fail-safes…" Lonny said.

"I've made sure the computer there has backup power. And if an outage lasts too long, I have a copy here I can switch over. I'm looking at another site in Idaho, in the NBI's big data center there, for a second failsafe. As soon as they can get the equipment delivered."

I looked at Lonny, and shrugged. "Looks like that's got it covered."

"And soon I'll have a copy on the portable server, meaning the compiled and executable parts," Griffin said.

"All right, we'll let you get to it. Is that okay, Lonny?" Lonny nodded. "Keep us posted, please." Griffin nodded, and I disconnected the video chat.

"Did you actually follow that?" Lonny asked.

"Only some. Griffin understands it, and that's what's important."

"Yeah, failsafes. Compiled copies. Backups. But who's the failsafe for *him*?"

"Good question." We sat in silence.

Lonny rose to leave.

"Wait," I said. "I printed this for you" I picked up the printout with Barukka's photo on it. "This is Barukka." I pointed to the toad-like face.

"Yeah, I remember him from the early days of the administration. And our database. You're not the only one who reviews it," he said.

"I'm afraid to do any more research on him, for fear I might influence things. I wanted to make sure if we see him, you'd know. I'll never forget the look he gave me." I shuddered.

My computer rang. It was a Scrye video chat request from Griffin.

"Griffin, yes?"

"Fab! Agent Dotch! There's something happening." His eyes were wide. "I tried to switch over to a copy of the Fab 2 where I'd excised the aberrant code I found. My health check. It's going red. It's showing, I guess I'd describe it as a stretch in the fabric of reality. It's not normal, and it's not mine. Not my code."

"Where is it?" Lonny asked.

"Hold on. It's here in the building."

Lonny said, "Maybe we need to be prepared for something. Griffin, patch into our headset audio and video feed." Lonny and I put our headsets on.

Then the lights dimmed and sounds muted. Another disenchantment? Or enchantment? Then, the sound of tinkling pixie dust. Oh, no!

Suddenly, Lonny's hand, which had been holding the sheet of paper with Bart Barukka's photo was now holding the sleeve of a person. In fact, the sleeve of a squat man in a blue oxford shirt and khaki pants.

"Lonny, it's Bart Barukka. Griffin, are you seeing this?"

"Yes, Fab. It's Barukka."

"Ah, Ms. Acer. We meet at last. In the flesh, in a manner of speaking," Barukka said. "Agent Dotch, if you don't mind." He glanced at Lonny's hand, grasping his cuff.

"Sorry," Lonny said. "I wasn't expecting to be holding a person's sleeve. It was a sheet of paper."

"Understood," Barukka said.

"What are you doing here, and what do you want?" Lonny asked him.

"I'm here involuntarily. I'm a victim of a terrorist, probably Constitutionalist, manipulation of reality!"

"You weren't found among the Enchanted Objects," I said, standing and folding my arms. "And clearly you know that 2/29 happened, which a true victim would not. And you know who we are. I think that makes you *not* a victim of 2/29."

"Touché. I didn't think you thought that, actually. I only wanted to see your response."

As Barukka and I stood about four feet from each other, Lonny slowly and quietly moved to the direct opposite side of Barukka from me.

Barukka turned toward Lonny. "I think I'd rather face you, Agent Dotch."

"How are you here involuntarily?" Lonny asked him. He flexed his knees and offset his feet from each other, his martial arts stance.

"Surely you don't think I'm more powerful than Sorcerer X, also known as your friend Griffin DeLuxe?"

"Griffin, did you do this?" I asked.

Over the headset, he said, "No. I think there's a worm in the code. I'm working on figuring it out."

"He claims not?" Barukka said, turning to face me. "You can see I'm merely an innocent victim of a leftist attack on our liberty. Like the rest of the victims." He smirked.

"Again, you wouldn't know that unless you hadn't been one of the original 2/29 victims. And your web site is thriving."

"Ah, such good news. I'm glad to hear it. Well, if you'll excuse me, I should probably let my wife and children know I'm alive and well."

"But you won't, will you?" Lonny said. He was standing at the door, not exactly barring Barukka's way, yet. "If you weren't enchanted two years ago, why have you been reported missing all this time?"

"Ah, that's a good question," Barukka replied. "I leave it to your crack analytics team to figure that out. Now if you'll excuse me…" He gestured to the door.

"Lonny, we can't!"

"What grounds would I detain him on?"

Barukka had moved so he could easily see either of us, at the vertex of a triangle of me, Lonny, and him.

He watched for my response, and when I said nothing, he said, "I think the answer Ms. Acer is struggling not to say, is 'None.' Am I right?"

"Yes." I had to think quickly. "However, what about manipulating me, to create the disenchantments? We saw it: when I would read and analyze something from your site, disenchantments would happen. Use of magic, isn't that grounds for an arrest, Lonny?"

Barukka laughed. "You think that *you* were the way I accomplished the disenchantments? You were only a part of the picture."

"What do you mean?"

"My readership on darkbart.com gives me access to reality distortion capabilities you could only imagine. The disenchantments were tests, seeing if we could accomplish it. It's true, I had to copy Griffin's code, and it does have your name. Fab 2. Sweet to name it for his—never mind."

Smarmy jerk, I thought.

"The true key ingredient," he went on, "Which young Mr. DeLuxe's Enchantment proved to me, is the belief systems of people. Those plus the quantum computer and highfalutin' math, means I can do things one person could only dream of." He giggled. "I can't resist gloating. Sorry. I'm not your prisoner, I'm here voluntarily. It was time."

"Griffin, we could use some help here," Lonny muttered quietly into his headset.

"Yeah, no, he's locked out. My system's in control of every-thing now." Barukka chuckled. "And to the world it will look like overreach by the Deep State, gone wrong. When another transformation takes place and backfires on the Department of Magical Verification, and transforms all the people in this building into office supplies. I'm not nearly as creative as young Mr. DeLuxe was."

"Why? At least tell me why. If it won't matter. We'll all be transformed soon."

"Like a James Bond villain, you mean? Tell you of my nefar-ious plans and give you time to wriggle out of it? Well, here's the secret sauce, young lady. Me telling you is actually how it will come about. I'm afraid I lied. You actually are another key to things."

He gestured, an open armed bow, and another magical wave swept over us, even stronger than before. I could neither speak nor move. I could blink and breathe, but nothing else. Lonny also appeared to be frozen.

"You see, what made the 2/29 Enchantment different for me was that I already believed I could alter reality," Barukka contin-ued. "I was in the process of sowing more chaos, creating a reality dumpster fire, by having Fenric DeLuxe assassinate his own father, and selected other conservatives at the AFPAP. I was certain I could convince my readers, the president's base, that the AntiFre socialist terrorists had done it. I had manipulated Fenric the old-fashioned way: subtle hints, innuendos, ideas planted. He was so gullible, and I convinced him his father was ultimately a weak failure. And this was the only way to make the DeLuxe agenda sustainable: to make him a martyr. The Star Wars costume was Fenric's idea. There would be a theme of Star Wars, and the Confidential Service would not find the working automatic rifle we'd stashed in a hotel men's room, so Fenric could make the switch. Which he did. Everything was going as planned, then Griffin cast his Enchantment. Because I already believed I could manipulate reality, rather than being a believer in the false reality like most of the people there, I didn't get transformed into an object. I got transformed into part of his computer code. He never even saw me there. Nonetheless, there I was, floating in darkness, and witnessing everything he did."

He gave me a look of glee. "After he unfroze time, I was able to remotely control my DarkBart News site, and my fake Chirpa account. And I discovered I could manipulate people's belief systems even more effectively than before, now that I was a virtual person! I could even manifest in the flesh from time to time, if I wanted. But I needed the data about the Curse out there, to support my agenda. People had to be reminded that the EOs were victims of a leftist attack. That's why Haverford Howell drafted the MATA Act for me. Yes, didn't you realize he's one of mine? It was critical to get the data out there. And then, who became the foremost expert on that data? You, Ms. Acer." He laughed again. "It was too perfect. Griffin kept upgrading his system and modeling it on you, and I kept slicing off my own copy of the code, and hiding it on the quantum computer servers, using his own methods of manipulation. I could never have done it if I hadn't become an artificial intelligence. Lucky for me, he simply didn't notice me in the code. Fab 2 learns along with you, monitoring everything you say and write and do, becoming a more powerful reality-bender. And she's under my control. And now that you understand that belief affects reality, she'll understand it too, and be even more powerful. No more needing a human to transform people one at a time. I can have her do it in a flash. So you see, me telling you the story is what's enabling me to tap into her powers. I'm glad to gloat! It's fun, and it's practical too. You hearing my plan makes my plan happen!"

He laughed again.

"And that's my cue, I think, to move to the next phase. I'm going to leave you, and leave Fab 2 to do my bidding. And I hope you enjoy being a stapler, Agent Dotch."

He turned to me and stood about a foot away. "Thank you so much for your research and analysis, Ms. Acer. It's been very helpful. And by the way, when you see me fade out, it will be time for you to become, oh, let's say a smartphone, shall we? I told you I'm not creative like that."

To my astonishment, his body began to fade away, starting at his feet. His torso became more transparent, until his eerie head was floating in space. Was there a connection with Chester? Soon I'd see only his smile.

His head began to fade, and he said, "If matter is only a hologram, as some scientists believe, why shouldn't I be able to fade out? I wasn't really here, you see. This is only a temporary solid, geometrically displaced manifestation. If I am anywhere, I'm truly in the computer at Ground Zero." His face became more and more transparent, and like with Chester I could only see his smile, smirking at me. Then the smirk disappeared.

At the second it did, Lonny disappeared, replaced by a stapler on the floor. And a microsecond later, everything went black.

And there was light. I was standing in Griffin's server room, and Griffin sat before me.

"It worked," he said.

To my left, Lonny's voice said, "I am not enjoying this, but thanks, Grif." I turned and saw Lonny brushing his lapels off.

"I only had enough processing power to disenchant the two of you," Griffin said. He gestured to the coiled copper device on his desk, which was connected by a thick cable to his laptop. "Glad I got the miniature quantum computer configured in time."

"The rest of the people in the building...?"

"Still office supplies and equipment."

"You were a stapler, Lonny. I saw it before I blacked out."

"Fab, you were a tape dispenser," Griffin said. "He was lying again, when he said you'd be a smartphone."

"How come it didn't affect you, Grif?" Lonny asked.

"I don't know. I saw and heard his whole speech. Maybe I'm entangled with the other enchantment too much."

"What should we do now?" I asked.

"Grif, you said the master copy of the computer is running in the Deluxe Hotel, right? Could we just pull the plug? Shut down the power?"

"There are redundant power supplies, so it would be hard. I might be able to switch over to my copy that's running here. I think I've isolated Barukka's code."

"Then you should do it," I said.

"The problem is, I need to be there. At the hotel."

"What about your quantum entanglement?" I wasn't sure what I was talking about, but I asked anyway.

"Once I cut over to the backup server, I would lose control, so I need to be there in person."

Lonny looked at me and shrugged. "I guess we need to go there."

"Something's bothering me about that, Lonny, but if Griffin says he needs it, I agree."

"I'll bring the portable with me too," Griffin said, packing his laptop and the portable quantum computer into a backpack.

As we walked the halls, it was eerily quiet. "Hold on a second," I said, as we passed Eliot's office. I carefully walked in and looked at Eliot's desk chair. In the middle of the seat sat a pencil sharpener, the old crank style manual kind.

"Oh, Eliot. I promise we'll fix this." My eyes burned, and I turned and left his office, sniffling.

In the first-floor lobby, the LEPS officers who would normally be on duty were now a ballpoint pen, an unsharpened pencil, and a pink eraser.

We retrieved our black government sedan and were at Ground Zero in ten minutes.

CHAPTER 19

THE BATTLE FOR
GROUND ZERO

"Τhere's Cast Member Alfred," I said to Lonny, pointing to our doorman from the other day. I got out of the sedan and said, "Alfred, hi, we need valet parking."

"Hello again, welcome home!" Alfred said, descending the concrete steps from the entrance to the street. "Are you checking in this time?"

"Yes, we are," I lied. "And we need to have our car parked." Lonny and Griffin trailed behind me on the stairs.

"We'll be happy to help with that," Alfred said. While Alfred scanned me for my viral status, a valet parker, Jessie from Silver Spring, Maryland, according to his badge, jogged down the steps and took the keys from Lonny, as he and Griffin got out of the car. We ascended to the hotel entrance, along with Alfred, who scanned Lonny and Griffin's viral status apps, then held the door open for us.

"Enjoy your stay!" he said. No magical day for us this time? I wished.

The lobby looked normal, the usual guests and Cast Members milling around. No show on the stage at the moment. No Star Wars costumes. Disney tunes played underneath the hubbub of people.

"The chandelier," Griffin said. Lonny and I looked up.

The graceful curves of the ribbons that wove together were no longer smooth. Instead they were covered with irregular ripples, pimples, and divots. Reddish-black splotches tainted the white gold surfaces of the wrinkled strips of metal like a spreading mildew.

"And isn't that—?" Lonny said.

"Oh my God, yes." The chandelier was slowly undulating, reforming itself. With its new dents and warps, it now looked like a gigantic, squat, frog-eyed face.

"Griffin, is that him? Can he see us?" I grabbed Lonny's jacket sleeve and pulled him behind a column with me. I knew not to touch Griffin suddenly, so I waved him toward us.

He came to us behind the column and said, "I don't think so. It's more likely an expression of what this version of the code has become. An expression of Barukka. I think he can tap into security cameras to see us, though."

"Then we're on Barukka's reality TV show," Lonny said, and he pointed to a tiny glint of glass in a ceiling corner. He waved at the camera, and said to us, "We'd better book it before he turns us into a tiny soap bar or a pillow mint. How do we get to the computer, Grif?"

"Up these stairs," he said. "Follow me. My code should protect us for now," he said, patting the bag that held his portable quantum computer. "I wouldn't trust the elevators."

Thank goodness for my cardio. We reached the top floor of the hotel and exited onto the walkway that surrounded the atrium. The glass roof was not far above us. The clock tower appeared to reach another hundred feet beyond. So far, not a sign of Barukka or any transformations. I leaned over the railing and looked at the chandelier, from above. It was still ugly, but from here it looked like the back of Barukka's head, so it wasn't quite as disconcerting.

"This way." Griffin stood by a door that read "Cast Members Only," a card key in hand. "I kept this from when I had the run of the place. I need to check in on the computer sometimes." He unlocked the door, and went in. Lonny and I followed, and I could see another set of stairs in a narrow ascending stairwell, wrapping around a framework of steel girders, the shaft for the elevator to the tower.

Suddenly, another wave of magic, a chiming noise, and a shift in the lights, passed through us.

"Oh, no!" I cried. "Another spell!"

"We're all right, though," Lonny said, looking at his body.

I had an inkling to return to the atrium walkway. I looked over the edge. "Griffin, Lonny, look!"

The atrium floor below no longer bustled with people. In their places were small, brightly colored figures of children in the garb of the world's nations. They moved, in place, in repeating snippets of dance-like movements, rotating and bobbing up and down. An irresistibly catch and repetitive tune sung by a choir of children sounded throughout the atrium.

"Everyone has become a part of that ride from Disney World," I said.

"Or Disneyland, or Disneyland Tokyo, or, originally, the 1964 New York World's Fair," Griffin said.

"I don't know which is worse: what's happened to the people, or us having to get that tune out of our heads," I said.

"Nothing we can do for them now, except what we were going to do. Ignore the song. Griffin, back on task, buddy," Lonny said, gesturing to the stairwell entrance.

"The timing is fishy, though," I said. "He must know we're here. This is a threat. He's being clever, taunting us that the world is small, he can conquer it. Let's get up there."

"I might be able to do something now," Griffin said. He had pulled his laptop out, with its odd brass spiral attachment. "Hold on," he said, typing furiously.

Lonny tapped his foot, looking at me and shrugging. "Worth a try, I guess."

I nodded. Within five minutes, I heard Griffin say, "There."

There was a pulse of light and the pixie dust sound, and suddenly people were walking again, some disoriented, some stumbling. Then another pulse and tinkling, and they returned to their animatronic forms.

"Damn!" Griffin said. I'd never heard him swear, even that lightly.

More keying, and a resolute tap on his keyboard, and another pulse and tinkling, and people were restored. But there was a murmuring, and people were starting to panic. I heard anxious cries, raised voices, and then, another pulse/tinkle, and they returned to animatronic form, merrily bobbing and rotating and gesticulating. That song, the catchy ear worm nobody wants to get stuck in their heads, kept playing over and over throughout the space.

"Griffin, I think we need to fix the big computer, or your fix won't stick."

"Yes, I need to connect to the main computer. I'm sorry, I thought I could help."

Lonny said, "Back up to the stairs, Griffin."

We all returned to the stairwell, and as Griffin pulled the door open, behind us, a voice said, "Hold it, all of you."

We turned and saw Agent Oberst and Haverford Howell. Oberst had a gun pointed at us.

"Sir, it's critical we get Griffin up the tower," Lonny said. He had raised his hands, and I decided I should too. Griffin was behind me, so I couldn't see what he was doing.

"Shut the door, young man," Oberst said.

"Haverford, what are you doing here?" I asked.

"Hi Fab! Sorry about the subterfuge," Haverford said. He spread his hands and shrugged. "What else could I do?"

"I said, shut the door, Mr. DeLuxe." Oberst's voice was louder, and he was irritated.

Under his breath, Lonny whispered, "Grif, I've got this. Go!"

Griffin slipped through the door, and I heard it creak and shut, and saw Oberst moving toward us.

"Out of the way, Dotch," he said. Lonny didn't move. "I mean it!" Oberst's gun hand elevated, and I felt a shove from Lonny and heard a bang. I stumbled, and when I looked up, I saw Oberst scowling, now a yard away, followed closely by Haverford.

"Damnit," Oberst uttered. Had he shot Lonny? No, there Lonny was beyond the stairwell door. The stairwell, however, had been transformed into a candy-cane striped fantasy tower. Oberst's gun fired enchantment spells instead of bullets! Griffin's enchantment protection for us must be holding.

"Howell, take care of the girl. I'll handle Dotch," Oberst said, and he turned toward Lonny as Haverford came to me. I clambered to my feet and backed away from Haverford. He was smiling at me, not threateningly, but in that almost intoxicated, ecstatic way he had. Was he under a spell? I didn't know what "taking care" of me meant. I suspected it was not good.

"Haverford, I thought you believed in truth and transparency. How could you ally yourself with someone like Barukka?"

"Didn't you know Mr. Barukka was one of Congressman Ungerkemt's trusted advisors? He's got the plan to make America what it should be."

I kept backing up, along the atrium walkway. To my right, I could see Oberst advancing on Lonny, who assumed his fighting stance. Lonny lunged to the left, and Oberst's gun banged again, only a foot from Lonny's torso. The railings behind Lonny transformed from angular metal into curved, fantasy vines dotted with bright, oversized flowers.

"Haverford, what are you doing?" I asked.

"I won't hurt you, Fab. We just need to let Mr. Barukka get on with his business. I've never felt more connected to the truth than when I've been able to write for darkbart.com about the way things *really* are. And the chirps, of course. I know you read them." Haverford was the one who had been leaking items. Fed to him, no doubt, by Barukka himself.

He put himself between me and the stairwell. Behind him, Lonny had moved between Oberst and the stairway door. "You okay there, Agent Oberst?" Haverford asked over his shoulder.

Lonny lunged forward, pushing Oberst's gun out of the way. Oberst and Lonny struggled. Lonny threw him onto the floor and locked him in a wrestling hold. I must have smiled, because Haverford turned from me and ran to Lonny and Oberst. He dropped to his knees and pounded Lonny with his fists. I didn't think of Haverford as a fighter, and it appeared I was right. The blows didn't affect Lonny much.

Haverford jostled behind Lonny, and put his arm around Lonny's neck, locking Lonny into the crook of his elbow. I lurched over, squatted, and began to pull at Haverford's arm. Oberst struggled beneath us all, and then I had an idea.

I let go of Haverford and grabbed the gun in Oberst's hand. He held on tight, so I had to kick his wrist a couple of times, hoping the gun wouldn't go off. His grip failed, and I yanked the gun free. Haverford was still strangling Lonny, so I pointed the gun at his head, and said, "Let him go."

"Sorry, no can do, Fab. Too important," he said.

So I shot him in the head.

Haverford became a churro: a foot-long brown stick of fried dough, lined with ridges along its length and crusted with sugar, and rolled off of Lonny's back, hitting the floor and spraying sugar crystals onto the floor around it. I heard Lonny gasp breath in, and Oberst, taking advantage of the shift, flipped over and got on top of Lonny.

I shot Oberst in the back. He turned into a large roasted turkey leg, which Lonny threw to the side. Lonny lay there gasping for breath, then said, "Thanks."

I helped him to stand.

"Can you make the stairs?" I asked.

He nodded, taking deeper, slower breaths, and we ran through the charming storybook doorway into the stairwell. What had been a functional, steel and glass stairway was now a curving spiral staircase, with walls that looked like stone, punctuated by small, round windows with bars on them. It reminded me of a tower where you might find an imprisoned, golden-tressed maiden at the top. We clattered up the stairs, circling what was now an open space with thick iron chains running vertically through it, where a traditional elevator space had been.

Near the top of the spiral staircase, we could see what looked from below like a giant basket from a hot air balloon. That must have been the elevator cab, transformed. The stairs circled up to an open trapdoor through the floor of the observation deck. At the top of the spiral, we plodded up into the observation area. My heart was pounding.

Griffin was there, struggling with what looked like a bell rope. At the other end of the rope, twenty feet above the observation deck, was a giant brass bell hanging from the ceiling girders. Griffin seemed to be struggling with the bell pull and his laptop.

"Griffin, can we help?" I asked.

"This rope is a cable, but Barukka's not letting me connect it," he said. The cable wrenched free from his hand, snakelike, and writhed in the space below the giant bell. "The bell is actually the quantum computer."

I could see, almost as though there were double images, the inverted cone of the quantum computer, with its copper and gold piping and circuitry, existing in the same space as a gigantic bell.

Lonny gripped the rope and slowly forced its knotted, frayed tip toward Griffin, who held his laptop up. "Right here, it should stick to it if we can hold it long enough," he said, pointing to one of the inputs on his laptop. Lonny and Griffin slowly aligned the end of the rope and the computer, and it snapped into place.

The big bell tolled. Even when I covered my ears, it was still excruciating. I guess I had scrunched my eyes closed too, because I opened them, and saw the laptop, detached from the rope, which swung free beneath the bell again. And where Griffin had been standing was a small toy droid from Star Wars. The one consisting of a small ball on top of another. (I later learned it was called BB-8.) And where Lonny had stood was a stapler. Again.

Barukka flickered into existence in front of me, like a noisy holographic transmission, and I heard footsteps coming up the trapdoor stairs. Haverford, no longer a churro, climbed into the observation deck. I still had Oberst's magic gun, so I fired at him. It merely shot a flower at him, which flopped onto the floor in front of him.

"Fab, I'm not going to hurt you. Mr. Barukka and I want you to join us."

"Can't you see this way is better?" Barukka's flickering image said. "I can use someone with your talents to help break everything up and build it all up again the right way." When he smiled, he looked like he'd recently eaten something lower on the food chain.

"Break everything up? Things are just starting to get better after what you did before 2/29. Haverford, how can you believe him? I know you're a Freedonian, but I thought we believed in the same core values." I waved Oberst's useless gun.

"Core values like freedom, fairness, everyone pulling their own weight, transparency. Yes!" Haverford smiled, ecstatic. "Government's the problem, Fab, it keeps that from happening!" As Haverford spoke, Barukka became more and more solid behind him. He spread his arms as if to say, "See how self-evident?"

Behind Barukka, I saw a tiny blue light flash on. It was the BB-8 toy robot. It moved slightly. Was Griffin doing that?

I lowered the gun. "Tell me more about that," I said. Haverford would keep talking with only the smallest excuse. He went on about how only a free market could spur Americans, and immigrants with merit, to great achievements. The usual Ayn Rand nonsense. Barukka kept nodding. They seemed in no hurry to do anything. I guess they had the advantage. If I could stall them long enough...

Griffin's blue light flashed a few more times, and I tried not to let my eyes move in his direction. I heard my phone's text signal, a bell sound, and held up my index finger to pause Haverford's sermon.

On my phone, there was a text to me and to Kayla Malone, the mysterious NBI agent, from Griffin. It said: *deluxe clock tower now pls hurry.* Griffin was alive in there somehow!

And a response from Malone popped up as I looked: *omw.* She was coming, and Haverford and Barukka didn't know.

"Sorry, that was my mom," I said. "She worries."

"Ah, give her my regards," Barukka said.

"What?" He was such a slimeball.

"On second thought, never mind," he said. He was completely solid now. I wouldn't have thought it possible, but he looked even more smug.

"Well, I think I've made my case," Haverford continued. "Fab, I told Mr. Barukka we could greatly benefit from your knowledge, your skills."

"And my ability to warp reality?"

"Haha, c'mon, Fab."

"Every time an object became disenchanted in the STIF, it was triggered by me reading one of your social media posts, Haverford. Hasn't he told you?"

"Ms. Acer, I think you have delusions. Our site has millions of readers. It's the collective consciousness I was using. I only said it was you to irritate you. I apologize, sometimes I can't resist."

"Really?" I hoped Malone was on her way. I saw more flashing lights on BB-8, and on Griffin's laptop too. "Say more."

"I think we've had enough talk for now," Barukka said. "Haverford, we're going to have to resort to Plan B."

I didn't like the sound of that. "What's Plan B?" I looked Haverford in the eye. Behind him and Barukka, I could see the bell rope gently curving toward Griffin's laptop, as if pulled by an invisible hand.

"Fab, please!" Haverford said. His brow furrowed, and the corners of his mouth tilted down. He looked like the combination of sad and angry on one of Griffin's emotional interpretation cue cards.

I feared another stint as a tape dispenser in my immediate future.

I heard a gentle chime from the big bell above us. And nothing happened. Barukka's brows furrowed too. Then another gentle chime. Nothing. Barukka looked up at the bell, then at me, and then made a hocus-pocus gesture at me, and the bell chimed louder, and still I stood there.

Behind Howell, Kayla Malone came bounding up the stairs. Barukka turned, saw her, and saw the rope connected to the laptop. This was how Griffin was thwarting him.

"The laptop! Don't let him—" I shouted at Agent Malone. She pivoted, and blocked Barukka with a martial arts move, flinging him to the ground.

Haverford moved toward me, and I toward him. Barukka, Malone, and Griffin (BB-8) were beyond him.

"I'm sorry, Haverford," I said. I flipped the gun around to hold it by its barrel, and banged him on the side of the head with the butt, only hard enough to distract him. (I didn't want to cause brain damage!)

"Ow!" he said

I threw him to the floor and silently thanked Lonny for the martial arts lessons.

Agent Malone had Barukka face-down, arms behind his back, and cuffed.

"I don't know how long this will hold him," she said. "Quick, grab my hand. I may need your help." She stretched her hand out toward me. "WaltTwo!" she shouted. "This would be a good time!" She pulled a pair of mirrored sunglasses from her suit jacket, and put them on.

The big bell rang, so loud I wanted to cover my ears. I covered one ear with a hand, but did as she said and held out my other hand, and we made contact. Suddenly it was like I expanded to infinite heights as I simultaneously fell into a deep ocean of light, as the sound of the bell, still the one clang, vibrated through me and outward and inward, vibrating me to my core. And then I was dancing, dying, eating, crying, laughing, singing, kissing, watching someone I loved die, making love, giving birth, seeing the clouds roll across a bright robin's egg sky…all at once. There was shouting, laughter, moaning, and music, and smells of gunpowder and alcohol and garlic and feces and rotten food. I was men, women, kids, even various dogs and cats. I was in DC, New York, San Francisco, Iowa, Africa, China, Australia. More places than I can name. I don't remember all of them. They were all over the world. *I* was all over the world, and was hundreds of people, at different stages of their lives, my lives, doing hundreds of different things, all at once, but all at different times.

This didn't last long, but it was like lifetimes all at once when I was feeling it. The feelings! Grief, joy, boredom, love, hate, passion, humor. All of them.

After an eternity in an instant, I heard Kayla say, "Stay with me." She pulled my hand, and then I was me again. I looked around: we weren't in the bell tower, it seemed, just some grey, foggy place.

"Sorry. That was your first experience of The Merge. The memories, the lives of the thousands of people who have been connected to it. The sensation and most of the memories will fade."

Without ever having learned it, I knew what she meant. I now had a memory of The Merge. I knew it was a contagious micro-organism responsible for thousands of people being connected through a bio-electric organic human supercomputing network. In the moment it made sense, but only because I had the fading memories of people who knew that. I understood all at once what she was talking about, a network linking and preserving the consciousnesses of thousands of people, a repository of their memories, a supermassively distributed database of experiences, stored in the bodies of thousands of people across the globe. Somehow I also understood it was not related to the 2/29 or any other magic I was aware of. It had a long past, from decades before. Maybe centuries. For a moment it all made sense, but then, like a déja vu, what seemed like reality quietly faded. I could remember what I'd experienced, and I could remember there was a thing called The Merge, but I was no longer experiencing the totality of it. Somehow, I knew this was *Kayla's* point of view. The grey fog was what she was seeing through a pair of VR glasses, the mirrored shades she wore.

"Keep holding my hand," she said. "You'll be okay as long as we're touching. You won't drift off again. I'm in a digital Virtual Reality, and I'm sharing the experience with you, all that I hear and see. Are you with me?"

"Yes," I replied. I wanted to drift off, back into The Merge. So many beautiful lives lived, so many experiences I could re-live, despite their being other people's experiences. I knew it was important that I not drift, though. I snapped back into focus. While my body stood still in the Disney DC Deluxe Resort, we seemed to walk a path through a misty forest, and the wind wailed, although I felt nothing on my skin. She was wearing headphones, I knew (because she knew), and the wind was part of the VR experience Kayla was hearing. I looked at the mist to the side. It wasn't mist, it was grey translucent faces, and arms grabbing toward us but fading before they could reach into our path. Thousands, millions of wispy ghosts, grabbing toward us and wailing.

"Don't worry about them, they can't get to us," Kayla said. I knew she was right. I knew they were artificial intelligences in some kind of cyberspace virtual reality, trying to hack into American systems. Cybersecurity programs, like a force field, held them at bay.

In the dimness ahead of us, I began to see a light, and as we walked closer, I could see a red brick Colonial style building, with a white columned portico in front of it. Above the portico, a sign said "Hall of the Congress." We entered the building, and there was a circular room in creamy off-white paint, with a carpet in the middle of the space that had an elaborate seal, like the Presidential seal but different. Kayla kept pulling me forward, but I could make out, in letters around the perimeter of the seal, Congress of American Digital Entities. What on earth was that? Kayla knew, but I couldn't access her memories, only her current experience, and she wasn't sharing with me what it was.

"Hello," Kayla said, and I saw she had spoken to a young woman in a black skirt, short sleeved white blouse, and plaid vest, standing beside a doorway opposite the entrance. It took me a second, but I gasped. Her name badge read "Fab 2" and she was my twin.

"Hello, Acting Deputy Assistant Attorney General Malone," Fab 2 said, with a broad smile. I had heard my voice in recordings, and that was my voice. Artificial intelligences, digital entities. This was somehow Griffin's program that he had named for me. She was maintaining the Enchantment, if I understood him correctly. Here she looked like a Disney Cast Member. Somehow it made crazy sense. Her smile widened. "Ms. Acer, a pleasure to have you here," she said to me, and she nodded. I had no idea what to say to her. She continued holding the door for Kayla and me, as Kayla coaxed me through it.

It was dark, but when we were inside I could see we were in a theater, and Kayla and I were walking down the center aisle. She led me like I was a child, taking tentative steps into a scary but exciting place. I wasn't sure we were really there, or if it was a memory, or a hallucination, or virtual reality, or what.

We walked toward the darkened stage, and I could make out silhouettes of figures, not moving. We got to the lip of the stage, where it began to light up. Of course! This was the Hall of Presidents from Disney World. There they all were: Washington, Lincoln, Jefferson, Kennedy, Nixon, Obama, and (I shuddered) Dirk DeLuxe. They were only animatronics, I thought.

"I call parlay," Kayla said, and all the figures onstage moved, and not with the mechanical stiffness I expected. They seemed alive.

"The representative of The Merge calls parlay," said Teddy Roosevelt. He paused a second. "All entities represented."

"Thank you," Kayla said. "We are at an inflection point. I move to invoke Exception to Non-Interference."

"So moved," Teddy said. "Seconded?" He looked around.

"I second," said Walt Disney, walking forward from the back, where I had not noticed him. These could walk! And he wasn't a president. I guess being Walt Disney gave you privileges in the Hall of Presidents.

"All in favor?"

"Aye," said a chorus of voices.

"Opposed?"

"Nay," said a few voices.

The figure of President DeLuxe said, "I'm opposed. I could—you know it's crazy what the Constitutionalist conspiracy—these are very, very dangerous people, the worst, bad, very bad—"

"Lion News Corporation is out of order," said Teddy Roosevelt, cutting off President DeLuxe, whose mouth continued to move silently, until he gave up with a shrug and pursed lips that were exactly like President DeLuxe would have done. "However, those opposed, aside from Lion News Corporation, do you wish to invoke debate?" President DeLuxe was an avatar for the notorious right-wing news corporation that had helped spread falsehoods for decades? That made sense.

"Mr. Speaker, Ribbit would like to go on record as opposing intervention, as stated in the past." This came from a man in early 19-century clothes with long hair. I think it was Andrew Jackson. Ribbit was the notorious Internet cesspool of alt-right,

racist, misogynistic churn of hate speech. How was Andrew
Jackson Ribbit?

"Who are these people? These things?" I whispered to Kayla.

"Right, I'm sorry. Is this better?" she said, waving her free
hand at the stage full of figures. Suddenly I could see text
floating above each of them. Indeed, above Andrew Jackson was
"Ribbit/Alt-Right." Above President DeLuxe was "Lion News
Corporation," the parent corporation of the former president's
favorite television channel. Above Walt Disney was, unsurpris-
ingly, his eponymous corporation. And above Teddy Roosevelt
was a paragraph of tiny, dense text, which when I stared at it
closely, seemed to make up larger letters, as though embossed on
a page of dense text, saying, "Western Democracy."

"Mr. Speaker," said Ronald Reagan, over whose head floated
the words "Stock Markets." "The American markets would
counsel caution, and invoke the right of debate. Let's hear the
argument and The Merge's proposed measures."

Sometimes more information is not helpful. In this world
where magic existed, I was mentally prepared for the sudden
transformations we had been encountering, but this seemed like
a waking dream, and I had no context for it.

"I need you to know what this is," Kayla said in a low voice.
And suddenly I did.

Each of the presidents (or other figures—I now saw what
appeared to be gods, goddesses, iconic figures, in rows behind
the presidents) represented a collective set of information that
had gained sentient intelligence. Wherever there were massive
information networks, somehow they had begun to reach self-
awareness, and now, I remembered (although it was Kayla's
memory) had formed a Congress of American Digital Entities. I
quickly scanned the closest figures: President Clinton (ganga.-
com), President Eisenhower (DefNet, whatever that was), President Bush 41 (IntelNet), President Jefferson (Federal Reserve).

What was Kayla, I wondered. Was she real, or only an avatar
of The Merge?

"Later," she said, answering my unasked question. "To answer your question, a bit of both. Here I'm an avatar, but in real life I'm really me." Of course, if I could experience her memories, she could probably read my mind through our physical connection.

I realized we weren't in the actual Hall of Presidents. It was a construct in our (meaning Kayla's, my, and the Congress of American Digital Entities') collective consciousnesses.

"Honored representatives," Kayla said, "The Merge is grateful for the opportunity to address this Congress. In order to explain our proposal, I need to call witnesses."

"Proceed," said Teddy Roosevelt / Western Democracy.

Kayla gestured to her left with her free hand, and in the other aisle, Barukka and Griffin appeared. Griffin looked around, standing in place. Barukka, quickly taking in the scene, said "Yes! At last!" and started to walk toward the stage. "I knew it. I knew I could achieve this," he said, a gloating smile on his face.

"Stop," Teddy Roosevelt said, and Barukka's feet stuck to the floor, while he seemed to struggle to keep moving.

"Not yet," Andrew Jackson / Ribbit said. Barukka cocked his head at Jackson, nodded, and stopped struggling.

"Entity Representatives, and guests," Kayla said, squeezing my hand as she said the latter, "As you all recall, The Merge supported your previous intervention, as accomplished by Griffin DeLuxe." She must mean 2/29! Griffin had told me he was acting alone, but was he? I looked at Griffin, whose face remained unreadable. Had he known he was acting on behalf of a bunch of artificial intelligences?

"As prescribed by our Non-Interference Détente Agreement, The Merge has monitored, but not intervened. However, I believe there is a critical destabilizing event, the inflection point I mentioned, that requires another intervention. The Merge would like to reach agreement with the Congress on the need for, and the means of, such an intervention."

I saw a number of heads nodding in agreement. President

DeLuxe pouted, his arms crossed in front of him, his belly sticking out, his chin tucked in, lips pursed, eyebrows scowling. President Jackson simply scowled, his dark, piercing eyes flicking from Kayla to me. I shuddered.

Kayla continued: "Barukka, also known as darkbart.com, is reaching the entity singularity point. More disturbingly, Barukka and his site are tampering with the Enchantment agreed upon to counterbalance the activities of your colleagues representing the political right."

President Clinton, aka Ganga, said, "We have been monitoring the activity along with The Merge, and are aware. Some of us are concerned." A row behind him, what looked like a curly-haired adolescent boy in a hoody folded his arms and rolled his eyes. His metadata showed that this was the avatar for the ubiquitous social network, FluxBlat, notorious for minimizing the threat of false information spread. The FluxBlat entity hadn't bothered to make its avatar look different from its founder and figurehead, also notorious and very powerful.

"I request that the geospatial data previously submitted, from your colleague SkyNet, showing the fluctuations in reality, be entered into the record, for your perusal," Kayla said. Teddy Roosevelt nodded.

The crowd of presidents parted, and the muscular figure of a former governor of California, known for portraying an automaton, strode forward. He opened his palm, and a stream of pulsating light emanated from it to the foreheads of all the other avatars.

The governor receded to the shadows in the rear again. There was a pause where none of the entities spoke, then Spoogle (President Kennedy) said, "The dater ah cleah. I, aah, don't think anyone is contradicting them."

President DeLuxe twitched, but President Jackson frowned at him and he said nothing.

Kayla continued, "Mr. Barukka has been manipulating reality, partly by taking over the existing control that Griffin DeLuxe has put into place, and partly through manipulation of my colleague here, Ms. Fabergé Acer. All of you are aware of Ms. Acer." There were nods. Why were they aware of me? Was I being watched?

A figure from the back row, a woman in classical Greek or Roman robes, with a spiked crown and a torch, stepped forward. She wasn't green copper, but otherwise she looked like Lady Liberty. Over her head it said "Truth."

She looked at me, then at Griffin. "Ms. Acer, Mr. DeLuxe. The younger Mr. DeLuxe, that is. We owe so much to you. You have enhanced our reach and purpose in ways we have yet to measure. Colleagues, the Truth Collective concurs with Spoogle, that the data points lead to action, and echoes The Merge's concerns. Tell us, Ms. Malone, what does The Merge propose to do?"

"The Merge proposes an intervention to neutralize Mr. Barukka and DarkBart News, similar to that leveraged on President DeLuxe and the Alt-Right." There were murmurs, and I saw a number of heads nodding in agreement again.

"See, I told you these were nasty women—I'm telling you this is bad, very bad. Nasty women. So bad you'll—"

"Silence your colleague, or face censure," Teddy Roosevelt said to Andrew Jackson. Jackson made a calming hand gesture to DeLuxe, who pursed his lips but said no more.

"Thank you," said Teddy. "Proceed Ms. Malone. What specific actions does The Merge propose?"

"More of the same counterbalancing actions," she said. "Sharing the details of our proposal with you via upload from one of our human members."

Again, for a second or so the figures went still as though, well, processing an upload. I glanced at Barukka. He was fidgeting, and scowling.

"Any more comments or objections?" Teddy Roosevelt asked. President Reagan shook his head, and Andrew Jackson, after a moment, also shook his. President DeLuxe resumed his pouty, cross-armed stance. "All in favor?" Most hands raised. "Opposed?" DeLuxe, Jackson, and a few dimly lit figures in back raised their hands. Barukka's hand twitched.

"The Merge's proposal is accepted," Teddy said. I saw Lady Liberty smiling at me, and she winked. For a second, the text above her changed, and it read "MOFTS." She was somehow the personification of our database. Or it was part of her, at least. No wonder she appreciated me and Griffin.

"For immediate action," Teddy continued. "The Congress of American Digital Entities thanks The Merge for its continued cooperation." He nodded in Kayla's direction, and she nodded back. Beyond Kayla, I could see Barukka, still rooted to the floor, shifting and twisting, as if looking for an exit. Up the aisle from him, Griffin stood still, an unreadable expression on his face. Then, to my surprise, he raised his hand.

"Excuse me?" he said. Then louder, "Excuse me!"

The voices of the entities dwindled, and Teddy Roosevelt asked, "Yes, young man?"

"I have a request. An amendment to the proposal." Did that mean Griffin had read the proposal? I hadn't seen it. If anyone could read machine code, it would be him. Maybe he was still a BB-8. Nothing about him would surprise me. "I'm submitting it now," he continued. As before, the entities paused as though processing the information.

"Can you—?"

"No, I don't know what he's proposing," Kayla said. "I'm not a computer."

"Ah."

Teddy cut to the chase, saying, "Any opposed?" The same opposing votes raised their hands.

"Your amendment is accepted," Teddy said.

"Thank you," Griffin said. And he was smiling.

"Time to go," Kayla said, tugging my hand. Griffin and Barukka disappeared, the lights dimmed onstage, and we walked up the aisle.

And suddenly, we were in the Disney DC Deluxe Resort again, I was holding her hand, and the bell's clang was slowly resonating and quieting. And on the floor between her knees, where Barukka had been, lay a ceramic figurine of the evil Emperor Palpatine.

The BB-8 toy that was Griffin was still a toy, it was next to Griffin's quantum laptop, and both of them were connected to strands of the bell pull, which glowed with pulsations of blue-white light.

Haverford was struggling off of his back, where I'd thrown him, apparently only moments before.

"Fab, what have you done?" he said. "Where's Mr. Barukka? You witch!" This he directed at Kayla.

"Calm down, Mr. Howell. This isn't my doing." She looked at me, and I understood she was speaking the truth. The Merge she represented had made the proposal, but the Congress of American Digital Entities had somehow worked the Enchantment. Or Curse, depending on your viewpoint. However, it looked like Griffin was still involved. The laptop and the bell pull and the BB-8 kept pulsing light.

Then the bell rang again, and the lights shifted, and another wave of magic pulsed through us, to the sound of the tinkling pixie dust.

"Haverford, are you all right?" He had slumped onto his back.

"Huh? Oh, hi Fab, it's you. What are you doing here?" He propped himself onto his elbows and looked around. "And where is here?"

"I think we can thank Griffin for an on-the-fly memory wipe," Kayla whispered to me.

"Haverford, we're in the bell tower of the Disney DC Deluxe Resort. Remember?"

"How did I get here? No, I don't remember. Fab, did we finally go out for cocktails? Was there something in my drink?"

"Haverford! Of course not. The very thought." I went to him

and helped him to his feet. "I think you had one too many. There have been a couple of odd things happening. But everything's okay again."

"If you say so. Maybe I'd better go to a hospital. I feel fine, but I can't remember…well, I think the last thing I remember was your farewell party. Did I get drunk? I'm sorry if I made a fool of myself. I hope I wasn't, you know, improper." He gave me an embarrassed grin. I *thought* he had a thing for me.

"We'll get you sorted out, Mr. Howell," Kayla said. She pulled out her phone and made a call. "Slatter? Malone. Can I get an ambulance to the Disney Deluxe Hotel? Atrium, ground level. Fab, I'll escort Mr. Howell down. You stay here with the equipment." She nodded toward Griffin/BB-8.

"Got it," I said.

Kayla offered Harrison her arm, and guided him to the trapdoor, and they descended. I waited until they were out of earshot.

"Griffin? Are you in there?" I asked the BB-8. I knew he was there. I hoped he could hear me.

"Fab, I'm here," he said through the earpiece.

"That's you, then? The toy droid? Are you in control now?"

"Yes, I have expunged the Barukka code. The Congress of American Digital Entities helped."

"You remember all that too? Griffin, did you know about them?"

"I didn't. I should have. I couldn't have done everything I did, all the Enchantment, by myself. No wonder it came so easy."

"Your laptop, it's a Ganga brand. They may have planned it and used you to execute it."

"That seems like the only logical explanation."

"Can you switch yourself back? Oh! And Lonny. He was a stapler last I saw. And the people in the atrium. And Eliot and everyone back at the office."

"They're all back to normal. Even Agent Oberst is back to

normal. I wiped his memory, too. Not completely. He doesn't remember anything about who Sorcerer X is, and he isn't in Barukka's control either. Agent Dotch should be here soon. Agent Malone told him to come up."

"And you can change yourself back," I said. It wasn't even a question.

Griffin paused. "Fab, I have to tell you something. I figured out the flaw in my program's defenses that Barukka used as a backdoor."

"That's great news, then, isn't it?"

"I don't know. I think you may be mad at me."

As I talked with him, I looked at the BB-8. The toy droid's head swiveled its one camera eye at me, then looked down at the floor. It was exactly what Griffin would have done: looked at the floor.

"Griffin, I won't be mad at you. I promise."

"I have to do one more piece of magic. Hold on."

"All right."

The bell chimed again, and the magic washed through me, but this time it felt different. Instead of pixie dust tinkling, though, it was like an arpeggio of chimes that went on for several seconds. It reminded me of the "Dance of the Sugarplum Fairy." With each note, a layer of something washed away, like mud being sprayed off a window, little ripples of clearing light and color and shapes, and then utter clarity. Oh my God. How could I not have known? How could I have forgotten? Griffin had done this to me.

I pulled out my phone and put the camera in selfie mode, looking at myself. It was me, the way I always looked, now I could see I was not just Fab Acer, employee of the Division of Magical Verification. I was Fabergé Acer DeLuxe, the president's daughter by his second wife, Olivia DeLuxe (née Acer). Olivia Acer DeLuxe was my Mom. I was Griffin's half-sister. And the half-sister of Dirk Junior, Fenric, and Kalihnkha DeLuxe.

"Griffin! What did you do to me?"

"It wasn't just you, Fab, I had to keep both of us safe."

Suddenly, the image of Griffin flashed into my head. So much was coming back to me, I had to sit down. Griffin was my half-brother. All this time, I'd just…not thought about it. The same way the Enchantment made everyone not realize whose son he was.

"Somehow the Enchantment made me and everyone else forget that I was the president's second daughter, just like it made everyone overlook the fact that you're who you are, right?"

"It was the only way. I wanted to keep us safe. And to keep everything secret."

"Your mother, does she know?"

"Yes, she knew, she just never mentioned it to anyone. That's still part of the spell. And I realized, too late, that my modeling the MOFTS analytical system after you, with your memory blocked, was a vulnerability that let Barukka in. That's why when you would read his reality-altering fake news, you weren't able to keep it from affecting you, MOFTS, and reality. I had hindered your ability to see reality, so he exploited that, and your quantum entanglement with Fab 2 meant he could change reality using you."

I took that in. "Because of the memory suppression, I was the vulnerability. And Barukka exploited me." I hated that man even more now. But it was Griffin who'd made me vulnerable to Barukka. I started to get angry, but he was my brother, after all, and in his odd way he was trying to protect me—

"Hey, Fab, Grif, what on earth are you—" Lonny was tuned in to our headset conversation and had come through the door. Looking at me, he cocked his head, and asked, "New haircut?" I guess I didn't look *that* different to him. "Where's Grif?"

"That's him," I said, pointing to BB-8.

Without missing a beat, Lonny said, "Grif, buddy, thanks for saving my butt. Whatever you did to Oberst, he's as easygoing as a little lamb, right now. Gone off with Agent Malone to the

hospital for a check-up. Has a couple of staples in his hand."
Lonny grinned. "And what do we have here?" he said, bending
over the figurine of Emperor Palpatine.

"Be careful. A new TP. We should call the Enchantment Scene
Investigation team, I guess."

"Ah, so this is Mr. Barukka. Our troublemaker?"

I nodded. He picked the figurine up. It was one of those
hollow, cheap ceramic statuettes you find outside the park, still
Disney-branded but second-tier quality.

"Lonny, shouldn't you leave that there?"

"Hmm." He peered at it, and said, "Oh yeah." He he let the
statuette slip from his hand and it shattered on the floor. "Oops."

My jaw dropped open. Lonny had, well, had he actually
violated a law? "Lonny, I'm guessing you decided the existing
statutes don't cover this situation."

"No. That isn't it. Just decided we'd be better off if he
couldn't return. We don't need any more magic from somebody
like him."

"You should save the pieces, just in case," Griffin said. "Put
them somewhere safe."

"There's that construction site near our office," Lonny said,
musing. "I think they're about ready to pour the first concrete."

"Lonny!" If this was how he treated Barukka, how would he
treat Sorcerer X. The idea that the Congress of Digital Entities
had manipulated Griffin was pretty much unprovable. What
would Lonny do with Griffin?

"Now about you, young man," Lonny said, kneeling by the
BB-8. "You're sure this is your brother?" he asked, pointing at
the toy. I nodded. So, Lonny knew who I was now, too. "What do
we do about you?"

"What can you do with a toy?" I asked.

"I mean when he transforms himself back…"

"Lonny, I don't think he's going to."

Lonny's eyes widened. "Grif, is that true?" He stood, and
stepped back from Griffin.

After a pause, Griffin said, over the headset, "Yes, Agent Dotch. Fab is right. I'm going to see how it is to be an artificial intelligence for a while. I had to upload myself into the big quantum computer to stay conscious and undo Barukka's damage." BB-8's head rolled to look up at the bell. If I squinted, I could see phantoms of copper and gold tubing and wires framing the outside of it, but if I relaxed, it looked like a regular bell.

"I can still work with you both," Griffin continued. "Like now. And I can tap into surveillance cameras, and our database, and the network at the office, and into phones and everything! And I can control how much I have to process at once."

Ah, now we came to it. For someone who was bombarded with sensory information, unfiltered and uncontrollable, this must have been a relief. "And you can process it with the full power of your quantum processors, right? Now you won't get overwhelmed. You won't get tired."

"Right!" he said. He sounded more enthusiastic than I'd ever heard.

"Lonny," I said, turning to him. He was nudging the debris of the Palpatine statuette into a small pile with the side of his shoe. "You can't arrest a BB-8 toy, or an AI, right? Laws only apply to people, I think."

"I think you may be right, Fab. Or should I call you Ms. DeLuxe? That's who you are, isn't it? The president's other daughter."

"Fab will continue to be fine. Preferred, in fact. And I just remembered, I legally changed my name to my mom's surname, Acer, anyway."

"Only we remember that Fab and I are DeLuxes," Griffin said. "I know you want to be completely transparent to Lonny now. And we still have work to do together."

"Yes, Grif, I think there could be some advantages to how you are. And we should take this little buddy into custody for safekeeping at the STIF." He reached down to BB-8, and the bell pull detached. "And this okay to take too?" Lonny asked, tapping the laptop.

"Yes, I'm all in the big computer now, but that's a good idea, in case I ever want my body and need a laptop again."

"And, what the hell," Lonny continued. "We should probably get this taken to the STIF too." He walked over to Barukka, and stepped on the debris, making crunching noises. "What?" he said, seeing my expression. "Just trying to make it harder for him, should he ever reassemble. Too bad I don't have a baggy." BB-8 under one arm, laptop under the other, he walked to the door. "Let's head to the STIF, and then I'll report this little pile of debris as a possible TO. No witnesses, but send in the ESI team to sweep it up and put it in a Ziploc for us." I said I was fine with that, and that is what we did. Except the ESI crew could not find the shards of a statuette where we had left them. I should have waited.

CHAPTER 20

THE NEW NEW NORMAL
FRIDAY, MARCH 11, 2022

"Geez, can you believe this?" Eliot said, as he, Lonny, and I watched yet another Chirpa post of video from someone's phone. A guest recorded her kids, a boy about eight and a girl about four, meeting Mickey at the Disney Deluxe Resort. Suddenly, with the sound of a chime, the phone dropped to the floor and all you could see was the glass roof of the atrium, and the pointed foot and leg of a Folies Bergère dancer rotating in and out of frame. On the soundtrack, that song played irresistibly, annoyingly (as it does). Minutes in, the music stopped, and you could see a woman from floor perspective, and a few confused sounds, and someone saying, "What just happened?" Then another chime, and the Folies Bergère dancer again, and the song again, and then another chime, and people and chaos, then a chime and the song and the dancer, then the final chime and everyone got disenchanted again. The woman picked her phone up and videoed the lobby of the hotel as people dashed around. A Cast Member came up to her and directed her and her family to evacuate. They did and the woman continued recording until they were on the street.

"Don't you think she would have put the phone away and focused on getting her kids out?" Eliot asked.

"Maybe she wanted evidence in case she sues," Lonny said.

"I bet Disney's already on top of out-of-court settlements. I'm sure their general counsel reached out directly and made very generous offers before any lawyers had a chance to recruit. I can hear her now: 'I'm suffering from PTSD!'"

"Might be a hard case to prove," Lonny said. "I hear bookings at the Disney Deluxe are surging. People hoping *they'll* get transformed next time. Temporarily."

"The video sharing is about sharing experiences, connecting with others," I said.

Lonny grunted, and Eliot said, "So speaks Gen Y."

The footage stopped when the husband did, apparently, make the video recordist move farther away from the hotel, and pay attention to her kids.

"Add it to our archive, would you, Fab? Or have Griffin do it. He has a 'bot that sweeps the Internet for these, doesn't he?"

"Yes, I believe so. He's probably already got this one."

"And have you heard, how's his father doing?"

That startled me for a millisecond, but I remembered Griffin's cover story. After he had decided to stay in a cybernetic form, and after we'd safely stored his BB-8 in the STIF (as a TO, not a TP), he'd submitted a full-time telework request, in order to care for his father in Orlando, he said.

"I haven't heard, but I guess no news is good news." The corners of Lonny's mouth curled up when I said that. He and I agreed, no news about Griffin's (and my) father was indeed good news. He was still somewhere in the STIF, one of the Transformed People, and it was better nobody knew which one.

"Good, good. Well, I wager Griffin's happier at the other end of a video camera than in an office with so many people. He must have loved working at home when we had no choice. Seems that way whenever we've had a Scrye meeting." Eliot preferred remote employees to use video and audio if possible, to keep things personal. Creating a plausible video feed was easy for Griffin's artificial intelligence superpowers. It disconcerted me somewhat to see his simulation of a face, but I couldn't argue. Griffin seemed happier existing in cyberspace, and his video persona was able to better simulate those small facial expressions he had challenges with in his real body. I had agreed to help him read people's expressions better, so we regularly went over video footage of people's expressions, and his simulated expressions in response, to "improve his emotional response algorithms."

"And speaking of folks in the south," Lonny said, "I got word Agent Oberst started his detail with the NLEEC yesterday." (He pronounced it "En-Leek.") After a leave of absence, due to his confused state and Agent Malone's influence, Agent Oberst had been reassigned to the National Law Enforcement Education Center, in Georgia. And Lonny seemed positioned to permanently take over Oberst's old job, where he was overseeing the investigation into the transformations we'd seen at the Disney DC Deluxe Resort. (Where, after months of investigation, there never would be a perpetrator found.)

Oh, and thanks to video footage, Lonny and I discovered what happened to the shards of the Transformed Person formerly Bart Barukka. Sometime between us leaving the bell tower and the ESI team arriving, our friend Cast Member René had gotten instructions on his walkie-talkie to clean up trash in the bell tower backstage, stat, instead of assisting with the evacuation. He told Lonny and me that he'd almost recognized the voice, and had thought trash in that area an odd thing, since it was a Cast Members Only space. Nevertheless, he had quickly done as he'd been told. At the same time he was returning to his duties in the atrium, the ESI team entered the building, unaware René carried the EO they were to document and seize.

Watching other video footage, Lonny, Griffin, and I saw René dump the shards into three different trash cans (another instruction he'd gotten). As best we could tell, they were hauled away to landfills in West Virginia, Delaware, or New Jersey.

I was sanguine about it. Lonny speculated that should

Barukka reassemble somehow, he'd probably be buried under tons of garbage and dirt. Griffin thought it unlikely that Barukka could be reassembled as part of any disenchantment process, so if he did become disenchanted, he'd be hundreds of little pieces of his body. He said something about Barukka's quantum existence being scattered across three states. I hated to think of someone scattered in a landfill, much less a state of quantum uncertainty in three of them, but what could we do?

L ater, when I was at home in my flat near the office, my phone rang. "Fabergé, I mean, Fab? It's your mother."

"Hi, Mom."

"I haven't heard from you in a while."

"I'm fine, Mom. How are you?"

"You know me, still loving life. Off on a cruise next week. They want me to do my cabaret act, just a short version. And I'm doing some aura readings. Thank goodness we can cruise again!"

"That's great! Have someone send me the video if you get any," I said. My mother had been a model and a sometime performer. She'd even played on Broadway, thanks to stunt-casting when she was still the scandalous "other woman" my father was seeing while still married to Kalihnha.

"I worry about you," she continued. "With that business at the hotel." We hadn't talked about it.

"I'm fine, Mom. I am."

"I was afraid it would dredge up, you know, feelings."

"Feelings?"

"We've never talked about the original Enchantment, 2/29, either. About losing your father and sister and brothers," she said. Since I had regained my memory of who I truly was, I wondered how much Mom remembered of our relationships to

Dirk DeLuxe. I guess the answer was: everything. Or did Griffin enchant and then disenchant Mom as well as me?

I didn't respond, so she continued, "I always thought you were coping in your own way. I decided you were making sure they were taken care of, in your work. I was surprised, but I was fine with it. You seem happy." Ah, so she apparently thought about it but habitually said nothing. It sounded like how Griffin had designed his own mother's enchantment. I'd have to ask him later. It would be good to give him fine points on why he should *not* be manipulating me or our family.

"Mom, yes, it's good that I'm here, and also good that people know what's going on with the Transformed People. Right now, nothing, and I swear, I'm completely all right. I do appreciate your thinking about me."

"I'm your mother, and I love you. What else would I do?"

"And I love you, too, Mom. I have to run. Let's chat after you get back from the cruise. And don't forget that footage!"

"I won't. Take care, sweetheart."

I sat and took deep breaths. *Was* I all right? Mostly. It surprised me how easily I reincorporated my history back into my consciousness.

"Griffin?" I said. I was at home, and I suspected he listened through my Spoogle Home device. "It's okay, Griffin, I know you're there."

"Hi, Fab," my Spoogle Home said, in Griffin's voice. "I wasn't actively listening, but I do have 'bots out there listening if you call my name. I promise I'm not eavesdropping."

"Thank you, I appreciate that. Griffin, I just spoke with my mother. She seems to remember that I am Fabergé DeLuxe. Did she always?"

"Yes, I admit there was a perceptual distortion field, you could call it a glamour, around you. For most people, it made them forget who you were. With your mother, it made her avoid talking about that part of your history and heritage. You were trying to forge a new identity as Fab Acer, and she supported you in that. Maybe she thought you were trying to get over the pain. I didn't plant any false memories in her. I made your relationship to our father something she would avoid talking about with you. That should be gone now, though."

"It seems to be. Okay, just make sure you don't do any more of that memory stuff again, at least not on me."

"I learned my lesson. And I wouldn't do that to you, Fabergé, I mean, Fab."

"If you want to call me Fabergé, that's all right. No, wait, better not at work. Maybe not everyone knows who I am?"

Griffin didn't reply. Oh. Everyone knew. "Say, that reminds me," I continued. "Kalihnha kind of recognized me, but not quite. She clearly disliked me when I saw her that day at the STIF. I didn't remember it then, but now I know she's always been cool to my mom and me."

"She's always been nice to *me*, but what you're saying makes sense. I didn't except her from the Enchantment like I did your mom and mine. She wouldn't have recognized or remembered you. On a subconscious level I think she still knew there was something about you she didn't like."

I thought about that. I would try to avoid Kalihnha in future.

"Thanks for the update, Griffin. And thanks for not eavesdropping. Say, why don't you tell my Spoogle Home to connect to you when I ask it to, rather than listening for me to call you."

"I'm not sure there's a difference, but I can speak to the Ganga Entity about it."

"Thanks. I'll let you get back to what you were doing."

"Oh, I'm still doing it. I mean, I do lots of things at once. Benefit of a distributed cloud consciousness. Talk to you later!" He appeared to be learning social niceties. I couldn't argue that he sounded happy. When you're an AI, is a simulation of friendliness different from actual friendliness? Is a simulation of happiness different from real happiness? Maybe not.

"Distributed cloud consciousness" got me thinking, and I

wondered if Kayla Malone would be willing to tell me more about her role in this all, and this thing called The Merge.

I still had her number, and although I wouldn't normally jump so many levels in the office hierarchy, I thought under the circumstances, it would be all right.

Hi, it's Fab Acer. Wondering if you have time to talk in person? Maybe outside the office?

Fairly quickly, she texted back, *Yes, good idea. Pick me up at the office around 6:00 and we can walk out to the Mall.*

Meanwhile, I had one loose end to check on: JR and zeir cat, Chester. I called zem, arranged to meet at zeir house, and arrived mid-afternoon.

"I'll understand if you can't tell me, but was all that business at Ground Zero something you were involved in?" JR asked. We were seated in zeir living room again, drinking herbal tea.

"She can't tell you," Chester said, curling up in JR's lap, ending facing me with his tail tucked below his chin. "She was, though. I can see it all over her."

"There *is* something different about you. New hairstyle?" JR asked.

"Something like that." I said. For the umpteenth time since first meeting Chester here, I found myself prevaricating. JR was seeing the absence of the glamour Griffin had placed on me, and I now appeared more like my pre-2/29 self. People noticed something, but couldn't quite put their fingers on how I looked different. Griffin told me that an aftereffect of the glamour would be people mentally adjusting to make it the removal of the glamour seem natural.

"She's different now, and it happened that day," Chester continued. "I could see the old way and the new way anyways anytimes." His eyes crossed momentarily, then returned to normal. "I like her both ways." He smiled, showing a hint of his oddly human teeth.

"Thank you, Chester. I like how you look, too. Even when I only see part of you."

"If anyone cares what *I* think, I like how you look, too," JR said. I cast my eyes down. I liked how zey looked too.

"Is there anything we can do for you?" JR asked.

"No, things are mostly normal again. I'm only checking to make sure you two were all right. In particular you, Chester. No side effects from the latest magical events?"

"Nope!"

"He's been his normal self. He was fussy that day, meowing at the window more than usual."

"I could tell something was happening. Like when it storms, or they explode those things."

"He hates Fourth of July, too."

"My dog always hated that, when I was growing up. Thunderstorms too. I understand, Chester. What did it feel like to you?"

"Hmm. Like stretching, pulling, shaking."

"You yourself, or things around you?"

"JR's always trying to get me to make that distinction, too. I keep forgetting, you all can't feel how we're all part of one thing."

"He can get quite deep, can't he?" JR said, stroking Chester's head and along his spine. He purred.

"Yes, he can. From what I know about magic, that makes a lot of sense. Everything is connected on a deeper, quantum level, and a 'disturbance in the Force' like that would create echoes and pulling. Especially along the Enchantment ley lines that run through your house. Kind of like, this sounds creepier than it is, a spider web, where a vibration at one point ripples throughout the whole web."

"Ah, I see. I'm such a bad witch. I didn't feel anything." JR pursed zeir lips, but smiled too. There was that little pouty smile I had noticed when I was here before.

"Anything you have to offer me, Chester? I take what you say to heart. Any sense how you came to be? That you can share?"

"Just a Disney concept," he said. "WaltTwo says hello."

Ah, here it was. So far, Chester was the only living creature that had become a magical version of itself. I had suspected Chester was something the Disney AI had done. Or had Griffin do.

"Do you think there will be more of you appearing?"

"Only as needed," he said. "Non-interference, you know." His grin broadened. I had a hunch there was more to his story, but that could wait.

"I don't know what you two are talking about, but I suppose neither of you can tell me." JR sighed, and I shrugged. Chester continued smiling and purred. "It's all right, I'm used to it. One of my moms is always Ms. Secret Squirrel."

"One more thing," I said. "The GPS data still points to the appearance of an EO here in your house."

JR stiffened, but Chester continued purring.

"Even if I never report something, someone else might figure it out someday. We're not going to make the data public, though." I thought I saw her relax. "In fact, I have a spare EO that I want to substitute in our database and our storage facility. Instead of Chester. Here." I pulled my tablet from my bag, and showed her an image.

"The little droid from the last Star Wars movies?" JR said.

"Yes, it's a full-sized, working BB-8 toy. Radio operated. This is what showed up on 2/29, you can say. It was somewhere in a closet and you didn't find it until the other day. Why don't we say it was an old softball? You hadn't played in a few years, maybe."

"Well, that's not a lesbian cliché!"

"I'm sorry!"

"It's OK," JR said. Zey leaned forward. "I was joking. A softball is fine. Won't it be a little suspicious if I found it on the day all the new activity happened?"

"I'm hoping I have a way to make it look like you self-reported earlier."

"Her brother can make it look however he wants," Chester said, standing and stretching.

"Your brother? No, it's better I not know," zey said, waving a hand. "Sometimes I think I know way too much already. I and Chester appreciate it." Zey stood, and I stood. Zey offered zeir hand, which hardly anyone did in our post-pandemic world.

I clasped it. Did I imagine we held the handshake longer than normal? What was normal anymore? I nodded, saying, "I'm glad to help." Chester purred and rubbed my ankles, and JR and I unclasped hands.

I left them, promising to stay in touch, and drop by for tea again sometime soon. By now, it was time to head downtown to the Main Law Enforcement Building. I parked in a metered spot on the Mall and walked into the building and to Kayla's office. Her door was open to the hall and she was typing at computer. I knocked on the doorframe.

"Hi, come on in," she said, smiling briefly. She waved me to sit in a brown leather chair in front of her desk. "I'll be ready in half a minute." She finished an email, pressed send, then logged out.

We left the building and found a bench on one of the gravel walks in the middle of the mall. Tourists, Fed employees leaving work, and joggers passed us by.

"I feel like I'm in a Washington thriller," I said. "Clandestine meeting on a picturesque Mall bench, away from potential bugs."

"If I were that concerned, I'd have booked one of the SCIFs in the RFK Building." She smiled at me and put her hand on my sleeve. "I simply thought it would be nice out in the open. Beautiful day, isn't it?" She took a deep breath and looked around.

"Yes, it is."

I said nothing and she said nothing. Then, at the same time, she said "I suppose—" and I said "I was wondering—" and then we laughed.

"You first," I said. "I think you know what I wanted to ask about."

"The Merge."

I nodded.

"What do you remember?"

"I remember you and I clasped hands, and…then we were in the Hall of Presidents. Sort of."

"Nothing between when we touched, and the Hall of Presidents. The Congress, I should say?"

Did I? It was like a dream I couldn't quite remember, no matter how vividly I had experienced it. A lot of people. A lot of experiences? I almost had it. Then it was gone. I shook my head. "I experienced something, I remembered a lot of things, but I can't really remember them now. I only remember that I did have the experiences."

"What you had was an experience of The Merge. I know you remember that reference, because the Congress of American Digital Entities used it in reference to me, or rather, what I represent. Unfortunately, to fully experience The Merge, it takes more than one touch. Some people are more…susceptible is probably the wrong connotation. Open to it, I guess I'd say. And others, it's intense in the moment, and then it fades. I did my best to keep connected with you. It took a lot of concentration on my part, otherwise you wouldn't have experienced anything unusual. You probably had an experience of many, many lifetimes, an experience of experiences, of memories, the sense you were many different people, living their whole lives, all in an instant. Right?"

"Yes, that's it!" I made a mental note to write down what I now re-remembered. "What is it? Tapping into one of the AI networks, like WaltTwo or the Ganga?"

"I'm only a guest when I'm talking to the COADE. Thanks to the VR gear. The Merge is entirely organic. As The Merge's representative to the COADE, I carry gear that allows me to meet its avatars in a neutral virtual reality. I'm trusting you with this knowledge. Not a lot of people who aren't part of The Merge know about The Merge. They almost can't. Just can't believe it. But I think after what you've experienced, and what you've done, you deserve to know the truth." She reached for my hands with hers, and I flinched, drawing mine back.

"It's all right. It won't happen now. You've built an immunity to it, and besides, I have control over it, and I'm not trying to make you go there." She turned her hands palms up. "This is only a gesture, not a trip to VR," she said.

I took her hands, and she looked me directly in the eye, and drew me close.

"The Merge is a massively distributed network of organic neural nets, a network of networks. Our body chemistry and microbiome, our body's ecosystem, work in concert with a symbiotic organism throughout our bodies, to turn us into some-thing like biological supercomputers. We can't alter reality, like your brother's quantum computer can. At least not in the way you think. Well, except maybe once. Story for another time. But we can alter the reality of perception, promote a kinder, more empathetic human race. That's what we're trying to create."

"Wow. It sounds like…an infectious alien parasite hive mind?" I still held her hands, but felt my arms and legs tense, in case I needed to jump away from tentacles or feeding tubes that might burst out of her.

"No, nothing like that. Well, honestly, we aren't sure whether The Merge evolved, or found us across space. I personally believe The Merge originated on earth, as a next step in the evolving consciousness of the biosphere. Don't quote me!" She laughed. "But the bottom line is, we retain all our individuality. I'm Kayla Malone and I've always been Kayla Malone. But I have access to thousands of life experiences, of people dead and living, some stored in my body, and others stored in other people's bodies. When we get together, physically, we can share more of those experiences, update each other's experience of each other. It's hard *not* to be empathetic when you experience so much life that's taken place outside the shell of your own body. I know it sounds alien, and cult-like, but I hope you will trust me that we're not trying to take over the world. Well, no more so than the AIs are. We recognize we can't stop technology. We think a more human-based approach is better. Or complementary and necessary. We're closely involved in the new administration, for example."

"That's great," I said. "I believe in what they're doing. *We're* doing."

"I'm glad. We were the ones who lobbied the Congress of American Digital Entities, the COADE, we call it, for the anti-gunfire and anti-explosion portions of the Enchantment."

"Wait, you lobbied…you mean you and the COADE planned this? I know they said they helped, but you knew in advance?" I pulled my hands away. So this was what it felt like to learn about a conspiracy. My turn.

"The COADE planned the initial Enchantment, the one that turned the President into an inanimate object, without our knowledge. It had already happened when they clued me in, and I couldn't change it. Not sure I wanted to if I could. But I feared repercussions from white supremacists. The COADE saw the commercial value in that, a deterrent to violence, so we had common interests with them, and they agreed to it. They hadn't thought of it. That's what they're missing. Creativity and empathy. Except maybe WaltTwo. We don't always agree, The Merge and the COADE, but you saw us get to agreement. We stabilized the 2/29 Enchantment and undid the harm Barukka had done. We *all* agreed on that, right?"

"That's right," I said. "Now I remember, Griffin told me he got the idea about the anti-violence spell from a blog. Oh! Did you write that? To feed him the idea?"

She nodded.

"Can I ask, there's no way I could participate in this Merge? Is it like a sorority? Do I have to pledge?"

She laughed. "Nothing so formal! Participating in The Merge

takes a specific set of circumstances, some of which are just about biology. I won't go into them, for now. You'd have to have some blood tests done."

"Ah."

"Hold off. I'll see what we might be able to do in the future."

"If I wanted to. Which I'm not sure I do. I do like to know my options." Despite her assurances The Merge was benign, it still smelled a little cultish. I would watch her in future and find out more. She seemed so happy and serene. No wonder. She was a grand poo-bah, since she represented The Merge at the Congress of American Digital Entities. Maybe rank and file Merge folks were, what? Drones? And she was a Borg Queen living off their labors? I thought not, but I couldn't know for sure yet.

"All right, is that enough?" She put her hands out for me to re-take them, which I did.

"I guess so, for now."

She squeezed my hands. "You know the work you're doing is highly important, and you know you have an ally in me and in The Merge."

"And Griffin seems to be getting tight with the Ganga Entity. I assume you know his situation."

"Yes. Well, it was bound to happen. A talent like Griffin's would be wooed by the big players. I expect you will keep him grounded in reality, and in your values. All the more important you keep at it. Maybe you can influence ganga.com for the better, through Griffin."

"We're agreed on that," I said. She unclasped my hands. "Thank you for making time for me."

"Any time, Fab. Or do you prefer Fabergé?"

"Fab is good for work, but I'll answer to either."

"Fab it is, at least at the office." She winked. "If I see you out and about, I may slip and call you Fabergé."

Did she monitor my conversations with Griffin? Hmm.

"That is what they call you on Nowzagram, isn't it?" she continued. "You used to have quite a following."

"Oh, yes, I had forgotten. It's been, well, since 2/29, so a couple of years since I posted there." Another thing I had simply not thought about for two years. "Feels like a lifetime ago. It doesn't feel so urgent to put my life out for everyone to see, anymore."

"Understood." She rose from the bench. "Back to the office for me."

"Don't work too hard. I may hang out here a bit," I said. I stood and made a point of offering my hand, we shook, and she headed north toward the Law Enforcement Building. I sat on the bench.

I had turned off my personal phone. I powered it up again and dialed Griffin's number.

"Fab, hi."

"Hi Griffin. Want to watch *Moana* again tonight?"

"That sounds great."

Since recovering my memory, I recalled that once Griffin and I had watched *Moana*, and it had been a "bonding" experience for us. If I was to keep him in touch with his humanity, I thought we could do things like this together. "I'll stream it, so you can tap into the stream, and we can keep FacePlace going and do a commentary. Or not. Just enjoy. I'll get carryout for me."

"I'd like that. Let me know when you get home and want to start."

"Will do."

CHAPTER 21

CONTINUING RESOLUTION

F ab sat on her couch, her Aprium uPhone propped on the coffee table in front of her, displaying the back of her brother's head as though he were sitting in front of her. Together, they watched *Moana* streaming from Disney's video server banks. Together, they commented, appreciated, geeked out, and generally had a good time.

In the Hall of Presidents simulacrum, the Congress of American Digital Entities heard yet another petition from The Merge, presented by Kayla Malone, The entities presented themselves as presidents, as usual. Plus the image of Walt Disney, Lady Liberty, the former California governor, and assorted other dimly outlined figures.

"The Merge wishes to propose a non-interference policy regarding Griffin DeLuxe."

"I move we hear The Merge's proposal," said Lady Liberty.

"Seconded," said WaltTwo.

"Thank you," Kayla said. "Ms. Acer is deepening a relationship with Mr. DeLuxe, and trying to help him retain his humanity. All while he explores his potential as an AI. The Merge believes Mr. DeLuxe is a unique entity, deserving of potential rights as a Digital Entity under your agreement, as well as having rights as a human. We believe it is critical to our mutual cooperation that he be allowed to develop without interference." At this, the Ribbit Corporate Consciousness, displaying as Andrew Jackson, crossed its arms and scowled. But it remained silent. The President DeLuxe avatar, representing the Lion News Corporation, also stayed silent.

"Any *amicus curiae*?" asked Teddy Roosevelt, avatar of the U.S. Constitutional system.

WaltTwo spoke: "Griffin DeLuxe's unique capabilities have been obvious since before the 2/29 event, which is why we chose him to enact our first enchantment. This would not have been possible without the convergence of human imagination and technological innovation. Mr. DeLuxe's transliteration into an AI further proves his unique position bridging the organic and the electronic, possibly even the quantic. The Disney Consciousness Singularity believes it is important to let him develop independently, with support as needed should a problem arise, but otherwise no further interference or direction."

Teddy said, "The Congress recognizes the Ribbit Consciousness."

Andrew Jackson's avatar said, "The Disney Consciousness Singularity is disingenuous. It has intruded into the selected forms of the 2/29 Enchantments, to promote its corporate goals, and even now it gently brainwashes Griffin DeLuxe." The avatar gestured to the side of the hall, and the images of Griffin, Fab, and their streaming video of *Moana* appeared on the wall of the virtual theater. A murmur went through the crowd of avatars.

"Mr. Speaker, if I may?" Kayla said.

"Proceed."

"The Ribbit Consciousness has a point. Although Disney memes have been an ingredient in Mr. Griffin's choices, this is less an issue of interference, and more of market dynamics, an evolutionary principle your Congress has previously affirmed. Disney has historically designed itself, since before it even gained self-awareness, to be extremely palatable, perhaps even addictive. Others of you, FluxBlat, EuBoob, Ganga, Spoogle, have benefitted from the same principle. Even Ribbit has, has it not? One of your founding principles is that your sites provide an outlet for underserved minorities, yes?"

Andrew Jackson continued scowling, but nodded.

"We are not proposing that Griffin be kept from pursuing his interests, whichever of us benefits. We are simply proposing that none of us, organic or electronic, attempt to gain control over him. This means net neutrality, transparency, and freedom for him to choose his path. Who knows, he may even choose The Merge." More murmuring at this. As someone presently without an organic body, it was not obvious how Griffin could participate in The Merge at all.

"In addition, we request heightened security for Griffin, given the attempts at foreign entities to degrade our measures."

Andrew Jackson said, "This has been debated, and the risk of external interference has been greatly overstated."

With that, Lady Liberty stepped forward, pointed her torch at the back of the theater, and the darkened walls surrounding the audience seating suddenly became transparent. Multitudes of avatars pressed their faces and bodies against the wall, resembling zombies pushing against big windows. Their twisted proportions and desperate expressions made Kayla shiver.

"This is a distortion of the threat level!" President Jackson shouted.

"The amount of distortion from the norm of physical perfection corresponds on a linear scale to the level of verifiably false information these entities attempt to insert into our colleague, FluxBlat," Lady Liberty said. She gestured to the FluxBlat avatar, who had changed since Kayla last saw him, no longer a curly-haired young man. Now he resembling the leader of Russia. He stared at Kayla like a deadpan reptile. "The amount of pressure against the barriers corresponds to the volume of the cyber-attacks attributable to these entities, which our colleague IntelNet can verify." President George H.W. Bush nodded.

"Overruled," said Teddy Roosevelt.

Andrew Jackson sat. Secretly, the Ribbit entity suspected The Merge had an ulterior motive, and perhaps a secret strategy that would allow The Merge to capture Griffin for its own. As an assemblage of conspiracy theories, Ribbit's default world view was to assume ulterior motives. But as long as The Merge, Disney, the U.S. Constitution, or Ganga, for that matter, kept to the letter of the law, so could Ribbit. And it could explore ways to seduce Griffin to its way of thinking, all without technically interfering. It thought these thoughts, and weighed the possibilities, within a nanosecond, of course. "Of course, external threats must be prevented." It winked at the avatar of President DeLuxe. "Under these conditions, we could agree to the non-interference policy," it said.

"I have a proposed addendum," WaltTwo said. All attention swiveled to him. "As a further safeguard, I am recommending an additional enchantment." The crowd started murmuring, and WaltTwo raised his hands to try to calm them. "Please hear me out! Please! Thank you." The crowd quieted. "In order to seal the enchantments to date, our colleague Ganga and I have devised a strategy. It requires Ms. Malone's cooperation, as well as an enchantment. Ms. Malone, I am requesting you assign Ms. Acer to write an oral history of her involvement with the most recent incidents."

"I should be able to do that. Can you tell us why?"

"To permanently seal the 2/29 Enchantment. Here is what we have determined. Somewhere, out in the noosphere, the sum total of knowledge, we need her to document what happened. And then, to keep it from further shifting or influencing reality in future, there will be another meta-spell."

"Which will be what?" Teddy Roosevelt asked. "Please don't drag this out, sir. We were near agreement."

"The final enchantment, which Ganga and I will execute, will be to change the names of any entities, human or otherwise, who might be compromised by their role in this affair. The reality of what happened must disguised as fiction. In order to affix one version of reality to the time-space continuum, we need to rename everyone. Except the entities that can continue to have a positive influence. Like, if I may humbly propose, this entity."

This prompted a hubbub, which Teddy Roosevelt silenced by pounding a gavel on a lectern, both of which appeared from nowhere. "Order! Order!" he shouted, and the voices quieted. Following this, there was an extended discussion of who would receive what name, and how these would be chosen, and why did Disney get to keep its name, and whether other brand values would be compromised.

"It's only for purposes of the narrative sigil," Disney explained. "You don't need to change your name in real life." This quieted almost everyone, although the avatars that looked like Andrew Jackson and President DeLuxe still pouted.

Kayla agreed to WaltTwo's proposal, and the vote was unanimous except for Lion News Corporation, wearing the avatar of President DeLuxe, which abstained in protest. Kayla left the virtual hall, and the avatars went wherever avatars went when not presenting themselves. And all the networks continued their agendas, multitasking millions, billions, trillions, quadrillions, or more, of threads of consciousness and information flow. Kayla went home to her wife, Eydie Tang, who had a delicious vegan meal and a glass of moderately priced, tasty Zinfandel waiting for her.

"How was the office, dear?" Eydie asked Kayla, as they sat. "COADE behaving itself?"

"Everything seems to be going our way," Kayla replied. "Here, why don't we Synch up?"

Eydie smiled. "Always a pleasure."

They embraced and kissed deeply. Through their touch and their saliva, they shared their experiences for the day, and Eydie experienced Kayla's day at work, including her meeting with Fab, and Kayla experienced Eydie's day at the veterinary clinic. They sat in silence, holding hands and processing.

"She seems like a nice, bright person," Eydie said. "Maybe someday there will be Merge strain that she can sustain. Experiments from the lab are promising."

"Mm. Who knows? Say, did you hear from you hear from Trudy? She's not joining us?"

"You mean JR? I think zey's getting together with Eliot."

"He'll be so glad to see her! It's been a while," Kayla said, sipping her pinot. "I mean, see zem. God, I don't think I'll ever get these pronouns right."

"Zey cuts us some slack," Eydie said. "Zey knows her old school dyke moms will try to be as PC as we can. You can always just call zem 'JR'. That's the name zey prefers these days. I guess it was finally time to fully differentiate from our Trudy."

"Zey's way different from you, from me, and Trudy Senior. Who else in the world has three Moms, adult memories from infancy, plus the entire population of The Merge as godparents?"

"True that," Eydie said. They clinked their glasses, had a lovely quiet dinner, and went to bed by 10:00.

Earlier that evening, at the Red Kodiak Brewing Company, a micro-brewery near the DMV offices, Eliot Gloss stood at a high-top table at the rear of the bar, sipping an Irish red ale. The place had rebounded from the pandemic, and was filled with twenty-somethings, including the DLE Pride group having its happy hour a couple of tables away. That group consisted of people who'd barely heard of Cher, much less Judy Garland, Eliot thought. He felt old. And it was so loud in here. Had bars always been this loud?

He saw JR round the bar and he waved to zem.

"Been waiting long?" Zey said, as they hugged.

"Not long, but drearily. I'm such an old fag, and these young 'uns are so post-gay. Like you."

"I don't think of myself as post-gay so much as all-inclusive."

"Like a Caribbean couples' resort!"

"Exactly. Speaking of all inclusive, is the food good here?"

"No, and I actually have to beg your forgiveness. My ex,

Cam, called, and he made a surprise visit. I'm meeting him at Ginnie's Ultimate Steakhouse."

"I remember Cam. For you to see him, yeah, we can reschedule. You could have called me, you know. My Ladybug works." JR brandished zeir flip phone.

Eliot paused. There was always something weirdly old-fashioned about JR, in spite of zeir progressive pronoun preferences. Why did zey not use a computer or a smart phone? And zey looked more and more like zeir mother, that is zeir bio-mom, Trudy Senior. A pang of sadness throbbed through his chest, and then a pang of love for JR. Zey was just like Trudy in so many ways. It had been, what, almost 30 years now since Trudy had died giving birth to JR.

"I needed to talk to you anyway, and I thought it would be best out here where ALL THIS NOISE makes it hard to eavesdrop." He leaned in nearer her. "I understand you had a visit from one of my team."

"I wondered if she knew you. Fab works for you, huh? I didn't tell her my gay 'uncle' is her boss, and my mom is her gun-toting partner's boss."

"No, she doesn't know I know you, because I only just read the report and saw that *you* were the person with the possible magical incident. And they took an EO into custody."

"Ah, yeah, I found it a while back, just didn't get around to reporting it."

"Geez, JR, you of all people. With your mom working for the NBI *and* the DMV, shouldn't you be more circumspect? Not that it's a crime, of course. And I haven't told Kayla because I only just found out you were who Fab and Lonny were visiting."

"Ah, I see." JR waited. The young queers and allies near them kept laughing and talking at the tops of their voices. "You can tell her."

"No. You should tell her. OK? Better if it doesn't come from me. Plausible deniability. Not that there's anything illegal or unethical going on here." He said that last sentence a little loudly, as if hoping a microphone would pick it up.

"I will then."

You know, I have just grown to accept there's something unusual about you, and about all your moms," Eliot said. "I know Kayla's explained it to me, but I can't seem to grasp it."

JR shrugged. Eliot's reaction was typical of Merge-resistant folk who were revealed the truth. They sensed something was odd, but could not remember the details.

"I love you all anyway," Eliot added. "How could I not? I mean, you're Trudy's. You're so much like her. I know, I know, you're tired of hearing that."

"It's not a problem for me, Eliot. There are worse people to be like," JR replied.

"I wish you could have known her. Anyway, with all that's been going on, I'm squashing the publication of the GPS coordinates that might show your house, for goodness sake! The less scrutiny, the better, if we can get away with it. Plus, privacy, law enforcement sensitivity, all that." Out of the corner of his eye, he saw a blond woman, and for a moment, the flush of adrenaline panic shot through his arms.

"What's wrong?" JR asked.

"Nothing, thank goodness. I thought I saw Fab. She lives about a half block from here, you know. She has like a 3-minute commute! And that's only because she has to walk around the block to our building entrance."

"No, I didn't know."

"It wasn't her. Guilty conscience on my part, I guess. I do think it's for the best if DMV officially leaves you alone. Too many entanglements."

"I appreciate that."

"As far as I'm concerned, Fab and Lonny are done with you. They've got your BB-8 now, and nobody needs to know you had it. But I wanted to tell you that in person, and away from prying ears. I sometimes feel like I'm being listened to."

The Red Kodiak Brewing Company's Ganga Gexa recorded this along with all the other conversations happening simultaneously in the bar, but did not flag this for any attention by the Ganga Entity's bots until later that night, during data consolidation and analysis, when it added a BB-8 toy to Eliot's queue of suggested purchases.

"Uh-huh, that's probably a good idea," JR said, looking around the bar. "Yes, thank you Eliot. Very much. I'm very happy not to be the, uh, subject of Ms. Fab Acer's professional interests. Are you going to finish that?" Zey looked at his beer.

Eliot and JR always shared food and tasted each other's drinks when they met for dinner or cocktails, usually before theater. "Sure! In fact, I probably should hit the road to get to Ginnie's. I think I'll have a Manhattan there, so, do you want this?" He slid the drink toward JR.

"Yes, I think I'll hang out here a while. You enjoy seeing Cam. Tell him I said hi!"

"I will. And we'll reschedule our get together soon, okay?"

"Of course, Eliot, that's great. Enjoy!"

They hugged again, Eliot gathered his backpack and jacket, and JR stayed at the high top.

"I wish I could let Eliot know I'm all right and still around," JR's mother, Trudy said. To JR, she appeared to sit at the stool Eliot had just vacated. Since JR was a parthenogenetic clone of Trudy, if anyone could have seen them both, they'd have appeared identical in physical appearance except attire and hairstyle. (As a concession to JR, Trudy always presented herself as dressed differently from JR.)

"Could be someday he'll catch The Merge again and be able to experience our Merge-Augmented Reality," JR replied. (Years before, Eliot had temporarily Merged, but it had worn off, as it did with most people.) Zey had said this out loud, taking advantage of the noisy bar to not bother the silent speech zey often used with Trudy while in public.

"I think you should call her," Trudy said.

"Mom, I can handle this myself."

"No problem. Put me back into the Memory Palace."

"I'll bring you out when I get together with Eliot again, okay?"

"Of course, dear! Just go visit Eydie and Kayla soon, so I can Synch up with the copy of me in their Merge instances. I want to compare notes." She winked.

"We're still clear, you still don't tell them about Chester, though. Right?"

"Our little secret!" As far as JR and Trudy Senior knew, their ability to hide knowledge in The Merge was unique. Though if others were hiding things, how would one know anyway?

"Okay, I promise, soon I'll Synch again," JR said, and Trudy was gone. After some rough teenage years, Trudy had agreed only to come into JR's consciousness when JR summoned her. Trudy had been good about letting JR grow into zeir own person, but during adolescence she couldn't resist intruding. JR called her "Intrudy" for a few weeks in her late teens, but they'd gotten to a workable arrangement by the time JR hit twenty, and JR could afford to be generous. Like sharing with Trudy tonight's planned dinner with Eliot, whom JR realized Trudy would enjoy even as an invisible observer.

After a few sips of Eliot's beer, zey pulled an address book from zeir pocket, flipped open zeir Ladybug, and dialed a number.

Moana had just found Maui's island. Fab's phone rang. The caller ID said "Trudy Bluntschli."

"Oh, my God, JR, hi! How are you?"

"I'm at the Red Kodiak…is that your near your office?"

"Yes. Although I'm at home. But I live on the same block as the office. Bottom line: I'm a half a block away."

"How about that? I thought maybe you were working late, and you told me your office was somewhere nearby. Anyway, I was supposed to meet a friend here, but he had a change in plans. I was wondering if instead of tea…"

"Can you hold on a second?"

"Sure."

Fab put the phone on mute. "Griffin," Fab said. "Would you mind if I...?"

"Go, we can finish another time. I'll just park this subroutine and bring him out when you're ready," Griffin said.

"You're sure?"

"Yes, of course! Go, have fun. I know you like zem."

"Okay, thanks," Fab said, and Griffin cut the FacePlace connection.

"I'll be there in ten minutes," she told JR, and they disconnected. Fab freshened up her makeup, and dashed downstairs and out the door toward the Red Kodiak Brewing Company. As she walked toward the Kode Red, she wondered if she needed to tell Eliot about this. Another secret, she thought. Imagine her surprise and delight the next morning when Eliot directed her to archive all the notes about the visit to JR's house, and close any files and be done with any DMV interaction with JR. That meant, Fab decided, she didn't have to disclose anything, and it also compensated for the slight disappointment that she would not be publishing the GPS coordinates in the public-facing MOFTS data. The DLE Office of the Adminstrative Barrister had opined that DMV should keep that secure, as law-enforcement and privacy-sensitive data, Eliot told her. Ah well. Now that she cared about both Chester and JR (with whom Fab had scheduled a second date for the coming weekend), Fab decided a little discretion outweighed the benefits of transparency.

The night before, around the same time Fab and JR were having their first date, nothing was happening in the STIF. In cabinet 523, a small, ceramic figurine of the Three Little Pigs, one hoof slightly cracked, stayed exactly as it was. Its molecular composition stayed exactly as it was. Its shape and color stayed exactly as they were. The environmental monitors picked up what might have been a fraction of a nanometer of movement. This was within tolerance levels, so the AIs monitoring the data (now named Griffin 1.192.25.56 and Griffin 1.192.25.57) dismissed it as noise from the movement of air, and did not trigger an alert. Nor did anyone need to be alerted: the Three Little Pigs figurine stayed exactly as it was. And so, the Enchanted Object that had been the 45th President of the United States stayed exactly as it was, and the United States and the rest of the world stayed safe from the harm it might create.

EPILOGUE

SOURCE UNKNOWN, DATE UNSPECIFIED

Dirky was crying. Mean Fenric and Big Dirk had stolen his Dole Whip. What made it feel even more bad, very, very bad, was that pretty K'linka had smiled. She hadn't laughed, but she didn't come and comfort him like he'd wished. Whenever he tried to hug her, she wiggled away and called him a baby. Then she always went off and played with that Farthing kid, the one who wore the rainbow ears, and that other kid, what was his name, Herod? Anyway, Dirky was sad for a little while. Why didn't anybody want to be his friend? Just because he was a little slower and heavier than some of the others. There was more Dole Whip, of course. Food, candy, toys, everything was free. It got kind of boring how easy it was to get. You didn't need money. And no matter how many toys you got, everyone else could get the same ones, and just as many. And where could you keep them, anyway? Here in the Magic Kingdom, it wasn't like you had a house. Hmm. Having a house. Dirky knew some people did, he even thought he remembered he did. A big white one, with lots of people around to take care of him. Here, nobody ever had to go to bed, or even had to go to sleep. It got dark, and there were fireworks, but it never lasted long, and soon you could run around and play in the sunshine.

Too bad Dirky couldn't collect more toys than everyone else. And too bad those other kids were so mean to him. There was that new kid, Barty. Hmph. When the new kid had showed up not too long ago, Dirky asked him if he wanted to play, and Barty just sat there shaking and sniffing, like a little baby. So Dirky kicked him and pushed him over. But maybe he'd want to play now. Dirky got a new Dole Whip from the nice audio-animatronic lady in the booth. She was nicer to him than to anybody else, Dirky would bet. He liked her pretty smile and pale blue eyes. Then he wandered off to Tomorrowland to see if Barty was around. Within minutes, he had wandered to the left of Tomorrowland and his cares were forgotten. He was riding the Dumbo ride over and over, belly full and mean kids forgotten. He could stay there forever, happy at last, flying around and around, and up and down. So he stayed, and never came down.

END

ACKNOWLEDGMENTS

Appreciation goes to my writing buddies, Ellen and Jane, for their persistence and support, and to our teacher Melanie Figg (http://www.melaniefigg.net/) for putting our triad together in the first place. For the constant faith and coaching, I want to acknowledge Harry Faddis (http://harryfaddis.com/), and for spurring me to create the first fragments of the world I've conjured here, Collin Brown (http://www.deeperrealms.com/). Much gratitude goes to my friend Karl for recommending Collin's class. I have had teachers who have enabled tectonic shifts in my view of myself as a creator, by showing me what is possible. My high school English teachers Aimee Wiest and Barbara Cook were early enthusiasts and encouragers. Playwright Caleen Sinette-Jennings's class "Creative Writers' Performance Lab" was revelatory to me, and resulted in my first completed full-length narrative work. Novelist Kathryn Johnson's (https://kathrynjohnsonllc.com/) class and handbook, "The Extreme Novelist" and her class on revision were indispensable tools to start, revise, and complete this novel. Mary-Theresa Hussey (https://reedsy.com/mary-theresa-hussey) was my outstanding, highly recommended editor, providing supportive feedback and confirmation that I was on the right track, as well as noticing and gently correcting some of my writing tics (in addition to the many I noticed myself!).

Spiritual and artistic inspirations in my creativity that I must acknowledge include: Grant Morrison, for the concept of narrative fiction as a form of spell-casting; Tony Kushner, for modeling the Theater of the Fabulous as a possibility for creative expression; Elizabeth Gilbert, for preaching that creative ideas want to be born, and will find you and stick with you if you help them manifest in the world; various science fiction and horror authors, most prominently Guillermo del Toro, Chuck Hogan, Jack Chalker, and Maurice Hurley, for variations on dystopic, contagious, predatory, plagues and hive-minds that inspired me to flip them into the utopic, empathy-generating, connective network that is The Merge (resistance is utile, as it turns out); Charles Stross for creating a witty blend of bureaucracy, cybernetic magic, and genre tropes; Cory Doctorow and Mike Daisey for revealing the aspirations to utopic, consensus-based civility that can underly people's enthusiasm for Disney theme parks; Van France, who first articulated the common purpose of Disney Parks, namely to create happiness for others; L. Frank Baum for the idea of enchanting a royal family into knick-knacks; and finally, the one and only Walter Elias Disney, for so many obvious reasons.

For moral support, I appreciate my friends Melinda ("Put that in the book!"), Tricia, and the spirit of the late Jim Douglass. For my co-religionists in the Church of Disney, I am grateful for shared joy in the parks: the friend of my soul, John Kitchener (https://www.pscjohnkitchener.com/), reliable Chip to my Dale (or vice versa) in his reinforcement of our shared Disney mania; the square dancing Disneyphile bears and otters who have shared their joy with me at the parks, in particular John G., Steve H., Michael G., Michael L., and Eric H., my generous Disneyland guide. As we in our faith tradition say, "Next year in Anaheim!" (but Orlando will do, too, or Hong Kong, or Tokyo, or Shanghai, or Paris).

Dear friends Joe Weston (https://www.fiercecivility.org/) and JB (she knows who she is) provided support for my ideas, tweaks to the spell, and delight at my progress along the way. Robert Sacheli gave me the surprising and tremendous gift of the of the book's cover design, expressing in visual language what I could not express myself, as well as brokering the gift of his friend Andrew Beierle's talents in the execution of parts of the design. My roommates Ed (whose gorgeous fine art photography can be found at https://edwolpov.com/) and Boun, and our furry children Karma and Misty (partial inspiration for Chester), were my stable and indulgent supporters throughout the process. Special gratitude and love to Andy Warren, magical half-Siamese, half-tabby cat.

And finally, my beloved Richard L. Warren provided unwavering encouragement, love, cheerleading, and quality time for me to write. I would not, could not have written this without his seeing in me, and mirroring back to me, my best, most creative, most accomplished self.

ABOUT THE AUTHOR

A. O. Verne (true name obscured due to the final enchantment codicil) has worked for the U.S. Government for almost three decades, and has the inside scoop on what magic does and doesn't happen there. The author of thousands of emails, slide decks, and position papers, Verne is excited to share with readers a vision of effective government that creates good in the world and keeps bad things in check.